AND HERE THE WHEEL

by

John Harper

Published by Fantastic Books Publishing
Cover design by Heather Murphy

ISBN: 978-1-522895-30-5

Based on the space trading game
Elite: Dangerous by Frontier Developments.

This book is dedicated to my children

Credits

This book is dedicated to all of those Elite fans who supported my novel's Indiegogo campaign by purchasing a 'dedication'. All of these wonderful people are listed below (in no particular order). You guys and girls rock!

Chris Reeve, Mordant, Daniel, Darren Rees, Glen Sullivan, Jon M Horridge, Andreas Meyer from Hannover, Germany, Mark Cohen, Darrel Wollensack, Joe Scicluna, Stephen (Mort) Stuttard, Rob Cartlidge (The Dude), Rebecca O'Sullivan, Chris "CrispyLeper" Lepley, Chris Forrester, Chris Rudd, Andy Edgson, David Readman, Dan Atkinson, David JP Bodger, Martin de Ruiter, Graeme Harper (Thanks Dad!), Jay Selley, John Burton, Jonathan Hollingsworth, Matthew Cook, Neil Reynolds, Peter Brooks, Rich Green, Richard Thomas Harrison, Richard Davies, Robert Romano, Wendy Rowson, Susan Sparrow (Thanks Mum!), Paul Simpson, Matt Charlesworth, Simon Peacock, Andrew Craib, Stoo Collins, Andrew Bright, Darren Vallance, Carl Watson, Nik Clement, Rufus Glyn, Tim Palmer, RM Goodman, Rory Scarlett, Capper Deluxe, Mike Cook @ epubBooks.com, Andrew Wright, Adam Mellor, Dave Vint, Craig Cope, Gisle Martin von Hafenbrädl, Russ Fray, Steffan Westcott, Stian Davidsen, Bil Irving, John Purcell, Kirk Jewell, sono Mariangela and James Gibson. Grazie per rendermi meglio di quello che, Charles Morelli, Alan Stiles, David Burns, Jason Flaherty, Marcel Schoen, Mark Humpage, Mark Pidduck, Michael Brookes, Tal Musry, Andrea Schutenko, Brad Roberts, Matthew Benson, Phil Hibbs, Gregg Chamberlain, Carl Agnew, Steph Wyeth, Chris Gillie, Alan White, Commander Kevin Jameson, Kevin Alty, Lisa Wolf, Liz Barrett, Arto Heikkinen, Suzanne Woolcott, Stephen Link, Tim Do, and Robert Garrie.

Author's Note:

Elite: And Here The Wheel was born out of two things: My passion for the Elite universe and the unwavering support and generosity of fellow Elite fans. Some I knew, some I didn't but they helped bring Elite: And Here The Wheel to life by supporting my Indiegogo campaign to raise the required funds to buy an official fiction license from Frontier Developments.

Creating this novel has been an absolute dream come true. The teenager writing Elite fan fiction never dreamed this moment would actually happen! And it just could not have happened without the generosity of everyone who got behind me. So thank you very, very much to every single one of you.

Two days before my Indiegogo campaign was due to finish it wasn't looking very good. I still had over two thousand dollars to go. Due to the nature of the Indiegogo platform several would-be backers were put off, especially as it looked as if it might not succeed.

Success breeds success. I looked like a failure. Then suddenly I received an amazing pledge from a supporter. A man who I had never met, but a man who was so captivated by my passion that he halved my goal. Suddenly this crazy dream of mine looked achievable. And not just to me, but to everyone else. The pledges rolled in and I crossed the lined with about five minutes to spare.

That magic pledge was the turning point of the campaign. Stephen Link, thank you so much. You made my dream come true. I also need to thank Tim Do who threw in extra money at the last moment to get me over the line, and Robert Garry who 'purchased' the naming of the protagonist. I think I modelled my character pretty well on the real Robert Garry (but naturally any resemblance is coincidental and all that lawyer speak).

Enjoy the book!

John Harper – January 2014

Chapter 1

Robert hunkered down around the corner from the bridge of the Python freighter, yelling instructions through the main hatch. 'Throw us your weapons and we'll let you live.'

'If you want this ship you'll have to earn it,' came the reply.

Robert turned to his men, sweat pooling on their faces, hair slick with grime and blood, laser pistols running low on power, bodies running low on energy. Hadn't they done enough?

'What would you like me to do?' he asked.

'I want you to make it look like we put up a fight.'

'Deal.' Robert moved out onto the bridge. He stopped before the crew, his Colt Diplomat out in front at hip height; a faithful reproduction of a classic; a fine weapon.

The bridge crew was seven strong; three men, three women and a boy of eight or nine. The captain had a rugged look, trim but lined, a grease cloth strapped to his overalls, a clunky pair of magboots on his feet.

The bridge looked like the captain: round, worn, but functional, and perhaps a little bit proud. The pilot's console was the old two-dee version, straight out of the fifties. The three women, hair captive in tight buns, looked much like the men but for the slight swelling at their chests. They'd hold their own in a bar fight. The boy was a ragged collection of skin and bone, his stare locked on the captain.

'Bit risky bringing the family along,' Robert said.

'We'll not be staying at home by ourselves for months on end, thank you,' said one of the women, maybe the captain's wife.

'Fair enough.' Robert turned his attention to the discarded weapons that floated like a flotilla of warships; mostly low calibre pip-squeaks, but amongst them a Cowell

55 with a scope as big as the barrel.

He whistled and ten of his men appeared behind him. Turning back to the captain, he said, 'Now, the cargo.'

'Payment first,' the captain replied, spreading his arms wide. 'We can't go back empty handed looking like this.'

Robert studied the man's face as he stepped towards him. He looked like a worried father, for sure, but not like a father who had fought for his family's life. 'I see your problem. How about this?'

His fist connected, a snap shot, straight into the man's face, no real power behind it, but the captain rocked backward like an upside down pendulum. Away then back, magboots stuck to the decking. His left eye started to swell.

'There,' said Robert. 'Much prettier. Looks like you've protected someone's honour now, doesn't it?'

The captain straightened with barely a flinch. He pressed the heel of his palm into his eye socket. 'I'm afraid a black eye isn't going to do it.'

Robert pulled his bowie knife from his belt but kept it low by his side, fingering the grip. 'I have a rule only to gut a man who's trying to kill me or stop me stealing things. You're not in a position to do either.'

'We have medical supplies,' another voice piped up.

Robert swung his gaze to the second man who betrayed no anxiety in his tone. A surprise given what he was suggesting.

'And so does the Company,' added the captain. 'We'll be scanned, you can be sure of that. It's the new quarantine procedure.'

Robert nodded to one of the men behind him. 'Ralph here is my knife guy. He'll fix you up. Now, I've been told there's a lock on the cargo bay.'

The captain's gaze took in all his crew, pausing on the boy a moment too long. Robert saw his Adam's apple bob as though his neck had shrunk a size. 'Forty-two, Forty-two.'

Robert raised his link to speak into it. 'You read me, Dad?'

'Still here kiddo,' said Jordan Garry's voice in response. 'What have you got for me?'

'Forty-two, Forty-two.' 'Acknowledged.'

Rustling and electronic bleeps sounded over the comms.

Robert watched his boys canvass the bridge, each performing his allotted tasks. Two downloading the log – news and ship movements were as good as credits, two rechecking the crew for weapons, two more to create a little pirate-related sabotage, Ralph to do a little Salvador Dali and two to watch his back.

Jordan Garry's voice, 'Hatch is opening,' came a fraction of a second before laser fire shrieked across the link.

'Dad! Dad, what's happening?' Shock rippled Robert's skin. Every instinct screamed at him to run down there but he knew he must hold fast. 'Dad?'

His father's voice was gruff and unruffled. 'The hold is full of guys with guns. Your orders?'

Robert's glare snapped to the captain. 'So much for our growing rapport.'

The captain raised his hands. 'The Company … the new anti-piracy policy.'

Robert's stare never left the captain's face as he barked into the link, 'Kill them.' No one shot at his boys. No one.

A second frequency of laser blasts whined across the comms, followed by silence.

'Secure,' Jordan's voice told him. 'We'll start transferring the cargo.'

Robert pointed his finger at the captain. 'Don't lie to me again.' He turned to one of his younger boys. 'How's the rest of the fleet, Matt?'

'Most crews put up a fight, sir. Around forty percent survival rate. Two ships are already being unloaded. All of our ships accounted for, no losses reported.'

'Tell them to get a move on,' Robert said. They'd ambushed the convoy in the outer system, but distress calls would have gone out.

He looked at the captain. 'Now before we go and get you stabbed, let's talk about the women.'

'You won't be hitting them.' The captain's flinch betrayed his fear, but his tone was determined.

'That right?'

'You and I have an understanding sir, but if you start hurting our women, well, I might just start misunderstanding.'

Robert laughed despite himself. 'I'm the guy with the weapons.'

'I'm just saying.'

The captain's wife pushed forward. 'We don't need any special favours from the likes of you. We're perfectly capable of being stabbed.'

Robert shrugged. He didn't feel as sanguine as they did at the idea of hurting innocent people, but if he was going to stab a woman, it would probably be one like her. 'Fine,' he said to the captain. 'Stab your own women, then.'

As he turned away, the comms crackled. 'Son, you'd better get down here.'

'Back playing up again, old man?'

'Get your smart-arse down here now before I smack you stupid.'

Robert grinned and turned to Ralph. 'Do what you do best, but don't kill them. And be careful with the blood.' Blood and zero-gee would never be friends. 'Let them fix themselves up and tie them to that centre seat. Make it look convincing, and hurry it up. No point sitting here like viper bait.'

He backed out of the bridge hatch, speaking into the link as he went. 'What's wrong?'

'I think you'd better come see for yourself.'

* * *

The Clipper broke apart, thrusters careening off into the depths of space, micro explosions rocking the hull before it finally cracked open, spilling air, cargo and people into space.

Gunn-Britt Grotenfelt watched from the cockpit of her Saker Mark III fighter. She was at holding station and in formation. Sigma-12, the twelfth pilot in the squad of twelve. She had been instructed to watch while Sigma-1 made the kill. Watch, and listen to the long range scanner. They were in a busy dark system; A precisely chosen location, but dangerous because of it.

She reported on scanner blips, none of which turned out to be ships. Her voice was cool, professional, but an angry inferno raged inside her. Not that she would waste a moment's concern on the Clipper's owner, the Federation's Secretary of Defence who was bound to be guilty of some heinous crime.

But the Clipper had had a crew of eleven. All of them civilians simply going about their business, doing their jobs, piloting, astrogation, engineering, transporting the ship from A to B. All of them butchered in front of her.

And she'd let it happen.

The link squawked. 'Now comes the fun part,' said a voice sounding giddy with excitement. Her lip curled. Sigma-1, Commander Whithers, had been looking forward to this butchery all week.

'Bombs away,' he called. Space was silent but Whithers created his own sound effects as his Thargoid-derived laser drifted off the nose of his Saker. He pulsed his retro thrusters to create distance. A brief flash of light twinkled from within the laser. It slowly separated into a constellation of stolen weapon components.

Evidence.

'Okay team, good work,' Whithers said. 'Report back to base, double time. All ship logs are passing by the Architect's desk, remember.'

Gunn hated that Whithers had command of the squad, despite his kill count, but that shouldn't be the only requirement for leadership. She grunted and aligned her Saker for the hyperspace jump.

Timing her move with care, Gunn altered her coordinates as Sigma-11 hypered out. While the team flew home, she made a micro jump, in system.

Five precious seconds. Breath held. Nothing on the scope. No Sakers doubled back. She was alone. She reversed the jump and returned to the weapon debris.

Twenty seconds since Sigma-11 had jumped.

Her own laser, enhanced, speared towards the debris atomizing it until her own sensors were blind to it. The Federation government would sniff over every inch of this dark system. What would they detect?

Forty-five seconds; a suspicious delay. She stared through the viewport, hoping her effort would be good enough. Turning the Saker, she wiped the pilot log and hyperspaced out.

* * *

Robert jumped from the ladder to the loose decking of the cargo deck.

Rust crunched under his magboots. Grabbing the railing he marched forward.

This ageing Python Freighter, well past its best-by date, had a deliciously big cargo hold. At the starboard bay entry he passed Griff, wondering not for the first time how this clean-shaven, seventeen year old Scot, on course for some fancy college on Beta Hydri, had landed under Robert's wing.

'Was the manifest accurate?' he rapped out.

Griff stiffened to an instinctive salute that withered under Robert's scowl. 'Yes sir, maize, maize and more maize, but also seeds.'

'Seeds? What kind?'

'The type you put in the ground, sir. I'm no botanist.'

'Damn straight you're not. Get moving.' He ducked through the hatch. The space ahead and beneath him opened up as though it were exposed to the vastness of the universe. At the far end, cloaked behind shadows, walkways, ladders and fog, his boys worked hard.

'Dad?'

'Down here,' the response echoed back to him.

He made his way to where the Wayfarer was docked into the Python's port cargo hatch. A string of octagonal containers floated through the hatch on magnetic sleds.

Jordan stood inside the doorway of a small room, holding out a lamp before him, as still as vacuum-frozen hydrogen fuel, only the tendrils of his receding hair moving. He stared down at a long, black box.

Robert moved to stand beside him. 'What is it?'

His father didn't speak. Robert looked around the room. Its walls were corrugated duralium siding. A hammer and blow torch were strapped to one side. No shelves, no light panels, just the big black box. He put his hand on his father's shoulder.

Jordan flinched. His head snapped round, eyes the size of Coriolis stations staring at Robert as if he were death himself.

'Dad! Dad, it's me. What's wrong?'

Jordan blinked and shook himself. He threw a hunted glance at Robert, then turned back to the box. His voice was a coarse whisper. 'It was for you, kiddo. All of it. Everything I did, I did for you. '

Robert suppressed a shiver. 'Dad, you're scaring me. Let's get you back to the ship.'

'They'll come now. They'll come and they won't stop. They don't like letting go of their own. They'll come.'

'Who? Who'll come?'

Jordan ran his hand over the top of the box. Robert watched as his father's fingers traced an embossed crest, a bird with long, sharp feathers, a flattened beak, triangular body and two antennae, then ran on to the three words beneath. Robert thought they were Latin but couldn't read them. 'Okay,' he said. 'It's a coffin. We'd better see who's in it.'

'Don't.' Jordan put his hand on Robert as though to pull him back, but Robert shrugged him off.

He unlatched the lid and raised it. An old man lay on a bed of red velvet, the diamond-pattern cushioning glinting out at them.

Jordan jerked back, tripping as he did so, momentarily floating free before his magboots sucked him to his feet. The hammer clattered against the siding and bounced off at a tangent. 'We have to go. Now!'

Robert raised his eyebrow. It was just a dead body, although... 'Who is it, Dad?' The face was strangely familiar. He couldn't place it. The academy? His tour of duty? Villist? One of his father's pirates?

Jordan spun, catching Robert off guard and trying to lift him, the way he'd carried him as a baby. Despite age and the prosthetic leg slowing him, Robert had to struggle to keep his feet on the ground. 'Okay, okay. Hang on, old man, I'm coming.'

'Dammit kiddo, you have no idea what I went through to get you away from them. I'm not letting them take you again.'

Before Robert could respond, the link crackled. 'Sir,' said Griff's voice. 'The scanner is picking up something.'

Troubled, Robert glanced at his father. He could no longer see the scourge of the eastern sectors, the one-time First Guard of the Royal New Aberdeen marines. He saw only a jittery wreck. 'What kind of something?' he barked into the link.

'Ships.'

Jordan grabbed his arm, straining the sleeve's seams. Robert found himself pulled so close their noses touched. 'We. Have. To. Leave.' His father was white, shaking. This wasn't Jordan Garry.

'Okay, we're going. Dad, what is it? Who is he?'

'A Ceeper.'

Robert glanced back at the fossil. 'A who?'

'The Circle of Independent Elite Pilots.'

Robert's lip curled. 'Those Quixotes?' He slammed shut the coffin lid. 'Lucky he's already dead.' His father pulled at his arm again and this time Robert didn't argue.

'Tell the fleet to split,' he said into the link as he strode out. 'Sell their haul and get back to the meeting coordinates in a month.' Down below, he could see the last of the containers floating into the Wayfarer, two men guiding them in. 'Stop loading, boys. We're done here.'

'Only four more to go,' said one of them. A new guy; he didn't get the way Robert did things, yet.

'And I say you're finished. Get on board or you're staying behind.'

Robert stopped at the Wayfarer's boarding tube, Jordan in tow, as the hollow ring of boots on decking reverberated through the floor. Ralph turned the corner and winked.

'Those women

.. Fates I've never seen anything like it. I took care of the men. Everyone's patched and tied up.'

'Don't let anyone say you're not a good man,' Robert said, slapping his back. He gestured his father forward and followed them on board. He was always the last man off.

The last of his ragtag fleet entered hyperspace as he entered the bridge. 'Just us?' Robert asked Griff, seated at the conn station.

'And the others,' Griff said, pointing at the scanner.

Robert climbed into his acceleration couch and cloned the scanner to his console; twenty or so blips. On the edge of sensor range, but closing.

'It's them,' Jordan whispered. Robert frowned. 'You sure?'

'Check the scanner. They're warping in and out of detection. It's their ship paint.'

Robert watched. Half the blips disappeared while another group emerged from empty space. 'What the Fates?'

'Who are they?' Ralph asked.

'CIEP,' Robert said. 'The Circle.'

'Get us out of here,' Jordan yelled.

Robert nodded at Griff. 'Do as he says.'

The Wayfarer shuddered as the engines kicked into life. The Python shrunk and slipped from sight.

'Hyperspace?'

'Starting countdown,' Griff said. The rest of his bridge crew filtered in, magboots clicking, and strapped in. Tactical, weapons and communications systems activated. They were ready for anything. Kind of.

Targeting reticules on the viewport bracketed the Circle ships. 'Weapons range in forty seconds.'

'We're good,' Robert said, smiling at Jordan. 'Five seconds to hyperspace.'

The countdown hit zero. Robert flinched, that micro-moment before the jump when the brain was prepared but the body wasn't.

Nothing happened. 'Griff?' Robert asked.

The counter reached negative-five. The targeting brackets grew.

Robert's heart rate jumped a notch. 'Griff,' he repeated, forcing nonchalance. 'Where is my hyperdrive?'

'I don't know,' Griff mumbled. Ralph unstrapped, floated to Griff's station. 'It's gone.'

'Gone?'

'They're coming,' wailed Jordan. 'They're coming.'

Robert ignored him. 'Hyperdrives don't bugger off without asking, Ralph, where the Fates is it?'

Ralph reddened, hit a switch. 'Thirty seconds for reset.'

Robert turned to the new guy at the helm. 'I hope you know some evasive manoeuvres.'

Ralph kept pressing buttons over Griff's shoulder, his magboots clicking under the strain of acceleration. 'It's overdue for a service, it's melted down.'

'You'd better pray to your god you're wrong,' Robert warned him. 'Or we're all dead. And get back to your seat for Bruce's' sake.'

'Incoming,' Matt yelled from tactical.

The ship bucked as if sucker punched by a big fist. The lights dimmed. Ralph smacked into the console and drifted free. He hit the roof with a grunt and pushed back to his seat.

'Return fire,' Robert yelled.

Matt spoke so fast his words ran together. 'Twomorecomingin.' Robert glared at Griff. 'Where's my damn drive?'

A half visible wraith screeched past the viewport, spewing laser pulses. A steady beam retaliated from the Wayfarer's turret.

Blips crowded the scanner. More ships flashed past, fired a salvo and retreated, dodging the turret's laser beam.

Ducks in a barrel.

'Shoot them, shoot them,' Robert yelled, pointing. 'How hard is it shoot a bloody ship?'

Robert saw Jordan lean forward and grab his link. 'Turret? The left-most fighter always jukes before he backs out of range. Watch for it.'

The ship rocked again and an explosion echoed from down below.

'What did we lose now?' Robert asked the bridge. Strapped in place, out of his element, he felt useless. 'Anybody?'

A liquid cough echoed over the link. 'Fuel scoop,' rasped Gerald. 'Cargo?'

'Contained. Emergency bulkheads in place. They won't take another direct hit.'

Two Circle ships swooped in, juked and backed away. The turret beam lanced out and a Circle ship exploded.

'Shields failing,' yelled Matt.

Robert screamed at Griff, 'Get us out now or we're dead.'

'Go,' yelled Griff. He slammed down the hyperdrive initiator.

Chapter 2

The Architect stood over the holographic galactic map in his command cabin when Lieutenant John Graham entered.

On the map various colours represented the different human factions. And then there was the part of the map with no colour...

Several stars glowed, holographic news captions hovering above the simulated galaxy: the Federation Times, the Imperial Gazette, and other media feeds that would be the first to jump on any breaking news.

None mentioned the Federation's Secretary of Defence. The Architect glanced up and sighed. He expected that from the Times – a cover up would be guaranteed. The biggest surprise was the Imperial Gazette, their biggest news article highlighting the Prince's fly fishing prowess.

Not one media feed even mentioned the Thargoids.

His shoulders drooped. Another twenty-four hours had passed since their last attempt to educate humanity and nothing to show for it.

Lieutenant Graham continued to wait at attention. 'What do you make of it, lieutenant?' the Architect asked, sweeping his arm across the map. 'Hiding themselves from the truth, denying the problem exists?'

Graham's gaze tracked the map. He glanced at the headlines and shook his head. 'You can lead a horse to water, sir, but you can't make it drink.'

The Architect returned his attention to the map. Achenar glowed bright blue; a long distance between the Empire and their location, too vast a distance to travel in such a short time, unsupported and unready.

'That is where you are wrong,' the Architect whispered. 'You can make anyone drink anything. You just need to know how to motivate them.'

He shook off the dark thoughts. 'Report. Did Oberon reach home?'

Graham fidgeted beside him, the yellow light from the doorway dancing across the map and stone floor like a dull flame. The Architect didn't look up.

'What happened?'

'Pirates.'

The Architect kept his expression calm, but his stomach twisted into a tight knot. Did those parasites have no sense of decency, of letting a man rest in peace? All the Circle ever seemed to do these days was tackle pirates. Every day there were more people to save, more pirates to stop and fewer resources to do it with. And the Thargoids were still on their way...

'Did they take him?' 'No, but-'

'But what?'

The Architect looked up, impatient for an answer. He had thought fear made Graham reticent, but it was anger that filled his face, clenched his fists. 'Well?'

'They opened his coffin.'

The Architect turned and strode to the circular window; Reinforcements criss-crossed the glass, like a spider's web. He ran both hands over his stubby white hair. His technology had failed to keep Oberon alive. Now he had failed his mentor again, unable to even protect him in death. His first failure as leader, how many more failures would follow?

Barren rock filled the view outside, smooth, apart from the countless tracks of mining transports, overlapping like the streets of his youth. In the distance the remnants of an octagonal frame dissolved into the soil. Blackness filled the sky above, but the cloud that enveloped the planet brightened.

Another day had started; a day already slipping away.

'Are we tracking them?'

'Of course. The one that landed on Oberon's freighter flew a blue and white cross, a clenched knife superimposed on top. The heraldry of the standard suggests a link to ancient Earth. Picts.'

'Destroy them. They're pirates after all. You shouldn't have much trouble finding volunteers.' Lieutenant Graham nodded and turned to leave.

'One more thing,' the Architect said. 'Assemble the elders. It's time to make a decision.'

Graham stiffened then left. The Architect understood his hesitance, shared it even. How had it come to this? He had joined the Circle of Independent Elite Pilots to save people, to protect them from their own darkness. But there were other darknesses out there too.

He clenched the bracelet in his pocket. A present for his granddaughter.

The clouds brightened outside, turning the soil from dirty soggy brown to festering brown. The lightening colours didn't change anything though. The planet still held the same secrets. Their responsibilities to humanity hadn't changed; they were the same people with the same horrific choices to make.

The Architect shook his head. Instead of clarifying his thoughts the view had muddled them further. If only you had lived a few more months, *Oberon*, he thought. Oberon's vision had always been clear, his conviction almost a second presence. He would not have had doubts.

The six elders arrived together in single file, black cloaks dragging along the ground, their hoods off and nestled against their necks. They formed a half-circle around him, trapping him against the window.

It still felt strange. He had been part of that half-circle, watching Oberon and waiting for his guidance. Now the circle looked to him. Now he was doing the guiding, theirs, and humanity's futures weighing on his shoulders.

'Friends,' the Architect started, turning. 'We stand at a crossroads. Our decision will decide the future course of humanity. You've read the Thargoid reports, you're aware of their movements beyond the fringe.'

He gestured to the galactic map. 'Once again not a single government has responded to our latest operation. Our attempts to nudge them away from their squabbles and toward their common foe have failed. Subtlety is not understood by the President of the Federation nor by the Emperor.'

The Architect spread his arms wide and kept his gaze at eye level, picking out points between each of the elders. 'I don't take this step lightly. It will weigh on my mind for the rest of my days.' Was he trying to talk himself into it? Or the elders out of it?

The elders stared at him with stony faces but they all leant forward, listening. 'A thousand years ago a man from Earth said, 'The only thing necessary for evil to triumph is for good men to do nothing'. Gentlemen, we are those good men. We have the righteousness, we have the knowledge and we have the power, to do something.

'Another saying I have read is, 'Monsters are not those who purport evil; monsters are not those who condone evil; monsters are those that choose not to stop evil'. We are not the pirates that disrupt society. We are not the bumbling machine of the Federation. We are not the smug, self-appreciating nobles of the Empire. We are not the money hungry Pilot's Federation.

'We are the Circle of the Elite. We are the ones who stand between the light and the darkness. We are the ones who must step forward and help humanity when it can't help itself. We are the first and last line of defence.'

The Architect took a moment – for effect – but also to gauge the reactions of the half-circle. Old Tom, white haired and deep wrinkled; Rapier Rick, the youngest of the elders and still quick with a blade; Hamer the fisherman; Dominic the Greater, and the rest. They shared the same firm look of conviction that Oberon wore, the same look that the Architect wished he had now.

'And so with great sadness I propose that we proceed with project Endure.'

The Architect breathed deeply and stepped back against the window. It was cold, leeching enough heat to make him shiver. Watching the men, he waited, praying, but not sure what he was praying for.

Oberon had devised the plan. Could the Architect see it through to completion?

'Aye,' said Old Tom, who would have followed Oberon into hell if he could have. Hamer went next, pounding his big fists together. Then Rick, Dom, Giovanni and Swenson chimed in with nods.

The Architect exhaled, feeling one weight drop from his shoulders and an even bigger one take its place. 'It's unanimous. We have started.'

The elders nodded, bowed and left. They had little time for ceremony these days. The Architect watched them go, wondering if they secretly shared his doubts.

The bracelet weighed heavily in his pocket.

He reached for the link console by the holo-display, arm infused with lead and fingers stiff as rock. He activated the link. 'Get Commander Tybalt in here. He has a job to do.'

* * *

Gunn snapped her head up above the console.

Half crouching, she stared down the passage toward the computer core's exit. She'd heard something – a voice, a footstep, something, but now only silence greeted her.

Her thighs burned but she froze, not wanting to miss the slightest sound.

She breathed through her mouth, slowly, quietly, waiting.

She lowered her gaze to her wrist chrono: zero three hundred hours; absolutely no legitimate reason for her to be in the core at all, let alone in the middle of the night. If someone found her there would be hard questions asked.

The light beyond the passage was dull, but steady. No sound, no shadows. The core's toroidal shape played tricks with noise, amplifying the tick of a distant coolant pump to make it sound close by. Maybe she'd imagined the noise. She eased back down behind the console and checked her reader. The progress bar crept across the screen as it mined the servers.

She froze. A voice. Deep, but quiet, and familiar. She replayed it in her head. The memory was fleeting, unsubstantial.

She'd been thorough. The Alioth Intelligence Service had taught her how to break their best systems. What if she'd made a mistake? What if the Circle's systems were better?

The progress bar grew another centimetre. Was it too late to escape back to her cabin? Even if they knew someone had mined the core they wouldn't know who. If she could get out without being spotted she could salvage the whole operation.

A muted thunk echoed from the exit. Combat boot on the floor? Ammo charge clicking into position? The passage light remained steady.

The reader beeped.

Panicking, she tried to muffle the sound. She snapped her gaze back to the door, expecting guards to rush in, weapons out, screaming for her surrender.

No one came, no one yelled, no bullets drilled into the computers. It was just her, a torus of computer terminals and a cooling vent trying in vain to keep the area cool.

She glanced from the list of files on the reader to the empty passage, beckoning her out.

At the centre of the torus a ladder dropped down a shaft to the inside of the core. There were only two passages out to the rest of the station. Two ways in, two ways out. She'd put a team on both passages, out of sight, linked so they moved as one, trapping the target in the middle, or use one team to flush her out, straight toward the other team.

She was unarmed.

The armoury had strict sign-out rules, every weapon logged and traced. She could take down two or three unarmed, maybe four if she surprised them, and if she hadn't been awake for thirty hours straight. Her hand drifted to her empty holster. Right then she longed for her old Detective Special, locked away back at Montgomery, along with her flask. Fates, she wanted that flask right about now.

The coolant vent hushed. Distant pumps hummed, carrying oxygen, water, coolant. Normal sounds, all of them.

'Torpedo it,' she murmured and dropped to her backside.

There were twenty files on the reader, comms to and from the base commander. The first was personal; humiliating, but irrelevant. The next few she filed for later reading.

The subject of the last message almost stopped her heart. She tried to breathe, holding her chest as if it would shatter if she didn't hold it in place.

She heard the noise three times before it registered past the blood roaring in her ears. Shit, shit, shit. Time to go. She downloaded the reader to the crystal in her forearm, deleted and cleared the reader's memory, removed any digital tracks she might have left, folded up the reader and climbed to her feet.

The way looked, sounded clear; ambush or not? Safe or not?

Her legs held fast. At Montgomery they'd taught her to control her fear, but they couldn't surgically remove it.

She'd have to bluff it. She untied her long brown hair, ruffled it across her face. She unfolded the reader, opened it to her private link account and stepped forward.

The exit passage intersected a grey corridor bathed in blood red light unaffected by shadow or person. The on-duty technician's workshop was out of sight to the left, easily big enough to fit twenty armed people. It could be loaded tighter than a Lakon freighter on a milk run and she would never know.

She glanced back to the computer console. She'd hidden behind similar things as a child. Toyboxes, cabinets, too scared to move or scream while drunken foster fathers raged, while pirates raped, pillaged and destroyed.

But she wasn't a stupid, cowardly girl anymore. She controlled her future. She straightened her shoulders and marched up the passage.

The corridor was empty.

She stopped in shock, shoulders still bunched tight, ready for a confrontation. She slid her right foot across the polished steel floor, transferred her weight, slid her left forward, quietly moving through a tee intersection and up to the workshop's hatch.

Empty, save the technician, squeezed in behind a motion desk, eyes glued to the monitor, hands waving past the receiver.

Her shoulders dropped. Had she—

'Hey!' yelled Whithers behind her, his voice like grinding gears, unlubricated.

Gunn stiffened then relaxed immediately, an amateurish reflex, and turned to her squad commander. Whithers filled the corridor, his face contorted in red angry wrinkles. She felt a sudden urge to pee but that wouldn't fit her character. Instead she stared up at him, channelling insolence, annoyance and irritation – an easy reflex now – and gave him her stock standard growly-scowl.

'What?'

'What are you doing? You know the rules.'

The curfew, she'd forgotten about that. All active pilots were in lockdown, Circle wide, due to the leak.

'Can't sleep. That a crime?'

Whithers stepped forward, raised his index finger. Gunn stepped back. 'You touch me with that thing, you'll lose it.'

The finger stopped, half raised, pointing at her toes, then snapped up to an inch from her nose. 'Get to your quarters. I'll be informing the station commander about this.'

'You do that,' she sneered. She turned and marched down the corridor. The moment the hatch of her dark quarters slid shut behind her, exhaustion overwhelmed her and she slumped back against the door. Every muscle cried for her to slide down and sleep where she collapsed, but her bunk was five steps away so she stumbled forward, kicking something over. She landed in her bunk.

Fatigue crashed over her in waves but she couldn't sleep. She rolled toward the wall and activated her reader. She flicked through the station commander's messages; one to his wife – obviously a patient woman – and one to his superiors mentioning 'the leak'. The commander had proved his base was clean. She fought the urge to laugh. She almost wished they'd caught her, just to prove him wrong.

But those messages were irrelevant. She flicked through to the last one. From the Architect.

The head of the Circle of Independent Elite Pilots and with Oberon's passing, the undisputed leader. When first undercover she'd had a 'try-to-fit-in' drink with her squad (grape juice for her though) when the Architect was brought up in conversation. Her squad spoke of him as if he were a god, that he knew what was happening before it happened. A pilot said he had been born on Soontill, the lost Thargoid world, but everyone had just laughed. Still, a sense of awe surrounded him, an aura so blinding and so thick that no one knew anything about him, his age, his appearance, if he was even human. The technology she had seen made her wonder…

She read the subject line again, her veins going cold.

Project Endure is live.

The message had been sent to seven individuals, four she recognised as base commanders. Were there seven bases or were they merely members of renown? She still didn't fully understand the leadership of the Circle. She was at the bottom of the pile. And a woman. Just being an Elite pilot didn't make her special, but being a man would have helped. There wasn't much she was prepared to do about that though.

Sexism was their weakness.

She kept reading. The Architect had authorised the Circle to proceed with project Endure, Commander Tybalt in overall command. She skimmed the next few lines – a lot of umming and arring – and got to the meat of it.

Gunn's heart beat a slow, distant thud, the throb of a ship's engines if you put your ear to the hull, the loping, erratic idle of a misalignment.

The weapon is operational and we shall proceed to unify the human race against the Thargoids and wipe away the last remnants of the cold war.

It took a moment for the words to sink in, for reality to be absorbed through her consciousness. Her hands shook. This was it. This was why she was here, why the AIS had thrown all that training at her, why she had spent those two years beefing her pilot ranking up to Elite.

Because AIS had known, or at least suspected, that this group of freedom fighting, pirate murdering, humanity protecting scumbags, would turn on those they'd sworn to protect.

The last remnants of the cold war. The Federation? The Empire? She loved neither, but to destroy them completely? Sweeping changes to the face of humanity bracketed as a project task?

Project Endure. A second time around the name made her shudder.

She forced herself to read the other messages, though her mind was travelling to the other side of colonised space where a war was about to start…

A punch to the shoulder woke her up. 'You snore so loud you can't even hear your alarm?' said Jessica. 'We're on.'

Two words that woke up any pilot; Gunn snapped upright, shrugging off the sleep.

Oh four hundred hours. She'd slept for thirty five minutes. She closed the reader – on standby – wriggled off the bed, flicked off her shoes and squirmed into her flight gear, prepped in a pile on the floor. Step into the boots, pull up and seal the pressure suit, shrug on the overalls and zip up. Her body raced through the motions while she thought back to last night.

Project Endure.

She shrugged it off. Not the right time. 'What's the mission?' She realised she'd left her clothes on underneath. That would make her acceleration couch even less comfortable.

'A pirate stole Oberon's body before he reached home,' Jessica said, grabbing a necklace from her bunk and securing it in her flight suit's velcro pocket.

'Bastards.' Gunn may have been undercover, purposefully distrusting everyone, but even she had fallen prey to Oberon's charisma, a man as obsessed about freedom and justice as she was.

Jessica patted herself down and nodded. 'Let's go. Whithers is waiting.' Gunn could tell from Jessica's mocking tone that she was rolling her eyes. They stepped from their quarters. Being undercover had its perks. She didn't mind waking up in the middle of the night if it meant eliminating pirate filth, making the galaxy that little bit safer for everyone else.

She'd memorised the AIS statistics on pirates. On average, each pirate tallied twenty six and a half victims before they were arrested or killed, a damage bill of over five hundred thousand credits. One dead pirate made a big difference.

A thought suddenly struck: The foe of my foe is my friend. Before she had handed in her AIS badge and slunk off to reappear in a sleazy bar frequented by the Circle, her boss Trotsky had given her his final instructions:

Fit in, do what they do, be one of them. Use your skills, find assets, use them wisely. And listen. Listen, and wait.

What was her plan anyway? She couldn't just make contact with the AIS, not while surrounded by the Circle. And Trotsky had commanded her not to break cover unless ordered to. She'd spent three years preparing her cover. Once she broke it she couldn't get it back.

A little free labour to help her do a bit of ground work would be a good idea, but it would be impossible to implement.

Jessica and Gunn entered the lift. The artificial gravity weakened as the lift shuttled downward. Her magboots engaged and her hair drifted upward. She gathered it in a vertical pony. Her business hair.

She glanced at Jessica. The woman was a few years younger than Gunn, with the skin tone to prove it. She tied her curly hair into a bun but her eyes were wide, focused on an imaginary point in the distance. Her lips moved to a silent mantra, repeated over and over. They had flown together, staked out pirate bases together, protected humanity together. They were a team.

If you betray the Circle you will be betraying *her*. The lift indicator flashed past the last deck.

She shook her head. Jessica was one of 'them', not a friend. And neither was the pirate.

The lift opened onto the launch bay and Jessica ran out ahead. The bay was a long rectangle of steel and lights and ships. Enhanced Sidewinders and Saker Mark III fighters were latched in docking clamps along the walls and roof. Small, fast, deadly and painted in Elite black.

There were other bases like this; Hundreds of Elite pilots and an adoring public who would follow them.

She was just one person.

'Think fast,' Jessica yelled, tossing Gunn her helmet. She caught it – just – and tugged it on.

'Time to pick up the trash,' Gunn quipped, a Circle motto she agreed with. She raced up the boarding ramp of her Saker. She was surrounded by enemies with no one she could trust, in a situation she didn't fully understand, but she climbed into the pilot's chair and it no longer mattered. Just her against the pirates, ship-to-ship, pilot-on-pilot, and that was something she understood just fine.

Chapter 3

The Wayfarer punched out of hyperspace into the CD 32-331 system. 'Towards the gas giant, go,' roared Robert before the hyperdrive could wind down. He watched the pulsing hyperspace vector from a rear view camera. 'Collapse,' he whispered. 'Collapse.'

This was their fourth jump since the ambush, three empty dark systems and now here, two gas giants and a settled rocky planet further in system.

The Lanner's main engine expelled plasma across the rear view and they blasted forward. The vector shrunk, its pulses growing smaller and weaker.

Robert leant forward, heart racing, eyes riveted to the scanner.

The vector flashed, and collapsed. Robert exhaled in relief just as the final pulse reflected off a sharp black surface.

A ship.

'Incoming!' he yelled. He turned to the main viewport. The gas giant Middleton grew before them, a sea of blues and greens, maelstroms raging across the surface.

The black shapes formed into metallic birds of prey, swept forward wings, pointed beaks and a halo of engine wash stretching for kilometres behind them.

'Four of them,' yelled Ralph.

'More'll be coming,' Jordan whispered. 'They hunt like Vipers, in big packs.'

Robert checked the sensors. They were half an astronomical unit away from Middleton, a quarter of a unit ahead of the Ceepers, who were at least three times faster than the Wayfarer. Not good maths. He searched his console for inspiration. He needed extra speed, distance, anything.

'Dump the cargo,' he yelled.

'Wait,' Jordan said, 'I have an idea.' Robert's eyes widened. 'Jack in the box?' Jordan winked. 'Jack in the box.'

'Jack in the box?' asked Griff.

The distance to the Sakers dropped, the readout switching from AUs to KMs. Their engine plumes faded then grew from their wings, retros at full fire.

Robert activated the link. 'Gerald?'

'Yeah?'

'You in the cargo bay?'

'Where else?'

'Load the mines and grenades into the cargo containers. Anything that explodes.'

Gerald's voice crumbled. '...I'm strapped in.'

'We'll slow down, but it gives you less time. Eject them as soon as they're done.' Robert switched the link to the gun turret. 'Jimmy?'

'Sir.'

'Get ready for a Jack in the box.' Jimmy's voice rose in pitch. 'Yes-sir!'

Robert turned back to the viewport, watching the readout drop. 'Keep it steady.'

The Circle struck fifty thousand kilometres away from Middleton.

Four beams shot out, criss-crossing the darkness, smashing into the Lanner's shields.

The Lanner jarred and shrieked, the lights dimming as energy routed to the shields. A bass tremor ran through the ship as Jimmy's turret retaliated. A distant flash of fire erupted.

'Clipped one,' Jimmy yelled.

'Clipping's not going to cut it James,' Robert said. He switched the link. 'Gerald, where are my damn jack in the boxes?'

Out the viewport one of the Sakers spun around and fired its laser. The shields sizzled, collapsed. An explosion rang out. Buckling steel groaned from under the deck.

'Ready,' Gerald rasped over the link. He sucked in a breath. 'Depressurising cargo bay.'

The Lanner shivered. Fourteen cargo containers tumbled past the rear camera and into the distance. The Sakers split around the containers and fired back.

The turret laser shot out, scything through the containers.

Fire erupted behind them, a chain reaction of oranges and reds and then a bigger explosion. The vacuum extinguished the flame, revealing only three Sakers, one hanging in a cloud of smoke and fuel.

A warbling alarm cut through the bridge. 'Missiles inbound,' Ralph said.

Griff activated the electronic counter measure system. One missile wobbled, its nose gyrating in an ever increasing circle then it spun out, trailed a figure eight and exploded.

The other missile kept coming.

'Jimmy,' Robert called, but Jimmy yelled, 'On it.' The missile raced forward, its red nose cone reflecting the greens and blues from Middleton.

'Jimmy,' Robert repeated. He saw the guide vanes on the missile, the thruster nozzle gimballing as Matt threw them into a spiral.

Jimmy's laser narrowed in, veered away as Matt chucked the Lanner through another dive, and closed back in.

The missile exploded. Klaxons blared and the Lanner jarred sideways.

Laser beams flashed past the viewport—

—and then the clouds of Middleton engulfed them.

The darkness blued, tendrils of fog and gas building, buffeting the Lanner. The scanner became grainy and died.

A Saker burst through the gas one hundred metres behind them.

'Fire the retros then dive,' Robert commanded. 'Ralph, hit the kill switch.'

Ralph's fingers twitched. He turned to Robert. 'You sure?'

'Do it.'

The thrusters illuminated the viewport, plasma igniting the surrounding gas. The Saker flashed past, caught off guard, then Ralph pressed the kill switch and everything went dark.

The Lanner keeled over, tumbling downward into the depths, the greens shifting through blues to purples. Inside the gas giant, Robert's sense of down spun from the roof to the floor and across the walls. Only the cushioning inertia compensation kept him from vomiting.

He closed his eyes – a marginal improvement – and counted to thirty. He whispered to Matt. 'Activate secondary thrusters only. Get us out of this dive.'

'With pleasure.' Matt waited for Ralph to energise the thrusters then manoeuvred them to an even keel. The swirling gas outside stabilised until it could have been any dark snowy night back at New Aberdeen.

'What's our thermal status?' Robert said.

Ralph checked his screen. 'Good. The vents are near ambient.'

'Okay. Bring the infrared scanners online.'

The gas giant was a relatively cool smudge across the IR scanner, but two blobs of intense heat blipped in and out of range. 'Our friends,' Robert said.

Two more blobs appeared, then another two until Robert lost count. 'How many?' he asked, not minding if no one answered.

'Twenty-four,' Griff said. 'Two squadrons.'

'Can we wait them out?' Ralph suggested.

Jordan shook his head. 'They won't give up. They'll work in shifts if they have to. They can keep watch on this gas giant long after we've run out of power and air.'

'Which won't take too long,' Robert said, half listening. He was watching the blobs. Their movements were sharp, defined and aggressive.

He'd been on the other side before, hunting for prey, waiting them out. It wasn't easy. Initially perhaps with the adrenaline, but boredom eventually seeped in, no matter how vigilant you were.

He kept watching, waiting for the scanner blobs to slow down, for their search patterns to grow sloppy, but they didn't. Hours passed and despite them searching for a neutron in a flare-star they were still probing the gas giant with rigour.

It felt personal.

His men were walking around, stretching, Ralph nearly bending in half. Griff and Matt leant against a console, gesturing to each other, while Jordan sat perfectly still, staring out the viewport. Dad, the lone guardsman. Gerald and Jimmy appeared at the hatch, both patched up after their scrapes in the battle. 'We need more medical supplies,' Gerald said.

Robert shrugged. They hadn't been to a trade port in two months. They were running out of a lot of things.

'What was that?' Jordan asked.

'What?' Robert said, climbing out of his couch. His gaze followed Jordon's finger out the viewport. A patch of gas lightened briefly and faded. Wind buffeted the ship.

The others crowded forward. 'Lightning storm?'

Another flash, closer this time, bloomed. The Wayfarer rocked, like an old sailing ship on choppy seas.

'I don't think so,' Robert whispered. He dived back to his chair, checked the scanner. The flashes were big bright splotches in infrared. He saw their pattern immediately. Not a random, natural pattern.

A regular, canvassing pattern.

'Sonic depth charges,' he yelled, strapping in. The bridge clanged with magboots on deck as the others dived into their seats. Jimmy and Gerald raced out the hatch. No swearing, no fuss, just straight back into it.

'Can we go deeper?' Griff asked.

Ralph shook his head. 'Not in a Lanner, too much pressure.'

'They're depth charges, you idiots,' Jordan said. 'There's no place to hide.'

Robert scowled at Jordan but nodded anyway. 'He's right. Those charges have a big radius. We're leaving. Matt, get us out of here.'

Ralph brought all systems back on line and Matt swung the Lanner around and away from the charges. 'They'll send us straight back to the Bruce once we clear the gas giant,' Jordan said.

Robert ignored him. He stared out the viewport at the thinning clouds, brain racing for a solution.

'Robert,' Jordan said. Robert didn't say anything.

'Sure would be good to hear your plan,' Ralph said. 'Don't really feel like dying today.'

'Just shut up for a second.' Robert closed his eyes, thinking. He couldn't fight his way out. He couldn't keep jumping for ever – he was using fuel, the Circle were hitchhiking. He couldn't reason with them, couldn't tempt them with cargo. There was no one around to help.

'Mis-jump,' he breathed.

Matt choked, Griff inhaled sharply and Ralph growled. 'Do you want to kill us all? You can't mis-jump a gen three drive.'

Depth charges exploded to either side, sonic shockwaves pummeling the ship, the hull rattling as the energy dissipated.

'I've seen it done before,' Robert said calmly, though the memory was anything but calm.

'Sirius Corp ran extensive tests,' Matt said. 'They couldn't make it work.'

Robert ignored him and turned to Griff. 'Charge the drive, destination anywhere. I want to jump as soon as possible.'

'But Sirius—' Matt started. Robert cut him off.

'I'm not going to kill you, Matt.' *I hope.* 'Just fly her straight. Whatever you do, don't manoeuvre. Move us off course and we die. Do you understand?'

Matt was young and his hands shook but his face was firm, his eyes narrowed. 'Yes sir.'

'Griff, you need to activate the hyperdrive twice in quick succession, the second time just as we enter the vector. Not when we're inside, not before we enter. Clear?'

'It won't have enough time to recharge.'

'Doesn't need to. Hyperspace quirk.'

Ralph caught Robert's eye. 'How do you know this is going to work?'

I don't. 'Trust me.'

They burst out of the gas giant. Two Sakers were in high orbit facing downward. Time stalled for a moment, the Sakers hanging before them, the gas giant behind them, the darkness of space unmoving and uncaring. Then Jimmy fired the turret, shredding a Saker into cosmic rubbish. He tracked around to the other Saker which fired its own laser then snap-rolled away.

The hyperdrive controls counted down.

'Keep it steady,' Robert reminded them. 'No sudden moves.'

'More Sakers incoming,' Ralph called.

Robert saw them out the viewport, grey-black twinkles trailing blue engine plumes.

'Five seconds,' Griff said. 'Four. Three. Two. One.'

Space distorted ahead of them, stars stretching, brightening. Robert held his breath, gaze glued to the viewport, counting. Each moment seemed disjointed from the rest, a slow, jerking fall into the maw. If he got this wrong …

'Now!' he yelled.

Griff slammed his hand down again.

The stretched stars twisted like a tornado. An invisible hand grabbed the Lanner and smashed it sideways. The vector ripped apart and blinding white filled the viewport.

* * *

Admiral McKowsky stood before the full height window of his command room, staring out at the infinity, the hull of the Behemoth stretching out to a distant point.

He couldn't see home. A million stars out there but he couldn't see, or just didn't recognise Sol. Nothing to be ashamed of in that – they were as far from civilised space as one could get – but it still felt like a betrayal to his family, to his flag and to himself.

He'd been away for too long, hiding in the darkness, just waiting. He closed his eyes and sighed. He'd look again tomorrow.

He returned to his desk, magnetic cane tapping on the floor. Together with his boots they formed a waltz. One, two, three, one, two, three; a frustratingly slow waltz, but at least he was still dancing. 'You don't look a day over ninety-five,' he cackled to himself.

The desk was a duralium monstrosity, twice as wide as he was tall and almost as deep. He couldn't reach half the things on it without standing up and leaning over. An archaic, impractical monstrosity with sentimental value.

He sat down in the chair, strapped in and pulled in under the desk. The chair's magnetic couplers re-engaged. He ran his hands over the desk. It had been the side of a ship once, salvaged and honed to perfect flatness. It still wore its history though – a starburst of carbon scoring here, half worn lettering of 'AAAI' stamped there, and the signature of its foolish pilot etched in with a plasma torch before its maiden, and final, voyage.

He activated the tablet and looked through the day's paperwork. Dry and of no value, McKowsky still made himself review every report. Routine was all they had to maintain their discipline; routine, and the odd sortie. That would change soon enough though. He doubled the emergency drills and live fire combat sessions. They had to be ready.

The door chimed. 'Enter,' said McKowsky.

A level down, the hatch slid open and Commander Criddoch stepped through, datapad in hand. He gazed up at McKowsky with wide eyes and a slight smile, the look of unquestioned reverence. McKowsky nodded and placed the tablet back on the table, a deliberate movement, hard learned in a low-gee environment. Criddoch's boots clicked as he climbed the steps and stopped by McKowsky's right shoulder. He snapped his heels together and gave a quick-smart salute; as crisp as ever.

'Report,' McKowsky said.

'It looks like it's started.'

A flash of annoyance wrinkled McKowsky's eyes, but it passed. When they had first lost their power, their backing, their prestige, such intel would be cause for a demotion. Now, 'looks like' was the best he could get. What does a puppet master do when his puppet strings have been cut?

'Any problems?' McKowsky said, letting go of the past. *Adapt, migrate or perish*, that was what Father had always said.

Criddoch didn't reply. McKowsky glanced up, saw Criddoch's jaw working, as if chewing over the best response instead of delivering it. 'I asked you a question, Commander.'

'Maybe, sir,' Criddoch rushed.

'Maybe? What do you mean maybe?' Now McKowsky was mad. Two indistinct answers from Criddoch in two minutes was a first. A third would see a reprimand. He knew better.

Criddoch stepped back, his body angling toward the exit. 'There was a pirate.'

'What of the scum?'

'Our listeners intercepted a message, a pirate has upset their plans somehow.'

'Somehow how? What could a pirate do?'

Criddoch took another step back, then stepped forward to recover. 'We're not sure.'

McKowsky stared into Criddoch's eyes, filling the moment with disappointment. Then his gaze dropped to the pad. 'Leave it.'

Criddoch placed the pad on the desk then stepped back. He held his hands behind his back, staring into infinity, ready for a dressing down.

'Find some answers. You're the Commander of the Crimson corps. Use them. Don't come back until you have concrete information. Now get out.'

Criddoch saluted, spun on the spot and marched out as fast as his training would allow.

McKowsky let him. He reviewed the all too brief report. Yet another incident on the Eastern fringe, an attack against a pirate fleet. Circle activity had increased across the board, but was this an isolated incident or something far larger at play? He knew of the theft at Eta Cassiopeia, the destruction the Circle had caused. He knew what the Circle had stolen he just didn't know what they would use it for; or when they'd do it.

Fates, he needed more damn intel.

The small of his back started aching and he pushed the chair back to stand. Twenty minutes at his desk, the best he'd done for two months. Perhaps the coming events were rejuvenating him. He stepped back over to the window, not searching for home but this pirate, and how he could cause enough fuss to upset the Circle of the Elite so.

Chapter 4

The explosion ripped through the Wayfarer. The bang of emergency bulkheads slamming into place reverberated through the hull. The depressurisation slewed the Wayfarer around, bringing the horizon into view, the stars a hazy blur beyond.

'Dive,' Robert yelled at Matt. The hyperdrive had scrambled after the mis-jump. There was only one way to go.

Sakers flashed past, banking in the upper atmosphere then turning for an attack run. 'Jimmy, shoot them for Bruce's sake!'

They had been less than ten kilometres above the surface of Skardee IV, halfway down the gravity well, when the Circle ships had surprised them.

The turret gun stayed silent.

'Jimmy!' Robert yelled. He stared at the link as if that would Jimmy answer faster. The link normally glowed green when a connection was made.

The green light wasn't on.

Robert's chest felt crushed, riding six gees without dampening. The bridge quietened, the beeping controls, the air conditioners, everything muted except his breathing and his thoughts. 'Jimmy?'

The silence stretched from one moment to the next, then laser bolts flashed out from below, smashing against the armour. The ship shuddered under the blows, shaking like an ore crusher.

'We're not going to make it,' shrieked Griff.

Robert caught a glimpse of the boy's stricken face – too young to die. 'Where are those damn Vipers?' he yelled at Ralph.

'Five klicks and closing,' Ralph said. A glance at the damage readout and simple maths told Robert he was two seconds short of a 'Get out of Ross 128 free' card. He had five men on board still. He wouldn't, couldn't let them die.

'Open the heat vents.'

'They'll wrench off at this speed,' Griff said. 'Do it. All of them!'

Hydraulics droned below decks and the level on the temperature gauge collapsed, pumps sending the fluid up to the vents like blood to the surface of the skin.

A Ceeper ship flashed past, another laser beam found its mark and the Wayfarer skewed downward.

'Shields gone,' yelled Griff, then his voice rose an octave, 'hydraulics overloading. They can't take the strain.'

Robert waited another three seconds until the temp dropped enough. The heat dumps would be glowing good and bright. 'Fire the chaff out the back ports. All of it.'

The ship rocked again, though Robert couldn't tell if it was from the chaff or another explosion.

The sky went white.

'Down, down!' yelled Robert, helpless in his chair, hoping Matt got the message. His stomach lurched, though he couldn't tell in which direction, the viewport still whited out.

The ship shivered and shook, Robert's teeth chattering and then darkness returned.

There was one less blip on the scanner.

'Ha ha!' yelled Griff. 'That'll show the buggers.'

'Four more incoming,' yelled Matt. He pushed the Wayfarer through a spiral, the hull groaning in protest. Robert winced. 'Don't break yet,' he whispered to the ship.

Four Interpol Viper Mark III's roared past, beam lasers spewing death at the Circle Sakers. One of them disappeared off the scanner and the rest fell back.

'Get us out of here, quickly,' Robert said, 'before they realise they're shooting at their friends. Find us somewhere to hide and lick our wounds.'

And think.

Those might have been Circle ships, but they weren't the ones from Middleton. They were hunting him, singling him out, using multiple teams to track him, but he had no idea why. And if they hadn't hitchhiked on his mis-jump, how in Bruce's name had they found him?

* * *

The boys pulled out the emergency camouflage netting – a marathon in itself – and with Matt and Griff climbing over top and everyone else down below they were able to cover the ship. They'd half flown, half glided into the Red Wash and then park-cum-crashed under a rocky outcropping.

He personally checked the netting weights, pulling here and there, checking the ship from different angles, imagining its appearance from a distance and from above. Then he lined up the boys to check them for injuries. Some expressions were dazed, distant, but they weren't seriously hurt.

Next he scouted their surroundings to get a feel for the land – good ambush points, possible attack points, good defensive burrows. He wandered until he couldn't think of anything else that he could do.

Only then did Robert climb the ladder to the turret, each rung a mountain, a surge of will power required to gain that extra foot of height; rung, after rung, concentrating on the once-knurled-but-now-smooth texture against his hands, the clang of the ladder as he put his foot down. He kept his gaze down, delaying the moment for as long as possible, until he ran out of ladder.

It would have been a quick death.

Jimmy didn't have a home, or at least one he ever mentioned. The Wayfarer was his home. He'd joined Robert's crew to see the galaxy and get rich. The dark side of piracy never seemed to bother him.

There wasn't any wood in the Wash, just rock and sand and dust, so they rigged a cross out of the twisted melted girders of the turret and banged it into the ground. They gathered around, heads down, all of them silent.

'The cross tells a story,' said Ralph. 'He would have liked that.'

No one said anything else. They were probably all thinking the same thing: *It could have been me.*

Robert had ordered Jimmy up there, given him thirty seconds to climb up and strap back in.

He had ordered a man to his death.

He turned away, feeling the gaze of his boys on his back, and stared through the netting to the tally scribed into a landing strut. Something Malin had started. Each person he killed got a scribe. But what about those who he didn't mean to kill? He lifted his pressure suit pants leg, pulled his Sgian-dubh from his boot and reached up to scratch another mark.

A hand clapped him on the back, a strong, guiding hand; the hand that had steered him for so many years. 'Don't be too hard on yourself son,' Jordan said, stepping up shoulder to shoulder. 'You're the Commander. It's your job to command. They know it and they follow you because they know you put them first.'

'I didn't put Jimmy first though, did I?'

'If Jimmy hadn't gone up there we'd all be dead.'

'So you're saying seven deaths are not okay but one death is?'

Jordan's lips dropped into a sad line. His eyes pinched in that 'worried father' way. He grabbed Robert's shoulders and squeezed.

'It's Villist all over again,' Robert said. 'I came back to get away from that.'

Jordan pulled back but held onto both of Robert's shoulders. 'You could have stayed as my gunner with no responsibilities, but that's not you. You're a leader. You had to form your own clan, even though you knew what was at stake.' Jordan stared at him for a moment. 'You're something special. Remember that.'

Robert let the silence hang for a moment then turned away. 'I'd better get the boys organised.'

Even under the camo-netting the ship looked as if someone had dragged it through a shredder. The heat vents were gone, the hyperdrive initiators mere stubs protruding from the aft section. Half the hull consisted of emergency bulkheads. There was no top turret and way too many holes.

It was a wreck.

He considered abandoning it. Logically it was the right thing to do. It would make it harder for the Circle to track him, and the cost to rebuild would be astronomical.

But he was a man down. He couldn't part with the ship he'd grown up on, he'd lost too much already. Besides, there was still grain in the hold. That would help pay for the repairs.

His gaze turned to the Garry Standard emblazoned along the hull, a fist clenching a knife superimposed over the St Andrew's Cross. He couldn't have it towed to the dry-dock looking like that; ditto for the shark teeth and the thruster upgrades. It had to look like an innocent, stock Lanner.

'I'll get the jalopy,' said Jordan as he pushed the camo-netting aside and disappeared up the cargo ramp.

CHAPTER 4

The boys laboured through their work, movements stiff and stilted. Griff didn't laugh; Ralph wasn't overbearing. Matt walked back and forth, eyes wide and unfocused.

Robert clapped his hands. 'Come on boys. Life carries on. Do you want to die too or do you want to get off this rock and back to your lives? Get it done.'

He turned away from the mutterings. He didn't want to work either, but as Jordan reminded him, he was the commander.

A growl sounded from the cargo bay and Jordan appeared atop the jalopy at the edge of the ramp.

The boys called the jalopy the Bug, a squat platform with a control stick, half a windscreen and six thick mud wheels; perfect for sneaking into town to get supplies if things were too hot at the starport, an excellent investment.

The bug roared as it drove down the ramp, then it hit the sand and the big wheels dug in. Jordan pushed through the netting, swung around and Robert jumped on.

The Wash covered half the continent, red sand, red rocks and a littering of mesas. They passed the first rondavel hut in the early evening. It was an upturned coffee cup of red rock half submerged in the ground. Old turbine blades adorned the roof, scrubbed to a bright sheen by the desert dust, perhaps to deflect the sun's heat. Robert thought of the Wayfarer. Nobody was turning his girl into a house.

The red star slipped toward the horizon and the distant sand shimmered like liquid fire. A few shaggy dromedaries grazed on tufts of dull brown grass. The animals ignored the Bug as Robert and Jordan drove past.

As night approached the desert came to life, lizards emerging from hidden dens, insects warbling to potential mates. Something splattered against the windscreen. The sand changed to a natural desert pavement, eventually forming a road between two rows of rondavels. There were lights in the distance, growing brighter as the orange horizon darkened.

Technology became evident. Houses, shops, utilities, all of them appearing half submerged in quick sand, and finally the starport, its tall, synthetic construction standing out amongst the surrounding earthen buildings. Shops lined the starport perimeter, traders, suppliers, ship services and towies. The flight control obelisk and a ship hangar towered over the starport walls. Jordan stopped the Bug outside a towing office, a single light panel burning bright above the door.

'Going in?' asked Jordan.

Robert surveyed the shop front. Blackened glass windows and pitted aluminium framing that looked like they had spent a lifetime by the sea instead of slap bang in the desert. The fliers in the window, the 'i' missing from the 'Tom's Salvage and Towing' sign, all spelt out an owner who'd sell his own mother for a credit. No client confidentiality there. 'Let's try somewhere more .. reputable.'

They stopped outside on the south perimeter. The paint looked fresh, the sign, 'Sovereign Repairs and Salvage' illuminated and complete. Someone had put serious energy into making the place appealing; a new business perhaps? A young man with a dream and principles, who would hopefully not report them.

'Let's try this one,' Robert said. They dismounted and stepped through the entrance. A row of seats rested against the left wall. A digital chrono hung on the far wall. There was a door behind a small counter, just big enough for a credit machine. The neutral colour scheme matched. Either the man was married to a good woman or…

A rattle sounded from behind the door and a woman appeared, clad in blue overalls. Early twenties, a pointy chin, a smear of grease on her right cheek and a birds nest of blond hair half tied into a bun.

'Welcome to Sovereign,' she said, flashing a white toothed smile that said Robert's arrival was the best thing that had happened to her all day.

'I had some pirate drama up in orbit,' said Robert, only half lying. 'I landed out in the Red Wash.' Another half-truth. He'd never actually piloted the Wayfarer, and 'landed' was a bit of a stretch. 'She's a bit of a wreck. Are you able to tow her back here for repairs? The hyperdrive is scrambled, I think I lost all my heat vents and who knows what else failed in the landing.'

'Whoa, One step at a time, hun.' she said, raising her hands. 'We can pick your girl up no problem. Then we can give her a good coat of looking-at and put a quote together for the work. What is she?'

'Lanner Mark II.'

The woman physically cringed. 'Well this crash was the best thing to happen to you. The perfect time to upgrade to a ship that's, how shall we say, engineered? We can handle your insurance claim if you like.'

'Ah,' Robert said, wanting to avoid the 'insurance companies don't like pirates' discussion. 'No thanks, she's got sentimental value.'

The woman leant against the counter and laughed. 'You men, all the same, where would you be without your girls, eh?'

She glanced at a screen behind the counter. She waved her hand past it. 'Lanner, Lanner,' she mumbled, probably checking a list. Hopefully not Interpol's Most Wanted. 'Here we go. Someone trashed a Lanner here two months ago. Frames ruined but the hyperdrive's intact. The insurance company has been dying to get rid of it. You might not be hanging around too long after all. What are her coordinates? We'll pick her up at first light.'

Robert passed his pad to her. 'Fantastic, thank you.'

* * *

Criddoch stood in the centre of the hot, dusty street, trying to control his breathing. The Skardee sun was relentless. Even the buildings were decaying under the solar attack.

Pathetic. All of them; strength of character was a trait even a building possessed, imbued into the structure by its builder and his materials, but these buildings had none.

Sweat soaked his back – he was human after all – but how he dealt with the discomfort was what separated him from the rest of humanity.

He clenched his fists, felt the tug of the needles in his wrists, supplying isotonic water from bags up his sleeves. He wouldn't be dehydrating, not even if he stood out there all day.

And he would if he needed to. When the Admiral gave an instruction, Criddoch followed it.

The street emptied. The weak natives fled underground, a daily ritual that halved their productive hours.

A woman brushed past him, brown hair in a bobbing ponytail, piercing green eyes, the same woman he'd seen a day earlier at the starport. She'd given him a questioning look, eyes wide, mouth narrowed and he'd briefly considered removing her eyes and mouth, but the admiral's orders were quiet surveillance and the job took priority over his own feelings. The Admiral had made that perfectly clear.

The woman carried on, not recognising him, and disappeared into a bar. Criddoch waited, alone. His feet ached. Intense heat saturated him, but Criddoch didn't move. He wouldn't let the sun beat him into submission.

His link beeped; a call relayed through his support teams in orbit. The Admiral. 'Report,' came the firm voice.

'I've found the pirate and the Circle forces. They're all in one city playing hide and seek. There is only one way to the starport and I'm covering it.'

The Admiral grunted; a slight hint of satisfaction there? Criddoch thought so. He allowed a small smile.

'Remember Commander, the objective is intelligence. Learn, do not interact. Follow, do not destroy. No one must know you are there.'

Criddoch ground his teeth. Should he tell the Admiral? 'There's a woman here too.'

'Commander,' the Admiral warned.

'I think she's an Accer,' Criddoch rushed, not wanting the past to distract the Admiral. 'She may have figured me.'

'Alioth Intelligence.' The Admiral went silent for several moments. 'Don't kill her. This might be exactly what we need. Report back in six hours with an update.' He signed off.

Criddoch watched the street. He watched the doors. He clenched his fists periodically to keep the fluids flowing.

The sun moved across the sky. Solar noon came. Criddoch clenched his jaw and his fists and his quads. He wasn't going to move from this spot no matter how hot it got. The sun kept moving but the heat stayed. His breath was short, painful. His mouth burned, but he relished the pain of a job well done.

Another hour passed. The woman appeared from the bar. She stormed across the street into another building.

Criddoch kept watching. Moments later the pirate appeared; a twig of a man with two followers, one thin, the other wide and low, like a bull; a worthy foe.

The pirates shuffled down the road toward him. Criddoch kept still, watching, waiting.

* * *

Gunn watched the two pirates from across the bar. It was almost too dark to see, the patrons reduced to indistinct shadows. Then the door to the surface opened, lighting up everything.

The pirates had been easy to find. When the midday sun hit, everyone disappeared underground, drinking or hiding until they could get back to their business, and there were only so many places to hide.

The door closed and the bar returned to near darkness. The rush of air brought the sweet smell of Bourbon. She closed her eyes and breathed deep, savouring the charred fragrance. She hadn't drunk any in two years but the hunger had never waned. Her throat felt dry.

No Gunn, no! She got through yesterday, she'd get through today. She'd been staking out the pirates for two days. There wouldn't be a tomorrow. Whithers had finally made the connection between the blistering ship paint and the underground bars.

The two pirates sat in a corner booth nestled against the natural earth wall with a clear line of sight to the exit. They hunkered forward, cradling their drinks. They could have been studying the patrons, eyes out for trouble, but they wouldn't have been able to see much.

She sat in her own booth against the opposite wall, watching them, but there wasn't much detail. There simply weren't enough photons between her and the pirates and too many surfaces for them to hit and deflect. Simple maths; not enough light.

One pirate was wider and shorter than the other. He cradled a small slim drink. Alcohol. The slimmer one held a mug. Slim was still, composed. Wide was jittery, continually flinching as if he had a power cord plugged up his rear end.

Her first reflex was to put a laser pulse through them both. Two fewer pirates would mean countless fewer murders, thefts and an incalculable reduction in pain to people the galaxy over.

No one would ever know it was her. She wouldn't need to draw her weapon above the table. She considered the firing angle. She'd have to move seats to line them both up. Two squeezes of the trigger: tap, turn, aim, tap. Their heads would knock backward then their bodies would slump forward. Their glasses would skitter away or break, a common enough noise in a dark bar. They could even go unnoticed until the work day resumed and the crowds left.

Gunn squeezed out of her booth. Striking out of sight felt wrong. She wanted the pirates to know the law had killed them. She wanted them to know that despite running for so long, justice had caught up. She stepped forward, stopped, took another step. A man stepped past her in a hurry so she sidestepped and brushed against an empty table. She sat down.

She was two tables away now and able to make out more detail. She half turned away, worried Slim might pick her.

'Griff still doesn't have anything for me,' she heard one of them say; a younger voice, possibly Slim.

'He won't.' Definitely the wider one that time, an older voice, strained with age and perhaps, fear.

'They must have some technology to keep tracking us. Mis-jumps don't stop them. If we can figure that out, use that against them-'

'You can't win,' whispered Wide. 'They know everything, they see everything. They know what move you will make before you do.'

'They're just pilots, for Bruce's sake. They have friends everywhere, sure, everyone loves the Circle, but they have limited men and resources. And they can't see the future.'

Wide didn't say anything.

Gunn sneezed and dragged her chair a foot closer. Slim wore a reasonably snug jacket, a dark brown or blue, or green, they all looked the same in low light. Wide's hair was receding from his round face. He had big hands.

'They must have a base of operations,' said Slim. 'Maybe we can take the battle to them. I have a few friends too.'

Wide laughed. 'You don't understand, kiddo, it—'

'How about a distraction then?' interrupted Slim, 'Buy a new ship, register it under false names, disappear only to strike from behind?'

'The only way to make them leave you alone is to make them think you are dead.'

'I've been known to kill people from time to time, but never myself. Stage our own deaths?'

Gunn stood. She'd heard enough. They would never help her. Two quick pulls on the trigger then move on. She'd find another resource, one she could trust, one the Circle didn't know about; a second Gunn-Britt Grotenfelt.

She walked toward them. Six paces, five if she stretched out. Her pistol slapped against her thigh, heavy, comfortable, reassuring.

'There's a trick to it,' Wide said.

'I'm not buying,' said Slim. 'I have twenty other ships out there. Over a hundred boys being chased if they're not already dead.' He pointed at the media projector near the bar. 'You saw the news feed. The Circle just trashed our Hoopertown base. Thanks the Fates it was empty, but they're obviously targeting us. I'm not going to abandon my boys. I'm not going to have another Jimmy. Not today, not tomorrow. Now are you going to sit there sulking or are you going to help me supernova the bloody Circle?'

Slim's words stopped Gunn in her tracks, then angry at herself she raced forward, pulling out the pistol and jutting it out across the table.

Slim and Wide both flinched and dropped their hands but Gunn shoved the pistol forward, its focusing crystal a glint in the dark room.

'Hands where I can see them Gentlemen,' she said softly, calmly. Control, or at least the appearance of it, was crucial.

Slim and Wide's hands crept back up. Slim grabbed his mug, a coffee cup, let his shoulders settle and locked gazes with her. 'If you mean to use that thing, I suggest you do it.' His voice wasn't high or low, scared or threatening, but he spoke each word with deliberate pronunciation. 'Because I'm exactly five seconds away from sending you back to Soontill.'

'You're not that fast,' Gunn said.

She could only tell he was smiling by the gap in the shadow that was his face. It was a big, arrogant smile; the smile of a man enjoying himself. 'Try me.'

Her finger tightened. Wiping that smile off his face would be sweet justice, sweeter than a shot of fiery bourbon. And shooting them both would bring her kudos with the Circle. She would be above suspicion, free to sabotage the plot as she saw fit.

But sabotage took time; working from the inside took time. She needed answers now, actions now. And that meant external resources.

She lowered the weapon. 'I'm not here to kill you.' Slim kept smiling. 'I know.'

Gunn groaned; a cute pirate. Perfect. She lowered her voice to a scathing, cutting through ice pitch. 'I'm here to offer you a deal.'

Neither pirate spoke for a moment. 'Your uniform looks awfully black,' said Slim.

'It's dark. Everything looks black in the dark.' Slim laughed, glanced at Wide. 'I like her.'

'We're not interested in any deals with the likes of you,' Wide said. Slim elbowed Wide. 'Go on,' he told her.

'May I sit?'

Slim nodded and she settled into the booth. This close she could make out their features. They were related, probably father and son. Both had short black curly hair, though Slim more than Wide. Slim was lean, like a runner. Wide was built to stand still and tackle small starships; an interesting team.

Gunn studied the two cups. 'Why don't you gentlemen finish up?'

Slim gulped his, but Wide sipped; it gave her a second to think. She hadn't planned this. What would she say? How much should she say?

Slim finished his coffee then put his cup back on the table and slid it toward her. He waited expectantly.

She leant forward, trusting them not to do anything stupid, but unwilling to risk eavesdroppers.

'I'm with Alioth Intelligence,' she whispered. 'I'm undercover with the Circle.' Laughable that she could speak the truth to a pair of lying bandits like these, but they could go and repeat her words to Whithers or to the world right now. No one would believe them.

She had hoped for some kind of reaction but both of them looked half a speech away from falling asleep. 'The AIS have been investigating them for years. They might be smaller than the Pilots Federation, but what they've accomplished and how they do it

.. things didn't add up.' She paused for effect.

'I just found evidence that they are planning to start an interstellar war to eradicate the Federation and unite humanity under the Imperial banner.'

Still no reaction from Slim and Wide and for a brief moment she thought they actually were asleep, but Slim's eyes were definitely open, focused and staring at her.

She forced back the growl that formed at the back of her throat. 'I can't break cover yet so I need help. If you use your pirate contacts to help me stop the plot then you will be free from the Circle forever.'

'You want us to trust you?' asked Wide. 'A spy? You're probably a double agent trying to draw us out.'

Slim pushed in. 'We're pirates. We steal stuff and kill anyone that gets in our way. The galaxy treats us like shit, why should we treat it any different?'

'War is bad for piracy. Conscription, heightened security, all those extra military forces, and the war economy, the entire galaxy's production focused on construction. It'll be bad for business.'

'I'll take my chances.'

'What about all the innocent people that will die? Millions of deaths that you can prevent.'

Slim didn't reply but his mouth hung open like a short circuited disposal unit. When the words finally come they were so heavy and damp he sounded like a different person.

'Not my problem. Not anymore.'

'What about your other crews? Your 'boys' being chased by the Circle. Don't you care about them?'

Slim straightened, his body tensing up and she knew she'd pressed the wrong button. The air between them grew charged, a barrier of hostile air molecules.

'We're done here,' Wide said. 'Now walk away or my boy'll put a bullet through your heart.'

Gunn's eyes turned maybe five degrees, the pupils travelling perhaps six, seven millimetres from Wide to Slim, yet in that time a chunky lead thrower had appeared in Slim's hand.

She hadn't even seen him move.

The growl returned and this time she let it out. Couldn't the selfish fools see they were making a Phekda run in an unarmed Lanner? She thought she'd glimpsed some humanity, but they were just the same as every other pirate she'd killed. Except she'd let these ones get the jump on her.

'Misery merchants,' she spat. 'You're making a mistake.'

Slim snorted. 'Story of my life.'

'Fine.' She stood. 'Get killed for all I care. Do the galaxy a favour.' She strode away, past the booths, up the black steps to the halo of light and wrenched the heavy door aside. Heat and light smashed into her, almost forcing her back down the steps, but she couldn't stay another moment in the bar with those pirates.

The locals called the sun 'Killer', as in 'Don't stay long on the streets or she'll kill you.' She staggered up the steps to the street.

Every breath rasped, the air burning her throat on its journey to her lungs. She needed to get out of this heat.

Her ear piece squawked, Whithers asking everyone to check in. They answered in flight sequence.

'Waste of time,' she said hoarsely, looking back at the bar; *stupid arrogant fools*. 'They're not down there.' At least the person I was looking for wasn't.

She signed off, already crossing the road. There were four doors across the way, the fronts of the buildings growing out from a rock face. Their paint blistered and peeled, a plastic sign for a common house bleached white under Killer's bloody gaze. The buildings reminded her of huddling civilians, cowered and fearful as they were slowly ground into the soil. The dust burned her eyes. Sweat poured down her face. By the time she reached the relative coolness of the common houses' veranda her hair was drenched. She paused to recover. First, she needed darkness and fluids. Then she'd have to come up with a new plan to uncover the Circle's plot.

* * *

Robert watched the woman go, not entirely sure of what had just happened, but happy as heck she was gone. Still, they couldn't stay any longer. The Circle was onto them. He turned to Jordan to get his thoughts when Griff slid into the woman's seat.

'I was watching,' he said, eyebrows raised in an expectant way, a proud face waiting for recognition. The same look Robert had given his father after a good deed. 'I had a gun on her.'

Robert tussled Griff's hair. 'You're a good man. What have you got for me?'

'Trouble. The service crew uncovered the Garry standard. One of them recognised it.'

Robert swore. 'I told you to get rid of it.'

'How was I supposed to know they'd remove paint?'

Robert's mind kicked into gear. He'd never done anything criminal on this planet, but if one person recognised the standard, others might too and the Circle would find out.

'We're leaving.' He shoved Griff out of the way.

'But they're not done yet.'

'Is the hyperdrive done?'

'I'm not sure.'

'We'll have to risk it. Tell them to move the ship to a landing pad. Get the crew onboard. Do it now.'

They stood as one, walking swiftly towards the exit. The sun hit him with a double punch of heat and light. His skin tightened across his face, his eyes reduced to narrow slits, and his hair burned and insulated, cooking his head and its contents.

They strode down the road, everything whitewashed, like sunstrike. They moved at a fast walk, not a run – men had died doing less on this planet during the middle of the day.

Griff spoke into his link, recalling the team, his words punctuated by gasps. Robert struggled to breath even without talking, the air itself on fire.

The buildings shirked away from them, retreating into the rock on either side. The dugouts could have extended below the road but probably not all the way to the starport.

Their pace slowed. Sweat streamed down Robert's back. His skin itched and tightened. It felt like he was standing behind the Wayfarer's engines, radiation and heat turning him into a human crisp.

'I'd kill the Fates themselves for a bloody hat,' Jordan grunted. Robert put his hand over the back of his neck. The relief was small but welcome.

In the distance a man stood in the centre of the road, still, straight, watching them. He wore a hat and matching long black coat that draped through the dirt. He must have been roasting.

Jordan and Griff slowed, but Robert sped up. There was nothing between him and the man but dusty red cobblestones and heat haze, blurring the man's features and movements. Robert grabbed his Diplomat and held it against his leg. The gun was already hot in his hand.

Jordan caught up, wheezing. 'What do you think?'

'I was hoping you could tell me.' The man wore black, but Robert still couldn't make out any details. If off-worlders died in this heat though, surely they wouldn't stand out in the noon sun in a trench coat?

Griff stumbled, dropped to a knee. His palm hit the ground, he yanked it back and face planted. Robert swore steam hissed from the kid's jacket. He grabbed Griff under the armpits. 'It's just a little sunlight. You going to let a bloody star send you to the Bruce?'

'No sir,' Griff said, though his limp body suggested otherwise.

'Back to your feet, dammit.' The heat sucked the strength from Robert's arms so Jordan helped yank Griff back to his feet.

Trench coat didn't move. His arms hung loose by his sides. Robert couldn't see a weapon bulge, but he could have a scatter gun under there and they'd never know.

The Diplomat wanted to melt through his hand. He used his other hand to loosen his shirt tails then patted the ten shot L&F tucked into his belt. Just in case.

The man watched them, turning as they passed. His hands were empty but his eyes concealed something. Was he a distraction for an ambush? He was too big to be a pilot jockey.

But he didn't make any moves and as they reached their closest point Robert waggled the Diplomat.

'Problem?'

The man said nothing. Robert felt spiders crawling over his spine. He sped up, glad to be past him.

The rest of the road was clear. Still alive and unchallenged they hit their first patch of shade. They stopped to catch their breath. Robert's mouth and throat felt like sandpaper.

The dry-dock was an open ring backing onto the starport. The office was unlocked and no one was inside; hiding from the heat no doubt.

Sweat stinging his eyes and sunburn cracking his skin with every step, he pushed through the staff door and out to the dry dock. They stopped just through the entrance, a thin strip of shade affording them some relief.

The Wayfarer sat tall and majestic on her landing skids, nose slightly elevated to the sky. The wide bridge viewport stretched backward as if a god had given it a face-lift. The rear stabiliser wings were straight and undented and a large oval weld bead ran over the rear hull; where they'd installed the new hyperdrive. Hopefully.

Robert shivered. It didn't feel right. He stopped Griff with his arm. 'Ssshhh.'

The metal hull pinged and clicked under the sun's assault. A breeze whistled past above the building ring. There weren't any voices, no footfalls, no clang of spanners or the whir of pneumatics drills.

It was silent. Silent as a tomb.

The gangway hung open.

'Stay here,' he said, gaze fused to the gangway. He fingered the Diplomat, heart fluttering.

He strode out into the open, the build-up of dust muffling his footfalls. He put his first step onto the gangway and stopped, listening.

Nothing.

He took another step, rolling his feet across the steel to dampen any noise.

The sun filled the sky, each ray of light weighing on him like a tonne of cargo. The Diplomat slipped in his sweaty hand. His eyes stung. He tried to slow his panting but within seconds he was gasping again.

He reached the edge of the hull and pulled himself in. The relief was immense. *Out of the pot*

.. He stopped again, listening, but the only sound was his pounding heart.

To the bridge? It was the obvious choice, which made it the last place he should go. But if his boys were on board, that was where they'd be.

He kept moving, toe to heel, arms wide to stop his sleeves rubbing. He reached the first intersection. He leant out, glanced both ways. Empty. He stepped out — the floor groaned.

Robert snapped backward as he heard the swish of fabric. The light behind him dimmed.

Robert swung his gun up a fraction of a second before his brain caught up. Time became moments. His head turning, sensing black behind him, his finger tightening on the trigger, the action on the Diplomat sliding back, the muzzle flashing.

A man in black toppled backward with barely a sound. Footfalls sounded behind Robert. He dropped, spinning his arm back around as he fell against the wall.

The bulkhead exploded above Robert's head as he fired back.

Another man slammed into the far wall; a gout of blood and smoke bursting from his chest as he crumpled into a black rag.

Robert slouched against the wall, legs splayed out, gun shaking in his still outstretched arm. He was hyperventilating, mouth gulping like a fish while his head swished back and forth, scanning for more threats. His heart felt caught in his ribs, smashing and beating in a panic to be free.

Stand up!

The corridor was empty. His heart slowed, allowing his brain to restart.

The boys.

He jumped to his feet and raced to the bridge, Diplomat low, but ready. He burst in, eyes scanning for danger.

His crew were on the bridge.

They'd come when he'd asked, they'd done everything he could have ever asked from them and more. But they wouldn't be helping him again.

They'd been butchered.

Robert staggered backward, slamming into a wall. His gaze raced from one body to another; Matt, a gunshot between the eyes, Ralph, two to the chest. He turned away from Gerald's disfigured body.

Dead.

All of them. Dead, dead, dead.

He smelt the smoke from six years ago, tasted the blood in his own mouth, the depressurization alarm, the screams of his men, his own voice barking instructions. He stumbled away, running along the deck, blinded by smoke, fire consuming the valuable oxygen, his arms waving away the dangling pipes and cable trays. His ship was beaten and if he didn't do something quick they'd all be dead…

The shriek of a laser jolted him back to the present. He was on the Wayfarer, not the Tutankhamun.

Another laser pulse echoed from outside.

'Dad!' He raced back outside. Two men in black were trying to tackle Jordan. He threw one to the ground. Robert raised the Diplomat, shot them both. One hissed as he sagged, the other dropped sideways and made a satisfying thump as he hit the ground. Jordan looked up at him with relief, a stupid, lop sided grin on his face.

Then he fell to his knees.

Robert's guts dropped to the ground. His brain blanked. Someone screamed.

Then he breathed and sprinted forward, the distance between them stretching outward like a hyperspace vector, light years from one end to the other. His chest was a dense knot, his breath coming in rasps. He skidded to Jordan's side, hands out over his chest.

A wound. A big one; a crater with ragged edges, his shirt fabric flopping into the pool of blood.

Robert's hands shook as he pressed them into the wound. 'Help,' he whispered, meek as a mouse. 'Help,' he coughed, louder, but just as pathetic. His vision blurred, the blood kept pouring, his whole arms shook uncontrollably.

He didn't know how to fix the hole.

He jerked his head around in all directions; Griff lay nearby, a cauterized wound in his stomach. It didn't look that bad but the wide eyes told the story.

He was only nineteen years old.

No one came running. The siesta was still in full swing.

Robert's hands still held the wound, blood surging through his fingers, down Jordan's jacket to pool on the sand below. He curled his shaking hands into fists.

Stop panicking.

He scooped up his massive father – fear or adrenaline feeding him strength – and carried him to the ship. It was only fifteen metres to the ramp, but it was the hardest walk of his life. Heat and fear strangled his lungs, weighed down his legs.

'Don't you drop him,' he rasped, taking a step. 'Don't you bloody drop him.' Another step. 'He never dropped you.'

He made it up the ramp.

Griff's body was still out there. He glanced from his father to Griff to his father. Jordan needed attention now, but he'd made a promise, long ago, and he couldn't break it now.

He laid his father into the closest acceleration couch.

'I'll be right back,' he said, but Jordan didn't respond. He raced back down the gangway, scooped up the lighter Griff and brought him inside. He dumped him on the deck and ran to the medical station, a pathetically ill-equipped cubicle. Gerald's earlier words echoed in his head. Why hadn't he topped up the Fate-forsaking supplies?

He grabbed everything he could find and raced back to Jordan. The blood flow had slowed. Either the wound had miraculously healed or he was running out of blood to pump. Robert's arms shook as he rattled a bag of saline out of its packet. His fingers fumbled and he dropped it.

'Damn, damn, damn!' he screamed. 'Get it to-bloody-gether!' He clenched his fists and counted, 'One-one-thousand, two-one-thousand, three-one-thousand,' and unclenched them.

His hands had calmed, at least enough to work the saline. He ripped open the bag, uncapped the needle, rolled up Jordan's sleeve and lined it up on an obvious vein. He pushed the needle through and clipped the bag to the wall as high as it could go.

Step one: keep the fluid pumping. Step two: stop the fluid leaking.

He ripped open Jordan's top and sucked in a breath. His chest was a mess. How he'd kept fighting, how his heart could still pump blood … the spirit of the Bruce had to be running through him.

Robert sifted through the supplies; lots of absorbent pads and a tube of compound twenty-five, an artificial clotting agent. He picked it up gingerly. It could clot, but it could clot the wrong things. In the hands of an inexperienced surgeon, such as himself, it could be as lethal as a knife or a bullet.

Where was that standard foam stuff? They'd used a lot after the Wreaken platform raid.

He stared down at his haemorrhaging father. He couldn't go to hospital. The Circle were out there. He couldn't fly to another hospital in time, his father would die.

He opened the tube and poured it into the wound until it overflowed. Next he found a single syringe of something-or-other-ophen, a pain blocker, and added it to the saline bag. He leant close to his father's ear, unsure if he could hear him or not. 'You're not going to die. Not today, not on my watch. You get me? No one else is dying.' He packed the wound with pads and wrapped his chest in gauze.

He returned to Griff's body and dragged him to another acceleration couch. He raised the gangway, strapped in the rest of his crew, jumped into the pilot's chair, activated the ship systems and hailed flight control. They responded immediately:

Traffic control is busy at present. Please try again later.

It was then he realized he hadn't launched a ship since basic training, but the controls were idiot proof and the memories resurfaced. The ship's engines hummed, all the systems shone green on the systems console. The ship was good and ready. But traffic control continued to ignore him.

The scanner picked up three incoming ships; small, too small to be Vipers, and quick.

The Circle.

It was a trap.

Robert lifted off. The ship lurched into the air. The link filled with overlapping voices screaming for him to land, to surrender, to prepare to die.

Robert deactivated the link, pointed the ship upward and gunned the engines.

The Wayfarer powered for the heavens.

The Sakers above him came in fast. They sported wings and control surfaces like they were designed for the atmosphere. The Wayfarer was a blunt arrow head. And it flew like one too, but that was okay. He wasn't going to stay and fight.

Two more blips appeared on the scanner. Bigger and slower Viper Mark Ones. It was definitely shit-on-the-Garry-family day. *I should have shot that woman. This is her doing.*

No, it was his fault. He hadn't been careful enough. If she could track him to that bar the Circle could find his ship.

He had gotten his father shot and his whole team murdered.

The Wayfarer pushed for space as fast as it could. How high an orbit did he need to initiate the hyperdrive? Fifteen thousand metres? Twenty? Jordan overrode the safeties some years back, but to what? Regardless, he wouldn't make it. Air screamed against the hull, the ship tearing through the stratosphere. Below deck the engines growled, pumping out maximum wattage.

The first Saker swooped in, a black bird of prey screaming in for the kill, a laser beam spitting from its beak.

The Wayfarer rocked, but the shields held and the Saker screamed past then banked. Maybe seven to ten seconds before it could complete its arc.

The second laser beam slammed into the shields. The Wayfarer rumbled; the engines growled. Fore and aft shields dropped to sixty percent. And then the third Saker arrived.

The ship bounced and bucked. Warning klaxons blared but Robert ignored them. He could barely keep the Wayfarer pointing upward instead of falling back to terra firma. He dared a glance at the status console. He considered his chaff trick again but the service team hadn't reloaded the chute. He had the front gun, which he'd have to manoeuver to use, an unfinished turret laser, an engine at one hundred percent and a cargo hold of fuel.

Fuel …

Robert activated the automated fuel loader. What if he pushed it all through the main port? If there was too much fuel some of it might not ionize and get through the grids intact, ready for combustion. If the whole thing ran hotter than the middle of a neutron star he might just get a miracle.

More thrust.

The ship shuddered again and the shield hologram flashed red. Front shields critical. He raced through the control menus, found the fuel pump and cranked it up to two hundred percent.

A Circle ship banked in front of him. It seemed to hang there for a moment, suspended in mid-air, its pilot seemingly cavalier in lining up the perfect shot.

The engines coughed, spluttered then went offline. His insides clenched. He'd stalled the engines and he'd fall back to the surface, but not before being shot into a million pieces.

The Wayfarer launched and Robert's organs flattened against his spine, his unprotected arms flung back into the chair.

The Saker banked, trying to get clear.

The Wayfarer kept coming until Robert saw the whites of the pilot's eyes.

They made eye contact.

The crash wrenched the Wayfarer sideways. The shields sparked and died.

Spider web cracks filled the cockpit screen. The Saker exploded against the Wayfarer, twisted steel falling away.

The ship kept accelerating; numbers higher than he'd ever seen. The remaining Sakers pursued, closing the gap. The Vipers dropped off the rear scanner.

The Wayfarer popped like a series of exploding bubbles. Fresh alarms rang through the cockpit. The front laser's emitter tube was bent up past the viewport, the engine temperature was in the red and his rear shields sizzled.

Fifteen thousand metres. Where is the damn hyperdrive light? Oh crap.

What if they hadn't installed the hyperdrive?

The shields collapsed, a muffled explosion rang out and the ship slewed around as atmosphere vented from the ship.

Another alarm rang out but Robert kept it steady, one eye on the navigation console, willing, wishing, begging the hyperdrive hologram to appear.

A laser beam lanced past the cockpit then arced inward, slowly, steadily, ready to carve the Wayfarer in half.

Smoke poured from the air duct behind him. His ship was burning. He coughed and waved the smoke aside but it thickened, clouding the viewport. His eyes burned, but he forced them open.

The hyperdrive hologram flashed. He reached forward.

An explosion jarred the ship sideways and Robert lost his grip on the stick. He threw both flailing hands at the icon.

Chapter 5

The Architect stood before his desk reading the datapad. Outside the spider web window the dirty grey fog seemed lower than normal, as if the planet shared his feeling of suffocation. Opposite him stood Commander Tybalt, raven black hair wild and long, hands behind his back, legs spread, his wide eyes following the Architect's every move.

The Architect grunted and dropped the datapad on his desk. It made a tinny clap. He breathed in, clearing his thoughts. Each setback felt like a message, an omen. He clenched the bracelet in his pocket and felt the determination return. Finally he rolled his gaze toward Tybalt.

'You're sure?'

'Sure,' Commander Tybalt said in his usual stoic monotone. A confident bastard, arrogantly so, but that didn't necessarily make him right.

The Architect retrieved the datapad and re-read the report, just in case a third view would improve the numbers.

But the numbers didn't change. He could have held the datapad upside down and it still would have said the same thing.

They only had four weapons. Projections showed five were required. 'Is there any safety factor in five?' 'Not enough to go with four.'

The Architect swore. He turned to the window watching the fog roll by and time closing in. The bright patch in the fog meant the brown dwarf was at its zenith, but the surface below was still as bleak and dark and cold as always. The planet had been a blessing and a curse.

He turned away. There was no magical answer out there. They had a date with His Highness. It took so many days to travel there, it took so many days to make another copy of the weapon. The numbers didn't stack up.

'Can we target another system?' the Architect asked. 'He is visiting a few on his tour.'

Tybalt's jaw clenched, his mouth moving as his tongue worked at a response. If he was taking that long it probably meant he was toning it down. 'That would require a whole new plan,' Tybalt said, his cold and distant voice making his opinion clear. 'All Oberon's plans involved that one system. People have been paid, resources have been allocated, simulations have been run.'

'But is it impossible?'

'Close to it, at such short notice.'

The Architect ignored Tybalt's insolence. 'So it is possible.' Tybalt didn't say anything.

The Architect closed his eyes for a brief moment. He wouldn't get Tybalt to buy into that idea, if only for the fact that he had suggested it. That meant a Plan C or a different commander, but Tybalt had stolen the Federation prototype. He knew the guns better than anyone.

'Wouldn't four guns do enough damage?' he suggested, trying a different tack.

Tybalt shrugged. 'Depends if you want to guarantee success or just take a wild stab.'

The Architect bristled. He should have reprimanded Tybalt for such disrespect but that would not have been conducive. Instead, he rubbed his chin. 'I don't want to take a wild stab. What if you made the fifth on route?'

Tybalt's jaw moved a millimetre and stayed there. His suspicious eyes narrowed. The Architect could almost hear Tybalt's mental cogs.

'May I?' Tybalt asked, hand extended. The Architect returned the datapad. Tybalt flicked across to another report. 'If we change our course slightly we can go past certain planets to pick up the right components.' Tybalt drifted away, mumbling to himself, right hand holding the pad, the left writing script in the air.

'I'll need more men,' Tybalt said softly. 'Mechanics, engineers. Anyone good with their hands.'

The Architect leant forward on his desk, eyes wide. 'How many?'

'Everyone you can find.'

'You'll have them.'

Tybalt turned back to the pad for a moment. 'It'll slow us down. We'll have less time to prepare.'

The Architect nodded, waiting. His heart thrummed, a vein pulsing in his forehead.

'Can you do it?' Tybalt didn't answer.

'Commander?'

'I think so.'

'Is that how you answer a superior?'

Tybalt stiffened marginally. 'Sir, I think you are right. This is your best shot.'

'Then do it.'

The Architect sat down and put his hands over his head until Tybalt left. He waited for the relief to kick in, but a small part of him wished the first obstacle had been the last. He quickly pushed that aside.

He was the leader of the Circle of Independent Elite Pilots. He had to protect humanity.

* * *

The Wayfarer drifted along the coldest sea; a dark system, a dead sun, a collection of rejected rocks and a pitiful asteroid field.

A blank scanner, the damage board glowing red. He'd killed fire and cleared the smoke but every breath had an acrid bite still. He sat on a magnetised stool, one arm under Jordan's head, the other over his chest. The bandages were red and wet. The compound twenty-five hadn't killed him, but it hadn't saved him either.

The adrenaline had faded, clearing his mind, but he couldn't fix the wound. Not with what he had. He repacked it, gave Jordan more saline, and put new bandages on. He could do all that, but he couldn't even give him more pain blockers.

He'd had all the time in the world to stock up on medical supplies while waiting for the ship to be repaired. Instead, he'd put his finger up his butt and waited, worrying about the Ceepers.

The duct in the ceiling sighed as the conditioners kicked in. The ship was an organism, a million different systems working to keep it running, alive. Pumps, sensors, engines, heat vents. They all whirred and vibrated, adding together to the sensation of life.

His father on the other hand had no such sensation. He felt cold; cold, damp and still.

There was no more medical gear. He'd flown away from the closest hospital.

No matter what system he travelled to now there would be at least a couple of days sailing in system. The chances of finding a Federation medical cruiser out this far were non-existent and the first thing they'd do would be to throw him in the brig anyway.

Jordan would have known what to do. His father would have beaten such setbacks. His father was an unstoppable machine.

Had been. Now he was old. The lack of blood had turned him grey, clammy, sweaty. He'd aged thirty years in thirty minutes.

Robert's eyes moistened but he held back. It wouldn't do to have a Garry cry.

Jordan coughed and opened his eyes. Robert's heart skipped a beat and the shadows closed in another foot.

'Hey, you're okay,' Robert tried to say, but his tongue felt too thick for his mouth.

'Don't lie to your old man, kiddo.' Another cough.

'I got us away from the Ceepers, but I also flew away from the hospital. I killed you.' The same old helplessness filled his chest. He had all the desire in the world, all the people to protect and no Fate forsaking ability to do it. Every time someone depended on him, he fell on his face and failed.

'Chin up.' Jordan's voice was barely audible, yet still carried the authority from Robert's youth. His head lifted automatically.

'You didn't kill me, kiddo. You saved me.' Jordan paused for a breath. 'When you were born, I took one look at your perfect little face. Everything changed. You made me the man I am, kiddo.'

Another cough; blood spittled his lips. 'I've failed you. I tried to keep you away from them. I tried. But I failed. Now you have to go back. To the beginning, you have to go to Soontill.'

Robert sniffed, holding his delirious father tight. Soontill? Next he'd be talking of the Masked Mamba or Raxxla.

Jordan sighed and closed his eyes.

'Dad!' Robert yelled, shaking him. Jordan startled as if he'd been asleep.

'What? Oh, do you remember the promise?'

Robert nodded, the only thing he trusted himself to do. He wiped the sweat from Jordan's forehead and brushed his hair flat.

'A man is a warrior,' started Jordan, his right hand struggling upward.

Robert caught it. 'And a warrior is a man.' His nose was full of snot and he felt like he was talking underwater. They finished it together.

But all wars must end. And so too must all men.
So now I follow Bruce To glory and fortune
To my ancestors young and old
To join in one last quest.
To finally lay at rest.

Jordan's hand slackened in Robert's. He clenched it tighter.

'Dad. Dad?'

He cupped his Dad's face. 'Don't go.'

He felt Jordan's neck. He moved his finger back and forth. 'Just wait, Dad.' Where was the bloody pulse?

'Wait, wait. Please. '

'Dad...' He clenched his father in his arms. The shadows engulfed him as tears flooded his face.

* * *

The Wayfarer limped through the Arouca system and down toward New Aberdeen under autopilot. He stared out the viewport, distantly aware of colours and textures. He could have been under attack by the Circle and he wouldn't know. He didn't care. He didn't have the strength to focus his eyes, let along move his arms and legs to control the ship.

After a time he realised he'd touched down at Granite City, where it all started. Jordan might have been delirious, but Robert knew what he meant. The beginning, where they'd both been born and where his mother lay buried. Home.

He unstrapped, swung both legs over the edge of the acceleration couch and pushed off. He trudged from the bridge, each step a sequence of mechanical commands. Raise upper leg from hip, swing lower leg out around knee, lower back to the ground. Repeat on opposite side.

He hit an obstacle, nearly tripping. It was the remains of a Circle trooper.

Robert kicked it, again, and again, and again. Bones and cartilage snapped under his boot. He stopped. It didn't bring his father back. Nothing would. No future action he took would ever make a difference.

He walked to the gangway and lowered it. Icy flurries floated into the ship. Robert's legs carried him out into the snow.

The wind was gentle, cold and familiar, stirring him back to life.

Two men waited under an awning, hands enclosed in mittens, bodies wrapped in thick jackets. Their faces were hidden beneath their hats, but he could clearly see the 'not-terribly-impressed' grimace of a customs agent. They never liked it when ships arrived with dead bodies, especially ones with laser injuries. But Robert would jump through whatever hoops were required, do whatever was needed. He was going to make sure Jordan went on his last quest surrounded by his family.

* * *

He met with the three men in a small room of the starport. They sat in a row on the far side of the table, facing the door. There was a single seat on Robert's side of the table. The table was solid, brown, with scratches and nicks from a lifetime of use. Heat leached out the single core window to the right, light snow drifting past. The walls were granite, like the rest of the city, absorbing the light panel's meagre output.

Robert sat down and waited for the three men to talk. They had called the meeting. They introduced themselves but he was too distracted to remember them.

'We understand you wish to put your father to rest in our city,' said the man in the middle. He was the tallest, a brown handlebar moustache and small pinched brown eyes; an administrator, a paper pusher.

Robert nodded. That's what Jordan had wanted. Back to the beginning.

'Unfortunately,' said the man on the left, broad of shoulder, but with similarly small and disinterested eyes, 'we cannot find any records of your father's citizenship.'

Robert sucked in a breath. All Jordan's documents were on board his new ship, the Vista Oculto. Robert had no idea if the ship had been destroyed by the Circle, let alone where it was. He had assumed Jordan's documents were on file locally.

'He flew for the Royal Guard,' Robert blurted. Could that be why his records weren't available? Why else would there be no proof of his citizenship? Had Jordan done it to protect Robert? What about Mum?

The man on the right coughed. 'There are no records of a Jordan Garry in the Royal Guard either.'

Robert stood, pounding the table. 'Dammit, I'm not making this stuff up.' Stupid pompous arses – they have no business being in the Bruce's city.

The three men glanced at each other and turned back to Robert as one. Their expressions changed, from snobbish superiority to pinched brow, sad smiles. As if they'd had an epiphany and decided to dish out some pity.

'Don't molly coddle me you pricks,' he told them. 'My father deserves to be buried with his wife. He's a Scotsman, how can you deny him his final quest?'

'Where is your mother buried, lad?' asked the man on the right, the shortest and least pretentious of the three.

'Don's Garden Cemetery,' Robert said, no doubt, no hesitation. That was one name permanently etched in his memory.

Mr Right nodded a knowing smile. He opened a briefcase by his feet and placed a small datapad on the table. He spun it toward Robert and slid it across. 'Go on,' said Mr Right.

Robert sat and leant forward, arms under the table. The pad displayed a list of every 'resident' of Don's Garden. The Garry's in the list were highlighted. No Marilyn. He put his finger to the screen and scrolled down to the Paul's. No Marilyn Paul either.

He grabbed the pad and changed the search parameters to first names; four Marilyns, but none of them his mum.

He tossed the pad back on the table. 'Your list is incomplete.'

Mr Left straightened at the accusation; probably the curator. 'I assure you sir, the list is absolute and correct.'

'She's there, dammit. I helped bury her.'

His heart clenched, a crazy, stupid thought entering his mind: had the Circle been here first? Deleted all trace of Jordan's existence so that when they killed him it would be as if he had never been there? But to crack a government system and delete his mother? Could they not let the dead lie?

He pressed his index finger to the table. 'I'll find her.'

Mr Left nodded. 'Very good.'

'And about your father—' said the Middle Man.

'He was born here and he'll be buried here,' Robert said, 'and that's final.'

'How do you know he was born here? Have you ever seen proof?'

'He,' Robert stopped, brow crinkled, a lump in his throat. 'He, told me.'

Middle Man nodded, as if expecting that answer. 'Have you ever seen a birth certificate?'

'No, but—'

'The servers don't lie, lad. Don't take this the wrong way, but it's possible your father may have …'

'What?' Robert asked. 'Lied to me?' He stood, pointed a finger at Middle man. 'My father wouldn't do that.'

Mr Right stood, arms raised to placate him. 'We weren't suggesting that at all. Childhood memories have a way of distorting with time. When was the last time you talked to your father about this city? About your mother?'

Robert opened his mouth but no words came out. Mr Right continued. 'All we are saying is that we have rules and we can't break those rules. We can't allow him to be buried until proof of his citizenship is secured.'

Robert's legs weakened and he slipped back into his chair. It was a mistake, all one big messy mistake. He'd spent his childhood in this city. He'd seen Jordan work, seen his uniform. They'd lived and breathed this place for years.

Jordan must have done it himself, once he became a pirate, erasing his old life. But if he'd done that surely he would have kept a copy somewhere. Was it on his ship with his other belongings? And why didn't he tell him that as he lay dying instead of babbling about Thargoid legends?

He had to do something now. Not tomorrow, today. The Circle were likely already on their way.

'Fine. I'll get you your proof. But I can't take a casket with me. I need to cremate him.'

The three glanced at each other, three minds sharing the same thought. They turned back to Robert.

'We will allow you to cremate your father.' Middle Man said.

'As long as you take him with you again,' said Mr Left.

Robert stood and leant forward on the table. 'I'll be back.'

* * *

He was a terrible son.

Mum had rested in the same spot for twenty years, waiting for her family to visit, but he'd only been to her grave once, when he'd buried her. Jordan avoided coming back, claiming painful memories. Then Robert had enlisted in the Federation Navy and after Villist he'd run back to Dad and a life of piracy. He hadn't been home since.

The entrance to Don's Garden Cemetery stretched across the road, a grand arch of granite encased in a purple flowering creeper. He stepped through into rolling fields of trimmed grass, a small wall enclosing the gardens. Headstones dotted the fields in regular rows, criss-crossed by walkways. An empty mass-transit module waited at the main office. A few people wandered through the headstones, flowers in hand.

His memory of her grave was vague, thin tendrils of images and sounds and smells. He remembered a grave near hers, with bright yellow dandelions engraved around the tombstone and a marble encasement over the plot; to stop Zombies, or so the young Robert had joked. He had smiled for a moment, before reality wiped the smile from his face. Your mother is dead, your mother is dead.

The field had been a gentle rolling meadow, tombstones arrayed in a neat grid, a caretaker's building nearby, but in his memory everything was in greys and whites, a washed out, barely remembered scene that now felt surreal, more a dream than a memory, something watched from afar rather than taken part in. Details were fleeting, flying almost into reach just to disappear again.

It was a big cemetery.

He wandered in circles. There were many Garry's but not the right Garry. There were no Pauls either. It was an English name, not Scottish. His father used to joke that he had stolen from the English the way the English had once stolen from Scotland.

He walked past a grave with a small silver bell sitting before the headstone, a small photo of a newborn tied to the bell's handle. A lump formed in his throat. The photo was cute and sad all at once, but that wasn't what bothered him.

It was the third time he'd walked past it.

Again he walked past the east wall, back in toward a small electrical junction box. Again he passed the bin overflowing with browning Ladies'-tresses. He passed the rows of heroes from the Thargoid wars. He passed the balding white haired man sitting next to the cracked tombstone, chatting away with his long lost wife about their grandchildren.

He'd searched for three hours. First he'd walked from one side to the other, right across the meadows covering every row. Then he'd broken the cemetery into sections divided by walkways. Then he'd gone for a more organic approach, but still he couldn't find her.

Only when the caretaker stopped in front of him with a curious raised eyebrow did Robert realise how absurd – and suspicious – he looked.

'I'm searching for someone,' he said, eyes down, feeling sheepish.

'You find them?' The Caretaker's voice was slow but the words were still sharp.

'No,' Robert said. 'I didn't.'

The lump had consumed his throat now, growing down into his stomach and up into his mouth, a foreign thought, choking him. A thought that had grown since he'd finished his first search, but that he'd refused to acknowledge. But now it had grown to the point he couldn't ignore it.

There were over three thousand graves in Don's Garden, but none of them were from his family.

His mother wasn't there.

* * *

The crematorium occupied the second basement of the cemetery's main building. He walked down several long passages of dull brown and grey granite walls, clearly the only building material available. At the centre of the room was the crematory itself, a modest oven of ceramics and stainless steel and around it a mess of pipes and heat exchangers, and a chimney rising through the ceiling.

Jordan lay in a simple casket of kiln dried wood, Thin and dry, like a tinderbox, ready to burn at a glance from the crematory's burners. The casket sat on rollers before the furnace door. Normally a ram guided the casket in but Robert wanted, needed to do it himself.

The furnace was on. The operator had shown him what to do. He had left to give Robert some privacy. Fire raged beyond the door; a savage rush of flame, not quite a pure tone, but loud enough to make him cringe.

He stepped up to the casket and put his hand about where his father's head was. Cremation was for the best. He could keep his father with him until he could find the evidence he needed. Cremate his father, escape the Circle, connect up with his boys, get them safe, find his father's documents then come back to New Aberdeen to lay his father to rest; easy. Better to wait than for Jordan to go on his final quest alone in a strange land.

His hand curled into a fist. A splinter caught his little finger. 'Did you do this dad? Are you still testing me?' He stared at the wood, trying to sense his father beneath, make contact with him one last time. He breathed in once more, exhaled and unclenched his fist. 'I'm not going to fail you. I'll get you home, somehow. I promise.'

He was running out of excuses. It was time. He moved to the end of the coffin. His father's feet. He tested the weight against the rollers then pushed his father head first toward the flames. The door rose automatically, the roar from the flames deafening, the heat like a rectangular slap in the face.

The coffin picked up speed, left Robert behind and sunk into the flames. He stood there a moment, blue light dancing over the wood, new yellow flame bursting into existence, spreading along the dried lumber; first the sides, then up and over onto the lid, which cracked and sunk inward. Steam rose from inside.

The heat drove him back. He stepped aside and the door lowered, muffling the scream of the burners.

He'd forgotten to ask how long it would take, how long he'd have to watch his father be consumed by flame, turned into ash, forever removed from this galaxy, but right now he had nowhere else to be.

There was a glass port on the side of the furnace. Robert slid its lid aside but all he could see was flame and a shadow of wood within.

The power died.

The silence deafened. The room went dark, the oven's control panel blank. Inside the furnace the fires still burned, but lazily. Self-sustained combustion, the coffin and his father's body consuming itself.

He waited for the operator to come running back demanding an explanation but he heard no footsteps. On any other day he would have waited or got the Fates out, but neither were options just then. 'Hello?' he called. 'I've got a bit of a problem here.'

His voice echoed down the granite walls. The oven ticked and sighed as it cooled, muffled flames crackling inside the oven. The sides of the coffin fell away and the flames brightened for a moment then settled back into a wafting yellow cackle, throwing dancing shadows upon the dark walls.

A shiver tip-toed across his shoulders.

The roar of reversing turbines broke the silence. He heard at least ten, all decelerating hard, coming in from all directions.

The shiver carried down his back. His arms shook. The Circle of Independent Elite Pilots.

The emergency lighting came on, a soft dull red giving enough light to get out but little else. The roaring turbines faded, replaced with the hiss of coolant and the thump of landing skids on 'crete.

Robert spun, scanning the room for doors, vents, holes, anything to escape. There was just the one door he'd come through, and the oven, but he couldn't hide or escape through there. The flue was too small to climb through.

Footsteps echoed down the corridor; distant at first but closing, a lot of people, a lot of feet. The footfalls were loud energetic slaps, driven by minds with purpose, intent and a plan.

The Circle had chased him across star systems. They had scattered his fleet. They had killed his crew. They had murdered his father. And now they were here, on his turf, interrupting his father's cremation.

He armed the L&F, primed the Diplomat and stepped sideways to give himself a clear, unobstructed view of the passageway.

Because he was going to die. Here. Now. He was going to die a warrior.

He ran his eye over both weapons, and held them shoulder width apart, one aiming slightly up, one aiming slightly down. If he was going to die, he was going to take all of the Ceepers with him; every single one of them. They wouldn't get his father. Not while he had bullets and power cells, not while his arms could punch and bludgeon, not while his teeth could bite, not while he had one gasp of life left in him.

The furnace's traitorous operator would be busy tonight.

The footfalls grew louder; voices, short and sharp. They were coming for him.

Robert waited, his heart slow and steady, at peace with what would happen next.

How much ammo did he have? It didn't matter, the Diplomat made a good club, the L&F a good throwing distraction. He'd keep going until he ran out of strength or out of foes.

He half turned back to the furnace. He bit his lip, his heart heavy again. 'I did my best dad. It was never good enough, but I tried.' He turned back to the door. 'I'm sorry.'

One set of footfalls grew from the crowd, louder, faster, feet skimming across the granite floor, lightweight, like a …

Shadows moved around the corner. He tightened his fingers on the triggers … woman.

The woman from the bar; she still wore her black Circle pressure suit, but her anxious facial expression, her empty dangling arms, the open body posture, all screamed non-combatant. He relaxed his fingers but he didn't lower the guns.

'Out of the way for Bruce's sake,' he breathed, heart racing now. He swayed left and right to look past her.

She didn't move. 'You pissed a few people off, Robert Garry. Yes I know who you are. We all do. The Circle of Independent Elite Pilots is crawling all over this planet and the locals have welcomed them with open arms. They are friends here and you're an outsider.'

She stepped forward, still blocking the passage. The footfalls grew louder behind her. Boots squeaked on floor, guns rustled past clothes. And this stupid bitch wouldn't get out of the way.

'But you don't have to die here today,' she said, her eyes wide and green. 'I can show you another way.'

He thought of the Circle sliming up to the local officials, the three officials sitting down at the same table. They would say 'Yes, that man seemed a bit strange, said he was from here but we have no records. Yes, you are free to take him away.' He needed revenge. He needed to destroy them and teach them that no one stole from a Garry. He needed to take them down to save what was left, if anything, of his clan and his people. Could he trust this woman to give that to him? The footfalls were almost on them. Shadows moved around the corner. He could even hear their breathing. Suicide by gunfight or destroy those that took everything from you?

'Okay,' he said.

'Okay?'

'Okay.'

She withdrew an Investigator Special from her holster and aimed it at his chest. 'In that case I suggest you drop the guns and put your hands on top of your head.'

Chapter 6

Robert stared, fuming, the betrayal like a knife through the ribs.

Yet she hadn't altered her casual stance, off balance, primed for a counter attack, her head cocked backward as if listening.

His eyes widened in understanding. His guns clattered to the floor as he put his hands on his head, interlocking his fingers.

Two Ceepers appeared from the corner, carbines held at a low angle. They stopped, gazes flicking from Robert to the woman. One of them snorted. 'Allison? You know the orders, you're supposed to shoot on sight.'

'Gutless girl,' growled the other. Robert watched them raise their carbines as they stepped forward. The weapons looked huge in the confines of the crematorium. Robert shifted his gaze to the woman, heart rate steadily climbing. Sweat beaded his forehead. More footfalls echoed around them.

'This is for Oberon, misery-merchant.' The trooper on the right rammed the butt of his carbine into his shoulder in an overly dramatic way; he couldn't miss.

The woman's Special, shifted, fired, shifted again, fired and then dropped to her side.

Smoke erupted from the two trooper's chests and they sunk to the ground. 'I know my orders,' she said.

Robert's gaze switched from the woman to the bodies and back again. 'I think—'

'Shut up,' she ordered, kneeling beside the bodies, throwing one gun to Robert and pocketing the other. Robert grabbed his own two weapons and turned back to the furnace. Its door was shut and heavy; hydraulically closed. He'd need electricity to open it.

'What are you doing? She growled, footfalls nearly drowning her out. 'My father—'

'—Is dead. Do you want to die too?'

Robert closed his eyes, biting back a retort. She was right, but how could he leave? Someone would finish the cremation. Jordan would remain on New Aberdeen, he'd find him, someday, somehow, and put everything right.

The woman grunted and disappeared down the corridor out of sight. 'Beannacht leat go bhfeicfidh mé aris thú, Dad.' *Until we meet again.* Then he turned and followed her.

The woman ran, Robert at her heels. She took a bank of stairs in twos to a long corridor. He sprinted behind her. A dead end … no, a tee intersection. His heart thumped as two more Circle pilots appeared. Recognition lit their faces; the woman dropped them both.

She turned right. The wall became a full height window. Eight Sakers parked in the grass courtyard, black hulls and mean lasers. The woman pushed open the door to the courtyard. 'Okay it's clear.'

She turned to face him. 'I can't be seen with you I can't lose my cover. Take my ship, the middle one. Meet me in orbit above the farthest planet's polar cap.'

'What, Orkney?' He tried to peer past her. The Sakers' lower hulls were blued from the heat of re-entry, their landing gear compressing the frosted grass, small tufts of snow collecting in the nooks of the shield generators.

'Go.' She pushed him forward. Robert stumbled outside into the snow. The cold cut through his jacket and pants. He waited a moment for the sniper bullet, the rush of black suited assassins over the walls and out through the windows to mob him.

Then he ran.

The woman's Saker rested an easy ten metres away. Ice shattered underfoot, the crunch echoing off the courtyard walls. The air tasted warm and burnt from the ships engines. They were still ticking as they cooled down.

He hit the boarding ramp without a single shot being fired, squeezed through the hatch into the confined cockpit, checked the console – similar to the academy's training rigs – fired up the still warm engines and lurched awkwardly upward. He watched the scanner as he pulled back on the flight stick, expecting a swarm of ships to rise in pursuit, a hundred laser beams zeroing in on him as he fled, but no alarms rang out. The Saker handled easier than the lumbering Wayfarer and he pointed it for the stars.

It took him a moment to figure out the navigation computer. New Aberdeen was near its autumnal equinox but Orkney was at summer solstice on the other side of the solar system. He entrusted the ship to autopilot and studied the scanner; no contacts. He narrowed his eyes at the screen, suspicious.

He kept his eye on the scanner throughout the day long journey to Orkney. No pursuit.

The planetoid was an airless lump of brown rock, drifting around the edge of the system in an inclined retrograde orbit. A few times his father had talked about the government's plans to mine its heavy iron core. There was a small science outpost, Kirkwall, with a single bay starport, but nothing else of interest. He'd never been there.

The autopilot didn't know how to put him into a geosynchronous orbit above the polar cap but after a few hours Robert managed to get the ship into a close approximation.

While he waited he rummaged through the cockpit. A hand held signalling laser, two packets of freeze dried 'food', and the mother lode, an unbranded coffee-flavoured nutrient pouch. He settled into the pilot's chair, sucked on the coffee and waited.

A Circle ship appeared on the scanner; a Saker, identical to his own.

Robert checked the navigation computer. He was far enough away from Orkney's gravity well to make a hyperjump if it wasn't her.

The Saker dropped into a similar orbit and edged forward, sharp nose lit up from Orkney below. It closed on Robert in a relaxed, almost carefree manner, which felt very unlike the woman. Was the Circle trying to bluff him into giving himself away?

He dropped a hand to the hyperspace controls. Ready and steady. It came within two hundred metres then juiced its retro thrusters, stopping nose to nose. Robert watched it, eyes wide for any sudden movements. He wrapped his finger around the trigger. If the other ship fired he wouldn't have time to react, but the resulting explosion would destroy them both.

The other Saker closed. The link remained silent.

A small red light flashed from the opposing cockpit. Robert stared, unsure if he had imagined it or not, but pretty sure that things were getting too complicated for a simple trap; then he realised the light wasn't flashing. It was blinking.

Federation blink code.

Was it the woman? If so, why would an Alliance operative use a Federation code? Did she know his past?

Or were the Circle pilots from the Federation?

He tightened his finger on the trigger. What the heck is going on?

The code started again. He rewound his memory to the academy. Two short flashes, a long flash, a long flash, a long flash a short flash.

U – T – T – E

A code within a code – a secret Circle handshake?

The code repeated. Two short flashes, one long flash, a long break. Two long flashes a short flash.

I – T --M – E

Robert slapped his head. It's me. The woman.

Relief sagged his shoulders. He grabbed the laser signal and flashed it out the cockpit window.

O – K

W – A – I – T --T – H – E – R – E

Robert waited.

The woman's Saker drifted upward until all Robert could see was the landing strut doors and the crumbling ceramic of her atmospheric shielding. She goosed forward, reactive thrusters spilling plumes into the darkness. She edged closer and closer, then spun the ship around on its nose until her cockpit hung directly above his. Craning his neck back he could see her in her own pilot's chair. He waved, but she ignored him, unstrapping herself and disappearing from view.

Her Saker was so close he could almost touch it. Heck both ships were almost touching; fancy flying.

A bang echoed from within his ship. He jumped, unstrapped and stepped through to the boarding ramp. It was still closed but a small port above him irised open and the woman pulled herself through. She jumped down toward the floor, completed a zero-gravity handstand, flicked her legs behind her head then magnetised her boots. Her feet shot downward, clamping to the deck.

A killer and a gymnast, he thought. What a combination.

She straightened up to her full height, her green eyes meeting his.

There was nothing there. No soul, no life, no speck of anything that resembled a human. They were cold eyes, the eyes of a killer. They gave Robert the shivers.

'Hi, I'm Robert,' he said, extending his arm.

She stared at his hand as if he'd dredged it up from a sewerage pond. 'Don't touch me.' She pressed a switch embedded in the wall. The small port closed. She walked toward the cockpit. 'What did you do to my ship?'

Robert straightened as if he'd been slapped. 'Umm, hello? Thanks for saving my life?'

She strapped into the pilot's seat as he followed through the hatch. She reached for the controls.

His eyes widened. 'Wait.' He dived for the second chair, swung a leg over.

She accelerated the ship forward, tossing Robert into his chair. 'What in the Bruce did you do that for?' He strapped himself in as she put the ship through a roll. His head banged against the side of his chair. 'Fates, woman, what is your problem?'

The Saker stopped nose to nose with the other ship. She edged forward and up, closer to the abandoned Saker.

'Wait, what are you—'

Their laser emitter smashed through the other Saker's viewport and wedged into the pilot seat. The woman fired the main engines, nudging forward, using the manoeuvring thrusters to point them toward Orkney. Once she built up enough speed she fired the retros and the two ships disengaged, one to nil velocity, the other on a death spiral.

They sat in the still silence for an all too brief moment.

'Let's be clear,' she said, turning to face him. 'You are only alive because I have a use for you. If you didn't have value to me I would have been the first to shoot you. I'm an Elite ranked pilot – I kill scum like you for a living.'

Robert had no idea how to respond, but being Robert, had to try. 'I wish you had mentioned this up front,' he found himself saying. 'I would have preferred to die in the crematorium.'

The woman growled. 'Selfish pig, you have a chance for redemption, to make up for your piracy, yet you'd rather suicide?' She turned away. 'Maybe I should have left you out there.'

Robert didn't answer. He looked from the hardened steel decking to the green-grey bulkheads. Space dust rushed past the hex core glass of the cockpit shell, condensation beading on the parallel girders running down its length.

She sat before a one fifty degree holographic control console, orange and green holograms dancing before her, though he couldn't make them out from his angle. His seat's simple head-up display was blank.

He was running out of places to look that weren't her face so he cleared his throat. 'Okay, how about you tell me your name and what you want?'

Silence.

'You don't have to like me but if we're going to work together I need to know your name, or I'm just going to keep on calling you 'woman'. Your choice.'

'Gunn-Britt Grotenfelt,' she said finally.

'I'm glad to make your acquaintance, Gunn. I am Robert Garry, the—'

'—leader of the Garry pirate clan, a collaboration of scum that operates in the Eastern Systems, preying on the weak, stealing from the poor and killing the innocent,' she said.

'Now wait a Viper-baiting minute. None of the people I steal from are weak. They all make me work very hard to beat them into submission. And everyone I kill is trying to kill me, or stop me stealing something, so they're fair game.'

Her face creased into hard lines, her mouth drawn back revealing clenched teeth. 'Are you going to help me or am I going to throw you out the airlock?'

Robert dropped his voice an octave, speaking slowly to enunciate each word. 'Those bastards killed my father and invaded my homeland. I have over one hundred men unaccounted for.'

Gunn stared at him for a moment, blinked, then turned back to her computer with a grunt. A grunt of dissatisfaction perhaps, but alloyed with a hint of acceptance.

'There is an information drop. I can ask for intel but I have no idea when it will be cleared. We can't rely on it.' She typed into the computer.

'I know a guy,' Robert said, 'knows everything, pretty much. Maybe he can help. He's not too far away actually, we could-'

'No.' She said it as a statement, a finality not to be crossed.

'What?' Robert liked crossing boundaries.

'No more pirates.'

Robert threw up his arms. 'Then why the Bruce did you bring me along? I thought you wanted my help? My resources?'

'I've been killing pirates for thirteen years. No one else, just pirates. I've done it as a career, I've done it as a hobby, I've done it as the thing I do when I am between my career and my hobby. I breathe pirate ship hulls, I bathe in pirate blood. I want to gut you so bad it actually, physically hurts me not to do so.'

Robert leant away from the tirade, back into his couch, eyes wide.

Gunn stared at him for a moment, her chest rising with rapid breaths. Robert braced himself for another barrage, but instead she turned to the viewport.

'So, no. No more pirates. Not yet. I have a better idea.'

Robert shrank back further into his chair, suddenly suspicious of every nook and cranny in the cockpit. She could have all kinds of weapons stored away, just waiting to make him bleed. This was not what he had signed up for.

He watched her type away on the link. She wrote a bulletin board message asking for advice from knowledgeable pilots about her upcoming holiday to the continental reef. She hit the send button.

'Where is that going?' he whispered, almost afraid to speak for fear of flicking her psychopath switch.

'Leesti.'

'Figures.' Leesti was away from the regular communication channels. That probably made it easier to stay discrete. Leesti had a famous reef, but he'd only ever heard of it referred to as 'The Reef'.

The cockpit fell back into silence, punctuated by his breathing, the gentle rush of the air vents and a muted beep from beyond the hatch.

'So what is your idea,' Robert asked, wondering what role he would play in it.

'After terminating you our orders were to link up with the main fleet and escort our big ships.' She paused. 'It's the biggest gathering of Circle forces ever. I know they're doing something but all I get told is my orders.'

Robert shifted in his seat, tried to lean forward against his restraints. 'You think it could be part of this plot?'

'It makes sense. The Circle is composed of Elite ranked pilots. When you're doing something dangerous and risky you play to your strengths.'

Robert nodded. It did make sense. Of course those same Elite pilots had shown themselves quite adept at running around and butchering people too. 'So you might be escorting whatever it is through a system?'

She shrugged. 'Only one way to find out.'

'So, where is it?'

Gunn checked the link console and pulled up her orders. 'The Brohman system.'

Robert jaw and throat muscles clenched as one, as if power cables had just been plugged into his chin. He unzipped his pressure suit, struggling to breathe.

'What's your problem?' Gunn asked, staring at him. Her eyes were blank, unconcerned, but the eyebrows were pinched, as if to say 'You'd better not become a liability.'

Robert forced his muscles to relax, settled into his couch and closed his eyes, resigned.

'I'm fine. I love the Brohman System. I spent a bit of time there as a lad.'

'Perfect.' She pulled up the navigation screen and dialled in a hyperspace route.

'Sure, perfect,' he echoed, a knot forming in his stomach. Six years ago he'd run away from Brohman straight back to his father; now he was running from his father straight back to Brohman. He wondered if he'd repeat the same mistakes.

* * *

There were four starports on Villist, the main planet of the Brohman system and a quick fly-over showed Circle ships at Tranquille Base. At first Robert thought it strange they would be so open about their location, but he was used to thinking like a pirate, skulking around out of the public – and military – eye.

'I know Tranquille Base reasonably well,' Gunn said. 'I've been here a few times with the Circle.'

'That right?' Robert knew it well too. He'd been paraded around it enough times, had seen the devastation up close and personal.

'The Circle helped out during the unrest a few years back. Now the locals climb over each other to help them.'

'Unrest huh?' The media had given it far grander titles. Robert felt sick. The bloodiest chapter of his life glossed over by history, watered down to the wail of a hungry baby.

Gunn landed in the hills to the east, beyond the river Serene. They squeezed out of the hatch, down the boarding ramp and onto the hard clay surface. Only sporadic vegetation grew on this part of the continent. There was water and there was sunlight but the minerals in the clay made it hard work for seedlings. Those same minerals had started the unrest.

Gunn closed the boarding ramp and started walking. Robert jogged to catch up to her. 'So … are you still undercover? Should we be seen together?'

'Yes, and No.'

Robert waited for her to elaborate. She didn't. 'Okay then, tell me, where does the noble Circle go when they are in Tranquille Base?'

She shrugged. 'Depends what they need.'

'Well food, I guess,' he said. 'Everyone needs that these days.'

'They could get food from anywhere. Why Villist? What does it bring to the equation that nowhere else does?'

Pain and suffering.

'Maybe it's just a coincidence they're here. Villist just happened to be on the way, a place they knew they were welcome?'

'Do you believe in coincidences?'

Robert thought about it. A lot of things had happened to him in his life that shouldn't have. Some were his fault, some of them weren't. The rest had just happened. 'Tranquille Base used to have a few custom machinery manufacturers,' he said.

Before they got obliterated.

'Maybe they are after spare parts for whatever they are using? Or they just need repairs?'

Gunn nodded. 'Anything else?'

Robert pursed his lips. He'd spent six long years not thinking about Villist. Still, the memories came back. He'd never forgotten, not really. 'Telecommunications, a brown fur pelt the tourists like. You've been here recently, you tell me.'

Gunn walked in silence. They crested a small barren hill. The city lay before them. Robert took the break to wipe his forehead and take off his jacket. It was getting hot.

Tranquille Base had once had an organic feel, curved, twisting streets extending outwards in all directions as the city grew, buildings following suit, designed individually without any thought to overall aesthetics. Now the city was being rebuilt in a Federation grid with Federation designs. More than a dozen sky cranes stood proud over the skyline. The city slouched against the starport, the size of the buildings falling away until they dissolved into Desolace, the unclaimed ruins of suburbia. Some scars took a long time to heal. Before the war, the city had also expanded north, across the Serene, but the bridges were gone and the destruction had been left to rot. A single road headed west to Vaporum City and two bridges headed east toward the hills.

'I agree,' she said. 'Food and machinery. There are a few places of each we normally go to. But there are only two of us, so we have to make a choice. Fifty-fifty on both options or put all our bets on one table.'

'In times of war an army would ensure they were well equipped to fight then gather food as they travelled or set up camp. They couldn't bring enough food to last a campaign but they could bring enough weapons. The Circle aren't a military force though. Will they have that mind set? The pilots I know do the opposite: ensure they have enough food and water to survive the trip, and everything else is a bonus.'

Gunn kept her glare going for a moment then turned back to her ship, out of sight behind them. 'If you had just listened to me in the bar we'd have your father to help us investigate.'

'And my crew, which means this is all my fault?'

'You catch on quickly.'

He ground his teeth together. 'I'm a quick kind of guy.'

Gunn grunted. 'Fifty–fifty then.' She pulled a datapad from her jacket pocket, pressed the screen a few times then passed it over. The pad showed an overhead view of the city with the starport and four buildings highlighted in red. One of the machinery shops was to the east of the starport, the other to the far south. One food warehouse was situated in the central city, the second just outside the starport.

Robert glanced from the pad to the city, trying to visualise which buildings were which. The Circle would be in a hurry. They'd also be confident and arrogant, going where they wanted, doing what they wanted. They wouldn't be expecting anyone to be following them. For a big mission they'd want the most they could get in the quickest time. 'They wouldn't be expecting trouble but they will need reliable suppliers with stock.'

Harper and Buzzard Machinery then,' said Gunn, 'and Amalgamated Fisheries.' She pointed out the two buildings, the warehouse close to the starport and the shop to the far south. 'You take Amalgamated. That way you can also keep an eye on arrivals.'

The last Special Forces drama he'd watched on the three-dee feeds rolled through his mind. Digging into a stakeout hole, surrounded by expensive equipment, not moving to take a dump or piss for days. 'I'm not really designed for cloak and dagger. My specialties are stealing things and killing anyone that gets in my way.'

She studied him, a look of half annoyance, half exasperation then her shoulders sagged. 'Well, we'll probably get to that soon enough. Find a good vantage point, stay there and report anything to me.' She waved her link past his and then she was gone, running down the hill and out of sight.

'What in the Bruce have I got myself into?' he asked before half running half slipping down the hill toward the starport.

* * *

Amalgamated Fisheries was a big blocky warehouse, surrounded by road on all sides. The closest coast was five hundred kilometres away, though the river ran nearby. It was probably for temporary storage before the freighters arrived to haul the fish away. He walked the perimeter on the far side of the road, matching the pace of other pedestrians, sneaking glances every few moments. A long snake of MTV modules rolled down the road on mag-rails that criss-crossed the road like spaghetti. A module broke away, stopping just ahead of him. A knot of passengers climbed aboard and the module disappeared back down the road.

He felt foolish. The least Gunn could have done was give him some useful instructions. Stakeout one oh one. He imagined cameras picking up his every movement, step, stare, step, stare. Would a fish warehouse have guards? Were they on their way out right now? Were fish important enough to be guarded? Everything had a value to someone.

He watched his feet for a few metres then snuck another glance.

An alarm rang out. Robert snapped his head around but it was just an MTV's collision siren, a delivery truck forgetting the road rules. The traffic felt dense, but was that normal?

Refrigeration inverters pockmarked the building and what he could see of the roof confirmed his thoughts: the building was likely just one big freezer.

There were two fire escapes on the far end, a large delivery door down a side alley and the main entry at the front.

He studied the other side of the road; some residential stacks and a few commercial shops. There were two recessed doors where he could loiter, but he didn't want to risk vagrancy laws. Instead he strolled into a coffee shop. A poor angle to Amalgamated's entrance but he'd raise no suspicions if he sat here for a while.

Find a vantage point and stay there.

But for how long? Until business closed? His legs were already cramping at the thought of sustained sitting. He chose the window seat with the best view and sat down.

A two-dee menu pixelated within the table top. Robert selected a large soy latte, double strength, one sugar capsule. He glanced at Amalgamated's door as he swiped his ID. The table hummed, the menu retracted and a cup of coffee rose from inside.

Robert leant forward, his nose an inch over the cup and inhaled. It was a sweet deep smell, a hint of chocolate, some caramel notes, and already awakening his deadening senses.

Pure perfection.

Only then did he bring his hands up to cradle the cup. Warm and wide, just the right circumference for his two hands to interlink. Gaze resting on the fisheries entrance, he gently raised the cup to his lips and sipped. He sighed, content; a Tau Ceti brew. From the hinterland of Taylor's Landing, he reckoned, a popular choice among starport cities; milder and more legal than Riedquat Ultra, but with a smoother, nuttier taste.

He sipped again, smiling on the inside. Coffee just wasn't the same in zero-gee. It had to be drunk with gravity in an open ceramic cup, not from a straw and tube. He looked across the table to give Jordan more slip for not touching the stuff.

Robert blinked at the empty seat.

His chest deflated. The coffee warmed his stomach but his heart felt cold and empty.

He focused back on Amalgamated Fisheries and tried to think like a member of the CIEP.

Patterns and Processes.

He'd always had a knack for them, right from his days of ID-Scriffing for his father. Figuring out how people worked – what they thought, why they thought it and how to spot the resulting patterns in their behaviours allowed him to scriff without notice. His ability to decipher enemy movements had earned him the executive office of the Tutankhamun, but the skill had really come into its own on his return to piracy. Knowing where, when and how to strike had earned him many victories.

He didn't know much about the CIEP. They hated pirates and loved being adored by the public. They were intense and clearly dedicated to their goals, but every action they took spoke 'superstar'. They would take precautions but they wouldn't hide.

He checked his chrono; mid-afternoon. There was a window of opportunity an hour or two after lunch when requests could be processed, instructions could be given and transport could be organised. After that it all became too hard. People would put things off till the next day. They'd be worrying about dinner that night and getting the kids to sleep, not rushing through a last minute order.

If the Circle was going to make a move it would have to be soon.

No one went through the fishery's main door for twenty minutes. That probably made sense. A storage facility wouldn't have much traffic. But then a pair of men stopped by the front door, pointing and talking. They looked like locals, one wearing a green turtleneck, the other a black vest over a white shirt. Turtleneck was tall, Vest was mid-sized. Neither appearance screamed out 'pilot' but he was no expert. Pirates came in all sizes, shapes and sex and most of them were pilots.

The pair pushed through the front door and disappeared inside.

Robert felt himself standing, coffee only half drunk. What should he do? He sat back down, checking no one was watching him. He moved his link to his mouth. 'Two potentials here,' he whispered.

'Find out,' she whispered back.

'How?'

'Grow a pair of balls.' She terminated the link.

Robert curled his upper lip in an unspoken snarl. Bitch. He finished his coffee in a couple of gulps, stood and marched for the door. He was nearly running so he slowed as he pushed through the door. He crossed the road, dodging MTVs, delivery lorries and a personal car. He reached the far side and started toward the door, but his strides shortened, his legs growing leaden. If the plan was to go in guns hot and kill everyone he would have done it already. Sneaking around without killing and without getting caught was a whole new battlefield; a different mind set and different skills.

The doors were upon him before he was ready, but he was committed and he pulled them open.

The two men stepped out, laughing, the short one slapping the tall one on the back. They breezed right past without a second look.

Robert stood there for a moment before he realised he was sticking out like a blinking navigation beacon and he kept walking.

'A pair of duds,' he whispered into his link when around the corner.

The link scratched with static. 'I might have something. Standby, standby,' Gunn said.

Robert looked up. The pedestrians ignored him, probably buried in their own thoughts.

He held his link to his ear, waiting, but it was silent. He backed up to the warehouse, one foot up against the wall, hands in his pockets, and tried, and failed, to whistle 'Federation ships go sailing on.'

The link returned to life. 'I've got them. Get over here.'

Robert switched off the link and checked the sun. South was to the right. He turned left. An MTV snake hurtled down the road toward him. He jogged to the pickup point and climbed aboard.

* * *

The Harper and Buzzard warehouse was a survivor from the war; an isolated double storey tin building amid the ruins.

Roof vents banged in the growing wind. Several cars were parked haphazardly outside.

Gunn guided him past rusting iron and crumbling brick, all being reclaimed by nature, and to her hideout, a children's playground. It was a small pre-fabricated thing, built in a factory and planted on a mat of impact tiling. There was a lawn of grass and gnarled black trees, long dead but still intact. Builders had crafted a play hut from a scorched hull fragment, the eleven star standard of the Federation visible on the roof.

Robert's stomach shrunk on itself, pulling his other organs in with it. Everywhere he went he was reminded of his failures. Gunn had to know his past, intentionally dragging him down memory lane.

She leant through the biggest of the black trees, viewer over her eyes, watching the machine shop. Robert stopped two metres from the tree, unable to step closer. The dead branches seemed to twist toward him, long fingers reaching out for him, reaching out for justice.

'Get behind me you idiot,' Gunn hissed. He gave the tree a wide berth and moved to where she'd asked. 'Two of them went in the front door. Standard practice is to negotiate terms, leave then come back with transport.'

Robert watched the door too. A huge logo adorned this side of the building: An 'H' and a 'B' over a shield with a wheel in the middle. The car park was enclosed by a foot high plassteel fence.

'They're coming out,' she whispered. Robert stepped forward in spite of the trees branches and focused. They wore black and hurried through the car park but he couldn't make out any other details.

'What do we do?' Robert asked Gunn. 'Do we follow?' Cool steel pressed against the back of his ear.

Robert's heart thumped a cold slow beat. The steel was round and cool, yet gritty as if covered in a faint powder.

A gun barrel.

'I'd rather you didn't,' said the voice behind him.

Chapter 7

The Architect placed the keystone in the bridge of blocks. 'Masterful,' he said, smiling. His two-year-old grandson Alex sat cross legged next to him in the nursery. Alex clapped and pointed to the bridge.

'My bridge. My bridge.'

The Architect nodded. 'Sure is, my friend. That is your bridge.'

'My bridge?' asked Alex.

He couldn't help the laugh, a good honest hoot uncluttered by other thoughts; a moment of just him and Alex and nothing else.

He felt alive again. 'Your bridge. Now what else should we make?'

Alex moved onto his knees, straightened up and looked around the room. There were number and letter hologram posters over the walls and a bookcase covered in toys. The walls were still pink though. He'd meant to re-colour since … but he couldn't quite bring himself to do it; next year, maybe. He still needed pink in his life.

'Castle!' Alex yelled, mouth wide in an 'o' shaped smile, eyes staring straight into his, both a craving for love and a construction challenge. The Architect accepted both. He grabbed Alex and rubbed his tummy until he squealed with laughter.

'Okay buddy, you're on.'

The Architect's link bleeped and he sighed as the real world returned. For just a moment his only trouble had been how to build a bridge that stayed up, but responsibility landed back on his shoulders and he slumped forward. Alex gazed at the link and his smile melted in slow motion; a droop of sad acceptance. The Architect's heart bottomed out, a pang that made him reach backward for support as he struggled for breath. Alex didn't understand death. He still asked for his mother, confused and likely feeling abandoned. And now he had associated the link with his last family member leaving too.

The link kept bleeping but the Architect couldn't move. His eyes were locked on Alex, barely a toddler but already scarred by life. The Architect's mouth opened but the welling in his eyes kept him silent. He dragged his gaze back to the pink walls, to the little doll in the doll crib and the princess costume still in its package, unused. Much had been lost but there was still more to lose.

'I know it's rough buddy, I know, but I'm doing this for you. Please understand.'

The first three years were the most important. He'd read the studies as everyone else probably did. The foundation for an entire life was laid at the beginning. The brain made connections of experiences. Children needed love and attention and security, not death and trauma. Even if they didn't understand it they picked it off those around them.

He could be destroying Alex in his attempts to save him and the rest of the galaxy.

The link kept buzzing.

The Architect ran out of words. 'I'm sorry buddy. I'm sorry.' He stood and opened the link. Alex had already moved onto building the castle. He was good at independent play; too good. With a last gaze at the one thing he was trying to protect the most he moved to the far wall.

'Speak.'

'Commander Tybalt for you,' his Lieutenant said.

'Put him through.'

There was a moment's delay as the link unscrambled and re-scrambled. 'Tybalt here sir.'

'Report.'

'The weapon is seventy-five percent complete. We are waiting for the final components to make the fifth. Our engineers believe we are now ready to perform the test fire.'

The Architect repressed a shiver but it was just a test run. Not the real thing. 'Casualties?'

'It's still a construction site. It'll be midnight, local time; between shifts. There won't be anyone nearby.'

The Architect exhaled slowly, a bit of warmth returning to his chest. 'Your men are logging all the data? We can't waste this opportunity.'

'Everything is ready.' The words were perfunctory and stifled. He had bruised Tybalt's professional pride.

'I have full faith in you, Commander,' the Architect said quickly. 'Please keep me updated on the results.'

He closed the link before Tybalt could respond. He held it in his hand for a moment, staring. Such a small, unobtrusive item; plain, black, invisible to a degree, yet with it he could create destruction on a galactic scale.

He looked down at Alex building the castle himself, a lop-sided structure, one large wall shaped like an antenna and two lower walls at the back.

How many children would die before this was over? How many fathers would wake up without their babies? Their wives? Grandkids?

The Circle of Independent Elite Pilots would not be thanked for what they did. The history books would record them as traitors.

But at least there would be a history.

He sighed, watching Alex add a ridiculously high section to one wall.

Tybalt's message left him with more work to do. It was time to prepare for his Highness.

'Nanny,' he barked.

Alex clapped as the robot awoke and rolled out from the corner. It looked like a stack of garbage cans with caterpillar arms but Alex loved it. It simulated sentience with lots of sensor inputs and clever algorithms. It kept his grandson safe above all else and kept him company when the Architect had to work.

'I have to go now buddy,' he said to Alex. He squatted and spread his arms. Alex untangled his limbs, stood and rushed over, slamming into his chest. The Architect barely had time to close his arms around Alex before he rushed back off again and did the same to Nanny.

The Architect stood, watched for a too-small, precious moment, then turned and pushed out through the door.

* * *

Robert relaxed his body but the barrel pushed in harder, forcing his head to the side. 'Slowly turn,' came the voice.

Robert did as instructed, the pistol withdrawing as he turned. Before him stood two men, both holding laser pistols close to their hips, both slightly too far away to jump.

They wore silver two piece suits, a long tapered length of material tied to their necks and flapping in the breeze. The one with brown hair had shiny silver cufflinks; blondie sported bright yellow, straight out of the 3280s.

Robert sized them up. Jordan could have wrestled them down, but Robert would have to talk his way out.

'Phew. I thought we were in trouble there for a bit,' Robert said to Gunn. 'I thought they were with the Circle. But these muppets appear to have escaped from some retro circus. Should we call animal control?'

Neither of the men spoke, and surprisingly neither did Gunn. He thought she would have fired across an insult too but he saw that the three of them were sizing each other up, from shoe to frown, Robert seemingly forgotten for the moment.

'An Accer,' the blond one said to Gunn. 'FEDSOD,' Gunn replied.

Robert swallowed a lump in his throat and leant back, the Federation Special Operations Division, but that was an old reflex. They weren't his problem. Not anymore. 'Take a hike, brown hair. We're busy here.'

Brown raised his right eyebrow and seemed to study him with fresh eyes. 'You're not AIS.'

'Damn straight I'm not. I'm a pirate.'

'Your days at that are over,' Blond said, but Brown turned his head, as if looking at Robert from another angle would glean more information. 'You're a citizen.' A statement, not a question.

'You know they call you 'morticians'?' Robert replied, dodging the question.

Brown stepped closer, his shiny Ingram laser pistol shifting from Robert's chest to between his eyes. 'You're a deserter?'

Robert realised he'd just given himself up as ex-military; so much for weapon-like wit. The Special Operations Division trained on a special continent of Morgue's Mortuary. Only those who had also trained on the navy planet would know the nickname.

'I did my time,' he said, which was true in one sense.

Gunn stepped between them. 'Disregard this idiot. He's here because I thought he might be useful. We're both here for the same reason: the Circle. Let's work together.'

Blond shook his head. 'No can do.'

'That's ridiculous,' Gunn said, putting her hands on her hips. 'We can share data, apprehend that scum then go our separate ways if need be.'

'Our data is classified. We are not at liberty to divulge anything.'

Behind them distant words carried on the breeze, incomplete fragments of relaxed conversation. Robert half turned. The two Ceepers were on the street. Walking, but they'd disappear behind the construction 'borgs in moments.

'Come on guys,' Let's put away the weapons and team up to get the drop on those buggers.'

'I don't negotiate with people on the wrong end of my gun,' said Blond.

Brown put an arm in front of Blond. 'What my colleague is trying to say is that normally teaming up would be a useful temporary measure. However, in this case circumstances dictate that we pursue the Circle ourselves and without risk of interference.'

Robert tensed his arms and legs, readying himself. His own guns were tucked up in his clothes. He was still too far away from Brown or Blond to get the jump on them, but he wasn't going to go down without trying. 'That sounds like some kind of veiled threat.'

'Not at all,' said Brown in his casual tone. 'Just a statement.'

Robert accepted that with good grace but Gunn straightened, chest expanding, eyes narrowing. 'These are my targets and you're not having them.'

'Sure,' said Brown. 'Now turn around. You know the drill.'

'Typical morticians,' said Robert, 'cowards and bullshit artists.'

Blond panned his weapon toward Robert. 'I can shoot you in the face if you'd prefer.'

Brown stepped forward and cracked his fist into Robert's head.

Robert rolled with it, turning, kicking off and flying backwards. He pulled the L&F from his belt, aimed under his body and fired twice before slamming into the ground. The first shot took Brown in the arm, the other knocked Blond's gun from his hand and out of the game.

Brown screamed. Gunn pounced, arms and legs swinging. Robert heard three connections and Blond dropped. Brown cradled his bleeding arm and dived for his weapon, but Robert kicked it away and Gunn pistol-whipped Brown.

Robert stood up and made a show of dusting himself off. Gunn stood guard and the two morticians stared with small eyes, Blond's going purple, Brown's going white.

Robert laughed. 'You two just got played like a game of Saar duhm, tricked by a pirate and beaten up by a girl. Ouch.'

'I'd better trash them,' said Gunn. 'We don't want them coming after us.'

'No,' Robert said, arms up, then slower. 'No, don't kill them.'

'We don't have time to deal to them another way,' said Gunn. 'The Circle stooges are getting away.'

Brown's calm had returned though his voice was strained. His suit sleeve was red. 'Once a citizen always a citizen. You can't bring yourself to kill us.'

Robert shook his head. 'No, I've just caused enough Federation deaths in my time. I don't need to cause anymore.' He smashed his right boot into Brown's face.

Brown's lights were out before he hit the ground, a hollow knock against a tree root.

Robert danced on his left foot to relieve the pain, cursing. 'Dammit. Felt good though.' He gestured at Blond. 'He won't leave without his partner. That'll give us a big enough head start.'

Gunn turned. 'They're getting into a car.' 'Let's go.'

* * *

They raced across the playground, sacrificing stealth for speed. A muddy-blue ground car pulled up beside the Ceepers and they climbed into the back. Their buddies must have been in the front.

Four in total.

The groundcar had a boxy, un-aerodynamic grace to it. A head appeared through the window. It turned back, jerked and disappeared back inside. The car's small grip spheres squealed and it accelerated down the road.

Robert and Gunn jumped the car park fence. He slowed, looking through the car windows, checking for the best combination of speed and poor security. He passed an all-terrain vehicle, stopped, and turned back. It was slow but it sported big grip spheres and a strong chassis. Good for running other cars off the road. He fired the L&F through the driver window.

CHAPTER 7

A shrieking alarm pierced the still air.

Robert opened the door, swept the glass off the seat with the L&F and pulled himself in. He unlocked the passenger door then used the butt of the L&F to smash the control housing.

Gunn climbed in. 'Do you know what you're doing?'

'It's been awhile.' He'd jacked his last car twenty years ago, but Gunn didn't need to know that.

'Well your friends are coming, so do it faster.'

The casing cracked and he ripped it away. He glanced upward. Brown and Blond were racing toward them, pistols raised, collar fabric flapping behind them. Robert flinched in wounded pride. Brown should have been down for longer than that.

'Come on,' said Gunn, buzzing like an overloaded laser rifle.

Robert grunted as he yanked out a latching relay. The alarm fell silent. He wiped the sweat from his brow. Bypassing the security system was easy, but the owner's ignition tab had a quantum link to the car. Impossible to duplicate, reasonably complex to bypass.

'The employees are looking,' Gunn said, tone rising in warning. 'I think that's the owner.'

Through the ringing in his ears Robert could hear footfalls, fast and heavy. 'I'm going to have to start trashing people,' Gunn said. Robert heard her pistol slide past her clothing and the faint click of internal gearing as she readied the trigger.

Robert blocked her out, focusing on the two wires in his hand. Blue and red. One to start the car, one to permanently destroy the ignition. 'Pirate …' Gunn warned him.

He didn't know which wire to yank. He'd probably lifted a couple of hundred cars before he ran away to the Navy but there had never been a blue and a red wire. It had always been clear cut. His fingers twitched with adrenaline and the wires felt slick from his sweat.

'Pirate!'

He pulled the red wire. The electrics chimed alive and the car lifted a foot on its magnetic levitation.

Robert bolted upright and yanked on the control stick. The car raced backward and a laser pulse skimmed past the view glass. He flicked the stick around and the car spun on the spot, then the grip spheres dug in and the car launched over the curb and into the street.

He glanced at Gunn. Her eyes were wide, hands tight around the arm rests. A smile stretched across Robert's face, wide and stupid like a crazy man. There was nothing quite like the adrenaline rush of doing something incredibly stupid and getting away with it. He whooped, punching the air.

A blur of silver in the rear view caught his eye. Brown and Blond were flashing IDs at the gathering H&B staff. A woman pointed and the morticians ran to a car and Robert's euphoria disappeared. Now he didn't just have to find the Circle's car. He had to find it before the morticians did.

'Hmm,' growled Robert. The empty street stretched toward a distant intersection. Robert had the accelerator to maximum but the gearing was too low, the grip spheres too knobbly. He'd chosen poorly but the race wasn't over yet.

'Which way?' Gunn said, hands on the dash, head whipping back and forth as if repeated glances at the intersection could divine the answer.

Robert gave it his own cursory inspection. Three options: Left, right or straight. Left would lead into Desolace, right headed toward the starport. But is that where the Circle would go or were they savvy enough to try misdirection? No, the Circle crew were being chased on a strange world with only one way out. They'd go straight for it, balls to the wall.

The intersection was on him. Which way? A car pulled onto the road behind them; the morticians.

'Wishing you'd trashed them now?' Gunn said.

He raced through the intersection and took the next right, three hundred metres further down the road. Then down the long stretch, fallow fields turning to foundation pads, 'borgs erecting duralium columns, turning to completed industrial buildings.

Traffic became frequent; delivery lorries, taxis and personal cars. No MTVs this far out. He weaved in and out, hemmed in by the buildings, but he couldn't see the boxy blue car. Horns screeched as he swerved.

'You've lost them,' Gunn deadpanned, totally unsurprised.

'I know exactly where they are,' Robert replied in the same tone, before he wrenched the control stick around to miss a turning garbage scowl.

'How?'

'I don't need to follow them, I just need to know where they are going and there is only one way in and out of this place.'

Gunn grunted. 'The starport.'

Robert weaved again and she rolled toward him, but she grabbed the dash and dragged herself back to her door.

More honking behind them; the morticians were closing up. They had a faster car but Robert's quickly pushed through the traffic.

The traffic signals flashed red and the cars ahead slowed. Robert kept his foot down and punched a car out of the way. He sped across the intersection moments before oncoming traffic flashed past. His heart pounded in his chest but a glance over the shoulder made it worth it. The morticians were still battling through the stationary traffic.

The road was clear and headed for the next intersection. 'I hope you are thinking of a plan,' Gunn said.

'Call for backup?'

'Better than that.'

'Okay.' Robert flicked the stick left. The big spheres dug in and changed rotation direction, squealing against the road like a hyperdrive at critical pressure. He tossed the car down the side road. Straight arrows illuminated the next two junctions. They were coming back up on the main road. This time Robert stopped at the lights.

'Be right back.'

He climbed out the broken window and onto the roof. Cars behind him tooted their horns. A man screamed at him. A door opened and slammed shut and footsteps rang out on the road.

Robert looked up and down the road. To the right, maybe half a klick toward the starport, more horns and tooting carried with the wind. The ground car traffic thinned out, replaced with MTVs whose avoidance lights were flicking on and off.

Bingo.

He dived back into the car and speared across the junction, taking the next right to keep them parallel to the main road. The traffic was lighter but still slowed them. He dodged through, Gunn cursing beside him, drivers yelling at him from all directions. The next intersection showed a flashing red cross.

Stop.

Robert kept going. An MTV zipped out of a pickup point and joined the flood of other MTVs. The road was more rail than tarmac now, endless combinations that allowed vehicles to go anywhere from any point.

Robert drove straight into the current, trusting the autopilots to react.

Shrill alarms filled the intersection and MTVs jerked sideways as if his car magnetically repulsed them. He slid between two and glanced into another one then broadsided a forth.

It was a single module, six wide faces staring at him as it jerked from the tracks and capsized against a building.

Robert pushed the car through the spin, turning it into a three sixty degree turn, then punched the stick forward and kept going.

He felt eyes on him. 'It's not my first car chase.'

'Except you're normally the one being chased, aren't you?'

Robert said nothing. He did the sums in his head as he swerved around. In the time he had taken to cross the main road the Circle crew had probably covered an extra half kilometre.

He kept it straight, happy he'd chosen the all-terrain car. The rails made it rough going at high speed. Then he turned right, mounting the sidewalk to squeeze between an MTV and a street kiosk selling ketchup. It was two hundred metres back to the main road. The traffic signal was a flashing arrow, alternating green and red. He kept the stick rammed against the console.

The signal changed to a red cross. Four vehicles started across, only to brake and jerk away as a boxy blue car swerved between them.

Gunn didn't say anything. No accolade, no grunt of acknowledgement.

Robert smiled.

He slid through the intersection, barely missing a double module MTV and a small grey two door car. The Circle's car was just ahead, weaving back and forth. Robert followed them, move for move. An arrow flashed ahead. MTVs slowed. A delivery lorry joined the queue. The Circle car turned, shimmied sideways and crossed the traffic but then braked hard as a big truck lumbered through. MTVs piled up around it, their alarms shrieking.

Robert's smile grew, a smile of simple pleasure, a smile of a wild eyed scheme coming to fruition; he aimed for the stricken blue car.

The truck lumbered past, the Circle car accelerated, shifting to the left.

Robert smashed straight into them.

He didn't see the whites of their eyes, but he saw a crap load of sparks as their car bounced. It went airborne for a second, floating as if in zero-gee, just for a moment, before crashing back down.

Robert didn't stop. He kept on the Circle car, pushing it forward, forward, forward until the driver tried to flick his car around to escape.

Bad idea. Robert selected the all-terrain torque settings and sprang forward, pinning the car side on.

Now he could see the whites of their eyes.

The Circle car's spheres screeched across the road gouging two deep tracks as Robert rammed them forward.

And then they crashed straight into a wall.

* * *

A bullet ploughed into his headrest. Robert jerked awake, adrenaline exploding in his veins. The Circle car was pinned against a building, empty.

He turned, pain bursting from his neck, and punched Gunn in the shoulder. Four men in black crossed the road on foot. One was limping and two were supporting the fourth. They entered a paved area.

Gunn mumbled and he punched her again. 'Wake up, dammit.'

She snapped awake. 'Status?'

Robert pointed across the road. 'In trouble.'

She kicked her door which opened with a groan of steel and she half fell, half jumped outside. Robert followed suit and they crossed the road, dancing between the MTVs, and into the paved space. A statue stood atop a plinth in the centre of the plaza, a good two metres above head height. A tingle of foreboding wriggled its way through his stomach and he slowed as bile rose up his throat.

Gunn stormed past him. Their targets were ahead, stumbling as fast as they could. It would take twenty seconds to run them down and then the game would be over.

Buildings boxed the plaza in. A raised grass bed, ornamental benches and a few smaller statues littered the space. And people. There were a lot of people. The place became crowded, the Ceepers disappeared behind a sea of bodies and Robert realised they were surrounded.

Over fifty angry looking men and children. Scowls, clenched fists, knives. Things were about to get real ugly.

'We don't know what your business is,' said the man in front, a bearded guy in his early fifties, 'But you're messing with the wrong people.'

'We have no business with you,' Gunn replied, voice controlled but loud enough to be heard over the muttering. 'We are chasing suspected terrorists. Let us pass!'

They took no notice, but closed in. Robert's mental threat alarms were going off the map, bouncing from one local to another, leaving him little mental acuity to focus on anything but surviving the next few seconds.

Gunn raised her pistol and fired twice into the sky. The shot echoed off the walls, slowly dying away. The inward momentum stalled.

'I'll not ask again' Gunn said into the tense silence. She brought her own weapon down and aimed it at the leader. Robert narrowed his eyes. These were innocent people with nothing worth stealing. If she shot the man he'd take her down himself. He moved his arm up to her pistol.

'Hey it's him. It's Garry.'

The voice caught him off guard. It was young, high pitched and laced with reverence. He found it, a girl of eight or so, barely a toddler. She pointed up at the statue and he knew the credit coin had dropped. He craned his neck back, following her extended arm. The mutterings became whispers. The crowd gestured toward him.

His gaze reached the top of the statue and there was Robert Garry in all his bronzed glory, mounted atop a pyramid of chiselled rock, attired in a ripped Federation uniform, one foot on a piece of wreckage, one hand reaching for the sky. A plaque was fastened below his foot. Twenty three embossed words. Not harsh or nasty words, but words that would nevertheless haunt him for the rest of his life:

'We were dead in the water. Defeated. Gone. But I heard the screams and we came running. What else could we have done?' – Robert Garry, Commander, August 31st, 3293

Robert groaned. *Crap.*

Another man stepped forward his smile a gaping chasm between teeth. 'Robert Garry? Is it really you?'

Robert sighed, his shoulders slumping under an old weight, one he might never escape from. 'Yes.'

'Can you autograph my pad?' The leader reached for his pocket.

That made Robert angry. 'You want my autograph? I'm here trying to stop more people from dying and you're in my way. Move!'

The crowd parted immediately, their eyes glazed over, smiles so deep they looked etched into their jawbones.

Robert sprinted down the road, Gunn in tow, leaving the confrontation, and a nightmare of memories, behind. The four Circle members were navigating the next junction. A limping man turned, flicked up his pistol and fired. Robert flinched away, feeling the heat of a laser pulse. He snapped up his Diplomat and fired.

Limper kept limping; Robert's eyes widened in shock. He checked the Diplomat's barrel. He never missed. He snap-fired again and Limper spun and fell into the side of an MTV, spider-webbing the glass then crumpling to the ground.

Traffic screeched to a stop, MTVs, lorries and a couple of personal transports. The three other Ceepers turned as one. One released his injured compared, whipped up his pistol—

Robert fired again. His assailant's head snapped back and he sprayed the concrete with pink mist before crashing to the pavement.

That left two. Sirens echoed down the street. Robert reached for both of them. He grabbed an arm, and pistol-whipped one, the other stumbled back and fell on the road. A driver stepped out of his car. Robert straightened his arm and pointed the Diplomat at him.

'I need to borrow your spheres.'

The man looked like he was going to shit his pants. He nodded; his voice faint and mechanical. 'Okay.'

Gunn brained the fallen Ceeper and dragged him into the car. Sirens echoed off the MTVs and the buildings and from the plaza until it sounded like they were surrounded.

'In, in!' he urged, pulling his concussed captive off the ground and bundling him through the rear door. Gunn jumped into the control seat, Robert next to her, and turned back to aim at their prisoners. Gunn activated the window scraper to clear the blood and powered up the engine.

Blue and red lights flashed behind them. The traffic had scattered after the shots and the police had a clear run. Gunn wrangled the car down the road, through the traffic and around corners, trying to keep the police out of direct line of sight. They turned left, straight into a pair of police defence platforms.

Gunn spun the car around but her momentum was too great so she spun back again and raced for the gap. 'Get down!' she yelled as the policemen raised their weapons. Robert and the captives ducked down as the windows exploded above them. Metal screeched either side as they squeezed through the barricade.

Robert risked a look up. Four police cruisers chased them now, lights flashing, sirens wailing; the rest of the traffic pulling aside.

It was a race; them versus the police, the first to the starport the victor.

The scream of turbines echoed through the air and a Viper zoomed overhead, barely above the roof tops; it banked, coming around.

'They're going to fire on us,' Gunn said. Not a question, a statement, devoid of fear.

'It'd take a crack pilot to get us and not hit a civilian. They'd never get authorisation.'

A puff of smoke and fire belched from the Viper.

'Missile!' Robert yelled, trying to grab the stick. Gunn elbowed him off and turned the stick right.

Robert's restraints bit in as inertia threw him toward his door.

The missile grew bigger, shrieking as it split the air apart. They closed on an MTV. Gunn tapped bumpers. Robert's head bounced into the roof. He tasted blood.

Then Gunn wrenched them left.

The world went white. An explosion blew his window in, blinding and deafening him. The view outside skidded past, Viper, police platforms and the surrounding buildings. Road fragments and twisted metal flew past his shattered window.

A glass building reared up on them. Robert pulled his head back just as they slammed sideways into the building. Glass shattered and tinkered. His door ripped off and disappeared. His legs screamed in pain as red welled up in half a dozen places. He heard Gunn yelp but when he turned her face was a solid mask of concentration. The stick jostled in her grip as shattered glass rained down on the bonnet. The car bounced up and down, side to side. With a shriek that could have been from himself or the car, they jerked sideways and were free.

Robert twisted around to look back. Fire raged from the gutted MTV and two police platforms had stopped to assist.

There were still two more chasing them.

'Fate's sake,' he whispered, face white, heart pounding. 'We're not going to survive much longer out here.' He wasn't sure who exactly he said that to but one of the Ceeper's chimed in.

'That's what you get when you lead a life of crime.'

Robert smashed the grip of the pistol into his nose, spurting blood everywhere. 'That's what you get for being a dick.'

Gunn slid the car through a ninety degree intersection and straightened up onto a six lane road, the row of skyscrapers to the right, tall enough to make an artificial wall.

Robert glanced to the other side. Beyond a chain-link fence a lowered mag-lev line ran a good ten feet below the road; long haul and heavy cargo, maybe.

The arched entrance of the starport loomed ahead, beyond that, the MTV stations and customs waypoint.

Then he saw the line of security cars across the road, end to end, two deep; a solid block right across the entrance.

In the back one of the Ceepers groaned.

Laser beams flashed past from behind. Some went wide, some passed through the car like a vibra-knife through armour. Robert hunkered back down.

'Uh oh,' Gunn muttered.

Robert couldn't see a way through. Police in front, police behind, nowhere to go.

Bullets joined the laser bolts, pinging off the car and the ground, Gunn swerving back and forth to throw their aim off. The road block would be in range in moments.

'I'm trained to be subversive,' Gunn said. 'Hide in the shadows. Sabotage, earn trust, learn intel and pass it on.'

'What are you saying?'

'I'm saying I don't know what to do.'

'I'm a pirate. I'm trained to do as much damage as possible.'

The starport security officers crouched behind their mobile platforms, rifles resting on car bodies, heads behind weapons. Robert's skin tingled, tight, and his heart boomed like the last time he'd been here; a thousand Imperial guns; a thousand police guns.

The rear window shattered. One of the Ceepers jerked then went still, blood oozing from his chest. Gunn jerked the car sideways.

Through the roar of the engine, the rumble of spheres on the road, through the laser bolts and the bullets, Robert heard a new sound, the smooth whoosh of air and the song of magnetic choking.

A maglev train, about a kilometre back. It raced along the track, heading toward a tunnel under the starport walls.

Robert grabbed the stick and yanked it to the left. The car hopped and skittered and Gunn grabbed the stick back. She stiffened, clearly seeing what he was aiming for.

'Are you crazy?'

'Yes.'

His answer seemed to calm her. 'Okay.' The tarmac flashed past, empty lanes of traffic; the fence undulated, buffeted by wind as the maglev hurtled toward the tunnel, half a klick and closing.

Robert grabbed the stick again, straightening them up on the fence. Spheres squealed.

The maglev kept coming.

He sensed cars closing in around them. There were loud voices. A laser bolt slashed through the console between them making him jerk sideways.

They hit the fence.

Robert flew forward, restraints grabbing his shoulders.

The sky flashed past in a blur. Metal groaned, snapped. The floor became the roof. The Ceepers floated from their seats.

Overhead, the tracks, retaining wall then sky flashed past. The Ceepers flopped back down; Robert's stomach plummeted. He grabbed the console, readying for the crash.

They landed on a cushion of air, riding high on the magnetic tracks. The train hurtled toward them.

Gunn spun the control stick and mashed it into the dash. The car spun and shot off.

The maglev screamed as its motors reversed. From the road the train had seemed like a large beast. Fifty metres in front of it, it was a juggernaut, thousands of tonnes of steel bearing down on their tin-cup car.

The gap closed. The train's levitation dropped as the motors reacted. Its nose was a bulbous, streamlined cone ending at the right height to puncture their car. Robert looked through the train's window for the pilot but there was nothing but lights and consoles: sensors and crash defence algorithms.

'Come on, come on,' Robert yelled as a gruesome death closed to within twenty metres.

The tunnel waited a hundred metres ahead; the train was ten metres behind. The rail shook below them. The train closed; five metres, four. He could read the 'Core Manufacturing' logo on the nose. It kept coming, closer and closer, so all Robert could do was stare, lips white and pulled back, watching the reflection of the car grow on the train.

And then the reflection shrank and the train fell back ten metres, twenty, thirty.

And then they were in the tunnel and the maglev stopped, blocking out the light and dumping them in the dark.

The car's lights flared, lighting the duracrete tunnel as Gunn powered them toward the pure white key hole of the distant exit.

As it grew closer Robert became aware of the silence from outside; nothing but the clacking of the spheres on the rail and the thud of his heart in his chest.

His remaining captive remained frozen against the door, arms out for support, his face white, pupils dilated and unblinking, like a frozen computer that needed rebooting. His partner had stopped bleeding but an all too familiar coppery stench filled the car.

They blasted out the far end of the tunnel and back into daylight. They were inside the starport.

The track ended, a large platform rising up on either side. Gunn pulled the car off the track, up onto the platform. They roared past waddling loader mechs, spilling cargo containers as they spun away, straight toward the landing pads, arranged around a single flight control obelisk.

An eight sphered ferry turned onto the main thoroughfare, a pilot and his crew coming in from their ship.

Gunn leant forward. She kept the control stick hard forward. Sirens blared behind them. Robert spun; Starport security, inside and chasing them down.

The ferry blared its horn but Gunn either didn't hear it or didn't care. Her knuckles whitened on the control stick.

They closed the gap, small car against lumbering ferry; eight tonnes against two.

The ferry jerked to the side and Gunn swerved to slide up past it. Metal screamed against metal, sparks flying through his gaping door. He ducked away as the fireworks plumed and died. The car bumped and rattled and then it was past, in the clear, nothing but spaceships ahead.

The stench of burning hair filled the car. 'Which one?' Gunn asked. There were seven parked ships: an Anaconda, an Adder, a Lakon Type IV and four Sakers.

Robert shoved the Diplomat to the Ceeper's mouth. 'Which one's your ride, Quixote?'

The Ceeper shuffled backward and up to see past Gunn. 'The one on the right.'

Gunn swerved. A dozen security turrets emerged atop the outer wall as she aimed for the leftmost Saker; big flak cannons, designed for shooting down pirates, turning on grinding gears to point in and downward.

'Faster,' Robert urged. He turned to the dead Ceeper and searched his pockets. Fingers scrambling, getting caught in fabric, he grasped a small metallic entry pass and pulled it free. He grabbed the Ceeper's hand, swiped his thumb over the pass and spun back to the Saker.

The boarding ramp didn't detach. The turrets groaned to a stop on their gears, the big dark barrels pointing toward them. The security forces were closing in behind, blue and red lights splashing off the starport walls, reflecting off the ships hulls, the chorus of sirens like white noise.

Robert's heart skipped a beat. He swiped the pass again and again but the Saker didn't move. They were almost on it, out of time and out of ideas.

The turrets fired.

Twelve explosions of flame and noise and big artillery shells heading straight for them.

Except they weren't heading straight for them. They hit the Saker.

One second there was a ship in front of them, the next there was a cloud of smoke and fire and a smattering of debris on the landing pad. The smoke expanded, thick and grey and heavy, drifting toward them, and then they were inside, crackling fire and suffocating smoke. The car juttered over the debris, banging and crunching and shaking Robert's organs loose and they reappeared back into daylight, heading straight for a second Saker.

A Saker with a lowered boarding ramp.

'Well I'll be …' said Gunn, correcting slightly. The spheres flapped and skidded. They'd lost some rubber in the fire, and the car slowed. 'Not now, not now,' she squeaked, the first time he'd heard panic in her voice.

The turrets turned.

The distance to the Saker dropped, then the security cars materialised out of the smoke and fire behind them, a policeman hanging out the window of the lead car. He held a long cylinder.

'Rocket!' Robert yelled.

'What do I do?' Gunn screamed.

Alarms, ground noise, laser beams and the rush of artillery shells assaulted his ears and all Robert could think about was the Universal Scientist's statistic that no one had ever broken out of a starport and survived.

Gunn swerved, tossing him half out his door. Fire erupted to Gunn's right, and they were airborne. Robert's stomach flipped, his restraints loosened and Gunn's mouth formed an 'o' shape.

The rocket fizzed past beneath the car just as Gunn's side landed. Robert's restraints bit into his side. His head banged against the console. Gunn swore as she wrestled the controls, Robert powerless to help her. The view outside flashed toward one parked ship then another, turrets coming in and out of view.

Robert's side crashed down, the car skidded in an arc and screeched to a stop by the boarding ramp.

'Run!' yelled Gunn.

A bullet zipped through the gap where Robert's door had been. He clambered back toward the Ceeper, grabbed him by the jacket and hauled him out. Beyond the car two hangar doors opened, Vipers waiting inside.

Robert dragged the Ceeper up the ramp where Gunn had already disappeared.

They crammed through the hatch to the cockpit. The deck shivered as the engines spooled to life. The ship lurched upwards, unsteady, like a drunk stumbling home.

The Vipers launched. The roar of their engines cut through the Saker's hull and every other noise in the starport.

He shoved the prisoner into his acceleration couch and strapped himself in. Gunn turned the ship back on its engine nozzles and slammed the thrusters to their stops. Even then, his insides were trying to find a new home on his spine.

It looked like clear blue sky ahead but then two red blips appeared on the forward scanner and targeting reticles bracketed the incoming Vipers.

Zero piracy in a starport. Universal Scientist had collected the data from Imperial, Federation and Independent police forces.

Piracy above a starport, down twelve percent. Zero piracy escaping a starport.

But Robert had started inside the starport, so what statistic counted? The one that gave him negligible chance or the one that gave him zero?

They were at ten thousand metres, Gunn programming the hyperdrive, when the Vipers struck.

They were the new model, the Mark III, powerful and nearly as agile as the Saker. Two laser beams arced in. Gunn tapped the starboard thruster, corrected on port and grabbed the trigger. Her laser shot out and smoke poured from one of the Vipers, flame shooting from the engines. Gunn let it go, turning to face the other Viper as it fired its own laser.

Fifteen thousand metres.

Gunn swerved the Saker aside while keeping them climbing with the manoeuvring thrusters.

Twenty-one thousand metres.

The Viper dived, Gunn's laser glancing off its armour. Twenty-six thousand metres.

Gunn turned back to the heavens and max'd the main engine. The missile alarm screamed through the cockpit.

Thirty thousand metres.

Gunn's hand slammed down on the ECM trigger. A wave of writhing energy encircled the ship, pulsating in and out then slowly dying. Her eyes dropped to the scanner and she grunted. Robert knew what that meant: A hardened missile, impervious to ECM damage. A weight built in his chest.

'How far back?'

'Six klicks.'

'Are we going to make it?'

A pause. Small, but Robert heard it. 'I think so.'

Thirty-seven thousand metres.

Robert settled into his couch as best he could while sharing it. His arms shook, powerless to do anything but watch the missile's scanner blip inch closer and closer to the centre of the scanner. The alarm wail intensified as the missile crept inward, becoming a broadband scream across the cockpit speakers.

Gunn's jaw clenched. 'I don't think we're going to—'

The hyperspace icon flashed into existence. Gunn's hand snapped out. An explosion boomed through the ship.

* * *

They re-entered normal space before an asteroid belt, a familiar collection of thick rocks hanging in close orbits to each other. The rocks almost shimmered from the distant yellow sun, just like the ones at-

'We're still in the same system.' A sinking feeling mixed with the still pumping adrenaline. He needed to vomit. Or piss.

Gunn didn't reply.

Robert glanced at the Ceeper – unconscious by the look of him, then picked at his trousers, doing his damn best not to look at the asteroids. Gunn hunched over her controls, head down, veins visible on her hands and arms.

'You have a plan?' Robert asked. Gunn didn't say anything.

'You thought it might be best to stay local because if the Circle fleet was still here maybe you could stop the plot right here and now.'

Gunn still didn't say anything, though her grip on the flight stick tightened.

'You're easy to read,' Robert said.

'What was that about down there?' she asked quickly as if a new conversation would erase the old one.

'What was what?'

'That crowd. The statue.'

Robert's cheeks warmed; the bronze monstrosity. 'Mind your own business,' he snapped.

Gunn's eyes narrowed but she didn't retort. The silence returned, thick as a blanket.

Robert didn't care. He wasn't going to talk about it. Not ever under torture.

She upped the throttle, sailing them towards the asteroid belt.

'What are you doing?' Robert rushed. 'You're not seriously going to take us in there?'

'Don't be such a coward,' she snapped, 'they're just rocks.'

He grimaced away from the growing asteroids. 'Crap, crap, crap,' he whispered. She was playing dumb with the statue, but she knew. She had to. Why else would she torture him?

He closed his eyes as the first asteroids tumbled past. He couldn't watch the approach. Not without the moans of his dying crew echoing through his mind.

Think of something else.

The belt was just rocks. It couldn't hurt him. The locals called it Chamberlain's Despair, after the famous pirate who had come to grief hiding amongst the tumbling asteroids. Robert had also come to despair there, though not as a pirate.

The ship lurched to the side and his eyes snapped open, heart racing. Gunn guided them around two rocks on a collision course, a deft hand on the controls. The rocks crashed, showering the cosmos with millions of smaller fragments. Light played across the larger fragments, revealing tunnels, cracks, fissures and flat plains.

Gunn swung the ship around as the collision detector started barking. Robert could almost feel the thrum of his old deck beneath his seat, the viewscreen showing him a similar retreat into the belt. But back then broken electrics sent sparks across the bridge, burst pipes showered them with coolant and steam and bodies and equipment floated free, clogging the air and blocking the viewport. Once they'd reached holding stations he'd unstrapped and turned his CO's body over. The gash across his face completed the story that the wide dull eyes told. They'd taken too long to retreat.

Only two men had ever believed in him. He'd killed one of them there.

But that was then. Now, the other man who had believed in him had died too and he was drifting silently through the same place. Life had come full circle, except worse. The way of things, perhaps, but he had sworn that he would never let himself end in that situation again. *What in the Bruce are you doing?*

'This will do us,' Gunn said. She nudged the ship around and down.

There was a large asteroid ahead with a crater so deep it was almost a tunnel.

Robert kept one eye on the scanner. There wouldn't be any fighters following them in today, but he struggled to shake the memory.

She slowed the ship to a near standstill, nudging ahead at mere metres per second, into the crater and down. She dropped the landing gear. Details grew from the crater floor, stalactites (or stalagmites?) and jagged rocks; a perfect place to land. The ship juddered on touchdown and she killed the engines.

Robert unstrapped and stood, his body buzzing from repressed memories and adrenaline. He trained the Diplomat on the Ceeper. Unresponsive up till now, he sat up. Bruises swelled his forehead but the spaced look in his eyes had gone; an Elite ranked pilot and an actor.

Gunn unstrapped and stood up before them. 'Hello Seamus,' she said, deadpan, hiding any emotions she felt at this reunion.

'Hello Allison,' the Ceeper said. He straightened up, his upper lip curling as if caught in a fishhook. 'If that is your real name.'

Gunn gave a toothy, forced smile. She reached into her pants pockets and pulled out a small wand. Two prongs shot out and a small arc buzzed between them. She stepped forward, staring into his eyes.

'It's not.'

Chapter 8

Gunn climbed back into the cockpit. Robert watched her silently. The noises from the engine room hadn't sounded like two old mates shooting the breeze.

She settled into her acceleration couch, adjusted her straps and fired up the engines. He stared at her; she stared at her controls. She fiddled this setting or that setting. She checked the viewport here and there. She pressed a button. She checked her straps. She looked everywhere else except at him.

Robert cleared his throat. 'It's funny. You're on the right side of the law and I'm on the wrong side of the law, yet I've never made anyone make those kinds of noises before.'

Gunn's head panned around like a slow automated turret, eyes narrowed to laser beam slits, her jaw clenched so tight it could have snapped a duralium rod.

Robert leant back and raised his eyebrows. 'I'm just saying.'

She stared at him for another moment, her gaze gouging into him, then panned back to the controls.

'We're going to the Lanaest system.' Robert opened his mouth to ask why but she beat him to it. 'They're testing the weapon.'

'On who?'

Gunn's answer came a split second too slow. 'He doesn't know.'

'Are you sure?'

'I'm sure.' No pause that time. She lifted the ship from the asteroid and nudged the Saker around and out.

'Hey, what about him?' Robert asked. The Ceeper would quickly get uncomfortable without an acceleration couch.

'He's fine.'

There weren't any other acceleration couches on the ship. 'Not unless he's … oh.' Robert's eyebrows nearly lifted from his face. 'Wow.'

Gunn didn't face him, but her words were spat with a venom as tough as a Cobra's. 'Squeamish, pirate?'

'No, I just thought you would be.'

'I'm trying to save the galaxy,' she said, stressing the 'I'. 'My whole purpose is to protect. I've spent years getting to this point,' a pause, eyes going distant. 'My whole life.' Now she turned to him. 'Do you think I'm going to stop because one person is in my way?'

Robert studied her. Her hair was in a regular pony tail now, no longer pulling on her face so her sharp chin and cheekbones appeared more rounded. Before she had looked like a weapon.

Now she looked human.

Her long fingers were bent around the controls, her legs were tensed, who knew what was happening in the torso. It was as if her whole body was working in unison toward a single accomplishment, a unified goal.

'No,' he said. 'I guess you wouldn't. But when would you stop?'

She growled. 'An ethics lecture from a pirate?'

He shrugged. 'Many people justified worse for less. As long as you have a line drawn in your head, is all I'm saying.'

Gunn gave her usual grunt and adjusted her trajectory. Once clear of their asteroid she opened the throttle. Robert spared a quick thought for the body in engineering. 'You stow him?'

'I'm well aware of what gee forces do to a human body, if that's what you're asking. I've mopped up the results before.'

They worked their way out of the asteroid field and the hyperspace controls unlocked. Gunn loaded a jump sequence through six dark systems to get them to the Lanaest system. Then with a quick jab of her middle finger she activated the hyperdrive.

Robert sighed in relief as the hyperspace vector enveloped the ship.

So long Villist. Let's not do this again.

* * *

There was nothing in the Lanaest system; at least nothing that the long range sensors could detect. The navigation database showed no population and the sensors confirmed it. No obvious human traffic, just stars and gas giants.

'The sensors working?' Robert asked but Gunn just glared at him.

Out the viewport an orange star caught his eye. Holographic brackets targeted its three Trojan gas giants. 'What about there?'

CHAPTER 8

Gunn switched the sensors. 'Baleton Gas has a stake on all three gas giants but they haven't claimed them yet.'

'Let's check it out.'

Gunn squared the Saker on the distant orange star and fired the main engine. The primary star shone a dull red, bathing their controls in blood.

Gunn reported in to her Circle base as they sailed in system. She had lost her team but chased Robert across four star systems and requested reinforcements to some fake coordinates. 'That should stop them worrying about me for a while,' she said.

The scanner pinged two astronomical units from the star. Nothing malicious, just a standard radar pulse, but it did mean that someone was listening.

'The Circle?' Robert asked.

Gunn said nothing but her shoulders lifted an inch, the best version of a shrug he would get.

They closed to within half an astronomical unit of one of the Trojan gas giants when they saw it.

The scanner detected metals, but the other readings were gibberish. As they approached, targeting brackets overlaid something long, thin and invisible. Their eyes met for a moment, a silent thought passing between them:

We're too late.

Garbled results filled the scanner, then 'the something' twinkled like a starfield, thousands of tiny sparkles.

Gunn slowed them to a hundred kilometres per hour. Robert's eyes shifted from the scanner, now a snowstorm of tiny readings, to the viewport.

A twisted girder tumbled past, spinning around its long axis like the blades of an old VTOL plane. Then a second girder came past, then another, then a whole lattice of structural steel appeared from the darkness, a shadowy grid to their left so darkened by carbon scoring it looked like an apparition, only half there, shifting in and out of existence as he tilted his head. He fought back a shiver.

Gunn brought them to nil-velocity in a cloud of debris of all sizes. A large chunk of duralium casing spun around, the sun catching the remains of a logo, a four sided diamond backed by a cloud of gas. A faint 'B' was etched in the duralium, darkened by carbon.

Robert frowned. Baleton Gas. Debris could be misleading in terms of size, but whatever it was had to have been big. Very big.

'A harvester?' Robert glanced at Gunn. Her gaze was glued to the console.

'Bigger. Refinery station perhaps.'

Robert swore. He'd raided a refinery station once – accreted gas fetched a high price – and they were absolutely huge; a platform as long and wide as a coriolis space station and about a tenth as high. Flares and fracking towers littered the top deck while loading docks and gas condensers occupied the lower side.

They housed over three thousand staff at peak season.

'Any remains?' he asked calmly, maintaining a level of disinterest in his voice.

Gunn shrugged again, not turning from the screen.

Robert turned back to the carnage, mentally putting the pieces back where they belonged, trying to imagine what could have caused that much damage. Not a single bomb – the platforms had redundant structures in them – but a string of them?

No, not bombs; that was a terrorist's tool, not an assassins; a fleet then? The Federation could have mustered enough ships to do this, but the Circle? If they had that many ships they would be a superpower.

'How?' he asked, turning his palms upward.

'What are the Federation up to?' *A weapon of some sort?*

Robert raised an eyebrow and whistled. *Oidhche mhath*, Empire.

A new ping registered on the rear scanner. 'Finally,' Gunn said. 'Some answers.' She turned the Saker toward the distant ship, a small black arrowhead against the orange gas giant. Robert didn't have the best angle to read Gunn's console but it looked like a modified Lakon, perhaps a Type IV.

'A wake harvester,' Gunn muttered. She activated the broadband link but she got beaten to it by the Lakon's pilot.

'What the Fates happened here?' came a slow thick drawl.

'We were hoping you'd tell us,' Gunn said, in a calm professional voice. 'We're here to inspect the refinery.'

'Thought they'd done the certification last week,' came the drawl. Robert winced. What were the odds that this waker was well-informed?

Gunn's voice shifted to grumpy. 'I've just discovered trillions of dollars of losses for my company and the best you can do is wonder if the certification was done last week?' She paused for a microsecond, just long enough for the waker to draw in air before she blasted him again: 'Transfer all your sensor logs immediately.' She shut the link and a hurried second later the data transferred across.

'We should bail before he realises you're full of hyperdrive fumes,' Robert said.

'There might be more evidence.' She turned back to the debris and moved them in closer. She transferred the sensor logs to Robert's console. 'Pretend to be useful for a moment.'

An artery flickered in Robert's eyelid. His gaze lingered on her for a second, though she was back to ignoring him, then he loaded up the logs.

Harvesters carried good sensor suites, though they were normally aimed down into the gas giant. He hoped these ones weren't aimed too well.

The logs went back a week. The waker had passed the refinery two days ago before it had been destroyed.

The Lakon had run the same orbit around the gas giant for the last two weeks with an orbital period of ten standard hours. Which meant Robert and Gunn were likely less than ten hours behind the Circle, wherever they were.

Robert paused. Four hours ago the Lakon picked up radiation indicating five large hyperspace clouds.

'Check this out,' he said, swiping the data back to Gunn's console. She glanced at it.

'Five large hyperspace clouds. So what?'

Robert rolled his eyes and sighed. She wanted him to contribute yet rejected his input immediately. 'Look how big they are. Panther Clippers at the minimum. Why five? Why out here? How many convoys of Clippers would you see all the way out here? They have to be Circle ships. Maybe this super weapon needs five ships, one to carry it and four to maintain it, or it has to draw power from five ships at once, I dunno, but it just can't be a coincidence.'

'Perhaps,' she allowed.

'The sensors couldn't pick up the rest of the fleet unfortunately.'

'They're probably piggy backing on those five big ships. Saves fuel, improves cohesion.'

The scanners chimed and a new dump of data appeared on her screen. She sucked in a breath and leaned away from the computer. 'Thargoid weaponry.'

Robert laughed, but a small part of him worried. 'You're kidding, right?' He only knew the Thargoids from myth and legend. Not exactly 'happy ever after' bed time stories.

'No. Well yes and no. The remnants are showing the effects of Thargoid weapons, but that's because the Circle use Thargoid derivative weaponry. It's part of their plan.'

Robert chest deflated, the pressure easing. 'How do you know?'

'Because I've helped plant evidence like this; they were trying to convince the Federation and Empire to work together. That was Plan A. This is Plan B.' She kept reading the data dump. 'But this wasn't a normal Circle weapon. This was a plasma weapon on a scale I've never seen before.' She shook her head, her tone dropping an octave. 'This is unbelievable; off the scale.'

Robert studied the remains again. If it would take the whole Federation fleet to do this much damage how could the Circle do it with five ships?

Goosebumps fettled his arms. 'Let's get out of here.'

'Where to?' We don't have any clue on direction.'

'We need to go see my guy.'

Gunn shot him the kind of look a silenced pistol would give its mark. 'I said no more pirates.'

'Do you have any better plans? Anything else up your sleeve? No. We're out of options. Get over yourself already.'

'One pirate is too much. I don't even know I can trust you.'

The scanner warbled an alarm, cutting off the argument. Gunn spun almost before it started. Robert's eyes widened. He recognised that sound too. It wasn't one of the usual alarms of combat: missiles, weapons or link broadcasts.

It was the proximity alarm. Ships.

Gunn pulled the ship through a manoeuvre. He grabbed his console and held on. The ship jerked him sideways and stars twinkled across the cockpit.

He wiped his face with the back of his hand and realised the Saker had stopped. It took him another moment to work out why.

They'd been disabled. And as a pirate he knew there was only one reason to disable a ship.

To board it.

He fumbled at his belt for his Diplomat, wondering why everything felt slow and realising he was bleeding, a cloud of blood forming around his head.

He found his pistol, whirled around to aim at the cockpit hatch as he heard Gunn yell, 'Watch out!' But the blood confused his vision and his arms seemed to be moving through a tub of thickened lubricant. Something grabbed his arm and wrenched his elbow. He lost the Diplomat and then the deck came up and slammed into the side of his head and everything went dark.

Chapter 9

Arms tied behind his back with valves and other engine plumbing digging into him, Robert studied the two men from the comfort of his corner of the engine bay. Still, it was better than the alternative.

hey were Imperial agents, or at least what he thought they looked like; bright flashy clothes, tall sharp collars past their ears, blond hair, prominent cheekbones, wide chests. Expressionless faces, as if they'd been engineered with dormant face muscles.

Clones.

Gunn was awake beside him, eyes wide and studying them. Robert tugged on his restraints but gave up. They were high grade fibre; he'd never pull that apart. So he switched to his next weapon. He turned as best he could to Gunn.

'What kind of intelligence operative are you? Do they teach you nothing in secret service school? This is the second set of counter intelligence operatives to get the drop on you.' She opened her mouth to offer a snarky comment but he cut her off. 'If you flunked training this bad, why the Fates did they put you out in the field?'

'It's been your fault both times,' she snapped.

Robert eyed the clones. The two of them stood by the hatch, talking in heavy accented Imperial. They weren't biting.

'My fault?' he quipped. 'That's the catch cry of the useless. I'm better off allying myself with these buggers.'

'Don't you dare,' she boomed, and for a moment Robert wasn't sure if she was acting or genuinely scared that he'd turn his coat.

Robert shrugged. 'You're probably right. These guys would never buy it. The morticians might have. Maybe I should have taken my chances with them. These Imps wouldn't have the balls.'

The Imp on the left nudged the other and gestured at Robert. The other Imp walked over in precise, programmed steps. 'Pirate: elaborate on your dealings with the FEDSOD.'

Robert creased his brow, his gaze wandering as if he were worried, while inside he gave himself a fist pump. *They didn't engineer away your human nature though, did they*? People were so stupid.

'They're investigating the same thing as you, they just got onto it a lot quicker.'

'You could not possibly know what we are investigating.'

'An assassination threat against the Emperor.' Robert guessed – what else would clone agents get involved in? – then shrugged. 'Old news.'

Something flashed across the clones' face in the tiniest fraction of a second. It was so fast Robert couldn't even be sure what it was, but the clone quickly hid it which meant whatever he said next would be a lie.

'Incorrect.' Bingo.

Robert sneered and turned back to Gunn. 'The morticians even lied better than this. We should have given all our data to them; they might have actually been able to do something with it.'

Gunn's eyes widened, her head shaking fractionally. The clone stepped forward and yanked Robert up. His arms pulled taut to his restraints and he bit back a cry. The agent released the restraints, pulled up Robert's arm and put his own wrist up. 'Transfer all data to my crystal immediately.'

Robert punted it away. 'I don't roll that way, Impy. I deal in datapads. '

'There are no unaccounted datapads on this ship. Explain.'

The clone released him and Robert straightened his clothes. 'Look, I'm real sick of being treated like garbage. Even the bitch here is doing it.' Robert pointed at Gunn. He gave the talkative clone his get-down-to-business stare. 'So let's start talking like real men and trade.'

'We don't trade. We are the Empire. We take what is rightfully ours.'

Robert nodded. 'I see, I see. And how is Villist working out for you?' He tensed for a blow to the head but the clone ignored the comment. Time to change tact. 'Let me offer you a gift,' he said, stepping over to the only removable panel in the engineering bay. 'We both know who is behind this threat.' Another guess, but if he was wrong it was a good ego stroke. Do clones have egos? 'So we got a member of the Circle and roughed him up real nice to give us the details. Here he is.' He turned, unclipped the latch with his hands, pulled and stepped away.

A flood of blood and bone and fragments of body parts drifted away from each other. The clone turned to his partner. 'Gather the brain matter. There may be some memory cells intact.'

Robert cringed, unable to tear his gaze away from the man scooping up pulverised gore into a sample cube. The clone looked up at him. 'We are committed to our Emperor. We do whatever is required.'

Robert coughed. 'No kidding. Now here's the deal. We share. We investigate our angles, you investigate your angles, then we compare notes; twice as fast.' Robert started pacing, trying to gesture with his arms tied behind his back. 'Now I offered FEDSOD the same thing and they tried to shoot me. No bloody vision, don't you think? No Emperor to protect, just a bunch of claustrophobic and strangling rules. There's no passion there. You two on the other hand are devoted to your overlord.' He gestured at the remains. 'No angle too disgusting.' He glanced at Gunn. 'Getting help from a pirate is pretty disgusting, wouldn't you say?'

Talker leaned toward brain-scooping clone and whispered but his eyes never left Robert.

Talker straightened up. 'You will provide us the plans and coordinates of the CIEP forces in twenty four hours or we will terminate you.'

Robert's jaw clenched. Twenty four hours was probably quite lenient. 'This is a Circle ship. It's untraceable.'

Talker pulled a small shiny torus from his pocket. 'This bug is un-untraceable. Your ship is very traceable. We will find you.'

'Umm,' Robert said, stalling, groping for a retort, but the clone kept talking.

'Twenty four hours. We will program your link to our receiver.'

Brain-scooper finished and the two disappeared without a word. The access iris amidships hissed and sealed.

They were alone.

Robert turned back to Gunn, a big shrug in his shoulders and a lop-sided grin on his face. 'How about that?'

'You talk too much,' she said, standing and freeing her arms from behind her. The cord hung loose from both wrists.

'How the Bruce-' he started but she slapped him across the face; fast and strong, knocking his head sideways. He sucked in a breath through clenched teeth.

'That was for calling me a bitch.'

He cracked his neck and straightened back up. 'At least you're not afraid to touch me anymore,' he conceded. 'You were working on your own plan, huh?'

'I'm an Alliance operative. We solve problems.' He couldn't be entirely sure but he thought he saw a slight curve to the end of her mouth.

Robert smiled for her. 'Now you're getting into the swing of things.' He slapped her on the back. She flinched, but didn't comment. 'Come on, let's go find my pirate mate.'

She stared at him for a moment then sighed. 'Where?'

'Epsilon Eridani.'

* * *

They landed at Masseyville in New California when Gunn's mailbox pinged.

'Download it and check it later,' Robert told her. The Worldcraft corporation rep would be waiting outside. Gunn grumbled but did it anyway. She knew the score. You didn't stuff the corp around on their turf.

Gunn lowered the boarding ramp and hot dry air rushed in, leaving Robert sweating and wishing for his kilt. He hadn't seen it since the Wreaken Platform raid a month ago.

The opening ramp revealed a perfect cloudless blue sky, the distant starport wall and then it slammed onto the landing pad a few inches from three pairs of feet.

The welcoming committee.

There were two pleasant smiling women with blonde braided hair and small features and a man with a forehead and cheeks that were almost cro-magnon, and eyes that were small, recessed and dark. Instantly Robert didn't like him.

As he stepped down the ramp a massive rush of wind and screams sounded from the distance. He looked up to see a lev coaster flash past behind the starport wall, reappearing a second later. Beyond, a Ferris wheel clacked and clicked as it turned. Inside the walls, the only sounds were Robert's footfalls, the hiss of coolant from the Saker and the muted grind of cargo loader gears.

The welcoming committee stepped forward, hands at their sides, smiles cranked up to full wattage.

CHAPTER 9

'Mr and Mrs Ryder, welcome to Masseyville,' said the man, extending his hand. 'My name is Murray Sturgeon and I'll be your primary host for the duration of your stay on New California.' He pointed to the ladies on his right. 'My lovely assistants Ann and Alice are here to help with whatever you need while you enjoy our hospitality.'

Robert grabbed Gunn's waist and pulled her close. Every muscle under his touch froze and she inhaled sharply, but she didn't slap, head-butt or shoot him; small mercies.

He kissed her on the cheek for good measure. 'Great, Allison and I have never been here before. We're really looking forward to it.'

Murray pulled a datapad from his belt and glanced at it. A frown crossed his face. 'And I see you have requested lodgings in one of our more 'rural' settlements.'

Robert showed his best dopey-in-love-with-nature smile. 'Absolutely. Thank you that would be perfect.'

Murray turned to wave across the skyline of neon and steel and lights. A small capsule flew into the air and straight back down again. A hundred excited and terrified voices screamed in unison.

Robert knew that beyond all that would be sound shells, auditoriums, stands, sideshows, spinners, and dart runners.

Everyone came to Masseyville to enjoy themselves, empty their wallets, and bugger off again. No one came for the quaint rural life.

'We have taken the liberty of organising a schedule for you to truly experience what Masseyville has to offer. Would you not consider staying locally to enjoy what the Federation Times calls the 'playcentre of humanity'?'

Robert paused. They had to tread carefully. They couldn't raise suspicions, but they couldn't sit around idly while the Ceepers marched on. 'Perhaps on the way back? I promised Allison I'd show her the Esperi falls. 'He stepped forward and put his hand up between his mouth and Gunn. 'She's a water feature nut. I don't get it either, I just go along with it.'

Murray nodded, his smile back. 'Esperi is one of the great wonders of our world. Ann and Alice will be your tour guides. We have transport waiting.'

Robert forced a smile. Getting rid of the girls would be tricky; without using violence anyway. He gave Gunn another sloppy kiss on the cheek. Her skin chilled his lips. 'You hear that honey? We're going to Esperi.'

'Wonderful.' A sanitary worker could have conjured more passion but at least she managed half a smile.

'It was a long trip,' he said to the girls, raising his palms in a conciliatory way. 'A good night's sleep and she'll be back to her normal self.'

'Enjoy your trip,' Murray said, waving them forward. He passed his pad to Ann who took the lead. He imagined the corporation's motto stencilled into Ann's back:

Worldcraft: Supervised love.

The starport was the standard design, like the one he'd just torn up on Villist. The starport walls channeled them down the walkway to the interchange. Freight jalopies growled around, ferrying cargo between ships, MTV stations and warehouses. A maglev hovered at the station, ready to take passengers and cargo into the city. To the left a huge bay door ratcheted upwards. Inside, an Eagle Explorer sat on its landing struts, tiny bots buzzing around the ship's nose installing a new beam laser. Ann led them past customs, a few shops, then straight out the main gate. His skin tingled and he knew he'd been scanned, but he'd left his weapons on board and the guards watched on, silent. They weren't uniformed but their posture and pistol bulges were obvious.

The noise was madness. Millions and millions of screaming voices, different octaves, different pitches, all out of sync, some of them pure mortal terror that transformed into absolute joy as they crested a ride, the rest at different points on the spectrum.

Queuing guests choked the pathway. No roads, just paved access ways, android powered rickshaws weaving through the people.

Ann led them through the crowds, the clowns, jugglers and musicians, beelining for a small MTV platform. A single four-seater module waited for them. The doors swooshed apart.

'After you,' Ann said, waving them in with a smile. Robert ducked down into his seat without acknowledging her. The fake charm was wearing thin and he wanted her where he could see her. Gunn climbed in next to him.

Ann and Alice sat down opposite them. The doors closed and sealed, attenuating the noise. Robert's ears were ringing.

'I must be getting old,' he told Gunn. 'Fifteen years ago you couldn't have dragged me away from that.'

Gunn didn't say anything. The faint flickering of an eyelid capillary said enough. She was pissed about the kiss – kisses. He'd pay for them later, he was sure, he just wasn't sure how she would extract the payment.

'Check your mail,' he said to distract her. She blinked and pulled out her pad.

The MTV shot off down the track, leaving the jugglers and fire breathers behind. They soon passed the first building, a guard station and then they moved out into the city proper. The MTV tracks mixed and merged. Another module briefly attached to theirs before going on its own way. They passed rows of dark grey residential stacks, each sporting a holographic billboard. The local elections must have been next month. 'Worldcraft recommends Honourable Deema Silva for Governor,' read one. 'The Honourable D. Silva is the right candidate,' read another. 'Let's keep up the good work – reinstate the Honourable Deema Silva,' said the two next signs. There only seemed to be one candidate; democracy in action.

'You'll like this,' said Alice, turning in her seat. Robert followed her gaze. In a gap between the buildings lay a grass field at least the size of two zero-gee cricket fields. There were grand stands on the far side. On the field hundreds of men dressed up in ancient battle tank and aeroplane costumes ran around. There were pyrotechnics and mock battle gear disappeared behind explosions.

Robert's heart exploded into overdrive. He felt the explosions through his bridge's deck. The Imps had fired on them without warning. 'We're under attack!' Robert yelled, diving back into his acceleration couch. But he was alone on the Tutankhamun's bridge. Then Alice laughed and the bridge disappeared. 'It's a re-enactment, silly. The Battle of Madrid 2044.'

Robert blinked the vision away. Gunn ignored him; Ann and Alice watched the field. He eased back into his seat. 'Madrid, of course.' His history was hazy but a lot of bad things had happened in Spain during World War III.

'A lot of Worldcraft employees are actors. The tourists love the enactments. There are twenty purpose built stages around Masseyville designed for specific events, from the Battle of Hastings to the Insurrection of Alioth.'

Robert wasn't sure what to say. Wasn't war the first time around enough? No one who survived it would want to do it again; removing the dead, cleaning away their fluids in zero-gee. Writing the letters to family... Once, his own lieutenant had been the next of kin.

That had been a hard day.

He glanced at Gunn. She saw him as a sick virus on society, but romanticising war? That was sick.

'Neat,' Robert managed.

There were more high rises – stacks and offices, though no coffee shops and Worldcraft billboards as far as the eye could see, as if the corporation was bludgeoning their citizens into submission through mental overload.

He realised they hadn't passed another MTV since leaving the city centre. 'Where's all the traffic?' Robert asked.

'There's no need for travel at the moment,' Alice said. Everyone is back in the city working or enjoying themselves. Tourists don't normally leave the city so we don't have a high level of traffic.'

'I like to be a little different,' he confessed then settled into his seat to watch the scenery go by. At some point he would have to think of how to ditch the two blondes.

Gunn nudged him in the ribs and passed over the datapad. It was a message from Melkvin Trotsky of the Alioth Intelligence Service; Gunn's boss probably.

It was a brief message, the sentences clipped as if each word cost a fortune to transmit.

Of interest? Retain cover. Maintain secrecy. At my desk.

The message was clear enough. But it was the third line that interested Robert. He cast fresh eyes at Gunn, studying her for a change in body language or any sudden movements. If they cracked this case would he find a knife in his back?

He opened the attached file. It was an AIS document, a report with censored sections.

Alioth Security
Council Information

NOTICE

This document contains Alioth Security Council Information.
It is to be read and discussed with persons only authorised by law.

Persons handling this document acknowledges that he/she knows and understands the security law relating thereto and will cooperate fully in any lawful investigation by the Council into any unauthorised disclosure of classified information

TO: MONTGOMERY SITUATION OFFICE NEW ROSSYTH, ALIOTH INTELLIGENCE AGENCY NEW ROSSYTH, DIA NEW ROSSYTH, DA NEW ROSSYTH, DEPARTMENT OF JUSTICE, NEW ROSSYTH, DIRNSA, NEW ROSSYTH

AICNCS TRANS INTEL AFB TI INTEL OPS, MAXIN AFB

PROPOSED USE OF FEDERATION WEAPON 'STARBURST'

_____ *planning to execute new operations against the Alliance of Independent Systems. Weapon development aimed at combating recent naval tactics. Weapons suggests an optimum number of five for _____combat effectiveness. Potentially an array of combined compromise of power and_____*

The report continued for several pages, each one harder to read than the last, some paragraphs reduced to single words. But he got the gist of it. The précis could have read: 'The Feds have made a super weapon designed to destroy the Alliance navy but we don't know much about it other than it is small and may use several small ships instead of one large ship'.

But there was an addendum to the report. The weapon had never been tested in anger because forces unknown had stolen it from Eta Cassiopeia, the naval stronghold of the Federation. The Feds believed the Circle of Independent Elite Pilots were involved but had little proof and were investigating through FEDSOD.

There was nothing else in the report for him. He handed the datapad back to Gunn. 'Our Federation friend's story checks out,' he whispered.

'What's that?' Alice asked. She smiled but her eyes were cameras, her ears microphones, recording every detail and nuance to report back to her corporate masters.

'We have friends who live in the Federation. They said this place was to die for and they're right. It's simply beautiful.' Robert waved his arm toward the window, hoping for a picturesque view. He wasn't disappointed. They drove along an avenue, shepherded in by trees that grew up beyond sight, taller than any tree he'd ever seen. Each tree's leaves were a different colour, sardaukar green, autumn red then yellow. There were hues of blue and pink and even grey, the colours alternating like a rainbow as they drove past.

'Another recreational tool,' Alice said, turning away. 'Beyond the trees are gardens manicured by the finest arborists in the whole corporation. They win the Galactic Garden Awards every year.'

'I can understand why,' he said with an exaggerated nod.

They drove in silence, Robert afraid to say anything with super-hearing-girl sitting opposite. He turned to Gunn, smiling for the blondes. If he'd known they would receive this level of ... service he would have thought of devising a code with Gunn. She probably would have just grunted anyway.

They passed small towns where traffic picked up. Alice explained that those not directly involved in tourism were farmers supporting the tourism industry. Worldcraft, at least on Epsilon Eridani, was a self-contained, self-supporting system.

The track forked and they followed the sign to Esperi Junction. After a two hour ride the track stopped before a lone pre-fab building, the Worldcraft logo emblazoned across the closest wall. 'A supervision station,' Ann explained. Robert nodded again. Everyone had to report to someone.

Two Worldcraft-blue ground cars rested on their spheres outside. A narrow road continued on past the building, perfectly erect green grass running from the road side out to the distant hills. A perfect mid-dark blue filled the sky despite the sun shifting from east to west.

Ann pulled open the MTV's doors and Alice smiled her thin-as-duralium-foil smile. 'We'll just check in, organise lodgings and transport and head out to the falls.' As Alice climbed out Robert nudged Gunn and nodded toward the girls. He'd find out in a few moments whether she understood the message.

He climbed out after the two ladies. Ann led while Alice pulled in behind Robert and Gunn. They walked toward the front door. Ann swiped her ID chip at a scanner and the door parted. She walked across the foyer and through a door labelled 'Corporation Employees of rank 3 or higher only'.

'We'll wait here,' Alice piped up from behind, but Robert didn't stop. He stretched out his pace to catch Ann.

'Hey!' Alice yelled. Robert heard the double impact of elbow against skull and skull against wall. Gunn had taken care of Alice.

Ann turned, mouth opening, index finger rising, then she saw Alice and her jaw dropped; Robert head-butted her midstride, powered through the door and down the corridor to the far door.

Consoles ran the perimeter of the room, lists of personnel and tonnages cycling through large holographic displays; four inhabitants. Two computer jockeys, two guards. Rifles slung over shoulders, pistols in holsters.

The closest guard reacted first. His right hand pulled at the rifle, his left dropping to support it.

A rookie mistake.

Robert skipped inside the rifle's long arc and gouged his thumbs into eyes.

The man howled, tumbling backward. Robert spun into his arms, yanked the rifle up, aimed across the room.

The jockeys were already reaching for a big red button. Robert fired twice, shifted to the far figure, fired again.

The man pooled onto the floor like a boneless chicken. The jockeys slumped from their seats, nice neat holes through their heads.

Robert danced aside as the blinded guard pulled at the rifle and swung his fist at Robert.

Robert dodged the fist. He backed up into the range of the rifle. The man must have sensed the distance as he raised the weapon…

Gunn swung a flame retarder into his head and the guard tumbled head first into the ground.

Robert's gaze flicked from Gunn to the guard and back again, his chest rising and falling as he sucked in great big balls of air.

Ten seconds.

He'd just wiped out a corporate station in ten seconds; a new record. 'Thanks for the help,' he rasped.

The retarder clanged to the floor. She gave him a withering stare. 'You didn't have to kill them all.'

Robert shrugged and kicked the unconscious guard. 'Still three of them breathing, they were about to raise the alarm. Then I'd have to kill a whole bunch more. Which would you prefer? A few or a whole bunch?'

Gunn grunted then ducked back out the door. She returned dragging a docile Alice.

'Are you terrorists?' she asked through chattering teeth. She face was white, her lips a pale blue. Her eyes quivered.

'Of course not,' Robert said, a little hurt. 'I'm just a man who enjoys a bit of privacy.' Alice stepped backward into Gunn. She shivered. Robert stepped forward till they stood nose to nose.

'Now I just need a couple of hours and I'll be out of your hair. Do you want to stay alive while I do that?' He asked her in a matter of fact tone as if he were asking her what market she shopped at.

Her whole body shook. She was doing good to hold onto her bladder. 'Ya… ya… ya… yes,' she stammered.

Robert smiled, and not just for her benefit. He had never killed in cold blood and here wouldn't be a good place to start.

'Good. My associate here will tie you up real nice so you won't bother us. Then before you know it we'll be gone. But you have to promise not to try to escape or do anything that would upset me. You wouldn't do that would you?'

She shook her head, but her body was still, a glimpse of survival making her braver.

He and Gunn locked the living in a side room and plundered the dead; two good pistols, a little cash. Then he clapped his hands together.

'Ready to meet my mate?'

CHAPTER 9

Gunn ran her eyes over the three dead. 'I'm not going to enjoy this, am I?'

'That's the spirit,' Robert said with a smile.

* * *

Robert eased the stolen Worldcraft car to a halt outside an isolated wooden cottage. As the engine died, he heard the rusty grind of the iron chicken weather from the cottage roof. He smiled at the small patch of red grass enclosed by a rickety fence. The place hadn't changed.

He stepped from the car. The gate opened without a whisper but from inside a dog barked. He marched across the grass, Gunn in tow, and stopped at the front door. He turned to her, palms up.

'Just,' he paused, trying to figure out his next words. 'Just don't be a Squeaker, okay?'

'I'll be fine,' she said, though her stiff posture said otherwise.

Robert pursed his lips but nodded and knocked on the door. The silvered wood was heavy and gave a bassy thump.

'It's open,' came a voice from inside.

'He's awfully cavalier about security,' Gunn mused.

They stepped into the lounge, filled from floor to ceiling with bookcases and stands blending into the wooden walls. A worn easy chair sat by a free standing lamp. No trace of modern technology.

Leonardo Ramanujan stepped through the far doorway; a big man with considerable girth and massive arms and fists.

'Robert!' he boomed.

'Leo you old rascal.' Robert stepped forward as Leo spread his arms wide and they hugged.

'The Hero is back,' Leo said as they separated.

'Shut up,' Robert said, giving him a shove. 'How you been?'

'Good, good, no complaints. Life is good, lonely, but good.' His eyes drifted beyond Robert's shoulder and jerked in surprise, his whole body stiffening, hands rising to his shoulders.

'Oh, right, sorry, this is-' He half turned to wave at Gunn. She held a pistol up at eye level, pointed straight at Leo.

'Hey!' Robert said, jumping in front of the gun. 'I told you not to be squeaky.'

'You're under arrest,' she said to Leo, oblivious of Robert.

Leo stepped back, a little colour draining from his face, but his eyes were focused on Gunn, not the pistol. Good ol' Leo.

Robert took a half step forward. 'This is my friend and we need his help. Do you see me going around pointing weapons at your friends?'

Gunn's eyes slipped from Leo to Robert. Just for a moment, a fleeting seed of doubt appeared on her face then her gaze snapped back to Leo. 'Do you have any idea how many crimes he has committed?'

'Not as many as me and you haven't killed me yet.'

Gunn's jaw worked overtime, an internal battle raging inside. The pistol shivered. 'I have a duty. The damage this man has caused, will cause-'

He put his palm up to the barrel. 'Bigger picture, remember? That's what you told me. Now stop acting like a fate-forsaking policeman. You don't have to solve every crime at once you know.'

'I can't trust anyone else to do it.'

Robert frowned, his mouth puckered to one side. Her body was tensed, aimed, purposeful, but her eyes were hazy. Her mind was elsewhere.

He edged his hand across the pistol and waited a moment for potential backlash. There was nothing in her eyes, as if she wasn't even in the room. He eased the pistol down.

'You can trust me. If you can't trust a pirate, who can you trust, right Leo?'

Gunn jerked away from him. 'Don't touch me,' she spat, but the pistol stayed down.

Robert similarly jerked at her reaction. He looked at his hand. It was clean. 'I'm not diseased.'

Gunn didn't move.

Robert shrugged. Crisis averted, for the meantime anyway. He turned back to Leo, keeping himself between them just in case. 'We need your help. The Circle of Independent Elite Pilots are plotting to start a war between the Federation and the Empire, or something.' He thought about the two Imperial clone agents. 'It could be an assassination of the Emperor.'

Leo's eyes lit up. 'Where?'

'No idea,' Robert said. 'We don't know where or when but we know we have to stop it.'

Leo's smile pulled at a hundred different facial muscles. His arms shook with barely contained glee. 'Sounds fun.' He waddled over to the table and sat down. Robert chuckled at the reaction.

'You must be getting bored.'

Leo threw his arms up. 'You have no idea. You're the only person who brings excitement to my life.'

'Glad to help.' Robert explained everything they knew then Leo's eyes switched off. There was no other way to explain it, like the moment a person dies and the muscles controlling the eyes and pupils relax for the last time and you realise there is no one back there anymore. That was how Leo looked, yet he continued to sit up and breathe just fine.

'What is he doing?' Gunn asked, having snuck right up behind him. Robert tried not to flinch, the commander's words still fresh in his mind. *Maintain secrecy*. How many times would she sneak up on him before she silenced him?

'As you know he's a wanted man so he's hiding out, trying not to be traceable. Hence he has no computers except those installed inside him; and no connection to the link.'

'So how does he find out information then?'

Robert shrugged. 'How should I know? I'm just a pirate. I steal stuff and kill anyone who-'

'Tries to stop you,' droned Gunn, 'I know, I know.'

'He keeps me up to date on Galactic goings-on and I analyse the data to figure out the good places to hit. Nothing like reliable intel, right? I don't ask how he does it.'

He craned his neck back, his mouth close to Gunn's ear. 'Can I trust you not to start squeaking while I go out the back?'

'What's out the back?'

'None of your business; can you control yourself in here or do you need to go piss off?'

Gunn clenched her jaw, the grinding of teeth a deliberate and precise sound.

She lowered her head a fraction, her eyes locked across at his. An agreement and a promise; a promise of payback.

'I'll be back.'

* * *

Gunn growled as Robert pushed through the back door. The door swished shut behind him.

'Pirates,' she muttered. Why was she even here? She should have trashed him the moment she met him. He hadn't actually been that much help. It was his fault they'd been caught by FEDSOD and the Imps. She would have been better off by herself. That was the only way to make sure things were done right. No interference, no mistakes. No repeat of Thomson's World. Partners always screwed things up.

Her right hand shook and she grabbed it with her left. She didn't need a drink. It was just the pirate winding her up, nothing more. She didn't need a drink. She was fine. No repeat of Thomson's World.

'Don't be too hard on him,' said Leonardo. Gunn jumped, reminded of his presence. He sat rock-still, like an upright corpse, dead eyes staring blanking, almost invisible in his immobility. 'He doesn't handle celebrity status well.'

'What?'

Leonardo's mouth opened a fraction then closed. He held his hands together. 'He didn't tell you about Villist?' He chewed his lip, rubbed his chin. 'Well it's not really my place.'

Gunn sat down next to him. The wooden chair creaked, though it felt solid and dense and strangely comfortable. 'Tell me anyway.' Robert had seemed almost scared of Villist. That statue, the people in the square, what didn't she know about the unrest?

'I'm from Villist. I know what the Alliance tried to do there. They caused the war. What do you call it, the 'Villist Massacre'?

Gunn grunted. 'Unrest.' She was in no mood to defend the Alliance to this criminal. 'Why did you leave Villist? Local problems?'

Leonardo laughed. 'Naturally, my fame after the battle went straight to my head. Thought I was untouchable; hacked into one too many accounts. You know the rest.'

'I know enough.' Leonardo had singlehandedly tried to destabilise the government, and cause a coup through leaking sensitive information to the government's opponents. But he had gotten greedy. He had also tried to destabilise surrounding systems which were looking for Alliance membership, like the Lave group. Her trigger finger started to itch. She slipped her hand down to cradle her pistol and her finger relaxed.

'Listen to me, such a poor host. I have food from the finest farms in the Empire and whisky from the distilleries of 61 Cygni. Are you hungry? Thirsty?'

Fates yes. 'No thanks.'

Leonardo shrugged. 'Well anyway, you know me, so you know what I can do. I can track pretty much anything. Take the Circle of Independent Elite Pilots for instance. They have to be the easiest people to follow while in centralised space. They leave a huge wake due to their popularity. Resources taken by the Circle are flagged as such. Some governments give companies rebates for donating a percentage of their products to the Circle.

'And their ships are giveaways. No imagination. They stick to the same ships year in year out, making them easy to track.'

Gunn nodded. She couldn't argue that last point. She'd never seen anything other than a Saker or a Sidewinder while undercover.

'With time I can make a cloud plot of their standard movements. Anything out of the cloud stands out like horse shit.' He put his hand up, pre-empting Gunn's question. 'Sure there are holes, and an obvious curve to their visits to starports but the way these change with time make it obvious that they are operating on a radius from a base, until they move to a different base and the pattern repeats.'

Gunn stared at Leonardo, soaking in his words, forgetting for the moment he fronted the public enemy list, and wondering why Montgomery hadn't come up with the same idea. They could have nailed the Circle in the coffin if they'd been able to track them at all.

'It's a Federation weapon,' she blurted out, then grimaced at her haste. 'Who told you that?'

Gunn ignored him. 'So how do you hide on a corporate world? To call

Worldcraft slavers is putting it mildly; an untapped asset in their midst? If R.I.G. got hold of this story you'd be headline news.'

'Lucky for me Random Intergalactic Gossip don't have an office nearby,' Leonardo said. 'To answer your question I keep a low profile here the same way I had such a high profile on Villist.' He tapped his temple. 'I find the data and manipulate it. As far as Worldcraft are concerned all resources are accounted for and fully utilised.'

Gunn shook her head and looked around the room. Everything was old, or designed to appear that way. It could have come from the original settlement of New California. The wood looked like Gum or Birch. It reminded her of an old friend's house, the one she had stayed in after the tent orphanage and lived in for two weeks before the Calsace pirate clan came and murdered the whole town, before Gunn had figured out why so many things went wrong around her …

She blinked away the past. She had killed the last of the Calsace years ago. 'What else do you have?'

'Hmm,' said Leonardo, his lips pursed. 'That's odd. The non-standard movements have revolved around robotics, computers and high end mechanical components like plasma focusers. They normally take food, textiles, basic equipment to keep them running.'

'Are they building something?'

'I don't know, but they're running a straight line to Imperial space. It looks like they are heading to Cemiess, or something further on.'

Gunn considered it. Cemiess had a history of strife between the Federation and Empire. A Federation weapon striking there would cause some consternation, but enough to start the war the Circle were trying for?

'Too vague.' Then she remembered what the clone agents had said. 'Is the Emperor on tour?'

Leonardo snapped his fingers. 'Let's see what's on the Imperial social network.' He went back into a dream state for several minutes. Gunn heard heavy breathing out the back and a few whispers, the bleat of a distant sheep but otherwise the place was quiet, too quiet. No motors whirring, no fans spinning, no electronics buzzing. The house sounded dead, like the house of her youth after the attack. She had stood in the charred remains, silent and still, listening, but there hadn't been any sounds then either. No one crying out in pain, not even wood collapsing or shifting weight as it cooled. It was as if that one house had been transported out of time and out of place, frozen between moments so no sound or movement could penetrate it.

'A lot of happy citizens buzzing about this and that,' said Leonardo. He rattled off a list of things, most of them related to fashion and status and slaves. 'The Emperors three-quarter centenary tour is causing talk too. He is visiting every single Imperial system.'

'So which system will they hit?'

'Well I don't have the official plan but based on where he has already been, what is close to his current location and the straightish line the Circle are travelling, then one of the three systems around Cemiess is your best shot.'

Gunn considered the options. Three systems were too much. She couldn't defend three. Not without backup. She still didn't have authorisation to break cover, but surely she could justify it? She had a suspect, a methodology of sorts and a target. This was the end play – she didn't need cover anymore.

'Hello, what have we here?' Leonardo said with a sudden interest flavouring his words.

'What?'

'Looks like his Imperial Majesty has been delayed; the Mariner Doldrums have flared up, irradiating space between Cemiess and Vequess. He's going to stay to officially open a new space station.'

Gunn's chest swelled. She leaned forward, though she couldn't see anything except Leonardo's dead eyes. 'How long have people known about this?'

Leonardo shrugged. 'These things are pretty vague. I'm checking people's personal data, not galactic almanacs.'

She rubbed the goose skin on her arms, feeling cool. The Circle were always quick to react, almost as if they knew about things before everyone else; the word of the Architect. If they had been mobilised, already in motion, waiting for what they needed …

'How long have they been buying up machinery?'

'Three or four months,' he said. Gunn's jaw clenched. About the same time the weapon was stolen.

'How long have the doldrums been acting up?' Being undercover had put her out of date with Galactic events.

'A few weeks, based on what I can see here.'

Gunn cocked her head to one side, thinking. The Circle's main skill set was piloting, but they did have some base form of stratagem. Security forces the galaxy over were at their most vigilant at the start and end of their shift. Any attack would wait until just before the end, when The Emperor concluded his tour of a system. Not on the way out, but the day before, when everyone were already mentally preparing to move out.

'When is the Emperor planning to leave?'

'Seven days.'

'And how far away is the Ceeper's straight line from reaching Vequess?'

'It's a vague plot; a week, a bit more, a bit less.'

Gunn was already running to get Robert.

Chapter 10

Gunn burst out the back door into the corral. The pirate sat on the ground, back against a wooden post, a labrador lying with its head in his lap. He roughed it up, scratching it hard around the ears. Its face was stretched between a grimace and a howl of joy, in too much ecstasy to move. He whispered to the dog in a baby voice with a clean Federation accent.

She sucked in a breath as the dots connected. 'You were at the Battle of Villist with the Feds. You were in the navy. You saved that planet.'

Robert kept roughing up the dog, whispering with squeezed lips. The dog's tail pounded the ground. Gunn stood there, feeling awkward, heart racing but body still.

'You burst through the door to tell me that?' he said. No anger, which surprised her. Villist had been a touchy subject for him.

'I know the Circle's target. We have to leave now.'

Robert patted the dog between its ears. 'Okay bud, time for me to fly. See you around.' He pushed it aside and leapt to his feet. Gunn followed him inside. Leonardo was standing, his eyes focused. Robert gave him a hug, thanked him and promised to stop by 'afterwards'. Leonardo wished them good luck as they left.

It was dark by the time they returned to the theme park. The MTV stopped at a public terminal on the far side from the starport. Lights lit up the still turning Ferris wheels but the noisy crowd had diminished. The night was cool and only the young and drunk were out in any force.

They dumped their stolen weapons, then without trying to look hasty, hastened back to the starport main entrance. There were six armed guards but the gate stood open and no questions were asked. Customs let them go. They climbed aboard the Saker and after a quick conversation with traffic control about their stay in lovely Masseyville, Gunn lifted off. She flew them straight out of the gravity well and headed to the nearest gas giant. She dropped them into orbit, turned off the main engine and retrieved her pistol from the concealed locker.

She breathed in. Cold steel against her skin made her whole again; back in control, ready to make a difference.

'We need to get to Vequess in six days.' She opened the navigation screen. Robert unstrapped and came to peer over her shoulder. Resisting an urge to flinch away, she said, 'What was your rank?'

Robert kept his gaze on the screen. 'How long to get there?'

'Eight days.'

'Sounds like you're talking about breaking the laws of physics then.'

Gunn growled and leaned away. 'We need some hired muscle.'

Robert clicked his fingers. 'I know. There's this group: well-armed, well organised, have the same belief system as you.'

Gunn stared. What was he talking about? 'Who?'

'The Alliance; say, don't you have links with them anyway?' Gunn's right hand dropped to her pistol. *Retain cover.*

'I said no.'

Robert had opened his mouth to reply when the link chimed. Gunn breathed in long and deep and closed her eyes for a moment, readying herself for the conversation. This was an untraceable Circle ship. The only people who knew the link code were the Circle and the Imperial agents.

She activated the link. The lead clone agent filled the holograph display. He wore a frowning, disappointed-but-not-surprised look, like Father McDiel, the orphanage director. 'Tsk Tsk, Grotenfelt. We've been expecting your call for some time now. My partner suggested we come find you but I preached patience. I'm glad to see I was correct to wait. I assume I am correct?'

'We've been busy.' she said.

The agent nodded. 'I trust you have, which is why we won't be taking action against you and your families immediately. But I do require an update.'

Gunn paused. The booby trap. She'd looked everywhere inside the ship without success. Either they'd planted it on the hull – hopefully burnt off on re-entry – or it didn't exist.

'We got something all right, chatty boy,' the pirate said, leaning into view.

Gunn shoved him back and muted the feed. 'What do you think you're doing?'

'They're Imperials. Alert them. Let them deal with it. Chances are they'll get there before us.'

Gunn almost slapped him, but

.. perhaps he was right. It would get them off her back while she headed out there with her own forces. And they'd do their best to protect their Emperor, though vat-grown flesh couldn't really understand. It was humanity she worried about.

She unmuted and explained the situation. The agent showed no outward sign of excitement but his lips thinned, drawing across his face. Stress on a clone's face? Could they even feel stress? It had been right to tell them, if only to see that look.

'You have done well. We will be in touch.' The link died and the pirate's mouth curled in a silent snarl.

'I bet you will. Bastards.' For once Gunn agreed with him.

Neither of them moved for a moment. Then Robert said, 'You'd better get your buddies down there too.'

Gunn checked her information drop in vain hope but there was nothing. No information, no instructions, no hints to go on. She was on her own, again. *Retain cover.*

'I can't call on the Alliance.'

The pirate pounded her command chair. 'Dammit woman, they could have a fleet right next door and we wouldn't even know. How are you going to find out if you don't ring the bell?'

Gunn unstrapped so she could stand eye to eye with Robert.

'You have no idea what I had to do to get undercover. I was already an Elite ranked pilot before I started all this, but I had to make a new identity. I had to start all over again. I had to get back to Elite to get them to notice me with my clean sheet. I spent two whole years drifting through Phekda and Riedquat and every other pirate infested hole in this galaxy waiting for smugglers, waiting for pirates, waiting for people like you so I could blow up their ships and claim the kill.'

She jabbed him in the sternum. 'I've killed over twelve thousand pirates and invested five years of my life on this operation and I'm not going to blow it on the whim of some Scheiße like you. The Circle still think I'm chasing you. If I blow my cover I won't ever get it back. Ever. So don't you dare tell me what to do.'

The pirate recoiled from her jab and just stared at her. His eyes round, soft, as if he had just uncovered some clue about her. 'Pirates killed your parents, didn't they?'

'I didn't have any parents.' She returned to her chair and gave him her 'down-to-business' glare. 'The Alliance is not an option. Think of a Plan B. That's what you're here for.'

She became aware of a softer expression overlying the rugged sea of stubble and undulating lines on his face. It made him look less like a murderer and a bit more like a human. 'At least use that information drop of yours.

Maybe your boss will decide to contact you.'

'Fine.' She typed a request into the link and sent it.

He nodded. 'I'll put out some feelers. I know some people who like to fleece this region of space.'

She yielded the link and he sent out a request for help. When she queried to who, he said 'People you'd like to kill, I bet.'

They sat in silence. Robert lay in his couch, hands behind his head, eyes closed, seemingly unconcerned.

The numbers on the chrono flashed by. From memory she uploaded dark system coordinates to the nav maps. She reckoned that could get them to Vequess in seven days. With that done she wanted to get moving – every second spent motionless was a second lost – but they needed help and that meant waiting.

The link snapped, fizzed and a woman's face appeared on the receptor. Her surgically straight blonde hair brushed her shoulders as she turned sharp eyes to the screen, showing cheek bones too well-defined to be real. The unzipped front of her seam-straining orange pressure suit plunged out of the link's view. 'Garry?'

The pirate pushed past Gunn and waved at the woman. 'Varia Malin, you're a sight for sore eyes. We need your help.'

Malin, tried to look past him. Gunn recognised green eyes when she saw them. 'Who's the broad?'

Gunn's fingers tightened around her pistol.

'She's an Alioth Intelligence agent,' Robert said. Gunn kicked him. 'Yowww, ah, listen we're out of time. We really need you, you nearby?'

Her eyes burrowed into Gunn. 'We?'

The pirate snorted and Gunn could tell he was smiling. 'Me, obviously, I'd be lost without my psycho lawyer.'

Malin gave a wide toothy smile. 'I still have your kilt,' she oozed, the flirtation dial off the scale.

'Oh, I'd been wondering about that. That must have been from
..'

'The strike on the Wreaken Mining platform.'

He glanced quickly back at Gunn. 'Ha, yeah, that was a good day.'

'And a good night,' Malin winked and licked her lips.

Gunn rolled her eyes. 'Are you two going to have link sex or can we get on with it?'

'We've had more than link sex, girl,' said Malin. 'All that killing and looting makes a woman horny.'

Gunn looked the plastic-thin woman up and down and sneered. She leant forward – the pirate swiped at her face, blocking her from view. 'Yes we killed a lot of people and resolved your issues. How would you like to do it all again with money in the pot?'

'How much?'

He turned to Gunn. 'How much?'

The concept of giving any money to that woman made her retch, but the big picture took priority. She recited the line from memory. 'For assisting in matters pertinent to the Alliance, Twenty thousand credits for you to disburse to your crew as you see fit.' Her handlers had had some foresight thankfully.

Malin rocked her head on her neck. 'Honey, I don't get out of bed for less than fifty. You'll have to do better than that.'

'You owe me,' the pirate said. Malin pursed her lips and looked up to her left. Gunn recognised the classic sign of impending bullshit. Her handlers had trained her on basic body language too. 'You're asking me to put my men into battle for you with no possibility of plunder just a small retainer of twenty? You'll owe me afterward.'

'Deal.'

Malin blew out a breath. 'You're lucky you're handsome. What do we need to do?'

Robert laid it out. 'Get your little butt to the Vequess system. It'll be crazy but we're looking at an attack against the Emperor. We don't know who or what it is but we think a group of five big ships, Clipper size, acting together to make some kind of weapon. We just have to keep our sensors wired and strike fast when we see it.'

Malin grunted. 'Are you sure we can't just raid a depot for you? That's what we're good at.'

'Sorry, not my idea. It's the Circle of Independent Elite Pilots.'

Malin sucked in a breath. 'Those Quixotes? You should have said. I would have taken them down for free. I lost four corsairs to them in the last month alone.' She learnt toward the link, her face uncomfortably close. 'They're striking harder, defending more systems. Everywhere I go, there they are, trying to stop me. Who do they think they are? The police? I'll bring everyone I can muster.'

'I'll see you real soon.' He closed the link, moved out of Gunn's private space and scratched the back of his head. His cheeks reddened. 'Ahh, I'm sorry you had to hear some of that.'

'So am I.'

'She's actually pretty nice once you get to know her, a bit rough maybe. She jokes that when we first met I was too straight around the edges. She had to 'scruff' me up.'

'I bet she did.'

'She won't let us down.'

'I guess we'll find out.' The pre-undercover memory clicked into place. 'That was Varia Joelson. She has a six figure bounty on her head.'

'Is that all?' he said, seemingly nonplussed. 'She used to be a lawyer you know, one of the best in Leesti. But her employer didn't appreciate her ripping him off. Now she rips people off as a career, kind of funny in a way.'

Gunn just stared at the deactivated link. She had a moral, professional and personal obligation to kill that woman. She should have been blowing up her ship and heading home for a medal. Instead she was paying that evil skank and asking for her help. How had she ended up here? Divert the Circle, save the galaxy, then kill them one by one.

Maintain Secrecy.

Then a second memory surfaced, a recent one this time.

'That was you that knocked over the Wreaken mining platform?' Robert turned away. 'You heard about that one, huh?'

'They found it adrift with all three thousand workers dead, their bodies mutilated or dismembered.'

'Well, the boys can get a bit crazy in the midst of battle. But for the record those workers were seriously armed and they were pretty determined to win or die trying. In those situations it's simple self-defence.'

'You were a Federation officer. Do you have no sense of right and wrong at all?'

'Sure. Killing my father was wrong. Killing those that killed him will be right.'

Her fingers drifted toward her pistol. If a man thought it okay to murder three thousand people for mere cargo, how could she trust him to help save lives? *I'll kill him first, then I'll dismember him. Or the other way around, see how he likes it.*

The pistol butt was right there, the trigger finger less than a quarter inch away. Get a strong grip, retract, rotate, fire. It sounded so easy; one, two three.

His gaze dropped to her pistol. His lips flattened but he didn't otherwise react. She pulled her hand away. *Save the galaxy first.*

'I'm taking us out of here,' she said. She needed a change of subject, quickly. She reactivated the drive and Robert hurried into his acceleration couch. She piloted them away from the gas giant. 'I think I can overdrive the engines. Get us another percent or two.'

'I'm no engineer so perhaps I'm not qualified to make this statement, but isn't that a tad unwise?'

'Do you want to miss the start of interstellar war by one minute? We have a duty here, a duty to others and a duty to honour, something you've forgotten since you left the military.'

'I haven't forgotten about my duty, or my honour. I remember them well, I remember how they knocked me down and destroyed me. That's when I realised that the galaxy doesn't care about you or what you've accomplished. It's always out to get you. All you really have is your family and yourself and no one else. You can't trust anything or anyone except that they will eventually become your enemies.' He stared at her when he said that.

'You're like a broken link, you and all pirates, bemoaning the galaxy for all your problems, that it's not your fault you couldn't hack a real life. Why don't you be a man and stand up for once in your life?' She was so agitated the ship jerked back and forth as she tried to pilot away.

Panting, she faced him, waiting for his response, waiting for the provocation she needed.

He looked away.

'I did stand up. And look where it got me.'

* * *

Nineteen hyperjumps later; fifteen dark systems, four solar, and they were on the edge of Vequess' oort cloud near a small failed star.

'Ready?' Gunn asked.

He nodded. 'As I'll ever be.'

'I'll navigate. You just focus on the link, controlling your

.. friends

.. and listening to everything in system. If anyone's voice even raises an octave I want you yelling at me.'

'Okay.'

'I mean it.'

'I can do this.'

Gunn stared into his eyes. They were wide and focused. Regardless of who he was or what he did, he definitely looked in 'mission' mode. He would follow through with stopping the plot, she could see that.

It was what happened afterwards that concerned her. 'Let's go.'

'Just remember not to shoot at a Lion Transport,' Robert reminded her. 'You won't be able to pay Malin if you kill her.'

'I'll keep an eye out for her.' *With my laser sights.*

They made the final hyperspace jump into absolute bedlam.

'What the

..' breathed Gunn.

Chapter 11

Robert gasped. He'd never seen a hyperspace exit point so crowded before.

Around two astronomical units out from the star, they should be alone.

There were ships everywhere. Imperial Traders, Couriers and Explorers. Small Osprey fighters and bird like Eagles darted across the scanner. Metallic blobs and stabilising thruster plumes choked the cosmos. Any ship design ever produced in an Imperial factory was there.

'What are they all doing? Why are they here?' Gunn snorted. 'Haven't you ever seen a parade?'

'This is a parade?' Robert couldn't look away from the sight. 'It's an Emperor's parade.'

Robert stared, mouth slightly agape. 'Wow.'

'What?'

'You're saying we jumped straight into a parade?' He stared out the viewport again. He tilted his head slightly; the mess of ships could have been a cylinder enclosing an empty central space.

'An Emperor's parade; everyone of Imperial birth or title has to come out and see him off. It would be a huge loss of face not to.'

Robert couldn't help smiling. 'Love your leader or be exiled?' 'Something like that.' Gunn filled him in on current events. Agnews'

Folly, the yet-to-open space station orbited the main planet a mere astronomical unit away. Gunn had activated a scanner. Holographic representations of all the ships kept flashing up next to the scanner, which was a mess of dots and blips. 'So how do we know which one is the Emperor and which ones are the bad guys?'

Gunn typed into the link console. Hundreds of overlapping voices played out over the cockpit speakers. She pressed another key and the voices dropped one after the other.

Everyone waited, either anxious, bored but unwilling to say it, or bouncing in their magboots. None had seen the Emperor's personal Majestic-class Interdictor.

The parade hadn't started yet.

Robert's scanner fuzzed into a link display and Malin's face appeared. 'Hello Sunshine,' she said with a wink. 'We're here. What's the score?'

'The Emperor is still on the space station,' Gunn said in a clearly controlled tone. 'Let's get as close as we can. We're looking for a small group of linked large ships.'

'Maybe,' Robert added. 'We don't know for sure. So keep an eye out for anything suspicious.'

'But don't make a move without my authorisation,' Gunn said.

Malin gave that toothy grin she usually reserved for prisoners before she gutted them. 'Wouldn't dream of it, honey.' She turned back to Robert. 'Just posted you a package, you owe me.' The link shut down and a new blip appeared on the scanner, a cargo canister, tumbling toward them. Gunn manoeuvred the Saker and used the magnetic scoop to pull it into the cargo hold.

She sailed in system at a moderate pace, along the cylinder of adoring civilians.

An Imperial Courier flashed out of the line and drowned them in bright lights, filling the cockpit with whiteness. The link snapped alive. 'Identify yourselves.'

Robert had heard those same words before …

Heart burst into overdrive. He gasped. He turned to the Captain. Dead. The Corvette was his.

'Transmitting ID now,' Gunn said in a calm voice. Robert's chest rose and fell. Gunn glanced at him.

'Control yourself,' she hissed.

The Courier's lights snapped off and it turned away.

'Everyone loves the Ceepers,' Gunn said with a snort. 'Or at least aren't worried about them outside the cordon.'

Robert hardly heard her. The Imps were everywhere; outnumbering them, twenty to one. His CO's face was white but his jaw was clenched in strong determination.

'We'll have to fight our way out boys,' he called, 'Punch through and circle around. Prepare to-'

The Imps opened fire. A million beam lasers arced toward him.

Explosions filled the viewport. Fire engulfed the bridge.

A scream faded behind him. Flagship gone. CO down. The bridge scrambled. 'Call the retreat!' he yelled, looking for the helmsman. The ship rocked from another explosion and the helmsman flopped against the side of his couch. Robert unstrapped and jumped across the open space. Gritting his teeth, he dislodged the body, strapped in and turned the ship around. He activated the fleet wide comm frequency. 'Fall back to the belt, everyone, fall back!'

'What the Fates?' said his lieutenant. She spoke with Gunn's voice.

The memory cleared. No smoke. No fire. Just the Saker, Gunn to his right, brow furled, eyebrows arched. Outside, the Imp ships faced away, uninterested in him. His heart slowed and he filled his lungs with clean recycled air.

You're not insane.

'What the Fates is wrong with you?' Gunn asked. Her whole face had signed up to her what-the-fuck expression.

'I'm good,' he said.

'You don't sound good.'

'I said I'm good.'

'You did say that.'

Robert turned away, cheeks reddening. 'It just takes a little bit getting used to, being surrounded by Imps and them not trying to kill you.' A natural trigger; he'd been told it would pass with time.

'Well if it makes you feel any better, if we screw this up they will all be trying to kill us.'

'It does actually.' Then at least the universe would fit into a shape that he recognised.

Robert scanned every ship they passed, the majority of them too small to match the hyperspace vectors they'd detected in the Lanaest system.

'They're using Imperial ships,' Robert said in realisation. He'd been thinking Clippers because the weapons were Federation, his mind set too, but the weapon could probably be adapted to anything.

He and Gunn stared at each other. 'Imperial Explorers.' They spoke simultaneously as Robert checked the scanner. They were a long bodied ship, like the Courier, but with its two nacelles extended up from the back, like aft-castles on the ships of old.

His mouth dried. Explorers were everywhere, singularly, grouped in pairs, fives, tens. 'We'll never find the right ones in time,' Robert said, gaze flicking from the scanner to the holographic representations. A trifecta of Explorers towed ridiculous ship-sized banners behind them, flapping from the flow of engine exhaust; the Emperor's standard bearers.

His voice rose in pitch. 'They could be disguised as anyone and we wouldn't know until it was too late.'

Gunn's knuckles whitened on the controls. She didn't say anything. 'Gunn,' he said, slowly. There were too many ships, too many kilometres, too little time. She ignored him.

'Gunn,' he said louder.

'They'll be close to the station,' she said. 'Just keep looking.'

Robert clenched his teeth, a familiar powerlessness clawing over his shoulder. What else could they do?

Another Imperial Courier popped out of the ranks but Gunn buzzed across their Circle credentials. Robert activated his link relay. 'Any other Circle ships here today officer?'

'Just you.' The gruff and possibly bored officer clicked off before Robert could question him further.

Malin checked in. None of her fourteen ships had seen anything out of the ordinary, or at least what passed as ordinary given the scene before them.

A wide band hook-up activated their link as the Emperor officially opened the space station. Robert tried to ignore it. An old man standing inside the station's command and control cutting a piece of ribbon; too much talking, too much old people.

'What do you reckon?' Gunn asked. 'Not terribly inspiring.'

Gunn growled. 'I mean out there.' She pointed out the viewport.

Robert followed her finger. He tried to think like a Ceeper trying to assassinate the most protected person in the whole galaxy. They had a secret weapon, they had a cylinder of innocent bystanders to fight through. Then they had to get past the undercover guards and the standard bearers and everyone else trained to protect his Imperial Majesty. Robert counted at least two hundred naval ships. Probably double that within the throng. An impenetrable barrier.

It was absolute genius. The supporters formed an effective layer of armour between the Emperor and any foes. Free body guards who didn't even know they were being used. The Emperor would fly through the centre of his adoring public then hyper out, flanked at beginning and end by his personal guards.

The Circle's only chance would be to attack from the far end of the cylinder, cut straight through his personal guard with the super weapon and blast him away. A high risk, low chance of success strategy and it would require more than Elite piloting skills.

Robert's neck shivered, a tremor that worked from his deltoids, up his traps to the base of his spine. It made him curl inward.

This was all wrong.

'The space station,' he breathed. 'They're going to supernova the space station.'

'The test,' Gunn said, bolting upright. 'They tested the weapon on a gas platform.' Robert rallied Malin and her ships while Gunn raced for the station. Robert studied the broadcast, suddenly interested in the Emperor. When would they strike?

They'd be close to the station, among the flotilla of fans, interspersed between other ships. They'd pull out and strike. When the Emperor had finished, or before? Security would be at its absolute highest as the Emperor left the station.

It would have to be now.

They were still point four of an astronomical unit away. 'What do you have?' Gunn asked.

Robert shook his head. There were five hundred Explorers on the scanner.

They closed in. His heart hammered in tune with the ships vibrations. His chest felt cramped.

The Emperor completed his speech. He cut the ribbon. The ribbon halves fluttered away under the rotational gravity. Applause broke out, so deafening Robert briefly thought the attack had started.

A ship moved. He loaded a holographic representation. A single Imperial Explorer reversed from the cylinder of fans and turned toward the space station.

'Got him!' He transferred the data to Gunn's console. 'Explorer making a move.'

Gunn shifted, throwing the Saker toward the Explorer. 'Nearly in range.'

'Attention Saker Mark III registration DBH-127, your flight path has registered as aggressive. Heave to for boarding and inspection or be destroyed. This is your final warning.'

Four angry looking Couriers angled toward them.

Gunn looked like pure distilled determination. White knuckles. Pinched face. Robert gripped his couch; one puny Saker versus four Imperial Couriers. They couldn't win this fight. Malin's ships were nearby but they wouldn't be enough either if it came to a firefight.

Robert's carotid pulsed. The Circle Explorer was out of their weapon range but it could fire on the station in moments. Where were its four buddies? Or was that a ruse? Misdirection? Did the weapon fit on one ship? He enlarged the Explorer hologram; an oversized weapon on its hardpoint. He'd never seen the design before; had to be the Federation weapon.

Where were the clone agents? 'Hurry,' he urged Gunn.

Blue Cherenkov radiation shimmered across the tip of the advancing Couriers' plasma accelerators. Gunn's pupils danced, a fierce determination burning in her eyes. He knew she'd rather die trying than give up.

The Explorer raced forward. Its engine exhaust plumed for kilometres. Malin's ships weren't on the scanner. More Couriers converged on them. It was Villist all over again; another failure.

The Explorer fired its weapon.

'We're too late!'

Rings of flashing blues and yellows and greens filled the cosmos, a brilliant web of colour, supernovas, comets and black holes, blossoming and dying in overlapping sequences.

The space station was still intact.

Robert's brain took a moment to process what he'd just seen. The Explorer wasn't carrying a super weapon.

It was carrying pyrotechnics. Fireworks.

'It's not him,' he whispered, still not sure if he could believe it.

'It's a ploy,' Gunn said. 'They're playing us.' She kept her bearing, leaning forward, eyes wide, fixated on the view ahead.

The Explorer completed its arc and headed away from the station. Other Explorers moved, shooting their own fireworks across the black.

'It's not him,' Robert yelled, the adrenaline crashing out of him. 'Stand down!'

Gunn burned the retros and the Saker lurched.

The Couriers fired.

Space cracked into prisms of blue and black, shattered by beams of plasma-fuelled destruction. Gunn threw the ship through a tight turn and weaved through the beams. More and more plasma accelerators fired up until space was more blue than black.

A beam carved across one of the Saker's wings. Alarms bellowed through the cockpit. Regardless of how good a pilot she was, Gunn couldn't survive this.

'Make the jump,' he yelled. Gunn shook her head. Her eyes were hazy, as if she were somewhere else, living another battle, an internal crusade.

Robert's gaze darted to the scanner. All the defenders were distracted; the perfect time to strike.

But ships were only moving in two directions: toward the Saker or away.

No one approached the space station.

They weren't here.

'Get us out of here, now!'

The Saker bucked under another glancing shot and wind sucked at Robert, pulling him toward the rear hatch, wrenching the air from his throat. He scrabbled to tighten his straps, panic suffocating him. He wasn't going to get pulled out into space. Not ever again.

A bang reverberated through the ship. The wind died; the auto-seal system.

He watched Gunn, panting. Her hands moved faster that he could follow, squeezing every bit of movement from the ship, manoeuvring through gaps between plasma beams, trying to stay one step ahead of death.

'It's over, Gunn, we have to go.'

'Can't,' she wheezed, breathless. 'Can't fail.'

'You're going to kill us,' he said, a touch of whine in his voice. Desperate times called for desperate measures.

'Please.'

She stiffened for the briefest moment though her hands and arms kept moving. She kept going, and going, and going, and then her hand slipped and hit the hyperspace controls and they disappeared into a hyperspace vector.

* * *

They arrived at an inter-system way point. Gunn made three further adrenaline fuelled jumps to throw off pursuit and they drifted to a stop in a nebulous dark system.

Alarms still screeched through the cockpit but Gunn hit a button and they faded away. Robert just concentrated on breathing, listening to his exhalations in the relative silence.

The nebula shone green and red and orange but inside the ship it was quiet and dark, dull red lights flashing behind him. Frozen coolant drifted past the viewport. As his breathing slowed he became aware of the clicks and bleeps of the controls, the rumble of a pump and the flow of fuel through the bypass system.

He unstrapped, took a step to Gunn's couch and slapped her across the face. 'You stupid bitch, what the Fates were you trying to do out there?'

Gunn's head rolled with the slap then rolled back to face him. There was no anger in her eyes. In fact there was nothing; nothing at all. 'I thought it was him-'

'You want to know what I think?' Robert said, looming over her. She tried to unstrap but he knocked her hands away. 'I think you've made this whole thing up, this damn conspiracy. You're crazy, genuine, escaped-from-an-asylum crazy. You're a crazy nut job, obsessed with solving the galaxy's problems and when you can't find one you make one up. You've invented a conspiracy to give your delusions something to do. And you brought me into it to help make it more real in your mind. You're probably not even an actual intelligence agent.'

Robert sagged a little, as if the words had held him upright and he dropped to his chair, watching her. 'I've seen your kind before. You're not the first person to act like this.'

They stared at each other, Gunn's face blank, eyes still, like a computer experiencing an unexpected shutdown. He'd never seen her like that.

'I'm sorry for hitting you,' he said, sinking his head into his hands.

The conditioners rumbled, the engine idled and alternating red bars flashed across the damage control console. A message appeared on the link but they kept staring at each other.

'I'm not crazy,' she said slowly, each word measured for maximum control.

'That's the catch cry of the crazy,' he said, 'but I'm sure it's all real in your mind.'

Gunn unstrapped, opened a pocket on her pressure suit and withdrew a small gold badge of a griffon with outstretched wings. It was a sharp edged bird, blocky, yet with fine detail, its beak, eyes and claws in exquisite detail. Embossed across the chest of the bird were the words 'E L I T E'; an impressive badge. He'd never seen one before.

'So that proves you've killed a lot of pirates.' 'I have another at home.'

'So you say.'

Her coolness wore off. 'Do you think I'd willingly spend time trapped in a small cockpit with a known murderer for shits and giggles?'

'Of course not,' he said. 'In your mind it's real.'

She turned and pressed her wrist to the link. The holo display shimmered and displayed a written document. Robert leaned closer. A letter or declaration from someone called the Architect.

'Project Endure?' he asked but Gunn didn't say anything. He kept reading.

The weapon is operational and we shall proceed to unify the human race against the Thargoids and wipe away the last remnants of the cold war.

The rest of the document contained little specifics in itself, referring to other documents. 'This is all you have?' he straightened up. 'A vague plan by some hack to start a war? He crinkled his brow, not sure how to gently vocalise his thoughts. 'That's one heck of a jump to go from this to a conspiracy to assassinate the Emperor.' He rolled back onto his couch, face in his hands. 'What have I done? I followed you into this to try and protect my boys. I would have been better protecting them myself.'

'This is real,' Gunn said, moving her arm. The image disappeared. 'I'm not making this up. You've seen the same stuff I have, the Imps, the Feds, everything is leading here.'

Robert shook his head, staring through his fingers to the decking. 'I can't believe I fell for it. Malin is going to gut me next time she finds me. '

'You were going to commit suicide by violent encounter before I saved you,' she said.

They fell into silence. He wasn't sure what to say. He felt as adrift as the

Saker, prisoner to the ebb and flow of the blackest sea. How long had they worked together now? Two weeks? Two weeks his boys had been hunted by the Circle. Were any of them still alive? Had he failed them all?

Gunn coughed and jerked back to life. 'Leonardo's data showed they were flying a bee-line for the Empire that took them through Vequess. The timing all lined up

.. They could be striking at a system further along.'

'Is the Emperor visiting any system further along the bee-line?' 'I don't know,' Gunn admitted.

A flash of light outside caught Robert's eye but when he focused on it, it disappeared. Behind the Saker the hyperspace vector collapsed. No new vectors appeared.

No one had pursued them. They were alone in an empty place between systems, a mis-jump to nowhere. It felt apt.

'You know this ship will be marked. The moment we reappear in Imperial space we'll be targeted and blown out of the sky.'

'Did you know Norman Vesuvian?' she asked.

'Who?'

'He's a pirate.'

'It's not a fraternity,' he said. 'It's not like there's a club we all hang out at.' He saw the flash again; cosmic rays. 'Are there any listening posts nearby?'

'I'm not breaking cover-'

'Fates, you're a broken link receiver. I was going to suggest you mine them and see if you can pick up anything interesting. You'll have passwords won't you?'

Gunn cocked her head slightly then pulled up the navigation screen. Robert watched as she flicked through the systems, maybe waiting for a name to jog a memory. Colour caught his eye and he glanced at the scanner.

Ships.

He blinked.

The scanner had been empty a moment ago. Now it was full.

His stomach collapsed like a dying sun forming a neutron star, dense and heavy. 'Umm, Gunn?'

The shapes surrounded them; a ring of objects, black and blacker, only visible by reflected light. Foils, heat vents and a cockpit caught a stray photon. They were ships, but none that he recognised.

'Scheiße,' Gunn spat.

He sat still, helpless, useless, a passenger to whatever happened in the next few moments.

They didn't die.

Their opponent's intent obviously wasn't to kill; straight away, at least.

He tried to count their number, but couldn't be sure where one ship stopped and another started. They were only half there, not quite visible, like ghosts. Beyond the ships though was something a whole lot bigger, as long and wide as a gas refinery platform, and it wasn't black. It was grey, almost neon against the dark background.

'The Feds,' Robert whispered. He didn't feel fear. He felt calm. He'd been running from this fight for six years. Now it was over. 'They'll not be happy to see me. Or you I'd gather. Best to go down fighting.'

'It's not the Feds,' Gunn whispered, her voice barely audible, drawing the last word out.

Navigation lights blossomed across the enemy ships; twelve of them, a standard squadron encircling them. Each ship sported a pair of crimson stripes along the fuselage. He pursed his lips, not sure who flew those colours. 'Who is it?' he asked.

'Someone much worse.'

Chapter 12

Robert stumbled forward as a sharp pain ripped across his back and stretched across his shoulders. Cord dug into his wrists as he fought for balance.

They were on the huge ship, the corridors painted in a depressing colour theme – he wasn't sure where the paint stopped and the shadows began.

Gunn walked directly in front of him, arms also tied behind her. Even from his angle he could see her neck and facial muscles were tight, her jaw working away. Beyond, a dozen soldiers marched in file. Judging by the footsteps there were another dozen behind. He turned to glance…

Steel crunched into his spine and he gasped, but the steel – a rifle butt – had felt misplaced and spongy, as if the rifle had moved in his attacker's hands.

They weren't professional troopers, he was sure of it, more like a bunch of pilot jockeys, just like the Circle.

But if they were Ceepers, Gunn would have staged it so he was her prisoner. She hadn't bothered.

They hit a T intersection and their leader turned right. He was a big, cobra-shaped man; four commander's stripes on his shoulder. A grey uniform he looked like he'd been born into. Robert couldn't wait to test some sarcasm out on him.

First though he needed a plan. He didn't know who they were and he had a limited understanding of their capabilities, but he learned with every step, playing scenarios through his head.

His biggest problem was the balance of weaponry, but given enough steps and a long enough corridor he'd come up with an answer.

He fake tripped into Gunn. She half turned. Robert nodded to the guard in front of her. Gunn turned away, completely disinterested. What had her spooked?

Perhaps Gunn actually wanted to see where this walk ended – did this group have something of value to her?

'You there, up the front,' Robert called, changing tactics. 'What's the story? Don't I get some prisoner rights?'

No response. 'I like your haircut,' Robert continued. 'I could probably set my chrono to it; military precision. How bland and boring. Just like you I bet. You've probably never had an original or exciting thought in your entire life.'

Still no response; sometimes you just had to keep plugging away.

'Were you actually told to take us prisoner? Or did you just chicken out from cold blooded murder? Does your military programming allow that? Are you human in there? Maybe I should gut you to see if there is any blood in that flabby frame of yours. Does your father know you're so robotic? I imagine he is quite disappointed. I don't have any kids but I can imagine a failed child would be the ultimate disappointment.'

That got a reaction. The leader spun, marched back toward Robert, grabbed him by the throat and slammed him against the bulkhead.

Stars exploded across Robert's vision. He couldn't hear the leader over the ringing in his ears but the snarl in the man's lips and the fire in his eyes gave Robert the gist of it. He'd file that little nugget away. 'Touch a nerve, did we?' he gasped through his constricted throat.

The leader's fingers clenched. The corridor darkened. Robert's uncoordinated arms flailed against the leader's iron-cored wrist, useless and ineffective …

The hand disappeared and the leader returned to the front of the queue. Robert gasped, hanging in the zero-gee and blinked back to consciousness. His tongue felt two sizes too big. A guard jabbed him back into the procession.

Fun crowd.

'Nice colours by the way,' Robert rasped. *When you've crossed the line, keep on going.* The scenery is more interesting. 'Crimson. Isn't that a girls colour? Old fashioned too. What is that, half Imperial, half Federation?'

Robert's heart stopped as if an invisible fist had clenched it tight. His lungs felt leaden, swapped out with quick-set 'crete.

Oh shit.

The leader turned and tried to smile, a slight puckering of his lips. Gunn glanced back at him, nodded.

Elite pilots.

Half Imperial, Half Federation Crimson paint.

Gunn was right. This wasn't just much worse. This was the worst case scenario. This was why Gunn was so scared.

The Independent Naval Research Arm.
INRA.

* * *

Their marched ended at a door. It was taller and wider than the others and didn't automatically open. Robert rolled his shoulders and cracked his neck. He'd fumbled through his verbal attack earlier. He'd have to bring his A-game for the man in charge.

A guard slapped a sensor and the doors whooshed open onto a large room, easily as big as a landing bay; a lower level, matching stairs leading to the upper level. He glimpsed an elaborate chair and desk, a separate holo-projector table and framed pictures of space battles but his gaze quickly locked onto a large sectioned window that filled the far wall.

They were in hyperspace.

Blue starlight, infinitely stretched, sped past them and spiralled out of sight. They were looking straight down the barrel, the infinite depth of nothingness.

That infinity drew him forward, his feet moving under an external command. He was in hyperspace. Mesmerised … sickened … mad.

Hyperspace madness.

'You can't stare at it for too long or you'll go insane,' said a voice that cracked like aged concrete.

Robert blinked. How long had he been staring? He blinked again to clear his head. Before the windows stood a white haired man in the same grey uniform, but his shoulder insignia bore a big wide gold band and five stars. A fleet Admiral.

The Admiral lumbered to his desk, walking stick in his left hand and lowered himself into the chair.

The brute shoved Robert up the steps until he was close enough to see the admiral's brown eyes. They were strong and his hair was bright white and thick. He had that wizened, crazy-eyed scientist look about him that made you expect the galaxy to break into a moody percussion number whenever he looked at you.

The Admiral locked onto Robert's gaze. 'Well, well, well if we don't have the hero of Villist himself and the Alioth Intelligence Service's undercover agent with the Circle of Independent Elite Pilots.'

Gunn stared open jawed at the Admiral, her poker face well and truly shot. 'You've got the wrong guy,' Robert said. 'I just happen to be piloting a stolen Ceepers ship; happens all the time.' He waved at Gunn who'd mercifully shut her jaw. 'And this one? I can't really explain our partnership, but you know how fate works.' He made a big show of eyeing up the guards on either side of him. 'But, I guess we are your guests, so how can we help?'

The Admiral smiled, showing yellow teeth worn into rounded stalactites and stalagmites. 'From saviour to scum to Alliance dog; no, Robert Garry, it is I that can help you.'

'No thanks,' Gunn interjected. 'Go on,' said Robert, surprised.

The Admiral opened a drawer in his desk and pulled out a shard of green alloy. Its edges were singed and rough, a hull fragment. He placed it on a stick pad on his desk. 'Go on, touch it,' he urged.

Robert glanced at the guards, expecting a trick, but they didn't lean forward in expectation so he prodded it with his index finger. It stuck for a fleeting moment. He sucked in a breath, yanked it back and sucked on it. 'It's cold.'

The Admiral nodded. 'Though it's just been floating in my drawer all these years; remarkable isn't it? It came from a very remarkable ship.'

'Ceeper?'

The Admiral shook his head. 'What do you know of history?'

Robert shrugged. 'People evolved, tried to kill each other, evolved some more, tried to kill each other some more, until here we are, out in space trying to kill each other.'

The Admiral laughed. 'I guess that is an accurate summary. But you have forgotten one crucial element. Do you know what we were originally called?'

Robert shrugged again. They had changed names?

'Our organisation was a joint effort between the Galactic powers. We didn't care about politics or favour one side or the other. The cold war was irrelevant. Our split command hierarchy ensured there couldn't be any bias. We were called the Independent Naval Reserve Arm, driven by one single goal.'

'Defeat the Thargoids,' Robert said, gaze drifting back to the hull fragment. He remembered the bed time stories of his youth. He'd seen the mass graves out past Leesti. New Aberdeen, Villist, nearly every planet had cemeteries for Thargoid victims. Humanity had stood on the brink, saved at the last moment by INRA. But power corrupted and the rest was history.

'Defeat the Thargoids,' the Admiral agreed. 'We stopped them, but we didn't defeat them. We didn't do it properly. We misunderstood the size of their civilisation; we underestimated a certain political faction. And now they are back.'

Gunn chimed in. 'Don't be stupid. The Thargoids have been back for years and they haven't fired a shot in all that time.'

'Are they really?' The Admiral asked. 'When did you last hear about them in the media? Any of the feeds? Any footage?'

Gunn scowled at the Admiral.

The Admiral smiled. 'The Thargoids are not happy, my dear. The word 'coup' may be a human word, used by Scots and Germans alike, but the term is not restricted to humanity alone. We'll be seeing the Thargoids again, and soon, and they'll be – what do you young kids call it these days? 'Packing heat'?'

'Packing a plasma pipe, old timer,' Robert said. 'I don't understand what any of this has to do with us.'

The Admiral turned his chair toward the window. The blue light raced by with no end in sight. 'I took command of INRA, well co-command with my Imperial equal, just before our secret was exposed.' He turned back and slammed a fist against a logo on his desk, the letters AAAI. There was some written scrawl next to it, a signature. Turner?

Gunn's gaze centred on the signature too; she inhaled sharply. 'You murderer,' she screamed. Robert sensed rather than saw her wind up to pounce but the brute swung his arm and she was flat on the ground before she could jump.

'He was a hero, an inspiration to billions. He led us out of the darkness and into the light of freedom. The Alliance wouldn't exist without him.'

The Admiral laughed. 'Inspiration? Perhaps. Hero? No my dear, he was anything but. Mic Turner's actions directly resulted in bringing the Thargoids back into the game and taking INRA out of it.' He shook his head and examined his veiny hands. 'I didn't fire the guns that broke up this ship, but I might as well have. We were all ostracised. Funding was cut, our links with White House and the Imperial Palace severed. My co-commander was ordered back to Achenar and my spies never heard of him again.'

The Admiral's lips moved in and out as if searching for words. 'Joseph may have been an Imperial but we saw eye to eye on many things. He was a good man and after so many years together I considered him a

.. friend.'

His eyes grew hazy as he stared beyond Robert's shoulder. 'I've seen the graves from the Thargoid wars, countless headstones stretching beyond the curvature of the horizon, little spots of reflected light dotting the abandoned continent

..' His eyes snapped back to focus, his hands curling into fists. 'INRA is the only reason that you and I are alive right now. It was INRA and INRA alone that saved humanity. I swore an oath to protect humanity so when I received the command to return to Mars I knew my only option was to run. We have hidden, between the stars, gathering knowledge, learning, researching, training, waiting for the moment when we were needed again.'

Robert rolled his eyes. 'I suppose that time is now.'

'Unfortunately, not. We weren't the only group watching the Thargoids.' He glanced at Gunn. 'Your Circle of Elite pilots were also examining them carefully. They knew what was happening internally to the Thargoids. They knew trouble was coming. They knew something had to be done.'

Gunn stopped struggling. Her eyes widened. 'The Circle planted Thargoid evidence in their assassinations to make the Federation understand the menace. They wanted the Federation to fight before it was too late.'

The Admiral smiled and nodded to the brute. The brute stiffened, stared at the Admiral a moment too long – why? – then released Gunn. She stood up and straightened her hair. 'You're smarter that I give you credit for Gunn-Britt Grotenfelt.'

Gunn clearly tried to keep her face slack but her whole body stiffened fractionally.

'Surprised? Don't be. I know your history better than Robert's. He pulled a pad from across the desk. 'Gunn-Britt Grotenfelt, parents unknown, born New Rossyth, Argent's Claim, Alioth, 3266. Six years in the state orphanage; shuffled between foster families until the age of eight when her host family were killed by pirates. A continual string of accidents led to substance abuse and a very public suicide attempt.'

Robert's gaze snapped to Gunn. Her neck blushed but her eyes were murder, locked onto the old man.

The Admiral continued, 'Her failed attempt nonetheless caused sufficient distraction to free thirty hostages from radicals of the KumByar sect. Invited to join Alioth Intelligence, she earned her Elite wings, but her substance abuse led to disciplinary action and almost destroyed the peace process on Thomson's World.'

Robert watched her flinch, but every muscle in her body tightened, like a snake ready to strike.

The Admiral finished, 'She was quickly pushed into a quiet role undercover.' He looked up from the pad. 'Did I leave anything out?'

'You forgot the part where I gut you like a fish.'

The Admiral smiled but it didn't show in his eyes. 'Charming.' He turned back to Robert. 'The Circle failed in its attempts to stir the Federation into action so it has moved onto its next plan.'

'Start a war between the Empire and the Federation, help the Empire to win and present a united front to the Thargoids. Project Endure. Old news.'

'Indeed.'

'So why did you say you can help us then?' Gunn asked. 'It sounds exactly like what you want.'

'You're not from the Federation my dear so you wouldn't understand. Your friend here would.' The Admiral turned back to Robert. 'What is the motto boy?'

'Fuck you.'

The Admiral stepped forward, uniform shining under the lights. 'Is that how you answer your superior officer?' he boomed.

Robert's feet snapped together and his right arm swung toward his temple but he caught it before he could salute. 'Once a citizen, always a citizen,' he mumbled.

'Once a citizen, always a citizen,' the Admiral agreed. He waved to the troopers surrounding them before stopping at Gunn. 'So you see my dear I might be the leader of these 'Crimson Corps' as the media calls us, but I am still a Federation citizen and I will not let it be subjugated by the Empire.'

'Help us then,' Gunn said. 'Bring your fleet; let's stop the attack on the Emperor.'

The Admiral stepped away from his desk and hobbled over to his projector table. 'It's not quite that simple my dear. Haven't you ever wondered where the Circle got all its wonderful Thargoid technology? How it could casually litter the cosmos with Thargoid evidence?'

Gunn's eyes glazed but every pirate knew that answer. 'They have a stash,' Robert said.

'And how are they always able to know exactly where they are needed? That despite their small size they are always able to stop pirate attacks on civilians? How they were able to find out about the Federation's Starburst weapon?'

Robert smarted. This clown had known all along while they'd been groping around in the dark. 'Pass.'

The Admiral raised an eyebrow at Robert. 'You're not so young that you don't know the name 'Dark Wheel'?'

'Treasure Hunters.' He thought of Dad, being tucked up in bed, covers up to his ears, listening to stories of the Ryder family and the monsters the Dark Wheel found beyond explored space. His heart ached.

'Elite-ranked treasure hunters,' corrected the Admiral. 'From a by-gone age, searching for Raxxla,' Gunn said.

The Admiral nodded. 'From a by-gone age indeed. They never found Raxxla. But they found something else.' He activated the holo-projector and a map of the galaxy materialised before him. 'Neither of you were born at the time but when the Thargoids made their first peaceful contact, an inter-species convention facility was established. In the initial meetings the Thargoids mentioned a lost world; a world that they had once colonised and where they had completed amazing technical work. A world that even to them held an aura of magic. But they lost contact with the world and were unable to find it again. Covert surveillance recorded them discussing whether to ask humanity for help, though ultimately they didn't respect or trust us enough.

'When we translated the covert recording, the name of the planet was 'Soontill.''

The floor shook beneath Robert's feet. His knees weakened. His forehead pounded in sync with his heartbeat. 'Soontill?' he breathed, hearing his father's last words.

You have to go back to the beginning. You have to go back to Soontill.

He knew that bedtime story too, a world full of Thargoid treasures beyond anyone's wildest dreams, an artefact that could allow a glimpse into the future. A whole generation of treasure hunters had searched for it and failed.

Had his father been there? No.

The Circle was there. The Circle was the Dark Wheel. They'd found it.

His thoughts became a jigsaw jumble. He shook his head as he stared through the floor and across space. 'I know a couple of guys who are looking for it right now,' he said, 'rich pirates, chucking in the lasers for nav maps and tall tales in taverns.'

Gunn folded her arms across her chest. 'So what exactly are you bringing to the table here?' The sneer on her face was almost palpable.

'If you defeat their Plan B, do you think they'll just give up? No, they'll go to Plan C and Plan D if they have to. And with Soontill they can.' The Admiral stepped close, his cane tapping on the metal floor.

'If you want to stop them, you have to find Soontill.' He clenched his free hand into a fist. 'And take it from them.'

Robert raised his hands. 'This is all starting to sound a bit more than what I signed up for.'

'How?' Gunn asked, ignoring Robert.

'Criddoch?' the Admiral asked the brute. Criddoch pulled a device his chest pocket. It looked like a crystal with wires snaking out of it but Gunn sucked in a deep breath.

'A retriever.' She said it with the reverence the devout saved for religious artefacts. 'Does it work?'

The Admiral chuckled again. 'I like her. Criddoch?'

Criddoch cleared his throat. 'It works in all our tests. But we've never had the opportunity to run it in anger.'

'We've been ready to download the Circle's computer core for some time now,' The Admiral said. 'We've just been missing one key ingredient.'

'Gunn,' said Robert.

'Gunn,' said the Admiral. 'You have access we don't. Download the data and return it to us. If there is anything there linked to Soontill, we'll find it and then we'll bring our ships and end this nightmare once and for all.'

Robert thought of the total destruction of his Hoopertown base, the roars of approval from the bar, of all his comrades murdered by the Circle. 'Chi mi a dh'aithghearr sibh.' *See you soon Ceepers* …

Chapter 13

'There's nothing out here,' Robert said, standing by the Saker's viewport and squinting into the darkness.

'They're there,' Gunn said, still strapped in and watching the scanner. 'And they're watching us.'

Robert pursed his lips, studying for movement. He'd never visited this planetary system. It registered explored on the maps, but was sufficiently far from civilisation to be of little interest; a common-as-hydrogen red dwarf star, an asteroid field behind them and a blue-green gas giant hovering in space ahead. And apparently orbiting the gas giant was Gunn's Circle base.

She didn't look happy to be going back.

'They'll turn on us,' she had said earlier. 'INRA only cares about INRA.'

Robert had agreed. 'Of course they will, but better here, free to devise a plan, than stuck in one of their cells.' He rubbed the swelling on the side of his head; a parting gift from Criddoch. He'd leaned in real close, hot moist breath billowing over Robert's face and said he was looking forward to the battle for Soontill. 'You'll have to watch for friendly fire, daddy's boy.'

I'm not a pilot,' Robert countered, wondering about the father obsession. 'I'd lose. Is that how you get off, picking on the weak? Now if you wanted to have a gunfight, that's a party I could come to.'

Criddoch had slipped a pistol barrel under Robert's chin. Fast, but Gunn was faster. Robert stifled a yawn. 'Best keep practising.'

Criddoch had brained him with the pistol. It had been worth it, until it swelled up.

Gunn still hadn't wanted to go but a message from her boss Trotsky had clinched it. Alioth Intelligence could not afford to be implicated in anything. Her 'display' in the Vequess system had raised all kinds of 'hell'. Trotsky wanted her to stay under cover while Montgomery worked their other channels.

'Bastards,' Gunn spat. 'They won't do anything except sit on their fat arses and chuck the blame elsewhere.'

Robert had nodded. It did seem her superiors no longer cared about her original orders. Maybe the Admiral had been right about Gunn's undercover operation. 'Other problems to worry about now?' he asked.

'They are the Alliance. They are about the people, not the politics,' Gunn said, speaking with indisputable belief. He almost didn't want to burst her hyperspace cloud.

'Governments are governments. They do what they do, no matter how noble their beginnings.'

Gunn had stared at him for a moment then dropped her head. 'It's all over.'

'It's not over till the Cobra parks at the Tionisla Wreckspace,' Robert had said. 'Let's do what INRA suggests.'

She had agreed, slapping the link off. 'Once again it's all down to me.' Her voice dropped an octave. 'It's always down to me.'

Now, sailing at reasonable pace toward the belly of the beast, Robert wondered what she had meant by that. She'd been even less fun than usual; on par with a 'crete wall.

He placed his Colt Diplomat on his console and dismantled it. An old lesson well learned. If a weapon failed when you needed it, you were dead. When the stakes were high, it was easy to justify a five minute check before the main dance. He'd have to stow the Diplomat on the ship of course, but the check was a soothing ritual.

It was a handy weapon, he knew well. In times of desperation you needed a weapon you understood, one whose recoil you automatically reacted to, whose foibles you instinctively corrected for, a weapon whose reloading function was muscle memory to your arms and hands and fingers.

He checked the rifling of the barrel, checked the reloading spring, the little arms and joints. He pulled the ammo case out and back in, heard it settle in with a satisfying crunch. 'So,' he said, groping for an ice breaker. 'You tried to kill yourself. That doesn't sound like you.'

A brief glance was her only response. Had she finally learnt to ignore him?

'So you saved a whole planet from destruction. That doesn't sound like you.' 'Touché.'

The cockpit fell into silence again. The click of sensors and readouts, the odd fizzle of space dust ionising against the shields. The air tasted stale, the recyclers likely needing a recharge.

Minutes passed. Gunn's expression was either of extreme concentration or extreme abstraction, staring at the nav map, pupils wide and unmoving but eyes narrowed in thought. Her hands lay still and her chest barely moved as she breathed.

Robert had dabbled in silence before but it had never really worked out. He liked talking too much.

'It was the Alliance's fault,' Robert said. They'd set us up hoping the Imps would take the bait and break the armistice, attack us. The Alliance hoped that we'd weaken each other to the point that they could sweep in as protectors to free the system, offer membership to the Alliance and get free access to the mineral.'

Gunn didn't say anything. Maybe she knew that already or maybe she didn't care anymore. She kept her hands steady on the controls. The gas giant grew before them, bands of white visible between the blue and green.

'And I'm not a ... hero,' Robert said, lowering his tone for the last word. Even saying it made him ill. 'I was just the last schmuck standing.' he paused.

'I still hear the screams.' The same screams he heard every night. White noise in its sheer intensity effecting everything on the planet. Comms links flinging out help messages, crying women begging for their children, grown men pleading for life, asking for anyone, anything to help them, and then screams as boiling plasma ripped people apart and razed the cities to the ground. His jaw worked like a binary loader, tense, loose, tense, loose, a programming loop he struggled to break. He sniffed back wet eyes. 'The Imps surprised us, a one-two punch, took us from the rear. We were just a rapid response group, no match for them. Before we knew it we'd lost two thirds of our fleet, the flagship, and my CO. I was the highest ranking officer left. I called the retreat. I was the one that ordered us away from the planet to wait for backup. Help was weeks away. We'd barely stabilised life support and engines before the cries came out.'

Now Gunn turned, pinning her top lip with her lower teeth. 'What happened?'

'We went back out,' Robert said simply. 'We couldn't stand there and listen as the Imperials torched a whole planet. No one else was coming, the Imps had eradicated the Alliance.'

'How did you beat them?'

Robert's gaze turned to the viewport, tens of light years away to a once insignificant planet. He couldn't even remember why they'd received orders to go to Villist. That whole year of his life was lost behind a fog. 'It was Leo. He was the hero. I didn't have enough ships to take them all on, but I thought I could have a chance if I hit them one by one. The Imps were so spread out across the planet that I thought if we were quick enough it might work. The Germans called it blitzkrieg; lightning War. We couldn't beat them all but every Imperial ship we took down gave the people another moment of life.'

Gunn kept staring at Robert. He swallowed. 'Leo hacked into our communication grid. He had done the same to the Imperial ships. He could block their communications and drop their shields just as we opened fire.'

Gunn leant forward, hand on her chin, her face soft, perhaps even relaxed, her defences down for the moment. 'So you did it. You saved the whole planet?'

'Leo did it. He's the hero. He hacked them so they didn't know we were coming. We smashed them, moving from one to another until they were all gone.'

Gunn stared at him silently then her features hardened again, soft hills and curves changing to angry glaciers and rocky walls. 'So you became a pirate? How could you do that?'

Robert couldn't tell if she was trying to bait him, was angry or just confused. She was the law and her parents had been killed by pirates. He was a pirate and his parent was killed by the law. Maybe nothing was supposed to make sense.

'Do you know how many millions of people died under that bombardment? How many homes were destroyed with husbands, wives and children inside? All of them innocent, crying out, crying out for me to save them. Their lives were on me, no one else, just me. They were asking me for help and they died; all of them. I was too slow. I was too slow and now they are all dead.' His voice rose so he sat down and breathed. 'But the brass paraded me around anyway. Everywhere we went there were levelled buildings. There were still bodies trapped under the 'crete. You could smell them. Nothing made sense. It was just flashes; one moment I stood on parade, the next the Admiral of the Fleet shook my hand. It was all wrong, just…wrong. I barely felt human anymore, completely numb. The doctors cleared me but I felt insulated, isolated from the rest of the world, screaming at them to stop but no one would listen.'

His chest tightened as he relived it. He caught his reflection in the cockpit window. Curly black hair, haggard skin, vacant eyes. The Thousand Klick Stare.

The doctors were wrong. I'm not okay.

'I couldn't take it anymore.' He looked at Gunn. 'I thought about ending it.' He released a long breath. 'So I got out of there, went AWOL. I went home to Dad. He needed help with a job, a raid. And it went from there. I have no idea if the Feds are still hunting me.'

Gunn's stare bored into him; her pupils jerking back and forth like a narrow beam sensor, scanning for an answer. She swallowed, mouth readying to open, but something holding it back.

'What you did that day was heroic,' she said. Robert turned away, but she kept going. 'It's obvious you cared whether those people lived or died and you're not going to let yourself forget that, but as a pirate you've probably killed or hurt more than you saved on Villist. What part of you is okay with that? The part which had honour, a sense of duty?'

'You have no idea what it was like. I was drowning. I was so deep I didn't know which way was up. Going home to Dad was the only thing that made sense, the only thing I understood; a rock in the river, something to hold onto while I tried to figure things out.'

'Sure, no responsibility, no honour; it's easy to avoid those when you're a pirate.'

Robert didn't say anything for a moment. 'Do you know how a father justifies piracy to his six year old son who wants to know why they are hurting people that haven't hurt them?'

'Some bullshit story,' Gunn snapped. 'Do you know how many pirates I had in my life as a child? Everywhere I went, pirates followed, hurting innocents, torching houses, stealing valuables, blowing up their ships. People would have accidents, people would get hurt. Nobody wanted to foster me. I was the unlucky kid. Befriend me and you died. And the Sisters had the gall to tell me it was all part of God's plans.' She gave him a withering look. 'I've drowned too, pirate. I've been too deep to swim to the surface, but it wasn't because of anything I did. It was because of people like you.'

Robert stared, dumbstruck. He had killed people; many, in fact, but they had all been trying to kill him, or stop him stealing their stuff. Their families probably looked at it a different way.

'I …' Robert started, but then the scanner bleeped and they were back in business.

Two ships closed in, retros firing to match speed. The link activated and a man's surprised face hovered over the projector. 'Allison? Where have you been? Never mind, thank the Fates you're alive. We thought we'd lost everyone.'

'No, not everyone. I'm fine.'

The face wore the smile of a man seeing his dead lover return. Robert scrunched up his nose. 'What happened to the pirate?'

Now Gunn smiled, like they were both in on some big secret. She turned to Robert. 'I have him right here.'

* * *

Robert landed face first in the prison cell, harder than he would have expected. That told him three things. First, the floor was a dense ceramic, two the space station contained purpose built prison cells, which meant he wasn't their first prisoner, and three: the station's rotation created Imperial standard gravity; all important facts.

The hatch energised behind him, the hum of three distinct plasma beams coming to life. Two sets of footsteps faded into the distance. One Ceeper had stayed behind; to watch him.

'Don't prisoners have rights?' Robert asked, voice muffled between his crushed lips and the ceramic floor.

The voice behind him felt like a snap-frozen knife buried in his heart. 'You mess with Oberon, you mess with all of us. Your hours are numbered, viper bait.'

'Are we talking single figures here or…?' Robert asked.

The voice snorted. 'You think you're tough now, just you wait.'

'I haven't anything else to do but,' Robert said. 'I'm actually pretty tired.' He inched his arms from underneath his body and tried to get comfortable. His face felt thick and numb from the beating and his arms had caught awkwardly beneath him but he wasn't giving the Ceeper any satisfaction. They'd have to earn that.

The worry was that they would get the chance. Gunn had explained the

Ceeper's interrogation techniques before they boarded the Saker: Good cop, bad cop, toy with him, extract what information they can get then execution. When he'd asked when she'd step in, she hadn't answered.

Robert slipped his hands under his head – slightly less painful – and faked a snore. Eventually he heard a grunt and the squeak of combat boots twisting on the floor and disappearing.

Robert turned over.

The cell was utilitarian white, a smooth cement covering the walls; nothing to grab, nothing to break, nothing to get a hold of. The only deviation was the hatch before him, a rectangle two metres high by half a metre wide, three plasma projectors in the top spitting columns down to receivers embedded flush with the floor.

Purple plasma. He assumed that was bad. The light panel above him glowed sodium yellow, smooth against the roof tiling; a plastic cover over top. Unsure if he was under surveillance, he lay still, probing the plastic with his gaze, for edges, rough parts, anything he could use to pry it open, gain access to the panel behind. It looked awfully secure. Too secure for fingernails.

He'd been in other prison cells before of course, with Dad in Olcanze, and the brig as a young recruit. The conversion to a legitimate life had not been easy.

This cell was different to all of those. There was normally a way out of anywhere, but even if the walls and roof and barriers were impenetrable, there was always the human element. The one thing all cells had in common was visitors. Prisoners cost food and power to keep alive. That cost was covered by extracting value from the prisoner, which meant talking to them.

Hours passed. Robert watched the plasma ripple and pulse, playing scenarios through his head. Before the interrogators arrived he'd need to be standing, one and a half paces back from the door. If the interrogator stepped through the hatch and to the right, Robert would be primed to strike. If the interrogator went left, Robert would be disadvantaged. He'd need to get in real close, too close for fists or elbows. Knees and forehead instead, a brawl more intimate than most love rituals.

Two interrogators would change the equation. He'd need to balance attack between both. The first strike would have to be momentarily crippling – the spine, throat or eyes – so he could put a few dents in the second person before returning to the first.

He'd have to be quick, precise and methodical, which worried him. He'd topped his class in hand to hand combat at the academy, but he'd tended to rely on guns since then; an oversight.

When they finally came there were three of them.

The far door beyond the plasma beams shuttled open and they stepped through, one after the other. Robert stood to match them. Each sported black hair and blue eyes. One had a beard, another a long drooping chin; they wore dark uniforms with long sleeves.

Wrists and traps came his old instructor's voice.

Thick wrists and triangular trapezium muscles were signs of a man who worked out, who pushed his body to its limits, who had actual physical strength. Not just gym muscle but real world muscle. Their hands were big, good for wrapping around a flight stick – but they weren't well used, not weathered. None of them had split open a knuckle trying to split open a head. Their wrists were small, good for flexing in a cockpit, not good for burying a fist into a stomach.

They looked like pin up poster boys for the Lave pilot academy.

The rear two Ceepers stopped. One stepped to the right, one stepped to the left. They pulled out silver laser pistols and aimed at him through the plasma beams.

Robert smiled at them, even as his shoulders slumped. They'd done their homework too.

The third Ceeper approached. He leaned to the side, access card in hand. Robert stepped forward, two feet from the plasma. He spread his legs slightly, turned his feet outward, pointing one at each of the gunners; if he could get this one to block the other two …

His arms hung loose by his sides, hands open, ready to grab, deflect and poke (eyes).

The plasma beams evaporated. Something erupted in Robert's chest; butterflies? No, he wasn't six years old.

The Ceeper stepped forward. So did Robert. A laser beam sizzled past his ear. Robert jerked, his gaze snapping to the shooter, pistol up at eye level. A crack shot. All Robert's plans evaporated.

The echo died. The room went quiet, no plasma hum, just the light panel above and two pairs of lungs, breathing slowly, steadily and in control.

For now.

Robert studied the Ceeper, but the Ceeper wasn't studying Robert. He checked the room, the flawless walls, the trim of the light panel, the edges around the plasma beams. If he was searching for attempted escape then there couldn't have been any hidden cameras.

The Ceeper stopped looking.

He turned his whole body towards Robert, his chest, arms, legs and toes and face, all aiming in. They made eye contact. The Ceeper showed a set of white teeth.

And Robert realised exactly how this was going to play out.

* * *

The Ceeper stepped back through the hatch, leaving Robert cradling his chest in the corner of the cell.

The plasma beams reactivated. The guards returned their pistols to their belts. The three turned and left through the far door.

Robert let himself breathe. He closed his eyes. Let himself feel the pain across his ribs. And stomach. And legs. And head.

It had been easy, but painful. The interrogator was an amateur, and Robert hadn't needed to lie at all. He told the real story right up to Granite City, up to Gunn storming in on his final stand. They didn't care about what happened after that. They didn't think Gunn was a double agent.

They did care about what he was doing on that freighter and why, and what he thought he had seen.

Robert told the truth. It was a coincidence. He knew a guy who'd watched the feeds and knew grain laden ships would be entering that system with all haste. Jordan always went after foodstuffs. 'There's always a market for food, kiddo, and a clean conscience as well'. The Garry clan hypered in, waited, and a whole fleet of transports jumped straight into his lap.

He didn't think they believed him and now he sat still, waiting for the next round, the flesh over his ribs feeling thick and swollen yet normal under his fingertips.

The wonders of technology.

He wondered if the next visitor would be the second interrogator, the 'good cop', the Executioner or Gunn. He found himself wishing to see her face again.

His luck was up.

Gunn appeared beyond the plasma beams. She didn't make eye contact. She glanced around, nodded and mumbled something inaudible over the buzz of the plasma. She tilted her head toward Robert, lips moving but nothing reaching his ears. A Ceeper came into view. He wore the same black uniform but this was no pilot jockey. Half as wide as he was tall, the kind of guard that sat on his stool and ate out of sheer boredom all day, every day. Robert thought that maybe his presence would help this fat bastard's bored eating problems.

He was wrong.

The fat man passed Gunn, access card at the ready. Gunn's hand reached around his neck, yanked his chin back, stretching the loose pale skin. A glint of steel in her other hand, a thin bead of a knife.

The skin parted, reds and whites curling away like snapping rubber.

The knife stopped, twisted, kept going then it was gone, a deep black hole in its wake.

Then the blood came; a flood, a wave, straight at Robert, boiling to steam on the plasma. A smokescreen of death.

The steam cleared and the guard lay choking on a fading fountain of blood. His limbs stopped their spasms.

Robert didn't move. He watched with mouth agape as Gunn wiped the knife on the dead man's clothes. She swiped the access card through the scanner and the plasma disappeared.

Robert stepped through the hatch; one gingerly placed foot at a time. He stopped before the congealing blood and looked at Gunn.

'I think you just broke your cover.'

He saw Gunn bite back a response then settle on her customary grunt of displeasure. 'You're not surprised?'

Robert took a moment to respond. 'Of course not; we both know I'm growing on you.'

Gunn grunted again. 'The armoury is this way.' she turned and marched out the door.

Robert locked the prison hatch. He chased her down passages of grey marble veined with gold, Elite emblems etched into the floor. Self-appreciation or whatever it was called. He lost track of direction as he weaved through the passages, trying to keep up with Gunn. He concentrated on trying to hear over his own breathing and seeing all around, looking and listening for trouble.

They reached the armoury. Gunn turned. 'They'll receive an alert for the open door. They'll send guards. We've got three minutes, tops.' Robert nodded and she swiped her card. The hatch flew up into the ceiling.

He stepped into a pirate's paradise. A utilitarian store room, bare steel shelves from ankle to forehead. Every surface was packed with weapons of every manufacture dating back at least a hundred years; gratitude from patrons, companies and people more than likely saved by the Circle. He passed weapons he'd dreamed of firing, ones he'd never been able to afford and stopped at the ones he knew, ones he could trust.

He settled on a Tollett and Marks Assault 'Scatter' carbine and a pair of Vega Corp Deathwreakers. He slung a pair of bandoliers over each shoulder and clipped extra power packs for the Deathwreakers to his belt. He turned to Gunn, a grin stretching all the way across his face. 'All I need now is my kilt.'

'You're an idiot,' she said, but there could have been the barest hint of a smile. She slipped a feminine Graves Mark IV 'Popper' into her belt and stepped out. 'Now we have to get to the core. Don't shoot before we get there. The internal sensors are primed for weapon activation.'

'But I can shoot them once I get to the core, right? You promised me.' This was what he was designed to do.

Back to the basics. 'Let's go,' he said.

* * *

Gunn led, Robert followed, bandoliers rattling and weapons shaking, making enough noise to alert the whole space station.

Round the first corner, Gunn almost ran full tilt into a man who stared at her open-mouthed before she pistol-whipped him and raced past.

It didn't drop him but Robert gave him another tap and he collapsed. They dragged him through a side door and locked him in.

Gunn whipped left around a corner and disappeared down a ladder. A quick glance behind him – passage empty – and he turned and scuttled down after her. He broke into a run to stay on her heels as she sprinted through a maze of empty passages.

'Where is everyone?' Robert breathed. The weapons were heavy, especially in the Imperial gravity and Gunn maintained a pretty good pace.

'It's three am,' she said. She gave a half laugh. 'There's a curfew because of a suspected leak.'

Robert grunted in response. Space stations were so artificial. Trapped in the cell he'd had no idea of the local time. 'Leaks, huh? I wonder who that was.'

Gunn didn't reply. They reached the core.

A standard hatch off the passageway, grey like everything else; Robert stepped through a short passage to a large circular room, an opposing passage off at an angle. Two rows of consoles around the perimeter, a lone figurine sitting atop a bottom row console.

Robert stepped forward into a conglomerate of blinking reds, blues, yellows and greens, his gaze following Gunn to a central ring of consoles, past a glide chair and a pair of gesture readers to a gap in the consoles, a ladder leading down a dark shaft.

'That's where I'm going,' Gunn said. 'I want a raw copy of all the data. If I access it like normal I'll get locked out. Down there it should work.'

'Should?'

'Should.'

'If it doesn't?'

'Then you'll wish you were back in your cell.'

Robert peered out over the edge. The ladder went down and down, a ring of soft blue LEDs every metre or so down to the very bottom. It reminded him of hyperspace.

The muted LEDs suggested a distant floor, a blinking green light that could have been a terminal.

'You're going to be pretty exposed down there,' Robert said. Yielding the high ground, nowhere to hide, improved chance of ricochets finding their mark. Everything about it said trap.

'That's why you're going to keep them off me.' She turned to climb down then stopped and looked up. Her eyes were hard, Business-Gunn as hard as he had ever seen her. 'This information has to get out. This data is more important than you. It's more important than me. One of us has to finish this.'

He didn't say anything as she disappeared down the ladder. 'I'm always the last one off,' he whispered. Then he turned away.

He had an ambush to prepare for.

Robert's gaze raked the control room. No useful defensive screens. Attack could come from either of the interacting access passages. In five strides he was up against the console, peering one way and the other. Down one passage he could see through to the main corridor where a light panel cast a hint of shadow; a crude early-warning sensor. The position left him open to attack from the other passage however. A few seconds manoeuvring, checking for the best compromise, showed no good position. The likely outcome would be a shot in the back, and probably soon.

His hand crept to his sporran but it wasn't there.

Watching, listening, he circled the torus again. His eye was drawn to the figurine; two inches tall, shiny pewter, a warrior with a battle-axe in hand. Robert stepped close and pocketed it.

He returned to the spot by the console. Far from ideal but it was his best bet.

He unslung the scatter gun from his shoulder, removed the ammo pod and checked the action, felt for resistance, any hang in the movement. He removed the first cartridge from the pod, gauging the spring's movement. Not keeping an idle gun loaded was another hard earned lesson. Springs were high tensile steel and when held out of their pre-stressed state for too long they lost their zing. No zing, no ammo, a potentially fatal issue.

The next cartridge slid into position however. The spring was fine. Good rifling down the barrel, no dags or filing damage. The sightings looked straight and true. The weapon was in overall good nick. He put it back together; the ammo pod sliding in with a gut curdling slunk of steel and pins. He waited a moment, listening to both passages, but he heard no running footsteps, no shouts of alarms.

He placed the scatter gun on the console and pulled out the two Deathwreakers. He smiled. The designer of the weapon was a kindred spirit. He ran his hand over the nearly foot long body, wiping marks away with his thumb. The oversized emitter glowed. The power cell sang a gentle hum and the heat sinks strapped below the barrel warmed his hand.

Primed, powered, ready to wreak a little death. And he had two of them.

Across the torus one of the screens flickered with scrawling text. His gaze snapped up; just a maintenance program.

He placed the Deathwreakers on the console behind him. He grabbed the scatter gun, held it aloft, dropped it, swung back for the Deathwreakers and aimed them down the two passages.

Too slow. He shoved the two weapons into his belt; safer, especially if he had to move in a hurry.

He reclaimed the scatter gun then wriggled his butt in against the console. Buttons and dials dug into his back but he preferred that to a bullet in the back. He was just lucky they wouldn't be using grenades. Hardened bulkheads had an uncanny knack for reflecting shockwaves.

He was as ready as he was going to be.

The room was quiet. He tuned out the beeping and slow clicks of the computers and the slow discharge of the air conditioners. He focused on human sounds. Footsteps, words, mumbles, the sliding of weapons past clothes, weapon safeties unclicking, anything that could be death in disguise.

He waited. The air tasted dry, and his tongue grew thick in his mouth and he thought of Riedquat Ultra. He hadn't drunk anything since the hyperjump in-system. He adjusted his butt against the console, relieving the pressure on one nerve ending and piling it on another.

Waiting was the hardest bit. Adrenaline wasn't easily controlled. Maintaining focus was hard. He'd read military papers on the problem. Most people couldn't keep their concentration intact for more than fifty minutes. Trained guards did a little better, but the mind was designed to be occupied and when distraction didn't come, the mind searched it out, becoming engrossed by the tiniest details, like the countdown to the end of the shift, blocking the mind from its true goal: to stare out into the distance for that one enemy trooper, minute after minute after minute.

He shook his head, blinked hard and rolled his shoulders. This was not guard duty. There was no second shift. There was him and no one else. If he died, Gunn died, and if Gunn died he'd lose the rest of his boys and his Dad forever.

'How are you going down there?' he called out to Gunn.

'Slower thanks to conversation.'

Robert poked his tongue out; charming as always. He waited. He waited some more. Then he stopped waiting.

Chapter 14

Brown floated in space.

At least that's what it felt like. The lights in his Kestrel's cockpit turned off, the sensation of the new-gen acceleration couch akin to a gel-bed, his arms spread wide and he could imagine he was soaring through the cosmos.

Free. Pure. Perfect. Nothing but him and the stars. The way it was meant to be.

A light flashed on the console and the illusion crumbled. With a sigh he activated the link and his partner's tight face and blond hair morphed into existence before him.

'Yes?'

'Interesting news from Command, it seems we have an asset inside the Circle after all.'

Brown felt an expletive rise through his chest, riding a wave of anger. He understood plausible deniability. He understood knowing only what you needed to do a job, but sometimes – no, often – Command didn't know themselves what he needed to know to do his job. 'Why am I not surprised? Have you activated him?'

'Still trying to get in touch.'

Brown rolled his eyes and brought up the nav map. He and his partner were drifting through an Oort cloud right on the border of Imperial space – as close as they could get without 'crossing the line'. They were in the unfortunate position of having to wait for more intel before they made their next move.

Waiting didn't sit well with Brown.

'How are your two friends?' his partner asked.

Brown checked his pad. The Alioth Intelligence agent and the citizen were beyond the frontier in an explored, but empty system. Either they had found the bug and were leading him on a goose chase or they had found something of interest out there. 'I have my own news on the citizen,' he replied. 'You'll never guess where he has been.'

He transferred across the upload from Command. His partner glanced sideways and whistled. 'Son of a bitch. THE Robert Garry?' Brown thought for a moment it was a whistle of admiration but saw his expression darken. 'I've been looking for that deserter for years. Next time I see him...'

'Steady on,' Brown said. 'Let's just see where he leads us first. He might take us straight to where we want to go.'

* * *

Alarms raged, rising and falling as if the space station itself screamed; infuriated that someone had invaded her core.

Robert started counting. Most of the Ceepers would be in their bunks. They'd jerk out of bed, get into their clothes, grab weapons and attack. But some would be on duty. They'd reach their nearest armoury and come straight away. They'd be awake, a little jaded perhaps, but with a head start on the rest. Robert gave them two minutes to show up, maybe one minute and a half to be conservative.

'How much longer do you need?' he called down to Gunn.

'Stop talking.'

'Dammit woman, I-'

'Stop talking!'

Robert growled, wondering how she'd like it when the guns started making noise. He pushed the stock of the scatter gun into his left shoulder, held its weight against the console then withdrew a Deathwreaker with his right hand. He aimed them down both corridors, up at heart height; a person's centre of mass; hard to miss.

The grip on the Deathwreaker warmed under his palm. Forty seconds passed. His fingers tingled. His focus narrowed down to the two corridors.

His internal timer reached seventy seconds, twenty second shy of his estimate when a black shape appeared in the left corridor. Robert fired the scatter gun and the Ceeper disappeared into mist.

Another Ceeper followed. His gaze dropped to his comrade, then back up, but Robert had already adjusted his aim and dispatched him to wherever Ceepers go when they die.

'Things are getting hot up here,' Robert yelled. Gunn didn't respond. She was going to get them both killed.

He heard them before he saw them; both corridors, simultaneously. He fired the scatter gun down the left. They were already there down the right; almost on top of him. They raised their guns to their shoulders, reared back for stability. Robert fired the Deathwreaker as consoles exploded beside him. He cringed away, firing both weapons as more Ceepers arrived.

The world became a numb torus of ringing silence. Flame burst from the scatter gun; light flashed from the Deathwreaker. Men fell. Mouths gaped in agony. Fire rippled across chests.

Robert heard none of it. He existed in a twisted shadow of reality, witnessing events but not in control. His arms adjusted, sagged. Imperial gravity drained his strength. Triggers were pressed, Ceepers collapsed. Consoles exploded around him. Something struck his hip. Numbness spread through his waist.

The scatter gun clicked dry.

Reality came crashing back, the numbness in his chest, his drooping right arm, the weight of the empty scatter gun, dead bodies piling up, live bodies scrambling to get through.

He had ammo, but no time to load. In that moment he wasn't on the space station anymore. He was above Villist, surrounded by Imperial ships slagging the crap out of the Federation fleet. As a young XO he'd called the retreat. That decision had turned his life on its head, and not for the better.

He dropped the scatter gun as he pushed to his feet. He wasn't going to retreat this time.

He fired one Deathwreaker to the right as he ran to the left, already pulling the second Deathwreaker from his pants. With the two pistols at eye level, straight out, shoulder width apart, he ran right at the Ceepers, firing as they fired back.

Robert screamed, trying shock to slow them down, throw off their aim. Laser beams erupted from the Deathwreakers. He saw faces, eyes wide with the thousand klick stare.

A shot glanced his shoulder. He collapsed, still firing, firing, firing, until there was no one left to shoot at.

A body pinned his legs. He struggled backward, kicking; more footsteps from the corridor. Where was his bloody gun?

There, just beyond reach. He clawed forward an inch at a time, fingers brushing the grip...

A Ceeper raced around the corner, rifle high. His gaze tracked down, the rifle lagging a moment behind.

Robert touched the Deathwreaker's grip.

The Ceeper lowered his head behind the sights.

Robert swung the Deathwreaker up, trigger depressed, spraying the passage with laser bolts. A laser pulse fizzed past his face as the Ceeper screamed out. Flame erupted from his chest and he dropped.

Gasping, Robert gave the body a final kick, stood, and raced back to the torus. A man stood over the chute. Robert fired, saw him fall as a second came from nowhere, leaping at him and slamming into Robert as he fired again.

Smoke burst from the man's back as his lifeless form crashed forward, pinning Robert to the ground, the Deathwreaker wedged between them.

Two more, rifles raised, barrels pointing at his head.

He writhed to escape the cadaver's embrace, grabbed at the trapped Deathwreaker and held down the trigger.

Laser pulses spewed from the back of the corpse arcing across the space.

The two figures collapsed backward and the torus settled into silence.

Robert lay there a moment, every muscle burning, his lungs screaming, his left side throbbing, his right side numb. He pushed the body off and stood, surveying the carnage, blinking, chest heaving.

His right arm dropped. The Deathwreaker fell from his numb grip.

There were a lot of bodies. Mothers, children, babies, flesh boiled from their bones, fathers huddling over their families.

Sound returned, his breathing, his heart spasming against his ribs, jacket crinkling as his chest expanded and contracted. The ticking of the Deathwreakers as heat conducted through their heatsinks and into his hand.

No screaming, no footsteps. He was alone.

For now.

He wasn't sure how long he stood there, waiting for his heart rate to drop from unrealistic to simply unbearable. Then he groped around the bodies for his second Deathwreaker. 'That's what you get for messing with the Garry clan.' He felt good for killing them, but it still wouldn't bring his Dad back.

Would Jordan have wanted the dead bodies?

Kill him so he doesn't kill you, Jordan had told him as a youngling. *But don't kill him just because you can.*

He found the Deathwreaker. His right hand could barely grip the weapon, let alone aim it, but if push came to shove maybe he could still shoot it. The right side of his waist was wet but he didn't look down. Until he actually eyeballed the damage he could pretend it was just spilt coffee.

He checked the Deathwreakers' power cells; five shots in one, four shots in the other. More if he turned the power down. He found and reloaded the scatter gun. He shoved the four shot Deathwreaker in his belt, flinching as the heat sinks burned through his pants.

He stepped to the chute. Down below, a dead body lay spread-eagled right in the centre. Bull's-eye.

Then he heard it.

A scraping sound and a cyclical thunk. Like a wheel with an off centre axle. Like the painful moan of a legless monster inching itself forward. He heard a murmur behind it; hushed voices perhaps? It sounded big. It sounded like it was designed to hurt him.

'Time to go,' he called down to Gunn.

'I'm not done,' she said, loud, rushed, dismissive.

'You're done. I'm out of ammo. Once they kill me they'll kill you. You're done. Get up here.'

She didn't respond. The scraping rolling noise grew louder. The ominous thunk reverberated through the torus. It reminded him of the Imperial repeaters he practiced against on Morgue's Mortuary. A weapon designed to intimidate with its appearance and cause maximum collateral damage with its bite. They called it the 'Emperor's Fist'.

'Gunn!'

She pulled away from the console and clambered up the ladder, two rungs at a time. Robert half stepped away, wanting to cover her but needing a better angle against the oncoming weapon. He checked over his shoulder. She was almost there.

Gunn climbed to her feet and slipped a crystal into his pocket. 'A back-up.'

He nodded to the other entrance. 'That way, go!' He raced after her, scatter gun at the ready, his five shot Deathwreaker back in his belt with its buddy.

They burst out of the narrow passage and into the main corridor, straight toward four figures.

Gunn froze. The men skidded to a stop.

'Drop,' Robert yelled as he raised the scatter gun. Gunn collapsed. He fired, shredding them to ribbons then yanked her up with his numb hand.

Thirteen shots left, four more dead bodies.

He took the lead, Gunn yelling instructions behind him. Every intersection had another wailing siren trying to numb him into submission with noise. The guns weighed him down; his lungs burned for air.

He was slowing.

His responses were fading, the scatter gun lowering as he fired. He took out a Ceeper's legs then had to fire a second time to kill him. The gun ran dry and he chucked it. Not the right weapon, not anymore. He pulled out the Deathwreakers. Five shots in his good left hand, four shots in his crippled right.

'Left, left,' Gunn yelled and Robert skidded to change direction. The wall became a large window through to the docking bay.

Gunn took the lead, running past the window, a cargo loader watching her. An overhead crane rumbled past.

The space doors gaped open. The magnetic containment was off. A vacuum.

Robert stopped.

'We can't go in there,' he gasped. Gunn swiped her access card at the airlock hatch but the panel flashed red after she swiped her card. She muttered and tossed the card aside. 'Escape pods.' She ran back the way they had come. Robert followed, more than happy to get away from the airless docking bay.

'What kind?' he wheezed, catching up to her. 'Stowmasters.'

'Hyperdrives?'

'No.' The word hung in the air for a moment. 'But I have a plan.'

Gunn zipped around the corner; a flash of light from her popper, the slump of a body to the floor. He turned the corner as she rounded the next, Popper flashing, voices yelling. He pushed faster, rounding the corner, finger squeezing the trigger before he registered the Ceepers ahead.

A Deathwreaker went dry. He dropped it. Four shots left.

Three ahead. The trigger depressed under his finger. Blood arced from a chest, a stomach then Gunn cried out.

Robert half turned as a hand grabbed his own, pushing it up and depressing his trigger finger.

The ceiling sparked and cracked, blinding Robert as he kicked out. The pressure dropped from his hand. The Deathwreaker died.

He glanced over his shoulder, breathing hard; four Ceepers on Gunn.

He turned back. His head rocked from a fist. He swung his own fists, sluggish as if in engine grease, while the Ceeper moved at light speed. Robert's eyes rattled from another blow then his back slammed into the wall and a hand squeezed his throat.

Robert gasped, choking as hot breath rushed past his ear. 'No one escapes the Circle, scum.'

'You're forgetting something,' Robert gasped, squeezing the words out.

He brought his right boot up, grabbed the Sgian Dubh. 'Yeah? What's that?'

Robert pulled the Dubh free and plunged it forward. 'I'm Scottish.'

His throat opened. The Ceeper leaned away, red soaking his stomach. He staggered back, his eyes rolled up and he fell.

'Slán go fóill.' *Bye for now.*

He turned back to Gunn. On the ground, Ceeper smashing her to a pulp, smoking bodies around them.

'Run,' she screamed, blood spraying with her words, before a fist smashed into her eye socket. 'Save them all!'

Robert felt the weight of the data crystal in his pocket. He didn't have to think twice.

He ran.

The alarms screamed. His footfalls boomed. The man looked up as Robert crashed into him. The floor banged into his head, ears ringing. He punched out, into thin air; hands grabbed his head, his hair, his eyes. He lunged the black shape over, smashed his knee forward, felt flesh sink inward; A loud exhale.

Robert rolled again. On top now, he smashed his forehead down on the head below him then used his fists, swinging again and again and again until the form beneath him felt limp.

It was only when Gunn shook his shoulder and he could feel his hoarse throat that he realised the screaming alarms had actually been him screaming.

He stared up at her bruised and bleeding face, his throat hoarse, knuckles prickling as if filled with glass, sweat dripping into his eyes. Then his gaze dropped to her hand on his shoulder.

'We're almost there,' she said softly, her voice all rounded comfort instead of its usual sharp tetchy self.

He dragged himself to his feet, legs leaden, right side throbbing, his whole body ready to crash.

Wall exploded by his head, showering him with dust. The ricochets rang out, deafening him. He pushed Gunn away. 'Go!'

He glanced a wave of black as he rounded the corner, bullets smashing into the walls around him. His right side burned with every step until they reached a blast door.

Gunn slammed her palm against a green button and the door dropped through the floor. Not a security door then. They pushed into a long and narrow room, pale red lights on the left, bright square white lights next to hatches on the right.

The door shut behind them. Gunn hit one of the white lights and it turned green. The hatch irised open and she bent to step through. Robert bent forward just as the blast door re-opened. People raced in, pistols up, searching for their target.

Robert dived through. 'Shut the hatch, shut the hatch!' Gunn dived into the cockpit. Her hands blurred across the controls.

The hatch shut. The capsule jerked forward, throwing Robert back and holding him against the hatch. 'Ummm,' he managed to squeeze out. It was just a few G's, but his ribs flexed under the load. 'Gunn?'

'Sorry,' she said. The pressure evaporated and Robert stumbled forward. The capsule was a small round space with bench seating and a nodule of a cockpit. Gunn filled the only pilot's chair. There were no straps in the seat.

No straps anywhere.

'Umm,' he repeated, searching every square inch of the pod again. 'Hang onto something,' she said.

Robert's eyes widened. 'Oh, shit.' He climbed onto a bench, wrapping his arms and legs around it in a tight hug, trying to remember basic training.; eyeballs in, vertical acceleration, blood to the feet okay, blood to the brain bad. He turned to put his feet to the back of the pod.

The capsule lurched forward. Robert cried out, eyes screwed shut, face buried into the bench, but the pull on his body faded and he realised it wasn't much more than one G, just a G completely arse about face. He lay down on the bench, yet 'down' was behind him, weak but steady fingers peeling him off the bench. His tired arms were already burning. He couldn't hold on much longer.

He raised his head an inch. Station booms and antennae intruded on the starlight beyond the cockpit. The stars shimmered slightly and he realised he was looking at the station's shields.

The shuttle jerked to the right and the ground fell out from behind him, a torque now trying to twist him off the bench. He buried his head back into the bench, fingernails digging into the flaking wood and held on with all his might. The acceleration shifted back behind him and slackened off.

'Where are we going?'

'Back in.' Her voice was rushed, hot, a breathless excitement that made Robert look up in panic. They were facing back toward the space station. In front an open door, and beyond, a large space filled with ships

.. the docking bay.

Robert's heart missed a gear, an explosion of power in his chest. 'What are you doing?' he yelled.

'I'm getting my ship back.'

The blood drained from Robert's face. He shook as the massive bay door grew larger and larger, filling the screen. The door jarred and rolled down. 'Gunn!'

'I see it.' She tweaked the controls. Robert's stomach lurched and he cried out. Details came into focus, individual Sakers and Sidewinders and the steel plates of the floor and then they were through, steel walls rushing past on all sides. Rows of ships zipped past until there were only two ahead, one of them a Gyr, one of them a beaten up Saker. Only then did he realise the escape pod didn't have a docking tube. There was no way to connect the two ships together.

He didn't have a remlok survival mask.

He couldn't stop the memories. Tongue boiling, eyes bloating in their sockets, the complete numbing of the nerves as they struggled to comprehend the lack of sensation.

He squeezed his eyes shut, trying to shut down his thoughts, but his arms shook and his voice squeaked out, 'We'll be sucked out into space!'

'Don't be stupid.'

'I can't do this,' Robert said but then the view out of the capsule window inverted. Walls spun past; a blur of vertigo. The distant stars came back into view, growing smaller and smaller through the narrowing bay doors.

'I can't do this,' he repeated, hyperventilating, each word a wail in its own right.

'Hold on tight,' she yelled.

Robert held the bench tighter and shook his head to stop the memories. 'Shit, shit, shit!'

The impact threw him from the bench and he slammed into the back wall. Pain ripped through his back and hips as his body crunched into the undulating shape of the wall.

The force holding him in place disappeared. For a moment he hung there, a weightless piece of stellar debris.

And then the whole capsule tilted around again and the ceiling rushed onto him and punched him back down to the ground.

Gunn kicked him awake. 'Get up. The bay door's closing.'

Robert struggled to all fours. His head pounded like a hyperdrive motivator in resonance, his hip throbbed and a hundred needles pierced his lungs with every breath. He waded through floating globules of blood to the rear hatch then stopped, shaking his head.

'No.'

Gunn growled. 'We'll die if we stay. We have to go. Now.' 'I can't go back out there. Not again.'

Gunn sounded surprised. 'You're scared.'

'I'm not. Scared. Of anything,' he said but his words came in short gasps.

'Afraid of a little vacuum? You call yourself a space pirate? More like a snivelling little girl.'

He could still taste the silent scream, the absolute emptiness. Mouth open, diaphragm down, but lungs completely empty. He stepped back up to the hatch, trembling. 'I'm not a Fate-forsaking girl,' he yelled.

Gunn shook her head. 'Men. It's like swimming except you don't sink so make your first kick a good one.'

Robert rocked back and forth. His fingers drummed blink code against his legs and either he was crying or his head was shaking because he could barely see her. He had to leave. He knew he couldn't stay, but no amount of logic could convince his legs to step forward. He thought of the vacuum and his brain seized, synapses shutting down, neurons stopping mid-flight.

Gunn took his hand in hers and squeezed. She looked into his eyes. She didn't have Business-Gunn eyes. She had normal-person eyes. 'You can do this. I'll go across first. Hold onto something tight and wait. Once I have the Saker's ramp open get your arse over there.' She dropped his hand and grabbed the release handle.

'Wait,' Robert yelled, a pressure filling his chest, crushing his heart, squeezing his lungs.

Gunn pulled the handle down. The hatch blew open.

A hurricane ripped at his clothes and fingers and he lost his grip on the wall. He tried to scream but the air raced from his mouth. Gunn disappeared through the hatch and he tumbled after her, barely catching the hatch before the wind died away.

He couldn't feel anything.

No air.

No sound.

No pressure.

It was happening again.

He turned, scrambled for the hatch, his arms reaching desperately, all his muscles moving together but disorganised, as if his brain had lost all coordination. His fingers shook. He couldn't get a firm grip. Gnarled fingers of dark panic stretched across his vision.

Thirty seconds. That's how long he had. That's how long he'd had last time. He'd been as near-dead as a person could have been. He'd been right there, salvation just out of reach, flailing and stretching and praying a silent scream as he'd watched the gash in the cruiser's hull, lights flashing from within, the cannon's controls waiting silently for their operator. He'd watched the gash knowing it would be the last thing he'd ever see…

There's no air in the pod.

He didn't recognise the cogent thought but knew it was true. The capsule was dead, as was he if he didn't turn around. His brain's commands seemed slow, a lag of seconds between thought and movement, but he did turn around.

Gunn stood two metres away, one arm wrapped around a ramp post, the other frantically waving him forward.

His tongue boiled, the roof of his mouth too. It was on fire, though it couldn't be because he was in a vacuum. The thought made him laugh, except that made the pain worse.

She wants you to come to her. She was dreamy, a beautiful goddess, a siren, calling him over. She wanted to have her way with him. She wanted to show him some immortal pleasure. Well, he sure wouldn't stand in her way.

Make your first jump a good one, said the Goddess. He knew he was going to die.

He couldn't feel any part of his body. His vision distorted, bending outward.

Gunn's arm grew longer. It swung up and down and then he was on the decking. Her arm was cylindrical and hard. Somewhere, something deep inside yelled two simple words: *Grab on*!

He wrapped two ballooning fists around the arm and he inched forward until he hit the boarding ramp.

Then he blacked out.

Chapter 15

Admiral McKowsky entered the pill-box bridge. He turned slowly to take in the near three-sixty degree panorama of space. For him, scanners and sensors weren't enough. He needed to see it for himself, to have a complete visceral understanding of a battle.

He watched as the rest of his forces arrived. The last of the frigates lumbered in from its jump point, forming up in an ever-growing INRA fleet. He shook his head at the sparse parade, an embarrassment to the McKowsky of fifty years ago. The McKowsky of today squared his shoulders as though the greatest military leaders of all time stood at his side. Leonidas, John Chard, James C Neill, Thomas McKowsky. History showed what a small group of committed individuals could do.

This was his moment; to save humanity, or die trying.

A squadron of Condor fighters flew from the frigate and docked with the Behemoth. The last of Criddoch's recruits, shoulder tapped from the Federation navy. More Condors appeared, brand new fighters appropriated from the Third Federation fleet.

The ship captain turned to McKowsky. 'Sir, another ship has just hypered in system; a Mark II Asp.'

Criddoch.

'Patch the link through,' McKowsky ordered. Across the sea of crewmen buried between couches and consoles, the main viewport shimmered and Criddoch's face filled the bridge. He was in a cockpit but still stiffened as if to salute.

'Sir,' Criddoch said.

'Report.'

'Transferring data now, no one is biting. The Alliance isn't making any moves, nor the Federation. Our Imperial spies were unaware of any massing of forces, beyond what is already deployed around the Emperor.'

McKowsky shook his head. He wasn't surprised. The Circle were buried deep in every single government in the galaxy. All it took was a few members in key high ranking positions, such as the Council of Admirals; small numbers, big influence.

Like we used to be and how we will be once again.

An officer pulled the ship captain aside. McKowsky saw a flashing red light. 'Problem, Captain?'

The captain turned and saluted. 'Sir we have more ships in bound.' An image of mottled space replaced Criddoch's face on the main screen, targeting brackets enclosing the distant ships.

McKowsky frowned. Everyone was accounted for. He stared, ready to order the ships' destruction if the captain showed any signs of dithering.

'Sir, they, they're our ships.'

McKowsky heard both fear and confusion in the man's voice. 'Why do you say that, Captain?'

'Sir, they are black ships, vintage circa 3250, impressive stealth technology, and they have the crimson stripe.'

McKowsky frowned. 'How many?'

'A full squadron, and an Imperial interdictor.'

His old heart skipped a beat. *Joseph, can it really be you?* How his old partner had survived his trip back to Achenar, McKowsky would never know but he couldn't wait to shake the old bastard's hand again. Another friend when needed the most; a good sign.

One of the bridge crew called up from his pit. 'Sir I'm getting strange readings from that interdictor.'

'Open the link,' the captain said.

'No response,' replied the crewman. The interdictor closed in. The squadron of INRA fighters were now visible as twinkling specks of light.

McKowsky stepped forward, a frown adding yet another crease to his forehead. 'Try again.'

'Nothing.'

McKowsky's frown deepened. Joseph wouldn't have kept him waiting like this, at least the Joseph he remembered.

'Criddoch, run a close scan on that Interdictor.'

Criddoch's Asp flew into view, running a bee line for the ageing, dagger shaped Interdictor.

McKowsky waited, gripping his cane tight. The Asp flew closer. The Interdictor maintained its course.

The fighters didn't.

They moved as one, a swarm of hornets, awoken and angry, opening fire on Criddoch.

'It's a trap,' McKowsky yelled. 'Destroy them! Fire all weapons!'

* * *

Robert jerked awake. He sucked in a deep breath; coughed. His mouth flaked away as he breathed. He tried to turn to spit out whatever clogged his throat but he couldn't move. His eyes snapped open. Bright red light, everything tinted in hues of blood.

He was in the Saker, strapped into his acceleration couch. And that was his blood he was looking through. Burst capillaries in his eyes, because of the vacuum. He knew the signs.

Red stars swirled past the cockpit. Gunn sat in her couch, facing him. She stared at him.

'You're not blind,' she said.

Robert shuddered and tried to reply, but couldn't. She kept staring at him. Not like an interrogation, not like her eyes were a body scanner recording every detail for later evidence. She was staring into his eyes, her pupils fixed, searching for something.

'What?' he managed at last.

She turned away, nestling back into her couch. 'Nothing.'

Now he watched her, hands moving across the touch screens. She looked like she was trying really hard to concentrate on the console. He unstrapped and tested his body out, arms, hands, fingers, legs, toes, back. He tried to breathe deeply but wheezed like an asthmatic, struggling to get a full chest of air. 'You fed me water.'

She didn't even look at him. 'And bandaged your eyes.'

'How long was I out?'

'A day or so.' She shrugged as if it were no big deal.

Robert swallowed. It still hurt, but not as bad as the last time.

He steeled himself for the big question. The last thing he remembered was the docking ramp.

'You saved my life?'

She nodded, still looking at the controls. They were in hyperspace, there was nothing for her to control, yet she did her best to look busy.

'Why?' he asked.

When she finally spoke her voice whispered, low and quiet, the voice of a woman talking to a man, not the voice of a scarred intelligence operative talking to a pirate. 'You saved mine.'

'I don't leave my people behind.'

Her jaw clenched but she kept staring at her controls. 'I'm one of your people?'

Robert studied her. 'I don't leave my people behind,' he repeated.

'I guess we're even, then' she said.

'I guess so.'

She didn't say any more. Robert stepped through the hatch to the mess. He could see a bit better. His eyes would be fine in a few days; with top level medical support, anyway.

He grabbed a hydration gel pouch, stopped, turned back, grabbed a second one and returned to the cockpit. He lobbed one at her and she grabbed it as it floated past. She sucked it dry before he could strap back in. He broke the seal on his pouch and put it to his lips as she wriggled back around to face him.

'You could have walked away from me. You didn't. You could have left Villist to the Imperials. You didn't.'

A weight settled in Robert's stomach and the pouch lost its attraction. 'I think I see where this is going.' Not thirsty anymore he sucked on the gel anyway, just to give himself space from the ensuing conversation. He gagged and brought the fluid back up. His throat burned like he had just downed a shot of whiskey, but not in a good way.

Gunn pressed on, oblivious to his pain. 'I think Villist scared you. I think you were scared of the responsibility of having so many lives in your hands. I think that's why you went back to piracy, where there was no responsibility. But you lead your own clan and you fight so hard to protect them and you're prepared to go to war to defend them. That is just as much responsibility.'

Robert watched her, lips sealed shut. He wanted more than anything to make her shut up but he couldn't move a single muscle.

'It doesn't make any sense. You feel such pain in your losses, all the civilians you failed to save, yet as a pirate you have killed so many more innocents.' She shook her head. 'I don't understand you. Can you not see the damage you do? Are you trying to undo the good you did at Villist? Is that what it is?'

The weight in Robert's stomach sunk him deeper into his couch. Finally he managed to make his mouth work. 'Do you remember me asking if you knew how a father justified piracy to his six year old son?'

Gunn didn't say anything. She leant forward, chin on her fist as if she wanted to hear the answer.

'The father explains that the Federation was once a great state, where the state helped the poor, where everyone had an equal chance at a good life, but that the Federation had become a bloated corporate controlled mess where the poor fell between the gaps. The role of piracy was to steal from the rich who could afford it and supply it to the poor.'

'You give it away for free?' A glimmer of her normal disbelief and smugness curled into one. 'I find that hard to believe.'

'Of course not. Equipping a team to attack and pillage the ships of the rich is an expense, so these expenses have to be forwarded on. If the pirate goes out of business, the poor don't get their shipments. It's a win-win for everyone except the rich, who can afford another shipment anyway.'

'Sounds like a bunch of bullshit.'

'It's more honest than your life,' Robert said. 'I loved my dad and I loved my mum and we went to sleep every night with a clear conscience. Could you say that? I still remember when I was ten, the blockade of a planet on the Imperial border. They were starving. The Empire was punishing the whole population for the crimes of their government. We snuck in with our stolen grain. Yes, they paid maximum value in goods they didn't need under a blockade. They didn't care we were pirates, they were just thankful they got to eat that night.'

Gunn nodded as if she were absorbing it. Then she turned away. 'I don't understand you.'

Robert rubbed his throat, trying to massage away the pain. 'Well understand this. Once we've handed over the coordinates, I'm out.'

Her head snapped back. 'You're out?'

'I'm out. Like you said, my clan needs me. They're being caught, arrested and slaughtered. I need to help them. I thought I was doing that with you, and maybe I have, but you have your coordinates and you have INRA. You don't need me anymore. You're heading for a space battle. I'll be a liability.'

Gunn's eyes were wide and still while her mouth chewed away. 'You can't be serious,' she said finally. 'After everything you've done, you're just going to turn away?'

Robert worked his jaw, pursed his lips. He lowered his eyes. 'Look, I just want to get to my boys, okay? I've paid for my mistakes. I don't need to go on a crusade to remedy them. I can't lose anyone else. I just

.. can't.'

'What about the galaxy?' she paused. 'What about me?' Robert turned away.

'I was wrong,' she said, her voice cold and hard, stripped free of any human nuance. 'I understand you completely.'

Robert didn't know what to say to that.

* * *

Gunn lowered the Saker onto the docking bay deck and shut down. She stayed in her couch. Coolant hissed from exhaust ports. The engine cycled down, vibrating through a rough patch. The hull clicked and sighed as it cooled.

Her gaze drifted to the empty co-pilot chair. Garry would have filled the silence with a dumb smart-guy comment, but he'd shown his true colours and she'd done what had to be done.

Two men waited for her at the bottom of the boarding ramp. They bellowed out their identifications then whisked her deeper into the station. She passed over the copy of the Circle data then found a sonic shower. She scrubbed her body clean then washed and conditioned her hair twice. She had physical and mental filth to wash away. The sonics dried her skin. She dressed into Alliance blues, a pressure suit with the Alioth rings on the breast. She sealed the front zipper and sighed in contentment. It felt good to be back.

She tied her hair in a loose, low pony, tidied up her face and headed to Command and Control. The station commander greeted her. His big calloused hand shook hers. His droopy moustache bobbled as he thanked her for her hard work. He guided her to his office.

Trotsky's face hovered above the link emitter. His brow was furrowed and his eyes seemed intently focused on her, though that could have been an effect of the link.

'I'll leave you to it,' the Commander said. He closed the hatch behind him.

'Report,' Trotsky said. No thank you, no hello, no 'great to see you back in the blues'.

Gunn glanced around the office. A desk, a hologram of a middle aged woman, the wife presumably, and a lone pad stylus. No decoration, no loose stationery.

'I'm alive,' she said finally.

Trotsky's jaw clenched, his cheeks dimpling. 'The pirate?'

Gunn didn't hesitate. 'Trashed.'

'INRA?'

'They've narrowed Soontill's location to three possible systems.'

'We need to get to Soontill before they do. I have approval from the Council of Admirals to conscript every available military vessel. Where should I send the fleet?'

She couldn't stop her glance away from the link. Trotsky inhaled. 'You don't know?'

'We have the same data as INRA. We're still processing it. Even then we'll still have three different locations to choose from.'

Trotsky leaned forward until only his was visible. 'Have you been drinking?'

Gunn flinched back, angry. 'Of course not.' Though ironically it was being undercover with the Circle which had helped her achieve that.

He leant back. 'If we are ever going to have equality with the Empire and Federation we need that Thargoid technology. Don't screw this up Gunn. If this turns into another Thomson's World, you're done.'

Trotsky disappeared and with him her faith in her cause.

Chapter 16

Robert woke to rain; hot drizzle. He opened his eyes. The sun peeked through fast moving clouds. He felt around. He was on a soft pliable hill.

Then the smell hit him. Garbage.

Each odour out-ponged the last. Petrified shit, decomposing food, degrading algae swarms.

He sat up, retching. He was on top of a big mound of rubbish, surrounded by similar mounds of rubbish, spreading out in all directions to the horizon.

Gulls flocked to the east. Hydraulics whirred nearby, a compactor truck a few mounds over.

He patted himself down. His clothes were soaking. The crystal was gone from his pocket but he still had the statue. No fresh bullet or knife wounds but his head pounded from Gunn's ambush. He looked up to the sky, big blobs of rain splashing against his face.

No scream of turbines. Gunn was long gone. The clouds raced along, working to their own plans, absolutely free.

Robert was free too. He pursed his lips. Free. The one thing he had wanted these last few weeks. Sitting there alone on a pile of refuse the concept no longer held much excitement.

He half slid half skidded down to the sodden ground. The surrounding mounds were a mess of rusting car components, plastics and rotting food. He almost tripped over an axle.

A rubbish field like this would have attendants, somewhere. He'd just have to find them and convince them to give him access to a link. He had a few calls to make.

He headed east.

* * *

He passed children playing amongst the refuse, running, yelling, chasing each other with sticks. They were playing Circle and Pirates. The Ceepers looked to be winning.

The clouds cleared and the sun beat down. Sweat soaked his pressure suit by the time he stumbled into the main street of town.

The metallic sounds of a hammer on steel rang out. Robert glanced across to a ramshackle steel barn where a man bent over a wheel, beating it into shape.

As Robert's footsteps crunched on gravel, the man stopped, his gaze tracking Robert as he walked by.

A small cottage leaned on settling foundations, its weatherboards rotten and crumbling. Beyond it was a pharmacy, 'Steve's Refrigeration' and another cottage, two small kids sitting on the deck weaving flax leaves.

A shot rang out.

Robert stepped back, hand reaching for his empty belt. A man flew backward out a door, scrambled up, fired a lead thrower back through the door and ran to a row of hover platforms. He jumped onto one, a board just big enough for two feet, leant against the handles and powered down the main drag, covering Robert in dust.

Two men leapt from the door, fired their own lead throwers and ran after him.

Robert watched them go, eyebrows raised. They weren't shooting at him. It felt strange. He shrugged and followed the murmur of voices up the street. Kids squealed in the distance, echoed by barking dogs.

He turned back to the door. 'The Owl and Duck' was hand painted above the entrance; an inn.

He leant through the entrance, the door dangling from a single hinge.

A bar stretched across the far wall, an older man standing behind it, watching Robert. Two men sat at a booth. The other tables were empty. A media feed played on a three-dee at the end of the bar.

Robert's heart stopped.

Behind the bar was a poster, held to the wooden wall with nails. The poster was of the Villist statue, a bronze Robert reaching for the sky. Emblazoned on the poster top and bottom were the words 'Villist Diaspora: 'We will remember.''

Robert stepped back outside, breathing fast. He couldn't escape it. Even in the literal rubbish bin of the galaxy he couldn't be free of it.

He glanced up the street. Everything else seemed closed. He could hear winches pulling on ropes, gulls squawking for scraps. Perhaps the wharf would be safer. Not much chance of a link there though.

He stepped back inside. Maybe they wouldn't recognise him. He walked up to the bar, wooden floorboards creaking under his weight.

The barman had mean eyes and a scar which ran from his right cheek to under his white beard; a hard man.

'You got a link?' Robert asked.

The barman tilted his misshapen head to the left. 'Out back.'

'Thanks.' Robert stepped away.

The barman's eyes narrowed. He stared at Robert for a second too long. 'You gonna order something?'

Robert paused. 'I'd kill for a coffee.'

'It's synth.'

'Okay.' He logged his ID onto the link. He was in the CD-73 253 system, the planet Tarlak. First he sent a grovelling apology to Malin and asked for her forgiveness. Not that he'd get it. She was a hard lady who had literally butchered people for less and profited from the results. Human meat had its markets.

Next he messaged his ships, the Vintage Flier, Barrel of Ale, Sherwood, The Healer, Despondence, Maximum Destruction, Platinum Alacrity, Jeff's Rig and Jordan's old ship the Vista Oculta. Then he messaged everyone's personal accounts. He asked everyone to get in contact so he could make sure they were okay.

Of course after what they had probably been through, perhaps they wouldn't want to get in contact.

A message came through immediately from Jessin McNaught, captain of the Vintage Flier and a real hard bugger. He and his crew were alive, tracking a Circle prison transport through a nearby dark system. Robert ordered them to divert to pick him up. They'd tackle it together.

He signed off. He thought of Gunn then growled at himself. He had what he wanted. He was free to gather up his boys and unite them.

But she hadn't killed him. She'd defied her orders. Why? He wanted to link her, but no, she wouldn't take the call.

Why did he care? The galaxy wasn't his problem. Never was. Whenever he tried to protect the galaxy the galaxy dumped on him.

He returned to the bar and paid for the coffee – barely passable – and an upstairs room. He needed a bath.

* * *

The balding man stopped midstride passing Robert's booth.

Robert slunk down on the seat, trying to hide behind his mug. Any chance of peace was gone now.

'I'll be the son of a 'goid, Robert Garry!' The man waved his arm to his buddies two booths down. 'Guys, its Robert bloody Garry,' he called, loud enough for the whole town to hear. His words were giddy. He sat down without invitation, sliding in too close. His friends rushed over, all of them mid-forties, all of them probably Villist survivors.

The balding man pried Robert's hand from his mug and shook it.

'A bloody honour, sir, a bloody honour.' The others crowded in, eyes and mouths wide in disbelief.

Robert pulled his hand back, shrank further into his seat, glancing from one face to another. 'How many of you are there?'

'Not many now a days,' said the sandy haired man. 'We came out here after the massacre. The corporation needed men, we needed houses and jobs. Most of us have moved on.'

'We made a statue,' said the brown haired man, beaming. 'Made out of scrap, but we got the look right.' He nudged his buddy and they butted fists.

Robert just watched them, lost for words. Now he knew why Gunn had dumped him here, alive.

'That's

.. that's great news.'

'What was it like?' the balding man asked. He leaned in close. 'Smashing those Imperial bastards?'

'Scary.' The answer was sudden, honest. 'I'd never been more scared in my life.' The men leaned back, glanced at each other. Robert kept going. Maybe they'd lean back far enough they'd go away.

'There were over seventy Imperial ships in orbit, most of them in good fighting condition. My ships were barely holding together at the fuse welds.

Some of them had failing life support, the crew breathing stale air. I had to dump a dead helmsmen from his couch at one point.' He shook his head. 'Each time an Imperial ship fired back I felt absolute terror, knowing a lucky shot would take out any one of my ships.'

His vision blurred as he thought back. 'Have you ever seen a person on fire in zero-gee? There is no up for the flame. It burns evenly across your whole body; your hair, your face, your feet, your fingers, every part of you. There's nothing you can do.'

'Seventy battles, that what we had. Each one lived at maximum, knowing that at any moment you would watch some of your ships and crew die. One of my corvettes lost its last laser. I ordered it to retreat but instead it rammed the Imperial, both of them disappearing in the blink of an eye.' He paused to breathe. 'It was scary.'

The men sat in silence. They looked everywhere except at his face. One of them coughed.

'All the feeds said you couldn't feel fear. 'Robert the Fearless'.'

'They lied.' *About a lot of things. The Federation needed a hero. They paraded me and put up statues and made me a galactic celebrity and for what?* 'So who mines the mineral now?' The negotiations had been leaning toward a fifty-fifty split. Half Imperial, half Federation, happy galaxy.

The men glanced at each other again, frowning. 'Some Federation company, I think,' said the bald man. 'Most people are just trying to rebuild.'

Robert nodded, disappointed but not surprised, and sipped at his coffee.

The bald man opened his mouth to speak when Jessin burst through the front door. Robert bumped the table as he tried to stand, ushering the men out of the way.

'Sir,' Jessin said, making eye contact. He stepped forward.

Robert grabbed his shoulder and hugged him. 'Good to see you, you son of a bitch.' He pumped Jessin's fist then pushed him to the door. 'Let's go.'

Steve the Slitter, Hamish and Vaughn stood on the street in a semi-circle, hands on their holsters.

Robert slapped each of them on the back. 'Where's the ship?' he asked.

Jessin pointed down the road. 'Out in the garbage fields. Nice and discrete.'

Hamish spun a Colt from his second holster and handed it grip first to Robert. Down the road two kids chased an automated ring world out into the garbage fields. Otherwise the street was deserted.

The sun darkened an instant before he heard the roar of reversing turbines. Robert looked up as a black hole coalesced in his guts.

A Saker screamed to a halt above them.

'Go!' Robert yelled, shoving Jessin forward. They split up, running for the cover beneath the shop verandas.

Robert climbed a railing after Hamish. They ran along a shop front, dust crunching underfoot and vaulted over the railing to the next.

The Saker dropped closer to the road, engines whipping burning dust over Robert.

'Attention, this is the Circle of Independent Elite Pilots,' boomed a voice from the Saker. We are here to apprehend four members of the Garry Pirate clan. Two thousand credits to anyone who helps us make the arrest.'

Robert's black hole deepened, swallowing his heart. Shit.

He leapt another railing and onto a shop porch. A man raced out the door. Robert slowed. A Villist survivor? The man straightened, turned, a rising pistol in his hand.

Robert fired the Diplomat. Point blank, maximum damage. The man collapsed. Robert jumped past.

Smaller engines piped up against the backdrop of the Saker. Across the road, men piled out of a repair shop. The last of the men tumbled forward, an axe in his back. 'Run Robert, Run!' yelled someone from inside.

Robert heard voices down the road. Men ran from the inn. Half of them armed, half of them not. They fought amongst themselves, pot shots flying past Robert.

They sprinted onto the street,

The road exploded in a geyser of dust and dirt. Robert glanced backward.

The Saker dropped between the shop fronts. Light danced across the laser's emitter.

The beam shot between Robert and Jessin, throwing up a wall of dust. 'Into the fields,' Robert yelled. He turned around. His foot found purchase. He started running.

The Saker roared overhead; too big to fit between the piles. Garbage exploded to his left. He ducked, twisted. He fired the Diplomat.

A bullet zipped past his head. He fired back, The Diplomat clicked empty.

The Saker zoomed past, blotting out the sun. Its laser ripped into the ground, nearly slicing Steve in half.

A crusher lumbered into view; cab at the front, compactor at the back. It swung around, big knobbly wheels crunching the soil then reversed into a mound, blocking the path ahead.

Robert's eyes widened.

Bullets pinged against the crusher. Hamish cried out, thrown forward.

His shoulder was red.

No one shoots at my boys. No one.

'Get to the ship,' he yelled as he fired back towards the Saker. 'I've got this bugger.'

Direct hit.

The Saker's laser screamed through the air, ploughing into a garbage pile. The cockpit exploded in a puff of smoke.

Robert ducked away, his hair standing on end. Then he heard the groan.

The garbage mound to the left reared over him, collapsing like an avalanche. 'Shit,' he yelled, rolling. A gesture terminal slammed into his knee. An MTV levitator smacked his face.

He slid back, metal cutting his back. He lay still, gasping.

An explosion screamed behind him and a ball of heat slammed into his back, tossing him forward. His back burned, thousands of tiny pinchers digging into his skin. Rubbish and burning fuel rained down around him. He kept running. Down the mound, onto the path and back up the next mound. Then he stopped to search the sky.

The cockpit had exploded before the crash. The pilot had ejected.

Robert was going to find him.

There, to the right, a wing suit, just about to touch down. Robert skidded and slid down piles of cars, across a path up and up a mound of food processors and rotting foot cartridges.

The pilot was folding back his wings, pulling off the suit. He turned, saw Robert. His pupils dilated. His legs tensed, half turned to leap away-

Robert crashed into him.

He punched the man, then head-butted him. Blood burst from the nose. Robert hit him again, and again. 'Why can't you leave me alone?' he yelled.

The pilot fell back, dragging Robert with him. They rolled down the mound onto the side of a crusher, working its way through the garbage.

Robert grabbed the pilot's collar and held him above the crushing teeth and rams.

'We never did anything to you,' Robert roared, shaking the man. Blood ran from both the man's nostrils, one of his eyes was puffed closed. His jaw was dislodged, maybe broken.

'Why can't you leave us alone? Tell me!' Everywhere he went, no matter what he did, the Circle were there. He couldn't protect his men twenty four hours a day every day for the rest of their lives. He was just one man. He couldn't sustain that pressure. He'd crack. And he'd fail. His arms shook, wild with anger. 'Tell me!'

Blood frothed from the pilot's mouth. 'Your team just attacked a cruise liner. Fifteen dead, twenty injured, all for a few tonnes of luxuries? The Circle will never let that lie. Never. Never!'

Robert watched this man, so defiant, so ready to die. How did you beat such fanaticism?

He dropped the pilot. He landed with a clang, head lolling over the edge. Robert stood over him. 'You're done here. Go home. Tell your masters to leave the Garry Clan alone. We're the least of your problems. You're busy trying to rewrite civilisation.'

The pilot's eyes narrowed, glanced sideways then back. 'We've caught his Highness hook, line and sinker. You'll never stop us.'

'Whatever. Just keep my clan out of it.' Robert turned away.

Pain shredded through his shoulder. He was tumbling; sky, soil, sky, soil, round and round. He flopped to the ground, lungs squeezed dry.

He lay there, stunned, shoulder burning; the shriek of a repulsion board, the grumbling crusher, police sirens, another bullet zinging past, this one just missing.

Move!

He rolled over, pushed up. His shoulder screamed, lava washing through the muscle.

There was an instant of numbness, a lack of sensation. Then the pain came.

It came in waves, big rolling balls of fire, washing through him again and again, a tidal wave, destroying everything in its path, nerve endings withering under the fire.

Robert screamed.

He sunk to his knees, clutching his stomach. Blood poured through his fingers as he covered the crater.

Dad had the same injury. *I'm going to die like Dad.* He started giggling.

He felt lightheaded.

The ground crashed into his head. He rolled onto his back. He needed a son to come and try, but fail to save him; a son to sing the promise with him; a son to cry over his corpse.

But all wars must end. And so too must all men.

A cold shiver racked his body. His fingers stiffened.

The world darkened, grey to brown to black.

Robert Garry died.

Chapter 17

The Architect sat at his desk, watching the relayed feed from the bridge of Commander Tybalt's ship. The hyperspace vector faded returning the viewport to darkness. Tybalt pressed buttons on his consoles then small orange boxes appeared on the viewport, bracketing invisible bodies.

It was the right system. They were too far away to see the mass of ships around the inner planet but he didn't need to. The media feeds were abuzz with the tour. His Highness was certainly creating excitement.

Ships zipped out of hyperspace before the viewport, filling space until the Circle's fleet had assembled. Over two hundred ships, all but five were small fighters, the best pilots the Circle had. If everything went to plan they wouldn't be needed, just the five Starburst ships with their forged identities.

The huge bridge was quiet. The Architect thought it ironic that a society based on slaves would develop such huge ships that could be piloted by a single person.

The smaller ships fired their engines and spread out across space, their engine trails a plasma-blue flower; a symbol of new life and new beginnings.

The Architect watched Tybalt. He sat very still, almost serene in his acceleration couch. Then he reached for the new console that the Circle technicians had installed.

The Starburst controls.

Four switches, four buttons and a master toggle. Tybalt hit the first switch. The lights dimmed for a moment and the engine whir dropped an octave before building back up. The button flashed green. One connection made. The viewport adjusted, panning through space to another Imperial Explorer. A plasma coupling pulsed between the two ships.

Tybalt flipped the last three switches, one at a time, allowing the engine to catch itself until all five ships were connected.

The Architect could feel the pent up energy even from over the link. Tybalt's arms rose, a prayer perhaps, and he puffed his chest out, almost as if the energy of the Starburst filled him, making him fizz like a bomb on the verge of critical mass.

Then Tybalt flicked the switches and the energy died away. He shrunk back into his seat.

The Architect fell back into his own seat. The final test was complete. No turning back.

Tybalt head in system to make history.

If humanity survived the next Thargoid invasion, the Architect thought, they would look back and say this was the defining moment, where humanity united its strength and was ultimately able to defeat the Thargoids.

The Architect moved in his chair, distracted. If it didn't work, Tybalt would be killed. If not there, then against the Thargoid fleets as humanity was slowly crushed like an escape pod in a black hole. All the pilots were volunteers. The Architect had personally asked each of them. They wanted to go down fighting, like any true pilot.

The Architect returned his gaze to the viewport. There was nothing but empty space between Tybalt and his target. Nothing would be able to stop him.

* * *

He floated above New Aberdeen, weightless, care-free, jubilant. He was in a vacuum but he could breathe. His whole body sung. He was a space creature, born to the vacuum's discomforts. New Aberdeen speared away from him, no, he speared away from New Aberdeen. He was flying. He spread out his arms and soared across the cosmos, faster than light, faster than hyperspace. He stopped above a dead world. Soontill, said a voice in his head. But he did not know this planet. Then he left it behind, flying again, faster and faster. He saw a Long Range Cruiser firing at a space station. He saw Imperial pirates and the plots of Bastards. Words hovered about him, keeping pace with his epic journey. Your Highness, read the words. Your Imperial Majesty, the Circle. But even the words could not keep pace with him forever and they fell behind. He flew into a swarm of faces. Some of them old, his father and mother, Malin and Leo, some of them new, some of them nameless, Imperial soldiers and Circle pilots he had killed. Some of the people had no faces, just a presence, people he had killed but never seen. His journey stopped above a blue and green planet; smaller than Earth but with a denser core and similar gravity. A net of Imperial ships surrounded the planet, the greatest fleet mankind had ever seen. But the fleet was disappearing, one ship at a time until there was nothing left but the planet. The Emperor was there, sitting by the side of a stream, a fishing rod in his hand. He draped one leg over the other, the tips of his cloak dangling in the water. 'There's nothing biting,' the Emperor said. Robert leant forward to check. The fish swam in their thousands, nearly choking the water. He turned to the Emperor, confused, but the Emperor was gone. Instead the Crown Prince was fishing. He wasn't in court clothes. He wore a woolly parka and a water proof suit. He stood in the river, fish tickling his legs as they swam past. He had the same rod as the Emperor. 'There's nothing biting,' the Crown Prince said. Then the planet exploded, like a supernova, but he was a space creature and used to such events. The glare faded and the planet separated into five points, five pulsing points.

Starbursts.

* * *

Robert awoke.

My boys! He jerked upward. His stomach burned and he clutched the bullet wound. Tender, but fused. He eased back down onto his narrow white bed, brain trying to catch up. There was a closed plassteel door to the right, a drab white wall to the left. There were no windows. There were no chairs.

By his right shoulder was an array of hospital gear – fluid bags, sensors, beeping lights, a graph of his pulse.

By his left shoulder stood the two morticians.

Brown and Blond.

FEDSOD.

They stared down at him, almost asleep in their stillness.

Robert sighed, sagging into his pillow. 'I suppose you've been waiting for me to wake up so you can dish out some payback. It's too bad you got here so late. If you had found me earlier you could have watched me die.'

'We did watch you die,' Brown said with his usual calm demeanour. 'Those were our Vipers. Your crew shot the Sidewinder but they didn't have any medical gear. We raced you here and got the docs to do their business and get you back to life.'

Robert's free hand moved under the covers to the wound. He felt a small indentation, like a filled-in ravine. It hurt less lying down. He glanced from Blond – skin wrinkled around his dancing eyes, mouth trying to hide a snarl – to Brown, plain and unreadable.

'Where are my boys now?'

Brown shrugged. 'They said they needed to catch up with a ship.'

The prisoner transport.

'And where is 'here'?'

'Somewhere safe,' Brown said. Robert wasn't sure if they shared the same definition of safe. 'Somewhere where we don't have to worry about the police.'

Robert exhaled and closed his eyes, a wave of fatigue rolling over him. He took a few seconds to re-gather. 'I don't suppose you're going to let me go?' He couldn't help the hope in his voice. Stranger things had happened.

Brown kept staring at him as he pulled a pad from his pocket. 'It's quite the record you have here. After Villist they threw enough medals at you to sink a harvesting platform. You'd only been promoted to captain for two days before you went AWOL.'

Robert pressed into the pillow. He remembered Brown's feelings about deserters. He raised a weak arm. 'I can explain.'

Blond spoke finally, leaning down to get right in Robert's face. 'You can't explain desertion away asshole. You're a traitor and you're going to pay.' Brown pulled Blond back. Blond straightened his cufflinks. This time they were bright green. Then he corrected the fabric hanging from his collar.

'What my colleague here is trying to say,' said Brown, 'Is that although we are bitterly disappointed in your actions seven years ago, I have seen enough in this record and of your actions lately to forgive that lapse in your judgement; for a price.'

'You're forgetting the thousands I murdered as a pirate.' He wasn't even sure why he said it, but he didn't regret it. A kid he told the story to had worshipped him as a hero. A murderer as a hero…

Brown swiped his finger across the pad. He glanced at Blond who had returned to his upright silent state.

'Interestingly there is no mention in Federation Intelligence records of a

Pirate Garry. You've committed no crimes against the Federation; which brings me back to why we are all here.'

Brown cleared his throat and puffed out his chest, 'Are you still a citizen Robert?'

Robert had to think about it. He had never committed piracy against the Federation. He had always told himself he had done too much damage already. Was that just another lie or was he simply trying to remove the Federation from his life completely? Had he even been in a Federation system since he'd gone AWOL? 'I think so,' he said finally.

Brown glanced at Blond, who shook his head. Brown chewed his lip and turned back to Robert. 'You know why we are here, don't you?'

'The Starburst.'

Brown smiled, nodded. 'Right, the Starburst. We want it back. I think that's fair enough. We did design, test and build it after all. What do you think?'

Robert coughed, closed his eyes, breathed. The pain in his abdomen kept building as his body awoke. 'That's fair.'

'Now our investigations have stalled. We know the Circle has it. We know they are about to use it. But we can't just go and tell the Empire. That would cause the war you, we all, want to stop. So we need your help to find it and retrieve it and to do it quietly. Do you know where it is?'

Robert closed his eyes. His dream replayed in the back of his head, flittering glimpses of events. But he remembered that it had made sense at the time. 'Yes.'

'Are you going to tell us where it is?' Robert nodded.

'On two conditions.'

Blond sucked in a breath to start a tirade but Brown raised a flat palm. 'List the conditions.'

'Once we find the Starburst I need to borrow it for a bit. Then you can have it for keeps.'

'Unacceptable,' spat Blond. 'That is highly classified equipment. We can't let it get into the hands of a pi—'

Brown put a hand on Blond's shoulder, silencing him. 'Continue.'

'You let me go in and get the weapon for you, with some help. If you barge in there with a fleet they'll escape and who knows what might happen.'

Brown looked up to the right, down to the left, his mouth moving like he was chewing over a morsel that he couldn't quite decide tasted good or not. 'I accept your conditions with my own condition.'

Robert snorted, smiling despite himself. 'Go.'

'We do things your way, but my colleague and I will accompany you.'

Robert only needed a second. He didn't have a choice and maybe a few extra bodies would help. 'Okay. Get me a link. I need to call some friends.' He pulled off the bed covers. He was in a hospital gown. He cringed as he stood, then followed Brown and Blond to a link terminal. He dialed in Gunn's ID. There was a delay as the link transmission jumped from relay to relay. Finally she appeared; her face drawn lines and narrowed eyes, her lips thin and white.

'It's not the Emperor,' he blurted out before she could yell at him.

'What?'

'Think about it. The Emperor is an old man, he's going to die soon anyway. Killing him wouldn't make a difference.'

Gunn stared at him across the link, eyebrows raised, waiting, not spitting venom at him.

'You didn't hear about the Fort Donald's attack? Look it up. The Circle want humanity to be a strong, unified civilisation, but who would lead that civilisation when the Emperor dies?'

Gunn's eyes widened. 'The Crown Prince.'

'-who cares more about fishing than war. He's a pushover. He won't handle the Thargoids-'

'But if you kill the Crown prince ..' 'The second in line takes power.'

'Hesketh,' Gunn said, a trace of awe in her voice. 'The Circle want to kill the Crown Prince so that when the Emperor dies Hesketh will lead humanity.'

'And I know where they'll do it.'

Gunn's eyes focused. 'Where?'

'We looked at his tour remember? Lagging the Emperor's by a few weeks, except the Emperor got delayed and the Crown Prince made a delay to match. He's at Delta Phoenicis.'

'How do you know that?'

Robert smiled. 'The third planet in the system is a water world. It's a fishing resort. It's right in line with his tour.'

Gunn's mouth dropped. 'How did you figure this all out?'

He shrugged. 'The Circle caught up with me again. They let some things slip. He mentioned 'His Highness', which is the honorific of a Prince, not 'His Imperial Majesty', the honorific of an Emperor. Plus he used a fishing metaphor. It all fell into place.' He didn't mention the dream that had tied it all together. He wasn't sure if that would strengthen his case or not.

Gunn's mouth moved a split moment before the link relayed the words. 'Bugger me.'

'Pick me up,' he said before he could stop himself.

Her teeth held her lower lip. She half smiled. She was light years away but she felt right next to him. 'Where are you?'

Robert looked up at Brown, who transmitted their coordinates. 'I'm in hospital; took a bit of a tumble. Come get me.'

'Okay.'

'Hurry.'

'Okay.' She signed off. The projector went dark.

Blond huffed. 'Look at you two love birds. You guys have a tiff?'

'Shut up,' Robert snapped. 'I need to send one more message.' He began typing:

You know the name, you know the legend. If you want a piece, meet at the Junction in four days.

He sent it as an open message to the underground channel feed, the Bounty Hunter Daily and then sent it to every pirate, smuggler and low-brow associate he knew. Hopefully some of them would answer. Malin wouldn't though, and she was his strongest ally; had been. Hopefully she hadn't poisoned everyone against him.

'Okay,' he said shutting down the link. 'Let's go save the galaxy.'

* * *

Robert wriggled down the air lock tube into Gunn's Saker. He turned, pushed down and landed. She stood a foot away, arms folded across her chest, hair up but loose so it didn't pull on her face. She'd ditched the Circle's black outfit for an Alioth navy one piece, a dressed up blue pressure suit with insignia, Velcro pockets and a utility belt. It was a tight, form fitting number.

It looked good. Real good.

He wondered why he'd never seen her like that before. She dropped her arms from her chest, eyes still locked on his.

'Umm, hi,' he said, head bowed but eyes watching hers, ready for any sudden movements. He had no idea what was going on back there. She could have changed her mind on the way to the rendezvous. She was dangerous to be around. Just like Malin.

'Thanks,' she said. It was soft, almost meek, perhaps her version of an apology.

'For what?'

'For coming back. To me.'

Robert's cheeks warmed. 'You're welcome.' He gazed into her eyes for a half microsecond before she pulled away.

'So you figured out the assassination plot all by yourself huh?'

'And I know where Soontill is too, but we can get to that later.'

'How?'

'I'm a pirate. I steal stuff-'

'And kill anyone who tries to stop you. I know,' she said with a straight face. 'But you're not a pirate. I left a pirate on that garbage world. A pirate wouldn't have come back to me.'

'How do you know that?'

'I know things. About people.'

Robert imagined she was probably right. When you were undercover all you ever did was watch people. Watch and learn, watch and learn and then maybe one day arrest them.

'I forgive you,' he said. Her shoulders loosened. She leant forward and her arms swayed as if she couldn't decide which way to move next. Then she pointed to the cockpit. 'Your seat is still there if you want it.'

Robert followed her through. It was just as he remembered it, though he'd probably only been away for a few days. He snuggled into his seat. It felt moulded to his body.

Gunn climbed into her own couch and activated both consoles. The two Kestrel Interceptors of Brown and Blond hung to their left and right.

Escorts or guards?

Gunn opened the link, audio only. 'We're ready.'

'If this doesn't work out Garry,' Blond started, his combative tone clear over the link, 'Then we're shouting you a one way ticket to the Ross 128 prison.'

'What my colleague is trying to say,' Brown interjected, 'Is that if we don't recover the Starburst to our satisfaction then we'll be shouting you a one way ticket to Ross 128.'

Robert tilted his head to one side, surprised. 'Hey, what happened to diplomacy?'

'The stakes are higher. I wanted to make sure the message was understood.'

'It was understood.'

'Then lead on.'

Robert nodded at Gunn, feeling an odd sense of foreboding. He was charging in on the back of a dream and disparate pieces of logic. He hoped he was right.

He was about to find out.

Chapter 18

Hyperspace evaporated returning them to the mottled backdrop of the black. Gunn set a course in system.

Brown hypered in five minutes later, Blond seven minutes after that. The three headed off at different angles, all just regular spacers, going about their business.

Gunn took her hands from the controls, leaving the Saker on autopilot. 'Now what?'

Robert wasn't entirely sure. There were four inhabited planets in the system: Benu, Anka, Kerkes and Garuda, the fishing resort. Would the Prince be there or had he left to wave to the crowds at one of other three?

He checked the system map on the navigation computer. He gave the screen a grumpy exhale. Benu and Anka were at opposing periapsis and apoapsis, Garuda orbited a gas giant, a few AU further out and then there was Kerkes slap bang in the middle of it. Everything stretched out, everything at its limit.

Gunn glanced at him and must have picked up his perplexed expression. 'Should we just follow the crowds like last time?'

Robert shook his head. He was starting to feel like an idiot, rushing in without an actual plan. But then he realised he didn't need a plan. 'Do we still agree the Starburst has to be on Imperial Explorers?'

'They wouldn't be stupid enough to try and get a Federation ship in here and your friends confirmed it wouldn't fit on anything smaller.'

'Then let's go find the Explorers. Wherever they are, the weapon is, and the Prince won't be too far behind.'

The cockpit speakers started tapping, a tight-beam digital link from Brown. Federation blink code. Gunn cocked her head to one side as she listened. Robert squeezed his lips and eyes half shut as he concentrated but only got every second letter or so.

'Your friend thinks we have company.'

Robert checked the scanner. It displayed a three-dee representation of an Osprey, keeping pace with them at the edge of scanner range.

'Legitimate Imperial guard?'

Gunn shook her head. 'Your friend doesn't think so.' The cockpit speakers kept tapping. Gunn typed as she listened. 'He's spotted two more. They're in a holding pattern.'

'The Circle's outer defence – an early warning team. Have they figured out who we are?'

'The first thing the techs did was scramble the transponder but they may still recognise the ship.'

'The Imps untraceable bug?'

Gunn's mouth opened, closed. 'Oops.'

Robert swore. 'Can we do one of those micro-hyperspace jumps?'

'He'd be able to follow us. It wouldn't accomplish anything.'

'Shoot him down?'

'Not before he calls his mates.'

Robert grunted. 'Send a blink code back to Brown. Tell them to angle back in and follow our lead.'

Gunn complied. 'Now what?'

'Slow down, one notch at a time, until the Osprey is in weapons range, then vent some fuel, open the cargo bay, give us some oscillation, whatever, but make us look damaged.'

Gunn's mouth curdled. 'That's a pretty crude trick,' she said as if he had offended her professional pride.

Robert shrugged. 'You have a better idea?'

Gunn grunted and dropped the throttle until their separation had dropped to half a klick. She gyrated the controls so Robert rolled back and forth in the couch. 'I've thinned the fuel out too; the engines should be visibly struggling.' She hovered a hand over the cargo vent switch. 'You ready?'

Robert checked the scanner. Brown and Blond were coming in. He nodded. Gunn flicked the switch and the Saker jarred to the right. 'Help,' Gunn yelled over a broadband link. 'We're under attack by an Osprey, registration AKZ-712. We're taking damage.' Her voice had just the right amount of rushed emphasis and stress.

The Osprey jerked as if the pilot had been slapped. 'Wait, I haven't fired,' cried the pilot, panic clear in his voice. 'You have an internal fault. Allow me to assist-'

The link scrambled into static and the Osprey disappeared from the scanner.
'There you go little lady,' said Blond. 'He won't be bothering you again.'

'You're so kind,' Gunn said. This time the acting sounded forced. Hopefully their little scene would be accepted on face value, a daily event repeated a hundred star systems over. Blond continued on his vector and beyond scanner range.

'Get us out of here,' Robert said. 'And tell them to split up and check Benu and Anka for Imperial Explorers in groups of five. We'll take Kerkes and Garuda.'

They dropped into the standard traffic orbit, deserted save a few Eagle Mark III fighters on patrol. Two Long Range Cruisers were docked at the orbital trading post. No show ships, no standard bearers, no admiring civilians.

'The planet surface?' Robert asked. There were two starports. The Prince wouldn't be down there without his entourage, but the Circle could have been using it as a staging base.

Gunn pinged each starport's control tower but they hadn't registered any Explorers in two days, an unusual occurrence itself in an Imperial system. 'Let's try Garuda.'

* * *

They were stopped half an AU out from the planet by a wall of Imperial Explorers. Purple stripes slashed across the sleek behemoths, the standard bearers of the Crown Prince.

'I count two hundred and fifty of them,' said Gunn as she followed traffic control directions into a holding pattern. She'd been assigned coordinates to allow her to gaze in wonder and admiration as the Prince's ship passed. A two dimensional array of ships was encircling a sphere of Explorers.

'Fifty groups of five,' agreed Robert.

'We're looking for a group of five,' Gunn muttered. 'It must be an Imperial thing.'

'Or a Crown Prince thing; the Emperor's ships weren't grouped that way.' He shook his head, annoyed it had taken this long to figure out. 'The morticians confirmed only four weapons were stolen. The Circle were shopping for components to make more. We know five large ships hypered out of the Lanaest system. I thought more meant more power, and maybe it does, but they actually chose the number five for disguise.'

'So your plan is to fly around the whole perimeter checking the hard points of all the Explorers until we find the Starburst?'

'What makes you think they are on the perimeter?' Robert checked the scanner whilst throwing an occasional glance through the viewport. The diameter of the dead zone inside the sphere of Explorers was staggering. Point one of an astronomical unit. That equated to a volume of space of around zero point five cubic milli-AUs that they couldn't search. Their scanners weren't powerful enough. He had a fair idea of what to expect though. There would be an inner cordon around the space station and the cream of the crop shadowing the Prince himself. If they were right about the Prince's obsession with the number five then the Circle could be anywhere, part of that inner cordon or even closer. In plain sight, free to do whatever they planned to do.

The scanner bleeped as the two Kestrels drifted into range. Not too close, but near enough that their blink code wouldn't draw attention.

What's the plan?

'I don't know,' Robert admitted. He couldn't see a way to do it. If they could locate their target then maybe they could blast through and take down the Starburst, but the instant they moved forward they'd be pursued by the entire Imperial fleet. They'd have seconds, maybe even minutes with Gunn piloting, but they'd need at least half an hour and that was beyond even her.

Gunn snapped her head around to face him. 'So what were you going to do then? Give up?'

Robert frowned, disappointed. Hadn't he proved himself to her yet? 'No. I was going to tell the Imps, let them sort it out. They can be-'

'-absolutely not,' Gunn interrupted. 'We can't trust them to get this right. What would you do if some stranger told you that one of your wingmen was a traitor? You would either not believe it, or you would squabble amongst yourselves and let them slip through your fingers.'

'I think they are a bit more efficient when it comes to the Duval family.'

'They don't understand the consequences. They don't know. They won't have the follow through. They won't believe us enough to put everything on the line. It'll only take a moment of distraction for the Circle to make their move.'

'Then we should really get a move on.'

They sat in silence. The same message tapped over the speakers: What is the plan? Gunn tapped back a short message.

'What is your plan then,' Robert asked. 'Fly in there and take down five Explorers singlehandedly?'

'Of course not. I don't need to destroy the Explorers, just punch through the shields and destroy the Starburst weapon.'

'And you think you can aim your laser to such pinpoint accuracy?' He said, incredulous, but she just stared at him with her calm eyes and firm mouth. She believed it.

'Okay, you can,' he said, 'but it still isn't going to work. How are you going to find the Ceepers before the Imps send you to the Wreckplace?'

She turned back to her controls. 'I have to try.'

Robert watched her for a moment. Though upright and awake she could have passed for a statue, bent forward in her acceleration couch, eyes and head perfectly still, stiller than sleep, stiller than death.

He exhaled. He knew what he had to do. He unstrapped.

'What are you doing?' Her eyes widened. 'If I have to accelerate-'

'-I'll risk it.' He climbed out of the couch and took the two steps to her side. He crouched down beside her, put his left hand on her right and looked into her eyes. She resumed practicing her awake-dead routine.

'Look at me,' Robert said; soft, but stern. Her gaze shifted toward him and then her head turned. 'I know why you are like this. I know why you think you have to save the world. It's exactly the same reason why I had to run away, hide as a pirate.' He squeezed her hand. 'You don't think you can trust anyone, but you can't save the whole galaxy by yourself. Let others help. Trust us.'

She stared into him, her irises brilliant, speckled with so many gradients of colour, like a rainbow saturated with green. Whenever he had looked at those eyes they had been hard, borderline cruel, shaped by pain and misery and determination. Now they were real, three-dimensional, filled with doubt and fear and hope. There was an actual woman behind these eyes.

He stared at her. She stared back, the cockpit tapping around them like that suspense music all the three-dee vids seemed to use these days. Her mouth opened, her lips stretching as they held together momentarily then finally parting.

'I trust you,' she whispered.

'Then let me help you.'

She nodded. He stood and climbed back to his couch. 'Link the guys…'

But Gunn had frozen. The tapping wasn't foley from a movie. It was the morticians. They were trying to contact them; four words. A short message repeated over and over, a message that turned Robert's blood to ice:

Get out of there!

Gunn slammed on the retro-rockets. A pair of Ospreys swung into view. Gunn was already spinning the Saker around as the Ospreys fired, their pulse lasers nearly splitting the Saker in half.

'How did they find us?' Robert yelled, but he knew the answer. The untraceable bug …

Looking straight at him, she told him quickly about delivering the data to INRA, the double cross that almost cost her her life and her escape.

Robert nodded, then turned back to the screen, focusing Gunn's attention once more.

Gunn completed the turn – straight into an Imperial Courier, a sleek shoe box with long engine nacelles on either side. Cherenkov radiation danced across the amplifying lenses of its plasma accelerator. More and more blips closed in around them, but none of them were firing, yet.

Gunn released the flight stick and used the thrusters to settle back to nil velocity. The Ospreys and the Courier closed in.

'Well I guess we blew that,' Robert said, trying to break the tension. Gunn shot him an accusatory look that said 'I could have tried it my way but you distracted me and now we're done.'

The link pinged and a face shimmered into existence above the projector. The perfect–model-of-genetic-engineering-face of the Imperial agent regarded them with a stern expression.

'Talkative Agent!' Robert exclaimed, actually happy to see him, at least compared to any other Imp. He artificially hyped his smile two notches up. 'Thank the Fates it's you. Where's Brain Scooping Agent?'

'Dead.' One word, one syllable, low, heavy, quick. Robert got the subtext immediately. It hadn't been one of those fun deaths he'd heard so much about. And Talkative Agent thought it was Robert's fault. 'Killed by your INRA friends.'

'No friends of mine,' Robert spat. So that was why the INRA fleet had been so messed up. The Imps untraceable bug had lead them straight to INRA. Criddoch had been right – it actually had been his fault.

'I'm actually a bit pissed you didn't destroy the INRA fleet. That would have saved me a bit of drama.'

He glanced at Gunn. What would have happened between them if they'd arrived at the INRA rendezvous to an empty system, or worse, an Imperial fleet?

Talkative agent smirked. 'I find it interesting how you promise cooperation with the Empire then proceed to gather alliances among our foes.' He nodded, as if revealing a trump card. 'I know about your friends in the two Kestrels.' To put words into actions, the Kestrels closed in on both sides, escorted by more Ospreys. The cockpit speakers began tapping. It would have been audible over the link, but even if the Imperial agent understood the message it wouldn't have mattered:

Nice work, morons.

'Look I know this may sound a bit clichéd, but I can explain everything.'

The agent smiled. 'Of course you can, and you will; in an Arcanorum detention centre.'

'Don't be dense,' Robert said. 'Why would we be here if we'd been lying to you? We're here because the Circle weren't going to assassinate the Emperor. They wanted to assassinate the Crown Prince. They're here, right now.'

The agent's smile flattened while his eyebrows rose into a peak. 'When we first met my partner wanted to shoot you both, destroy your ship, eliminate your families and anyone else connected to you. 'I disagreed, thinking you might be useful. I had never been wrong before. Now I have. I will make it my personal mission to destroy the Garry pirate clan.'

'Wait!' Robert yelled, heart racing, thinking of Jessin and Steve and the rest. 'You're not listening to me. The Emperor is an old man – he'll be dying soon enough anyway. The Circle want a strong leader for humanity. The Emperor is too old and feeble and the Crown Prince is a blouse.' Heat came off the agent in waves, almost frying the link circuits. 'It wasn't until I asked myself who was next in line that it all made sense.'

'Prince Hesketh' shouted the agent, straightening as if at attention. Robert's looked up. 'Umm, sure, who as you would no doubt agree, is the man who would win any war thrown at him.'

'He is undefeated. Humanity's greatest general,' the agent said.

Robert nodded. Flattery got you everywhere. 'With him in charge the Empire would be in a strong position for when the Thargoids attack-'

The agent laughed. 'You've been reading too many children's stories again.' He looked away. Robert was losing him. He thumped the link panel which would have screeched at the agent's end.

'Do you know everything about the Thargoids? I sure don't. But something has scared both the Circle and INRA. If INRA are worried, I think we should all be worried. The Circle don't care about politics. They aren't causing a war for fun. They think a unified human Empire is the only way to defeat the Thargoids. This is why they are doing this.'

Robert cleared his throat. 'So I'll ask you again. Do you know everything there is to know about the Thargoids?'

The agent pursed his lips, eyes refocused on the link.

'We also know that the Circle stole four secret weapons from the Federation to frame them in this attack. Yet we know the Circle are attacking with five ships.' He couldn't publish that statement in Universal Scientist but for the purpose of the conversation it was fact. 'Why five? Does that number ring a bell? The Emperor doesn't care about the number five. But your Crown Prince does.' He let that hang for a moment. 'Ask the morticians if you don't believe me.'

'Oh, I'll be talking to my Federation counterparts soon enough, have no fear. They've brought themselves a one way ticket to Peter's Wreck.' He wet his lips in apparent anticipation.

'You can't have them. I've taken them under my wing. They're mine now.'

The agent showed his teeth. A single wrinkle creased his nose; a scowl? 'Typical Federation arrogance. Why do you think it matters what you want?'

'Because I'm right and you're wrong and when your Prince dies you'll be working in the mines of Olcanze for the rest of your life.'

Robert dragged in a breath to keep going but Gunn jumped in, silent up till that point. 'Can you verify the identity of every single group of five Explorers in this system? Can you? Does it hurt to double check?'

A white blip appeared at extreme scanner range. While the agent narrowed his eyes and glanced upward in thought, Robert brought up a visual representation from the scanner. An Imperial Interdictor, the biggest of the big ships. Couriers buzzed around it like a swarm of gnats. That made Robert feel slightly better. The Circle weren't flying Couriers. Unless they were pulling the biggest triple bait and switch in the history of mankind.

The agent's eyes took on a faraway look, doubt creeping into his expression. 'I concur a double check cannot damage us once your crimes against the Empire are revenged.'

Gunn grabbed the flight stick, arm muscles tensing.

'We're not going anywhere,' Robert said. 'Not until you've stopped the Ceepers.'

'I'm afraid you don't have a choice.'

'Wrong. You've got the choice, comrade; waste precious minutes trying to take us down or concentrate on saving your future Emperor.' Gunn sent a one word tap message to the Kestrels: Fight? The response was immediate.

OACAAC.

Gunn raised an eyebrow at Robert but he understood and nodded at her. The expression he hadn't heard for half a decade but now seemed to follow him everywhere he went. Once a citizen, always a citizen.

Robert continued. 'You've got five seconds, comrade. Make a choice. Take us down or protect your Prince. Choose. The future of mankind is on your shoulders.'

The fleet of Ospreys hung before them, their bent wings giving them the appearance of angry hummingbirds. There were two dozen of them, at an average distance of two hundred and fifty metres. Well within firing range. So close that laser bolts and rail pellets would arrive almost simultaneously. The pilots would be given the signal to fire. They'd have to notice the signal, process it, and pull the trigger. The weapons themselves were separate from the trigger. Nanoseconds for the electrical impulse to travel down the wire. The mechanisms of the weapons would need to move or charge; a few more tenths of a second maybe. Bullets still obeyed the laws of physics. Capacitors didn't charge instantaneously. They could have a few fractions of a second to make a move.

Robert's breath misted, all energy routed to the offensive and defensive systems. His limbs were shaking. Temperature, adrenaline, fear?

How good was Gunn? She had once said that she was double Elite. If these Imps were all intelligence agents would they be Elite too? Probably. How many could she take down? What about Brown and Blond?

The link was quiet. The agent stared at them. He was breathing, mouth at half mast, eyes unblinking. Beeps sounded from his console.

Gunn's combat computer also diligently beeped warnings. There were armed ships nearby. The sounds felt muted, distant, out of place with the carnage and mayhem which was about to erupt.

Robert glanced at Gunn. She caught his eye. She didn't bob her head. She didn't raise her eyebrows. But her pupils dilated slightly.

Robert grabbed the edges of his acceleration couch.

Gunn yanked on the flight stick and slammed the throttle to its stops.

The Saker turned on its engine nozzle. They blasted away from the ambush.

Straight toward two Ospreys; laser pulses criss-crossed behind them. The two Ospreys held their ground, firing. Two pulses smashed into the Saker's armour. Gunn spun the ship around and down, the next two pulses going wide. She tweaked the flight stick. The cross-hairs skipped to the right most Osprey. She depressed the trigger for a split second. The Osprey exploded. She tweaked to the left, fired and destroyed the other.

Robert thought she would blast free of the attackers but instead she spun while drifting around in an arc. The Ospreys had all turned to attack and laser pulses tracked and overshot them. She bounced the Saker back and forth like a muon trapped in a laser, one way then the other, using all six thruster angles.

Robert's heart leapt into his throat as Gunn yanked him back and forth. Pulses flashed toward the cockpit, sure to strike, only for Gunn to spin them away then back, avoiding the pulse and getting her own shot off.

Robert watched her, her body completely still, her hands and feet blurring, the hurricane around an eye of apparent calm.

It was almost beautiful. She wasn't just an Elite pilot. She was something more. How many times had she put herself in such an outnumbered situation just to increase her rank so she could go undercover to kill more pirates?

The viewport was a child's painting of scribbled colours and blurred images, everything spinning around, splashes of different laser pulses, engine wash, yellow, orange and red explosions of Ospreys. He closed his eyes.

Any distraction …

He opened his eyes at the scanner. *Don't look up.* Reflected light lit the cockpit like a rainbow; cascades of colour flashing into existence, gone again.

They were surrounded by debris, but reinforcements kept coming. A unit of five Explorers seemed to be breaking the outer cordon to help. The rest of the cordon deflated, the circle of ships flattening from one side.

No.

The cordon wasn't deflating. One set of five Explorers were moving inward; toward the Interdictor.

He punched the link on. 'It's them,' he screamed. He read out the coordinates. 'They're making a move. Go, go, go!'

The Ospreys hurtled inward, lasers cannons spitting death toward the Saker. Then they stopped, turned as one toward the Interdictor and rocketed away.

'After them,' Robert yelled. He pointed at the distant Interdictor. 'Go!'

Gunn brought the Saker around. She was panting. Sweat beaded her white face. Her arms shivered.

Robert breathed in. She'd been scared. That realisation made him more scared than anything he'd just seen.

They hurtled after the Imps. The two Kestrels formed up on either side.

Smoke vented from one of them. The other had lost half a wing.

Robert tapped a message. *Okay?*

Brown responded. *Alive; can't let the Imps get the Starburst. Working on it.*

Robert saw Gunn optically zoom on the Interdictor; two kilometres long. Shaped like a pike, a habitation ring spinning around on top. The Interdictor yawed around, so big and slow it would be dependent on its escorts for protection.

The five Explorers closed on the Interdictor. They were arranged in a pentagon, energy beams surging between them.

'Faster,' Robert urged. He thought of the billions dead on Villist. He thought of a galaxy with a hundred Villists. A thousand. The entire population of humanity dying in a war that he had failed to stop. No one left to remove the bad guys. No one left to tell the next of kin.

No one left …

Comets of engine wash, Couriers, Eagles and Ospreys, screamed inwards toward the Circle's Explorers. The Ospreys fired their pulse lasers but the Explorer shields barely flared under the attack.

Then the Starburst fired.

A blue-grey laser beam, like a large plasma accelerator, fired out at an angle from each Explorer toward the centre. The beams collated instead of interfering. A huge shaft of light raced outward toward the Interdictor.

Then it hit.

'No!' Gunn yelled. Fire and smoke burst from the ship, then the beam punched all the way through and out again, hitting a group of Explorers which burst into fireballs. The Interdictor staggered sideways.

The Couriers opened fire. Plasma fire erupted across space, centering on the five Explorers which turned upward in perfect synchronisation. The Starburst gouged a canyon across the Interdictor. Explosions rippled across its hull. Robert could almost feel the energy from a distance. Whole sections broke away, fire gouging from the wounds.

The habitation ring flew free. The whole ship disappeared behind a cloud of debris and soot.

An Explorer pulled away. The Starburst shrank. 'What's going on?' Robert asked.

'Looks like our man Whithers came through,' Blond said. Gunn inhaled. 'Who?'

'It appears we had a unit undercover with the Circle as well,' Brown said, his voice without its usual confidence.

'Get us closer,' Robert urged. 'Follow the rogue Explorer.'

Two Couriers raced after it, plasma beams tracing across its hull. The Explorer's engines died and the ship rolled sideways. Small explosions bloomed across the hull then it disappeared in a supernova.

The other four Explorers kept going. The Starburst tracked across the

Interdictor. Fragments flew away. Escape capsules ejected across the ship, some disappearing in the Starburst.

Another set of five Imperial Explorers flew into the beam. They flashed out of existence in patriotic suicide.

The Interdictor's sharp nose appeared from the end of the smoke cloud as the fire died. The Starburst beam worked its way forward.

The Interdictor exploded. Gunn screamed.

One moment the big ship was there, the next there was just debris. Rage burst across the broadband link, the scream of millions and billions. Robert clamped his hands over his ears. He yelled to block it out. This isn't Villist.

This isn't Villist.

The Circle Explorers disappeared in a flood of hyperspace vectors.

Hundreds of ships swooped in after them.

Gunn quietened the link and Robert eased his hands away from his ears. She shrunk into her seat, deflated like all the water had evaporated from her body. Her expression had always been either anger or concentration but now it was neither.

It was defeat.

'I failed,' she breathed. She released the flight stick. She studied her hands. 'I failed.'

A snowstorm filled the scanner. The outer cordon collapsed. Every ship flew toward the Interdictor debris.

Robert turned to Gunn. What could he say? Any consolation would be hollow.

'We've still a got a weapon to steal,' he said instead. She was a woman who needed a goal. 'Let's go.'

She kept staring at her hands. 'All that training, all that time...'

The cockpit speakers starting tapping; Robert didn't have to decipher to know the message. *We need that gun.*

Imperial ships poured through the Circle's fading hyperspace vectors, but most of the Imps were corralling stricken civilians.

There was no order anywhere; absolute anarchy, the perfect time to stage a little theft.

'We made a promise,' he said. 'And the Circle still have Soontill. We're not done yet.'

Gunn kept staring at her hands. 'Okay.' She grabbed the flight stick and pointed them at the diminishing hyperspace vectors. The Kestrels formed up. They blasted past Ospreys and weaved through a trio of Couriers. The vectors kept shrinking. The distance dropped. A laser beam flashed past the viewport.

Robert closed his eyes.

* * *

They exited hyperspace. The four Circle Explorers hung at nil velocity. Wreckage floated around them like an asteroid field. Couriers watched, motionless, guns trained inward. Troop transports pulled away from the Explorers.

In through the fuel scoop cargo doors, Brown tapped.

Robert relayed. Gunn nodded. They dived across the open space. Orders yelled across the link, then threats and finally declarations of war.

'Faster, faster,' Robert urged. The Kestrels zoomed ahead. They split, heading to different Explorers. 'I hope they know what to do,' he muttered.

The Ospreys turned, bearing down on the Saker. Laser pulses flashed past.

The shots were wild, but would get closer as the distance dropped. 'Are you ready?' Gunn asked through gritted teeth.

'No?' He shot her a quizzical look. 'You're flying.'

'Can't you count? Four ships left, the Feds, me and yourself. You're flying one out of here.'

Robert shook his head, his heart jumping into third gear. 'No way. Uh-uh. I'm not a pilot.'

A plasma beam cut across space in front and arced toward them. Gunn threw the Saker into a twisting dive then wrenched it back up. The view out the cockpit had cleared but she yanked the ship sideways and another laser beam cut through the spot they had occupied a moment ago.

Robert's neck skin crawled. Her eyes seemed everywhere but nowhere, glances at every instrument without focusing on any one area. Her hands just seemed to know what to do.

He'd never had that. He'd bumbled through basic flight training, somehow scraping a 'Just Meets' grade. He could work miracles with guns, in the hand, or mounted on a capital ship, but as soon as he took control of both a ship and a gun he became an uncoordinated wreck.

If he had to pilot a ship out of here he would die; as simple as that.

Best to die fighting, though; he reached for his remlok – safely attached – then visualised the steps he would need to go through. Break the Saker airlock. Jump through the gap into the cargo hold of the Explorer.

He pulled on the remlok, rubbing it between his fingers. It was secure, it wasn't coming off. It would deploy as soon as he hit vacuum.

Open the Explorer's airlock, hope like heck there were no Imperial troopers on board, race to the bridge and hopefully piggy back through a hyperspace vector that Blond or Brown had opened up.

Easy.

Except for the dying bit, and the vacuum bit, and the risk of Imperial troopers bit.

'I'm ready,' he said, fingers working the remlok. He checked the gloves on his pressure suit.

The Explorers were close, a shield of Couriers between them. An assault transport pulled away from an Explorer. The Explorers still looked alive; lights shone from inside though the engines were dark. The Kestrels swooped past the Couriers, flittering past their plasma beams and disappeared inside two of the Explorers.

'They're not going to wait for us,' Gunn muttered. She leant forward, her whole body focused on piloting. Two sets of Explorer nacelles started rotating, their engines coming back to life. Small rows of thrusters ignited along their hulls.

The Saker barrelled toward the right-most Explorer. Then Gunn snapped the ship around, keeping their vector straight, tapped the trigger, and turned back before an incoming Osprey exploded. No aiming, just point and shoot. One shot, one kill.

'You're amazing,' Robert said.

'I'm an Alliance operative. We solve problems.'

Yes you do, he thought. Gunn pushed the Saker down as a squadron of laser pulses lashed at them, then turned back up until they were heading straight toward the Explorer's lower cargo bay door. It wasn't anything more than a slit with a pair of super magnets at each end; a fuel scoop, sucking up hydrogen gas, cargo canisters or anything else that come close. Today it would be a Saker.

The opening grew wider. Not taller though. Gunn didn't slow; closer and closer, a black rectangle waiting to gobble them up. The hole was too small. The walls reached out for them. They were going to hit. Robert shielded his face.

And then they were inside. Gunn spun around and brought them to a halt. Her gaze didn't leave the controls. He unstrapped, pulled the statue from his pocket and pushed it into Gunn's couch. 'If anything happens, take this to Smuggler's Junction; the LTT 2771 system. It's the key.'

'Nothing will happen.' 'I can't fly.'

She locked gazes with him, her pale green eyes blazing. 'There's something you don't know about me. I don't leave people behind either.'

'Okay.'

'Okay.'

He galloped out the hatch and up to the airlock. He put his hand to the remlok again, ran his hand over his pressure suit, climbed up into the airlock, ran the cycle through and the top door opened into vacuum.

Chapter 19

The remlok expanded and Robert closed his eyes. There was absolutely nothing out there he wanted to see. *Harden up, little girl.* He felt for the hand loops, pushed himself down against the bottom of the airlock and then kicked upward.

The temperature dropped immediately. His outstretched hands hit steel.

Right or left? He opened his eyes to get his bearings then closed them again. If he couldn't see the vacuum, the vacuum couldn't see him. He pulled himself to the right, hand over hand, until he touched the airlock and tumbled inside. He opened his eyes and slammed the control button. The airlock cycled, air hissed in and the remlok unfurled. His boots magnetised and he stood up. It had just been like holding his breath underwater. If he kept telling himself that he might even believe it.

The airlock opened. From a velcro pocket he retrieved a standard issue laser pistol, a small L&F point two-one. He stepped out slowly, listening with one ear, feeling through the steel with the other. No sound, no movement. If the transport had left a rear-guard then they were being quiet.

Robert ran; to the right, up steps, along the corridor, pushing as hard as he could in magboots. He rushed onto the bridge, a huge circular compartment with eight acceleration couches. He rushed past floating blood globules, noting the crack in the viewscreen and carbon scoring on the walls.

No dead.

Maximum prisoners; the Imperial way.

He strapped into the astrogation couch and activated the engines, scanner and link. A smooth almost musical thrum reverberated through the ship. The viewscreen shimmered as the shields activated. He'd never flown an Imp ship before. The control graphics were more decorative but the main functions seemed similar.

He fired up the combat computer and it immediately squawked at him; incoming ships. Ospreys were firing but the shields were recharging faster than their pulse weapons could drain them. Four Couriers swooped in. Robert tensed. They could cause serious damage.

Brown and Blond were already gone, hyperspace vectors glowing blue. A few Ospreys and Couriers followed through. The Saker wasn't on the scanner. Hopefully Gunn had commandeered the fourth Explorer. He turned his ship but it reacted slowly. A Courier bore down on him, firing into his broadside.

Robert flinched, the shock like a punch straight to the solar plexus. He swung the ship toward the Courier but knew he'd never get a shot on it. A second came into range. His shields shimmered and shrank as the shield energy swirled down toward zero.

Robert pushed the stick forward. One of the Courier's beams went high. Distant explosions reverberated through the ship. Warning alarms rang through the cockpit and the engines slowed.

One of the Couriers exploded. 'I thought pirates knew how to run away?' Gunn yelled across the link. 'Get moving.' Her Explorer came into view and fired again, slicing through the other Courier. 'Go!'

Robert froze for a moment, fingers hanging over the controls. *I'm always the last one off the ship.* 'I'm not leaving without you.'

'This isn't your game pirate, this is my game. I make the rules. You're not leaving me, I'm the one not leaving you.'

Robert hands couldn't move, his brain stuck in an endless loop. He'd never left a person behind before.

I'm always the last one off the ship.

'Robert, please!'

His hands turned the Explorer toward the fading hyperspace vectors. His name.

That was what did it. Not once had she called him Robert; pirate, scum, maybe even Garry, but never by his given-by-his-father name. She wasn't telling him to go for the mission. She was telling him to go for her.

He went.

Two more Couriers came in, laser beams scything toward him, but they were at the edge of firing range and his recharging shields absorbed the damage.

The hyperspace vectors shrunk; their blue hue darkening. How long did they stay open for?

The vector filled his viewport. Sweat beaded up his back and in his palms, the controls slicking in his hands. The ship was a monstrosity. What if he mis-jumped into Riedquat by himself? What if he didn't have enough gas to get back to where they needed to get to? Would any of those fates be any worse than what he would find here?

The vector kept shrinking. It didn't fill the viewport anymore. He urged the ship forward.

A boom rocked the Explorer. A depressurisation alarm sounded. Half the ship was open to vacuum, the engines were losing fuel

.. and then everything was gone; space, the Couriers, everything. Just the stretched starlight of hyperspace.

* * *

Robert emerged into a debris field. Imperial hull fragments whipped past the viewport.

He shivered. 'Gunn?' he called across the link. 'That's just the Imps that came after us,' Blond said.

Robert released his breath. He sailed through the debris toward two stationary Imperial Explorers, both in better condition than his. 'You better not have damaged the gun,' Blond said.

'What my esteemed colleague is trying to say is that you better not have damaged the gun,' Brown said, his diplomacy well and truly shot.

Robert laughed, despite himself. The fading adrenaline made him giddy. 'The gun is fine, I think, it's the ship that's struggling.'

Blond sneered. 'Don't you know how to fly?'

'No.'

The link went silent. Blond clearly had no come back for that. Behind him, the two hyperspace vectors evaporated.

'Gunn,' he breathed. He stared at the now empty space, a knot forming in his stomach. Had she been caught in hyperspace or was she stuck back there with the Imps?

'What do we do?' Brown asked.

'I don't know,' Robert said. His fingers were twitching. He couldn't go back, hyperspace vectors opened in the outer solar system. He'd never get to her in time.

'He was talking to me,' Blond boomed. 'Mortuary sent us out here to recover that weapon, not to let it fall into the Empire's hands. We have to go back.'

'With what fleet?' Brown retorted, a thread of unease in his normally flat business-like tone, as if for the first time in his life he wasn't sure of the answers.

Robert kept staring at the closed hyperspace vectors. He didn't care about the Starburst. The Imperials could do whatever they wanted with it. It was what they would do with Gunn that concerned him more. He couldn't bust through a fleet, but …

'If we go back, we can follow them, find out where they take her – and the Starburst – insert me and then I'll go kill them all.'

Blond snorted. 'Kill them all?'

'I'm a pirate,' Robert said. 'I steal stuff, or people, and kill anyone that tries to stop me.'

And no one's stopping me from finding Gunn.

Brown pulled in a deep breath. 'I hate to break it to you, citizen, but I don't think you're a pirate. Otherwise I like the plan.'

'What plan?' It was Gunn's voice. Robert's chest filled as he snapped the Explorer around.

Racing from a blue hyperspace vector was a blackened, smoking Imperial Explorer.

'You made it.' Robert tried not to let the relief show in his voice.

'I said I would.'

Robert smiled. The link went silent but he didn't mind.

'Oh, and we did it,' she said, voice choked with relief, 'heard it over the link before I hypered out. The Prince was on the habitation ring when it flew off. He's fine.'

Robert studied the link as his brain processed that. He released a long sigh, a sigh about a month old, a sigh laden with a lot of baggage 'We did it? The Prince is safe, war is averted? Everyone gets to live another day?'

'We did it,' Gunn repeated. Her pride washed across the link. He wanted to hold-

'Okay, okay, enough chit chat,' Blond growled. 'Let's get the weapon back to Eta Cassiopeia.'

'No,' Robert said. 'Those maniacs are still out there. That INRA Admiral may have been many things, including a liar, but he was right about the Circle. They are set on a course and have the access and technology to see it through. They see themselves above the rest of us and they won't stop until they succeed. This isn't even their plan A. It's their plan B. Plan C will be coming. We have to destroy them, forever.'

'How?' asked Gunn. 'People have been searching for Soontill for nearly fifty years. We didn't get the coordinates from INRA. How are you going to find it?'

'I don't need to find it. I know exactly where it is. '

'How?'

'I'm a pirate. I steal stuff.'

The link went silent. Brown and Blond could have been talking privately. 'We can't allow the Starburst to fall into another trap,' Brown said after a few moments.

'Tough. I promised I would retrieve the Starburst. I did. You promised me I could then borrow it which means you've promised me yourselves. We're doing this and we're doing it my way.' He waited a moment. 'I'm not wrong about this.'

More silence. Brown sounded like he was chewing something over. Blond ground his teeth.

'I have a battle group waiting to help,' Gunn said. 'But it might not be enough.'

'I know some people,' Robert said. 'I've called a meeting at Smuggler's Junction.'

Brown perked up. 'I'd very much like to come to that meeting.' Robert imagined he was visualising an endless sea of pirates to arrest and bounties to collect.

'No dice, mortician; just me and Gunn. You two are going to meet us—' he opened the navigation computer. Despite his bluster he didn't know exactly where Soontill was and Smuggler's Junction was a bit of a detour. He transferred coordinates. 'Meet us there. Give us a day.' He transferred a set of coordinates to Gunn.

'Gunn is an upholder of the law as well,' Brown said. 'She'll be the same as us. She would have dreamed of this chance for years.'

Blond chimed in. 'You pirates may have been hunting Soontill for half a century, but the military have searched just as long for Smuggler's Junction. If she's coming, we're coming too.'

Gunn hadn't said anything during the exchange. Were the morticians right? 'I'm taking two of the Starbursts with me to Smuggler's Junction. If you want to see them again you'll meet me in twenty four hours.'

Robert's hyperdrive controls glowed green.

'This is bullshit,' Blond said. His ship angled towards Robert's.

'Surrender or I'll fire.'

Gunn's Explorer turned on Blond's. 'I wouldn't.' Brown then turned on Gunn, leaving Robert to turn on Brown, but he didn't bother. They didn't need a Mexican standoff.

'You guys are absolute pikers,' Robert said. 'I'll see you in twenty-four hours.' He slammed the hyperdrive actuator down.

* * *

The Architect stood before the holo projector in his command cabin. He'd stood in the exact same place just before he'd authorised project Endure. He'd studied the exact same map with the exact same stars lit up. Again media logos hovered above the holographic galaxy. But unlike last time when the feeds hadn't shown him what he wanted to see, now the feeds showed him exactly what he didn't want to see.

Imperial Gazette: Prince survives laughable assassination attempt Federation Times: Luck, Ineptitude, save Imperial heir-apparent. Frontier News: Unknown technology used in Prince attack mystery. Random Intergalactic Gossip: CIEP arrest of pirates 'illegal'?

The Architect stared at the headlines forcing calmness. There was a chance, however minute that the holoprojector had voxelated gibberish and that the Prince was in fact dead. The moment he opened a newsfeed however, that fleeting hope would likely be dashed.

The Architect stepped back, lips pursed.

A total loss. What if another force had acquired the Starburst? What tyranny they would produce with it?

He shook his head and turned to the window, hands behind his back. All that planning, all that work, all that training, everything the Circle had done for humanity, squashed, by those they were trying to protect.

He allowed himself five seconds of despair, five long seconds, drawn out with breaths in between each one. He held the necklace tightly. Then he straightened up, turned back to the projector and brought up a new screen.

He'd had setbacks before. He'd recovered from all of them. He'd recover from this one too.

Removing the Prince and framing the Federation was the quickest way to their, nay, humanity's goal, but that avenue was surely closed now. The Prince's tour would be cancelled. He'd have extra guards, impenetrable security. There were other ways to accomplish Endure however, contingency plans – higher risk, lower probability of success – but still viable options. It was time to call the elders back.

The hatch buzzed open and Lieutenant Graham walked through. He marched straight up and snapped to attention. His expression narrowed, eyebrows and lips pronounced, his eyes little back orbs.

He knew.

'You have something for me?' Some good news would have been welcome.

'The latest on the pirate,' Graham said. He passed over a data crystal which the Architect fed into the holo-projector. 'He was last seen leaving Delta Phoenicis with Federation FEDSOD forces.'

'Federation?' the Architect whispered, the mental links connecting. 'He did this. The pirate, Garry. He was at Brohman as well. He stopped Commander Tybalt's team and stole the Starburst.'

A three-dimensional face appeared before the Architect with a column of two dimensional text beside it.

The Architect gasped.

Graham coughed. 'It was all the information we could find. No known date of birth, no planet of origin. He served for a time in the Federation, was quite the hero at one point.'

The Architect wasn't listening to him. He wasn't looking at the text, or lack of it.

He was looking at the face.

A face he had seen before. *Jordan, you cunning son of a bitch.*

'Evacuate the elders,' the Architect ordered. 'All of them. And prepare the defences. We're about to be attacked.'

* * *

Robert exited hyperspace before a distant red dwarf star. At that range it appeared barely larger than any other star, perhaps a stronger tint of red. There was little solar output at his distance.

It was a dark system, a collection of lost debris and planetoids, gathered up in a stable gravitational eddy, like a Lagrange point.

Gunn's Explorer shuttled in behind him, hitchhiking on his hyperspace vector.

'This is it?' Gunn asked. She didn't bother to hide the scorn in her voice, the upholder of the law casting disdain on the hideout of the scum she had spent her life destroying.

'This is it.' In truth he'd only visited Smuggler's Junction half a dozen times but he knew it and the approach pretty well, even if he hadn't always been the pilot. The first time he'd come here he'd flown a hijacked Federation Eagle fighter, numb, lost, confused, the screams from Villist playing over and over in his mind like a tortured personal theme song. Robert Garry – Murderer of Millions.

This time would be different. He was flying an Imperial slug for starters, and he'd barely slept the last few days. The nav computer's display was empty but the scanner slowly formed an image of the system; two rogue bodies, Mars size, an asteroid belt, and if nothing had changed in the last six months, one particular asteroid that would welcome him home.

He headed toward the belt, Gunn on his wing. She was quiet, but not abnormally so. It felt like she was concentrating, analysing the place, committing every detail to memory.

He turned to approach the belt. The shields flared as rock and dust vaporised against them. Then the belt thickened and the rocks grew bigger. The Explorer shook and rumbled like an ultrasonic sorter. The shield readout dropped with each shake, sometimes by half a percent, sometimes by two or three, but Robert wasn't paying attention. He didn't care about the shields. He cared about one particular asteroid.

There were thousands of them out there, some tidally locked as they orbited an invisible barycentre, others spinning in any number of axes, perfectly still or looping all over the place. They were round or oval, ones with big gashes in them and others that looked like miniature moons.

There! He saw it, a kidney shaped rock that looked as if a giant space monster had taken a bite out of its side. A completely normal looking asteroid but completely obvious if you were searching for it. It rotated around a single axis. Robert watched its slow painful revolution then turned the Explorer along the direction of the bite.

The shields dropped to sixty-five percent. Gunn weaved and threaded her way through behind him, but he'd probably do himself more harm if he tried that. Blunt and brutal was the way forward. A life motto perhaps?

He found the next marker, an asteroid with a circumferential valley running along the equator; man-made, but not obviously artificial on first inspection. Its pole pointed the way forward. He found the third and fourth markers and then he arrived.

He wasn't sure. Smuggler's Junction rotated around its axis giving it a form of artificial gravity. There was only one way in or out and as he approached it, it looked like just another big rock, except it hung in an area of clear space, the eye to the asteroid belt's hurricane. The asteroid kept turning and the docking tube came into view, followed by the antennae, piping and fuel scoops that sucked up any dust or gas that got too close.

'Fates alive,' Gunn breathed. Robert smiled. That was the reaction he'd been waiting for. It really was a fantastic sight. Buried deep inside a belt in a dead system that no sane person would venture through, they'd found a rock comprising maybe point zero one percent of the total belt's massand they were there with minimal damage and delay.

They weren't the only ones.

Some of the bigger ships were moored to the asteroid through docking arms bolted deep into the rock. In parking orbits nearby were Lanners and Gyrs, a host of Lakon freighters and even a re-purposed Saud Kruger yacht. He thought he spotted a lumbering Mantis bulk hauler in the distance.

Then he saw *The Sauntering Princess*. A Lion Transport.

Malin's Lion Transport.

Robert sucked in a breath. She wouldn't be there, surely, after everything that had happened?

Of course she would. She wanted revenge. He'd advertised his location. What better time to extract payment?

He panned the viewscreen to Gunn's Explorer. Any chance he would have of bargaining would be gone if Malin saw her. Malin had never liked other women.

'Gah,' he said to himself. He sent the nonsense code signal: 'The time has come for all good men to come to the aid of the party.' He waited for a response, counting. If he didn't get it in five seconds then he'd be turning around and getting out before the defence systems activated.

'Good to have you back,' said a woman in a rushed tone. Traffic control was a short straw assignment at the Junction. 'Docking tube is yours.'

'Docking tube is mine.' Then he switched the link to Gunn. 'We're in. This is the part where I remind you not to do anything stupid.'

'That's a bit rich coming from you.'

'Noted.'

* * *

Robert rode the Explorer's cargo elevator down to the landing bay. He stepped off onto steel plates riveted to the rock and the elevator rose and sealed against the hull. A boom shuddered through the flooring and he turned to see the massive inner airlock door close and seal tight.

Gunn parked her Explorer opposite his. Deeper into the cavern sat hundreds of ships of all classes and sizes. Diamond shaped Kraits, triangular Fer-de-Lances, snub nosed Sidewinders, Adders, Cobras, Vipers and even a Constrictor, a rare ship in this day and age. He took a few steps then deactivated his magboots. The rotational gravity was strong enough. He waited by Gunn's Explorer. The elevator separated from the hull and rode down on four hydraulic pistons. Gunn's head appeared over the edge. She stared out at the endless rows of ships. Once she reached the ground she locked him with a frown. 'Why did you bring me here? I just spotted twelve ships with bounties in excess of ten thousand credits.'

Robert grinned. 'Because you focus on the bigger picture and don't get bogged down in solving every problem anymore, do you?' He dropped the smile and chewed his upper lip. 'And I wanted to show you my side of the galaxy, you know, looking from the bottom up.'

'Why?'

'Because it's important to me.'

Gunn turned without a word and walked between the lines of ships. Cargo bots and ferries swooped back and forth while pilots shook hands over open cargo canisters. The Junction had always been a safe place to exchange stolen or scavenged goods.

Echoing footsteps, surging air conditioner ducts, loader hydraulics and chattering voices filled the cavern. There was banter and arguments and exclamations of surprise. People sounded at ease, comfortable, like they were at home; no one screaming, no one dying.

A nice change.

They passed a Krait he didn't recognise. Next was a Cobra Mark I with the name 'Devil's Reach' emblazoned in script down the length of the ship. The scored and dented remains of shark jaws were painted along the ship's nose.

Robert smiled. He'd hired the owner a few times to pad out his own crew for bigger jobs; a solid man with a solid reputation. The ship was sealed so he kept walking.

Activity increased as they walked. Mini cargo auctions went on around them. A woman harassed a man to swap Lavian brandy for furs. A man with ginger all the way around his face made eye contact. He dropped a trunk to the floor. 'Commander Garry,' he called and stepped over. He reached out, mashed Robert's hand and shook it. 'I served under you sir. Villist.'

Robert's knee-jerk reaction was to pull his hand away, but no, he wasn't hiding from Villist anymore. He vaguely remembered the man. 'Gunnery sergeant?'

Ginger beamed like he'd won the Epsilon Indi lottery. 'That's right sir. O'Reilly, Sergeant O'Reilly.'

'You're not in the force anymore?' Robert said, his right hand still entrenched by O'Reilly's two. Gunn stood a pace off to the right, a weird, S-shape to her mouth, but her eyes made it a smile.

'No, sir; honourable discharge. Did my time, lost my way a bit and ended up here.'

Robert nodded; a familiar story. When you spent your entire adult life following instructions in do-or-die situations, what did you do afterwards? Some filled the vacuum with families and babies while others went out on their own as Lone Wolves. Many filled it with piracy instead.

'So you heard my call?'

'Yes sir; another chance to fly with Commander Garry? Wouldn't miss it sir, thought it would be like old times.'

Robert's jaw clenched. He turned away, saw Gunn glaring at him, and turned back to slap O'Reilly on the shoulder. 'Just like old times.' *Except, hopefully without the millions of civilian and Federation deaths on my conscience.*

He considered running back to his ship, flying away and hiding. People would die in the next two days and they would do it under his orders. Could he live with that again?

Maybe.

Could he live with the Circle of Independent Elite Pilots continuing to plot war, to plot the deaths of trillions?

No.

Millions of deaths had nearly destroyed him. Trillions would be a bullet to the head. No muss, no fuss. No way he could live with that level of guilt.

He squeezed out a smile. 'Glad to have you with us.' He moved on before O'Reilly started reminiscing.

There were more ships he didn't recognise, but then he saw an Asp Explorer that he recognised beyond a shadow of a doubt.

The Healer.

He raced forward. Hayden and Tiwhe were leaning over a cargo canister arguing with each other. Robert spun Hayden around and crunched him in a bear hug. Just for a second though. 'You guys are okay,' he said. He let go of Hayden, stepped toward Tiwhe and punched him in the shoulder.

Hard.

'When your boss sends you a message to see if you are alive the decent thing to do is reply and say 'yes sir.''

'We're alive, sir,' said Hayden. 'The Circle chased us but we lost them in the Lesser Drift.'

Tiwhe rubbed his shoulder. 'How come he gets the hug and I get the punch?'

Hayden gave him a shove. 'Because I'm better looking.'

Robert laughed. They were both disgusting looking men. Unshaven, unkempt, clothes patched as if they had had a tumbling fist fight through a clothing factory, rolling from one machine to the other then into a wind tunnel for good measure. Hayden's empty eye socket was sewn shut and Tiwhe's whiskey nose almost glowed. But they were his guys and they were alive, dammit. 'Is everyone else here?'

Hayden straightened up, his face tightening to a bland expression and Robert's guts squirmed. He hoped he was reading Hayden wrong. 'Tell me.'

'Two ships didn't make the rendezvous. Plus yours.'

Robert closed his eyes. He steeled himself with a deep breath. 'Who?'

'Knucklebones,' Tiwhe said. 'And the Snake.'

Robert shuffled backward as if he'd been slapped.

You killed them.

You killed them.

You killed them.

'Their kids?' his voice the squawk of a pubescent boy.

'The Despondence is here. That's Snake's boy. Knucklebones had both his girls with him.'

That nearly knocked him flat. He'd met both the girls, one four, one eight, both in double pigtails with little pink ribbons at the end, laughing and running around Knucklebones' cargo hold as girls probably shouldn't, yet beautiful and happy and innocent.

And dead.

He turned, straight into Gunn. Her mouth and cheeks were flat but her eyes were probing his. 'I can't do this,' he whispered. 'I can't lead more men to their deaths. Not again.'

Hayden and Tiwhe exchanged glances then returned to their argument as if dismissed.

Gunn kept staring at him.

Then she took his hand. Electricity sparked. His fatigue lifted. He half expected her to knock him out again. But she just stood there, warm hand on his.

'Yes, you can. Didn't we have some agreement not to let the past affect our goals, or did I just imagine that?'

Robert looked down at her hand. It was real, warm, soft.

Knucklebones' girls had been real too. A price paid to get to where he was. How many dead children would it take to rid the galaxy of the Circle?

Gunn let his hand go and slapped him. 'Look at these ships. You told me you wanted me to see your galaxy? Well I've seen it. It's filled with people that worship the ground you walk on. It's filled with people that have willingly chosen to come here and follow you because they believe in you.'

'And Malin,' Robert said.

Gunn laughed. A real laugh; a great laugh. 'Her too.'

Robert watched the ships, the people. Gunn was right. They were united by one single person, him, for one single goal: follow him to glory, or riches, or whatever they thought was important to them. Either way they were his to command.

After Villist he'd shunned his heroic title, grew to hate the word. It embodied everything that was wrong with celebrating not everyone died.

But maybe it wasn't the fact that Leo had done the actual work or the fact he was too slow to save everyone. Maybe he inspired people, gave them something to live up to, dragging everyone up to a greater good.

Maybe that was heroism. 'Let's keep moving,' he said.

The bay became crowded toward the inner sanctum. People gathered around, filling the gaps between the ships. As Robert and Gunn approached, people nudged each other and the whispers died down, like a blanket suffocating the cavern. The crowd turned and stared.

Robert stopped, suddenly unsure of himself. He cleared his throat. 'Umm, thank you all for coming.' He stepped up the open boarding ramp of an Adder. 'I know some of you are here for me. I know some of you are not. But you are all here for Soontill. Admit it, you've all thought about it at one point of another; dreamed of that Thargoid technology, of an empty planet filled with enough alien items to make you rich forever.'

He thumbed his chest. 'Well I know where Soontill is.' A lie, but he'd know in an hour's time, hopefully. He let his statement hang for a few seconds. 'But it isn't empty. Yes it has Thargoid technology, but it also has defenders; the Circle of Independent Elite Pilots.'

The crowd jostled and grumbled, an angry murmur rolling toward Robert.

Nothing he heard complimented the Ceepers. He had his target audience.

'Who says those muppets have any right to the place? They go out of their way to make our lives difficult and the people of the galaxy deify them for it. They think they are bigger than the Fates, KumByar, or whatever it is you believe in. They think they are above everyone else, that they have the divine right to control the future of humanity.

'Well I say they are nothing but a bunch of delusional vigilantes. I say they have no such right. I say their power has gone to their heads. I say they probably aren't even Elite pilots. I say they are a bunch of bullies and it's time that we take them down a notch!'

He screamed at the top of his lungs. He swung his fist into the air. The crowd followed suit.

'Come with me to Soontill. Rid yourselves of the thorn in your back. Solve the riddle that has never been solved. Become legends that will live for a thousand years. Become richer than all the bankers on Andceeth. Come with me to avenge your losses.'

The men roared and Robert stepped down into the mob. Hands slammed into his shoulders and his back as he waded through the men. Someone grabbed his hand and shook it.

He bumped straight into Malin.

She was a tall thin woman, but her presence filled half the asteroid. The mob backed away. Her face had that I'm-going-to-gut-you-like-a-two-credit-slave-and-not-bat-an-eyelid look of almost disinterest. He backed off a step but there was no space and Malin stepped forward. Her hands were empty. There were no knives in her belt; bare hands then? It wouldn't be her first time. Her face continued to speak of a gruesome death. Then she slapped him, straight across the cheek that Gunn had warmed up earlier.

He rolled with it, a tingling smartness across his face but it felt much better than the alternative. He straightened up and looked her in the eye with as much regret as he could muster. 'I deserved that.'

She slapped his other cheek. His face went numb. She raised her hand again but he put his hands up in surrender. 'I think we're square now.'

Her hand dropped. 'You've got some explaining to do mister,' she said, poking him in his barely-healed bullet wound. Robert gasped as if his insides had just been rearranged and doubled over, cradling his stomach.

Her stern expression melted and her mouth fell into an 'o' shape. 'Oh my baby.' She cradled his head and kissed him on the lips and around his mouth. 'What did they do to you?'

Robert grunted, holding onto his knees to stay upright. He took a few deep breathes. 'Gutted me like a fish; which is what I thought you'd do to me.'

She kissed him again. A throat cleared behind him. Malin glanced over his shoulder and stepped back, her stare turning ice-cold.

'The broad,' Malin muttered.

'The pirate,' Gunn said. Malin threw her head back and cackled. She wiped a tear from her eye. 'Honey we're all pirates here. That's a compliment more than anything else, but if you have something you'd like to say feel free to say it.'

Gunn stepped closer but Robert put his hand up to block her. 'Gunn doesn't talk much these days.'

Malin grunted. 'I like her better already. Now you, mister, are going to owe me double for this venture. I might love you but my boys sure don't.'

'You'll have it.'

'We better.'

'You will.'

'Then what's the plan? How did you find Soontill's coordinates?'

Robert tried to laugh but waves of pain ricocheted through his stomach. 'What do you mean?' he gasped. 'I'm a pirate. I stole them.' He tried to stand up straight. 'But Gunn stole them back off me. She has the coordinates.'

Malin raised an eyebrow. She tilted her head at Gunn. 'This one?' Robert turned to Gunn. 'You've got the coordinates?'

Gunn's brow pinched as she pulled a data crystal from a pocket. 'How did you know?'

'You took the crystal before dropping me on that garbage world. The first thing you would do is decode it. You tell me what the coordinates are and I'll tell you which one is Soontill.'

Malin leant forward, staring at the crystal with wide eyes, as if gazing upon a holy relic. And in a way she was. Malin was the richest person he knew. Money didn't drive her. Infamy did. Doing things and owning things that others didn't – or couldn't – drove her. Soontill was her deity.

'I've got a good data miner,' she mumbled, still staring at the crystal. It looked like a cloudy, impure diamond, the carbon nodes overloaded with data. It was not a thing of beauty, yet Malin couldn't take her eyes off it. 'Follow me,' she said, her voice husky.

Robert took the crystal and Malin led them out of a sea of handshakes and back slaps to a Viper Mark III so new it still had its factory shine in places. 'Where did you steal this?' Robert asked.

'I didn't.'

A tall man appeared at the top of the boarding ramp. He had a finely chiselled moustache, bright pink and green dress pants, a white silk shirt with a black waistcoat and the butt of a Colt Diplomat peeking out from a shoulder holster.

'Thwaites?' Robert asked. He rushed up and shook his hand.

'Garry, you old dog. Good to see you; that father of yours keeping well?' Robert blinked, taken aback. The question stung. 'He's in a good place. What are you doing in a Viper?' Unlike most pirates Thwaites didn't like stolen or second hand gear so he always brought straight from the dealer, and always a Krait. Every time; no one knew why.

Thwaites shrugged. 'I happened to be at the dealer in Delta Pavonis and he offered me a good deal on this girl. I thought 'what the heck' and Jonty'd up; time for a change and all that. She sure turned a few heads.'

Malin cleared her throat. Thwaites and Robert shared a knowing smile. 'So your freelancing days are over eh?' Robert asked, nodding back to Malin.

'She lured me with her wily ways.'

'She has a knack for that.' He placed the crystal in Thwaites' hands. 'Decoded nav data, you just have to load it up.'

Thwaites yawned. 'You trying to put me to sleep? I thought the call to Smuggler's Junction was for action and adventure?'

Robert shoved him up the ramp. 'Get on with it,' he said with a smile. Thwaites ducked inside leaving Robert halfway up the ramp and Gunn and Malin on the deck staring laser beams at each other. Robert leapt down between them. He smiled at Malin and said 'I'm just going to show my guest around.'

He led Gunn away. When they were out of ear shot he whispered. 'Don't take this the wrong way, but she would have kicked your arse.'

'She could have tried.'

Their steps rung out across the floor; a plate creaked and Robert tripped over a rivet. He stumbled, cried out, his shredded abdominals trying to catch him.

Gunn caught him. 'You should be in a hospital.'

'I should be a lot of things.'

Their eyes met for a moment, then Gunn looked away. 'Is there anything else to this place?'

Robert shook his head. 'No. This is it. It stretches about a kilometre into the asteroid. It's not a commercial station. There are no services, except maybe a few tools lying around. Traffic control falls to the first arrival. It's a place to lay low, barter, trade information and hide while people like you are on the warpath.'

'I have warrants for over fifty people I've passed,' she said, her voice pulling back into its granite shell. 'Every fibre in my being is urging me to arrest or shoot everyone I see.'

'Please don't.'

'Why did you bring me here? To torture me? Why don't you think I'll come back after we are all done and set an ambush around this place?'

Robert stopped and took Gunn's hands in his. 'You think I'm a pirate and you think that's a bad thing. I wanted to show you that being a pirate is not a bad thing.' He waved at the people, laughing, joking, sharing stories. 'They're brothers, sons and fathers, trying to make it through their lives in a tough galaxy. They have kids. They love them to bits, they read them stories at night, they would all do anything to protect them.' He turned back to her. 'They're not scum and they're not sub human and they aren't people who should be eradicated just because of some title placed on them by others. They're human beings. I'm a human being.'

Gunn gritted her teeth. 'Didn't their victims have families too? We just passed the Black Platinum. Its captain blows male freighter crews out the airlock then rapes the women. I saw One-eyed Jiang in the crowd before. He targets medical shipments. Famines are worse because of him, thousands die of starvation.

'My foster parents... Did their killers love their children, hug them tight?'

Robert stared at Gunn's impassionate face, pain etched just under the surface. 'I...'

'Am I interrupting anything?' Malin said making Robert jump. She stood behind him, lips pouting, hands on her hips.

'Of course not,' Robert said. He stepped away from Gunn, who held her ground. 'Thwaites all done?'

'He's got thirty coordinates. You still think you can tell the real one?' Robert raised his eyebrow at Gunn.

'Thirty?'

She shrugged. 'Best we could do.'

He ushered her forward. 'We'd better go see what Thwaites has for us.'

They squeezed into the cockpit of Thwaites' Viper, an area twice the size of the Saker's cockpit. Thwaites passed Robert a mug of steaming coffee. Not a brew he recognised, but still magic to his deadened senses. Robert smiled in thanks.

Thwaites turned to a central console which projected a galactic map with thirty red glowing points, not three.

'Where is the Grandmort system?' Robert asked. Thwaites typed in the name and a blue point appeared near one group of red points. Robert walked around the map, checking height and width, considering the distance to each red point.

'What has Grandmort got to do with anything?' Malin asked.

'You know the system?' Robert said.

'I know never to bother going there.'

Robert nodded. 'That's what everyone knows. No one goes there. The bored go to Epsilon Eridani, the suicidal go to Phekda, the ship-spotters go to Beta Hydri. No one ever goes to Grandmort.'

He nodded to Gunn and she withdrew the statue from her pocket. 'My Dad had one of these. He'd was ferrying stolen goods from the HR 4790 system to some border world when he got jumped by a Federation battle group. He got the Fates out of there, just, and went to hole up.

'He ended up at Grandmort. There wasn't even a major starport on the planet at the time, just a flattened slab of rock to land on. It was a dismal place filled with fools that thought it was their promised land. Like you say there are no exports, no imports because they don't believe in impure material; certainly no tourism, absolutely no reason to go there.

Malin folded her arms across her chest. 'What's your point?'

'My point is if they're not slaving themselves to death or worshipping their god they are making these little statues of their god. Nowhere else in the galaxy would you find one of these. They're specific to their religion, and see how little light the statue reflects? Even the ore they mine is boring.'

He shook the statue. 'I found this statue in a base. Why would a Ceeper go there? There is no one to protect, no piracy to speak of, no goods that they can relieve the locals of. It offers the galaxy, including the Circle, absolutely nothing. Why would they bother?'

Malin snapped her fingers. 'Because they are also lying low, and because it's close to home; close to Soontill.'

'Correct. A Ceeper on rotation from Soontill brought the statue, then was reassigned to another station, where I found it.'

The cockpit was silent. Malin's eyes narrowed, analysing him. Thwaites studied the ground and it felt like Gunn was staring at the back of his head. When no one raised another question he nodded at Thwaites.

'Now highlight Brohman, Lanaest, Arouca and Delta Phoenicis.' Four new purple points glowed in a zig-zag across space.

'Remove Arouca. Draw a line from Delta Phoenicis to Grandmort and another through Delta Phoenicis, Lanaest and Brohman.'

Two near straight lines materialised like a narrow 'V'. Robert closed a fist and smiled. 'Extrapolate that one out, would you Thwaites?'

Thwaites pressed a few buttons and the lines extended to the edge of the map. Everyone crowded forward, eyes wide, bustling to get a better view. Robert stayed back, folded his hands over his chest and let his grin do the

the two lines sat one red blip. Soontill.

unty Katrina,' Malin said, a trace of reverence between the

'KumByar,' Gunn breathed. 'A dark system.'

'Of course,' Robert said. 'If it was in a planetary system the Thargoids would have found it by now, but it's been lost for a thousand years. Their hyperdrives jump massive distances in a single jump. They probably don't even know about dark systems.'

Malin lowered her face to within an inch of the glowing red dot, a tiger sizing up her prey. 'How many ships do we have?' She asked. Thwaites moved to another console. 'There's a couple of hundred here, only a few bigger than two hundred tonnes.'

'I have task force waiting for me,' Gunn said. 'Fifteen ships, Corvettes and similar, all military grade.'

'Plus we have the Starburst,' said Robert.

'What are we waiting for then?' asked Malin, standing up. 'I want to kill me some Ceepers.'

Robert raised his eyebrows. 'On that note, how would you like to pilot an Imperial Explorer with the biggest plasma weapon you've ever seen in your life?'

'Robert!' Gunn snapped, but he waved her off. 'I'm not flying that thing into combat again. The only person I'd kill would be myself.' He turned back to Malin. 'You'd need to fly in close formation with Gunn and two other friends of mine. Can you do that?'

Malin glanced at Gunn from under her bunched brow then turned back to Robert. 'For you, baby, anything.'

Robert breathed in deep. If they were lucky they could get there before INRA. If not they'd have to wipe them out once and for all. Either way there would be a big battle ahead.

He didn't know how it would end. He didn't know if they would be successful, but he did know that this would be what defined him. Not Villist, not his piracy, but what happened in the coming days, and that alone made it worth it.

'Let's make some history.'

Chapter 20

They emerged from hyperspace into the gloom. Normally dark systems held failed stars, or were sad collections of celestial leftovers, comets, asteroids, planetoids, a useful waypoint between systems and nothing more.

But this dark system was different.

It wasn't dark.

A brown dwarf glowed two astronomical units away, a pale purple blob so faint Robert didn't see it at first. There were rocks of all shapes and sizes in the intervening space, but it wasn't an asteroid belt. It was as if a giant hand had shaken out a fist full of space rock and left them where they lay. No pattern to their movement, an obstacle course of junk.

Then there was the fog.

Robert didn't know how else to describe it. He'd never heard of space fog, but there it was, an elongated cloud, like a giant comet's tail, deep inside the maze of rock. The fog was barely transparent. He could make out the shadow of a shape within, perhaps a planet, but he couldn't be sure.

Gunn cursed and slammed her palm against the sensor suite. 'Can't get any readings.'

'None?' He checked his own console. The brown dwarf emitted near infra-red radiation, the random rocks were some 'itium' metal he'd never heard of, and the cloud was

.. nothing. A discrete band of nothing surrounded the proto-star, as if the fog had left anti-sensor residue in its wake. There weren't any ships, there wasn't any space dust, there wasn't any mass at all.

There was just nothing.

'Have you ever seen anything like this before?' Robert asked.

'Never,' she said. They were alone on the bridge but with open communications at the Mortician's insistence. Brown and Blond's ships were visible from the viewport.

'Never,' agreed Blond.

'Once,' Malin said. 'But we'd just ransacked a freighter full of narcotics.

We thought it best to trial the cargo before trying to sell it.'

'Safe business practice,' Robert said as he gave Gunn a what-the-heck look.

The link went silent. Robert's gaze drifted to the scanner. The sign post rocks were so still they might have been painted on the viewport. Behind them were fifteen Alliance capital ships and two hundred and eleven pirate ships. But nothing else was there, nothing else moved.

No one waited for them.

'Where is INRA?' he asked. He struggled to believe they'd beaten INRA here, but if they had, where were the Ceepers?

No one answered. They were all staring at the fog. Robert squared his shoulders. Time to take charge. 'Let's take a look.'

The cloud roiled and twisted as they drew closer. Within, the circular shape of a planet was unmistakable. Gunn linked through to the commodore of the taskforce. 'Throw every sensor you have at that cloud. Get me some answers on that planet.'

'Acknowledged,' came the icy response. The commodore wasn't enjoying being told what to do by a 'spy', but he was following his orders from the Council of Admirals. Gunn had a way of putting people in their place.

Robert ordered the pirate fleet to spread out, hoping to get better sensor readings.

The fog darkened as they approached, its churning convections strengthening. Numbers and graphs briefly compiled on Gunn's sensors before shuffling back to gibberish.

'Commodore,' Gunn said over the link. 'You catch that?'

'Processing.'

The sensors kept beeping, pulses of data becoming frequent as they drew closer. Gunn grunted. 'It could just be anti-sensor chaff.'

They passed the last of the sign post rocks as the Commodore spoke up. 'It's a barren world; seismically active, traces of ammonia; negative one hundred degrees centigrade. There may be structures on the surface.'

'Ships?'

The Commodore paused. 'Insufficient resolution at this distance.' She turned to Robert. 'What do you think?'

'Let's just do this so we can take the Starburst home,' Blond said.

'What my esteemed colleague is trying to say is whatever you want to do, let's do it sooner rather than later.'

'Hey,' Robert said, perking up. 'You've reclaimed your diplomacy. Good for you.'

Brown didn't reply. Robert smiled at Gunn and shrugged. She forced a half smile. One day she'd get his humour.

'Nothing is going to happen while we wait out here. Let's go in, all weapons and shields charged.'

Gunn relayed the orders and they nudged forward. The Constrictor raced up beside them, tilted back and forth – a wave – and rushed forward.

The Explorer jolted as they entered the fog. An ethereal glow enveloped them, like smoke, disappearing as Robert concentrated on it.

'What was that?' Gunn asked, her head darting to the side. The viewscreen gave a flattened one hundred and twenty degree range of vision. She studied the far edge.

'What was what?' Robert leaned toward the link. 'You guys see anything?'

'To the right,' Brown said. Robert looked. There was nothing but faint wisps of fog.

He saw it; a shimmer, a distortion in the wisp. Robert's neck crawled. They couldn't see anything, couldn't detect anything. They were flying blind into an enemy fortification.

The perfect place for... 'A trap!'

His words soaked into the bridge for two and a half seconds. Gunn yanked hard on the controls. 'With me,' she yelled over the link.

Laser bolts flashed from everywhere. The Explorer banged and hissed and the shields flared and sizzled.

Pirate ships exploded, struck by wraith-like laser beams. A quarter of the scanner blips disappeared in an instant.

Screams filled the link, Anger, fear and death layered upon one another. 'We're being murdered,' Robert yelled. 'Lay down some covering fire.'

Gunn's mouth tightened. She pulled the trigger as she yanked the controls across. One quarter of the Starburst lurched out, carving a line through the fog. Faint explosions rippled in the distance.

'Get out, get out,' Robert yelled across the wideband link. 'Reassemble beyond the fog. We've got a fight on our hands.'

Light glowed on the Starburst panel and the Explorer buzzed as two plasma beams connected. Gunn rotated the flight stick, carving out a circle while the pirates fled. The Alliance ships were already gone. 'Where are your friends?' Robert asked Gunn.

She pursed her lips, grunted. She turned the Explorer around; the others followed in sync, Ceeper laser beams chasing them out. They accelerated through the fog, ship shaking like loose bolts in a rotary dryer, increasing in frequency and pitch to the breaking point

.. and then they were out in empty space. Robert had never been so happy to see the mottled black and white vacuum. Pirate ships ripped from the fog around them and raced toward the Alliance ships. The Corvettes laid down covering fire; some of the pirates circled back around, waiting, others fleeing for the asteroids.

Robert mentally cursed them then turned away. He had other things to worry about.

Laser beams fired from the fog. The cruisers retaliated. Lasers bolts criss-crossed, the fog glowing from the energy, then their enemy appeared from the fog.

Small ships. Dark in colour. Ceepers or INRA? Robert zoomed in. Sakers.

'Ceepers,' he growled. He thought of his father and his right hand curled into a fist. 'Payback time.' The Circle ships burst forward, lasers splashing against shields.

'Form up,' Gunn instructed. Small thruster jets pulsed across the pirate ships as they lined up on their chosen targets.

The Ceepers closed in; Sakers in the vanguard; nuggety Asp Explorers at the rear; thin profile, big gun, big problem.

'Standby, standby,' Gunn chanted, raising a clenched fist.

The gap shrunk to almost nothing but still Gunn held up her fist. 'Engage, engage,' she yelled, pushing the throttle to its stops. The Explorer lurched while the pirates raced forward, out through the Alliance shield envelope and into the fray.

Explosions rocked both sides, fire gutting ships before snuffing out in the vacuum. Gunn's Starburst fired into the incoming ships. Four Sakers and an Asp disappeared in a heartbeat. The Ceepers scattered; the pirates pushed forward.

The Sakers flipped back toward the pirates and fired, seemingly bending space around their hulls rather than turning through it.

'Holy shit,' Robert breathed, unable to believe the piloting skill. Pirates disappeared in fireballs. The survivors turned back to the Alliance ships. 'Dammit Gunn, get your buggers in the game,' Robert said.

Gunn changed the link frequency. 'Commodore make yourself useful or put someone else in charge who has a Fate-forsaking pair of balls.' She slammed the link shut and fired the Starburst through a pair of Ceeper ships.

'INRA!' a pirate yelled across the link. Robert's gaze snapped to the scanner.

A swarm of red blips ahead. Circle ships. Green blips around them; pirates and Alliance, more red blips to the rear and closing fast. The scanner zoomed in. A missile shaped Falcon. Black, two purple stripes.

Shit.

Trapped between two forces of Elite pilots, he'd brought all his men here to die.

No!

This wasn't Villist. He wasn't going to fail this time.

'Form up in twos,' he ordered across the wideband.

'Brown, Blond, form a mini starburst against INRA. Malin and I will take the Ceepers. Work in pairs, everyone. Protect each other, and shoot those bastards down.'

The morticians split off as the INRA fighters raced in. Had INRA been hiding in the asteroids or had they just arrived? Either way their tactics felt off. He watched them fire their lasers in sync – then Gunn turned their Explorer around and the INRA ships disappeared from sight.

Robert opened a private link to Malin. 'You okay girl?'

'Don't call me girl,' she spat, her rage almost enough to fuse the link. He grimaced at Gunn.

'She's okay.'

The wave of Circle ships split again. The Ceepers ran rings around the pirates, but the gunners of the Alliance capital ships were aiming true, their plasma cannons scoring more and more hits.

Gunn hit the link. 'Alliance ships, activate manoeuvre Hank-8.' She drove the Explorer into the destruction, Malin on her wing. Gunn fired the Starburst, vaporising the ships ahead, ploughing through the Circle lines and leaving a dead zone in her wake.

The Explorer's shields tumbled as the Ceepers retaliated. 'Rear shields failing,' Robert cried.

Gunn sightlessly flicked a switch and the warning hologram dissipated.

Shield energy redistributed.

The Explorer shivered beneath their couches as if it would separate into its constituent atoms. 'It's going to blow,' Robert yelled.

Gunn shook her head. 'Wait.'

The perimeter of the viewport glowed, a flash of light behind them. The ship juddered, pounded by shrapnel. The rear camera showed the Alliance ships concentrating all their fire on a point just behind the plasma wash from the Explorer's nacelles. As the Sakers swooped away from Gunn's attack run they stumbled straight into the ambush.

The explosions faded. The shields recharged. 'Neat trick,' Robert said, 'But they won't fall for that one again, any other bright ideas?'

The pirates regrouped behind the Explorers, covered by Alliance guns.

Then they burst outward, like air-fighters in an aerobatic show.

Half a dozen explosions scattered against the fog and then the Sakers spun on a credit chip and shot back into the fog. The scanner cleared.

It no longer looked like an utter cluster-fuck. 'What gives?' Robert asked.

The pirates fired their retros and hovered beyond the fog, waiting, except for the Constrictor, which plunged straight in after the Ceepers.

'We don't have time to find out,' Gunn said, turning the Explorer around.

Distant explosions blossomed among the asteroids.

'On us,' Robert said to his survivors. Nothing like fighting a war on two fronts to spice up a day. The pirates raced ahead of the Explorers. The distance felt like light years. Small shiny points darted about; too far away for any detail. 'Come on, come on,' he urged Gunn, but she had the throttle flat to the stops.

The mortician's Explorers lumbered in between the smaller ships, swinging the Starburst like a lance. They didn't seem to be doing well. They didn't have the advantage of the Alliance ships as backup.

Capital ships …

'Where is their ship?' he said.

'Too damaged to travel?' Gunn asked. Robert shook his head. 'It's their prime asset. They'd never leave it behind. He linked to the morticians. 'There's a giant craft out there somewhere, Federation design. A Behemoth.'

Brown panted between gasped words. 'Bigger problems here, citizen.'

Robert twisted toward Gunn. 'Can't this brick go any faster?'

Gunn growled then muttered. 'I'm firing.' The Starburst roared to life. A plasma coupling leaped out to Malin's ship and she fired a moment later. The beams combined and raced across the speckled darkness into the heart of the melee. The INRA ships sprang away in all directions, like flies from a rolled up piece of flimsy.

Brown and Blond fired their retros, sailing backward toward Gunn and Malin. A few INRA ships followed but the morticians knocked them out.

'Garry!' Yelled an all too familiar voice over the link. Anger rippled along the words like electricity through power cables, a keening hate that made Robert's heart bang against his chest.

Criddoch.

'I'm coming to get you, you bastard,' he yelled.

A scanner blip broke off from the INRA pack. A sand crab shaped Asp, the old military version; a Carrack Killer.

Gunn fired at the Asp but before Robert could vocalise his warning it danced aside and fired back, its laser smashing into the Explorer's shields.

Sparks and distortion filled the viewport. Gunn held the trigger as she tracked the Asp. The other three Starbursts joined with Gunn's but Criddoch was beyond Elite, making the ship perform acrobatics only seen in the entertainment feeds.

Robert glanced at Gunn, an unfamiliar doubt pressing against his chest; a pilot possibly better than her.

Gunn yelled at the viewport as she chased the Asp, but Criddoch's ship was more nimble.

The Explorer's shields collapsed.

Criddoch's laser pulsed, probably from thermal overload. He turned away as Gunn gave chase. Malin's coupling dropped out, unable to follow Gunn's manoeuvre.

'Do something,' Robert said.

'I'm trying,' Gunn said. 'You do something.'

'I'm not a pilot.'

'You've got a big mouth.'

Robert pursed his big lips. He grabbed the link. Set it to wideband. He wanted everyone to hear this.

'Go ahead. Piss your gutless laser against my shields, I don't care. You're not my target, boy.' He stressed the last word, wringing out as much contempt and derision as possible while his heart tried to burst from his throat.

'Call off your baby, Admiral. He's just a grunt that does what you tell him to do. No brains, no drive, just a set of hands. He's nothing.'

Criddoch snapped back around. Fired off a shot, but it went wide; an uncharacteristic mistake. He bobbled back to avoid the Starburst.

Was the Admiral even out there? He had to be. Robert had seen the greed in the old man's eyes. He wanted Soontill. He wouldn't operate remotely.

Three Starburst beams separated and fired at Criddoch, but he juked and dived between them.

Gunn bolted from her chair.

'Fates alive Gunn, get back in your chair,' he cried, reaching for her. 'What are you doing?'

'New plan. You get the Behemoth. And then get Soontill. I'm going to take care of this asshole.'

She left before he could say 'I'm not a pilot,' but he was the only person left on the bridge, soon to be the only person on the ship.

The pilot's seat was empty.

Criddoch strafed and backpedalled, raking Robert's Explorer with his laser. Klaxons screamed. The ship jerked sideways, explosive decompression down below.

Robert's heart beat like war drums, dull and bassy, building and building to some internal climax.

'Oh shit, oh shit, oh shit,' he panted, unstrapping. The ship jolted as he half dived, half crashed into the pilot's chair.

He fired the Starburst. He couldn't manoeuvre with Gunn running through the ship. The Explorer's engines were gutless but they could still ruin her day.

The other Explorer's closed in, overlapping their shields, firing their Starbursts. One by one they overheated and blinked out.

Criddoch seized the moment, firing again. 'I've got all day, pirate! You think you could steal Soontill? You're nothing but a two-bit operator. I'm INRA. I'm Elite! I've trained for this all my life. All you're good for is stealing old ladies purses. You're not even in the same league. Watch as I smash you under my heel.' The shields flared and sizzled before his eyes and he could do nothing to escape the damage. 'Get moving Gunn,' he yelled.

As if in answer, a Saker blasted into view. It fired its Thargoid-derived weapon at Criddoch, who snap-rolled away.

Robert clenched a fist. 'All day, Criddoch? You've obviously never pissed off an Alliance operative before. I give you two minutes, two and a half tops. Enjoy the rest of your short life.' He forced a maniacal laugh that he didn't feel.

'I've changed my mind, Admiral. No point seeking revenge against you. You're old; old and frail. You'll be lucky to live through the year. Why waste time hurting you when I can hurt those that mean the most to you? Make that last year as painful as possible?'

Criddoch's rage had always seemed centred about Robert's father. He had watched the way Criddoch looked at the Admiral. There was only one reason for that kind of look.

Love.

'I hope your bastard son has trained hard,' he said. 'My girl? Three times Elite pilot. She's killed so many pirates she got bored. Now she kills relics from a bygone age.'

Gunn flew circles around Criddoch. He kept rolling to escape her laser with few retaliatory shots. Gunn's laser cut out.

Robert frowned. He'd never seen that weapon overheat before. Criddoch spun instantly and fired. Even a glance would have been enough to destroy the Saker, but she deftly sidestepped the blast and fired her own laser. Criddoch swerved, figuring the trap a moment too late. The left wing exploded and tumbled from the Asp.

'Yeehah!' Robert yelled. 'Got to love payback, eh Admiral? Powerless to stop your boy dying right in front of you; so close yet so ineffective. What a pitiful excuse for a father.' He thought of Jordan. The words made him feel hollow, but they were his only weapon at this stage.

Criddoch's engines flared and he raced for the fog, Gunn in hot pursuit.

Robert watched them go then snapped his gaze to the warbling scanner. A nova-blue blip – off the scale large – materialised ahead. The closest asteroid elongated, stretching and narrowing to a kilometre in length, then two; the rugged craters shimmered and sharpened into weapons ports and hull segments.

The Behemoth.

Hundreds of laser bolts filled the viewscreen, flashing toward him. He pushed down on the stick.

Malin, Brown and Blond yelled over each other as they spilt away. An explosion blossomed to the right and the Explorer rocked like an ancient sea boat. Static screeched over the link.

'Who did we lose? Who did we lose?' he yelled, pulling back on the stick while laser fire kept hammering his shields.

'Here,' Brown said.

'I'm alive,' Malin said.

Static.

'Blond?' Robert said. He could barely spare an ounce of concentration as he tried to push the Explorer through some basic corkscrew manoeuvre but even straining his ears he couldn't pick up anything. 'Blond?'

'Once a citizen always a citizen,' Brown said, his voice stone flat.

That was all the confirmation Robert needed. Another person he'd lost. 'Fates,' he shouted, punching the console. 'Brown, take point, Malin take wing. Fuck that ship up.'

'On me,' Brown said. He pushed ahead and Robert tucked onto the left flank.

They turned as one toward the Behemoth. The plasma couplings engaged.

The Behemoth's laser assault intensified, the Explorer's overlapping shields straining and sparking.

Brown kept a bee-line, right down the barrel, right toward the belly of the beast.

He fired.

Robert's beam shifted, linking with Brown's and Malin's and a single massive beam lashed out across the cosmos and into the Behemoth.

A circle of flame burst from the centre of the huge ship's shields and down into its heart. Smoke and flame poured outward, filling its shield envelope.

The Behemoth's retaliation lessened as laser batteries disintegrated under the Starburst.

'We've got him, we've got him,' Malin yelled.

The Behemoth's bow and stern lasers kept firing. Missile alerts blared and overlapped on Robert's alarm console. Explosions strung out against his shields.

'I've lost my last generator,' Malin yelled.

'Don't die,' Brown said. Robert extended his shield envelope while lasers flashed out from the side, small ones, the INRA fighters.

'The ship is too big to disable this way,' Robert said. 'What did the Circle do to the Prince's ship? Take out the bridge.'

Brown shifted angle, Robert turning with him. The Starburst swung across the mass of smoke and flames and sparks, zeroing in on the hidden bridge.

The surviving pirates harried the INRA fighters as their laser beams danced across Robert's shrinking shields.

'You're out of alignment, citizen,' Brown said. 'Line up.'

Robert pushed back toward Brown. The Starburst brightened, its hum crackling across the link. The Behemoth's shields shattered. Hundreds of explosions burst out from the cloud of debris, an accelerating chain reaction, a symphony of destruction.

'My shields are gone,' Malin cried. 'I can't stay in formation.' Robert panned the viewscreen. INRA ships were swarming over her. Fire poured from hundreds of wounds. She was dying.

'We just need a few more seconds,' Brown said. 'Stay where you are.'

An INRA ship exploded and a missile slammed into its neighbour. 'Yeehah!' yelled a voice across the link. The Constrictor flashed past, its laser blasting through the INRA ships. 'The waves are breaking, against the shores of Aaymiay,' yelled the pilot. 'My heart is aching, for your return my love.' The Constrictor swerved to avoid one laser and ploughed into another. An INRA Falcon detonated.

Space went white.

The viewport polarised to pitch black but Robert could still see the wave of shrapnel rush outward.

The battle paused, mid action, the explosion blinding everyone. The Explorers rumbled as debris smashed into them.

The viewscreen de-polarised. Darkness returned.

The Behemoth was gone, replaced by a cloud of metallic fragments reflecting the pale purple light of the brown dwarf. The remaining INRA ships drifted. The Constrictor hung quietly. Fire raged inside Malin's Explorer, a burning piece of Swiss cheese.

Robert's heart beat, beat, beat, each beat a moment that felt stuck. The INRA ships turned.

A string of hyperspace vectors opened. Still the Explorers didn't move. Undulating static ebbed and waned across the link like the waves against a shore.

INRA were gone. Except for Criddoch. Gunn ...

He hailed the Constrictor. 'Nice flying. Did you see a friendly Saker by any chance?'

'Oh my beloved girl, come back to me, I could die of love for you. '

'What?' Robert said. Was the pilot singing?

'Ignore him.' A regal, Imperial female voice. 'He's drunk. We didn't see your Saker.'

'Drunk?'

The male voice returned. No slur, definitely not Imperial. 'I'm sure not taking on INRA sober!'

Robert nodded. 'Very wise.'

The Imperial growled. A lot like Gunn's growl. 'Don't encourage him.'

'You finished?' Brown asked. 'We're not done here yet.'

'Back to the fog?'

'Back to the fog.'

* * *

Brown fired the Starburst, clearing a hole through the battle raging over the fog. The Circle ships sprang away from the attack, straight into the Alliance ships' laser beams. The survivors fled into the fog.

'After them,' Robert yelled. His ragtag fleet ploughed into the fog. 'Don't stop to fight,' Robert warned. 'Maintain full speed until you clear the fog or ram into the planet.'

Malin's Explorer fell behind. 'You alright girl?' Robert asked.

'Don't call me girl. Ship's just a bit out of breath. I'll catch up with you.'

Robert's rear camera showed plasma pulsing from the fading ship's right nacelle. Malin would fly a ship straight down the guts of hell itself before giving up on a prize like Soontill however. He hoped.

The fog enveloped her and she disappeared. 'See you soon,' he whispered. Ahead, a sand storm, the Explorer wobbling as if he were flying through atmospheric turbulence. 'Come on, you bugger,' he muttered. The flight stick blurred as it shook, appearing as if in two places at once.

Sweat soaked his hands, his arms burned. 'Just a few seconds more,' he prayed. 'A few seconds more.'

The stick wrenched free, the Explorer spiralled away and he cleared the fog, drifting into clear space.

The far side of the fog glowed. Glints of metal twisted back and forth in the dead space ahead.

Soontill lay below him.

A uniform burnt brown ash colour. Dead, dusty, undulating hills without a single crater. Something had come through and burnt the place clean after the Thargoids left.

Or wiped them out.

The altimeter read twenty thousand metres, and he had to decelerate to try and pull the Explorer up. Ships were already landing, likely searching for treasure. Five ships hovered over the carcass of a Thargoid warship, so badly deteriorated it looked like a wire frame model from a child's computer game.

Brown was dead ahead. 'You on holiday, citizen? It's just you and me now.'

Robert pulled the Explorer around, its weak engines struggling against gravity. He formed up with Brown. They saw it at the same time.

'What in the name of KumByar is that?' Brown whispered.

Robert just stared, eyes wide, jaw hanging loose. 'I have no idea,' he breathed.

It was an earthen mound, as tall as a space elevator, a giant anthill with legs sprouting from the bottom, eight at regular spacings, but they had corroded away to hollow husks. There were openings throughout the mound but stains seeped from each one.

It was dead.

That was when he noticed the human designed structure behind it. A modest tower overlooking a standard ship airlock that burrowed into the ground.

'You thinking what I'm thinking, citizen?' 'Blow the airlock?'

'Blow the airlock.'

Robert followed Brown's trajectory, up toward the fog to gain altitude, then back around, screaming down toward the airlock.

The ground raced up at them but Brown didn't slow. He fired the Starburst and it smashed into the airlock doors.

Brown's aim adjusted, blowing another hole in the doors. Robert's heart hammered against his ribs, a weight filling his throat, choking him as he bared down on his death; too late to turn away now. The doors filled the viewscreen.

Brown shifted aim again and again, tearing a hole in the door and then a section fell away and the two Explorers raced through.

Chapter 21

Robert awoke. He unstrapped and rolled to the floor. The Explorer was on an angle. There was gravity.

He'd crash landed.

He crabbed along the passages to the cargo hold. The elevator still had power. He shrugged his shoulders, flexed his fingers, prodded his pressure suit and touched his remlok.

Then he activated the elevator.

The elevator jarred to a halt as one corner hit the floor. He lost his footing and rolled over the edge to the ground.

He dragged himself to his feet. Above, the jagged remains of the upper airlock door dangled inwards, one piece hanging precariously above him. A trench meandered along the grey-steel floor. The Starburst had burrowed deep into the soil.

Brown's Explorer crouched on the far side. Brown was running to a hatch built into the rock wall.

Robert chased after him, each step pulling at the repaired flesh of his stomach. He reached the airlock just after Brown. They stepped through. Brown pulled a Lance and Ferman from a pocket and handed it over. 'You know how to use one of these I assume?'

Robert gave him a raised eyebrow-you-can't-be-serious look, but Brown smiled, an odd look for his face. He was trying to add humour to his resume.

'Don't quit your day job.' Robert grabbed the laser, checked its action and tested the power pack. He turned back to Brown. 'I'm sorry about Blond.'

Brown met his gaze. 'He was a citizen.'

The airlock cycle completed. Brown and Robert raised their guns in readiness. The door shot upward.

No one was waiting for them.

They both stood there a moment, taken aback. 'Well,' Robert mumbled after a moment. 'I guess they're inviting us in?'

'Be rude to decline,' Brown agreed and he stepped through. He oozed forward in a half crouch – thigh muscles surely on fire – and swung his pistol back and forth. He nodded Robert forward.

It was a standard passage, identical to hundreds of other starports, the dirty blue-green walls made from that rough pre-fab stuff they'd used for the last few hundred years. The floor consisted of a plain matt pad of 'crete. The odd control panel blinked down the hall.

The place was deserted. It could have been four AM at any starport in the galaxy if it wasn't for the muted explosions from above.

'Where to?' Brown asked.

'I want answers,' Robert said. 'The control centre.'

They jogged down the passages, guns up, eyes and ears on full alert. Holographic signs pointed them towards rec centres, medical bays, the mess, crew quarters and finally to command and control. The sign pointed toward a pair of armoured doors. The handle was a thick rectangle of ship-hull grade duralium.

Brown studied the door. 'Four core. I'm sure there will be something in the Explorer for that.'

He turned to leave but Robert said, 'Wait.' He stepped forward gingerly and brushed the handle with his fingertips. No electric shock. Emboldened he wrapped his hand around the handle. He wrenched it down.

It unlatched.

'They've evacuated,' Brown said. Robert refused to believe it. They wouldn't have given up Soontill like that, unless …

'They knew we were coming,' he breathed. The realisation slapped Robert across the face but he couldn't believe they would just surrender Soontill like that.

'We'd better hurry,' Brown urged.

Haste was their friend. If there was an ambush he didn't have the time to get bogged down in it. He'd have to fight on the run. Left. Eyes up. Clear; down the passage.

The passage forked. They skidded to a stop, looked at each other, nodded. Brown went left.

Robert went right.

Grey walls flashed past; the red glow of a panel; floor shivering from distant explosions. Another turn, no troopers. Empty passage after empty passage; no defence of such a critical part of the base.

He turned the corner, straight into the C&C.

No Ceepers. He stepped forward, gaze probing behind consoles and control chairs, scanning the computer banks for a hidden sniper.

An enormous viewscreen wrapped around the far mezzanine wall. It displayed a satellite view of Soontill, small pinpricks of black dancing back and forth, laser pulses flashing between them.

A man stood before the viewport, disguised by his black cloak. He watched standing perfectly still.

'Welcome home Robert.' he said.

Robert blinked. His right foot stopped halfway through the step.

'Who are you?' Robert said to the shadow. The man turned. He wore a hood, his features shrouded.

Robert stepped closer, one step at a time, gun at eye level, up the stairs, stopping two feet from the man.

The man pulled back the hood revealing thick white hair, deep bushy eyebrows and river deltas for crow's feet. The eyes were sad, a deep green with no hint of deception, no hint of malice, just acceptance.

'You look just like him,' said the man, a glum smile on his lips. Robert's heart hammered in his chest. 'Like who?'

'Oberon Ryder.'

'My name is Garry. I'm a Scotsman from New Aberdeen.'

The man gave a tired laugh. 'No my dear boy, you're as Tionislan as the Wreckplace, but you were born here on Soontill, the grandson of our recently deceased leader.'

'What?' The walls leaned in around him. The air tasted bitter.

'You have his eyes, solid Tionislan eyes.'

Robert swiped his hand in front of him as if to erase the man's words but his hand slowed and dropped. The air cooled, his lungs felt small, squeezed from inside his chest, his heart beating bigger and bigger and bigger until there wasn't any room in his chest for anything other than one blood pumping muscle.

Everything fell into place. Everything. His gun dropped.

On one level his life had always felt like a lie. He'd never been at home in the Federation Navy, he'd left piracy only to come back to it, something just a little bit off kilter.

The statue weighed down the pocket on his pressure suit. He pulled it out. Stared at it. His father hadn't got it on a piracy job gone bad. He had it for the same reason as the other Ceeper.

'The dead man on that freighter, he was my grandfather?'

The man nodded. His mouth moved but Robert didn't hear him. Reality seemed muted, the colours fading to pastels, a numbness overcoming him just like after Villist, when he'd stumbled away, unsure if he was alive or dead, somehow finding his way to Smuggler's Junction, back to a life of piracy.

Clues, like jigsaw puzzle pieces came together. The dead man had freaked out his father, and had looked oddly familiar. Jordan had named his ship Vista Oculto. Hidden view.

Hide in plain sight.

No one knew his father back on New Aberdeen. He couldn't find his mother's grave, not because of a poor memory but because it wasn't there. She wasn't even Scottish. None of them were.

It was all a lie.

His father had read him stories as a youth, of dashing heroes, of people born to rise above the rest.

He'd become the hero he'd been destined to become and run away from it. But in running away he'd slammed straight into his past. He'd come full circle, back to the Circle.

He looked at his hands, turned them, seeing them in a new light. The hands were worn, rough, normal looking hands, yet the blood running within them was special. 'I'm a Ceeper?'

The man nodded. 'By birth. Oberon was our leader. Jordan was one of our best, until he died in an accident, or at least so we had thought.'

You have no idea what I went through to get you away from them. I'm not letting them take you again, echoed his father's voice.

Robert had written off his father's words as fearful ravings, but they were the literal truth. He had staged their deaths to escape the Circle. *Stage our deaths? There's a trick to it.*

Why? And why had he kept the statue? Had he wanted Robert to find out? Had he wanted Robert to come back at some point? To lead them?

Brown burst into the room. His pistol waved to the left, the right then snapped up to the cloaked man.

'What are you doing?' Brown said. 'We need to debrief him.'

'I believe you,' Robert said to the cloaked man, ignoring Brown. Then he raised his weapon to the man's heart. 'But it makes no difference. You've committed atrocious crimes against humanity and I'm going to make sure that it doesn't happen again.'

Brown holstered his pistol and stepped up to the Mezzanine. The cloaked man stepped toward Robert, who jerked his gun forward in reaction, halting the man's step.

'Robert, please, you are one of us. Surely you can see what we are trying to do? Doesn't the name Ryder mean anything to you? Did your father not tell you the stories?'

Robert nibbled at the obvious bait. 'The Dark Wheel.'

Brown laughed. 'Come off it old man. They're just a legend.'

'So is Soontill. The Dark Wheel has been around for centuries, always led by a Ryder, always hunting for Raxxla; until we learned of the legend of Soontill.

'At that stage Alex Ryder had two sons: Neptune and Oberon. Oberon believed he could find Soontill. Neptune considered anything other than Raxxla to be irrelevant. Arguments ensued and we split from the Dark Wheel. We followed Oberon and formed the Circle of Independent Elite Pilots with the goal of using Soontill's power to protect humanity.'

Robert snorted. 'You screwed that up, didn't you?'

The man shook his head. 'You have no idea what is out there, do you, Robert? The dangers? Humanity is on the brink. Once more our species stands on the precipice yet you want to look inward, close your eyes to the danger and maintain the status quo.'

The man cleared his throat. 'Three hundred years ago there was a big war. The Galactic Cooperative broke up, Independents formed into factions, armed by the Federation and the Empire. Humanity enjoyed a war economy. Full of weapons and munitions, factories ready to supply more, people willing to throw their lives away for patriotic glory.

'And then the Thargoids came. They were superior, they were in greater number. And they had genocide on their minds. Humanity nearly went extinct. Like the Dinosaurs, Robert, erased from history.' He brought this index finger and thumb together. 'We were this close to the end. INRA were able to stop them but the only reason humanity could even get close to counterattacking was due to the existing state of war, primed and ready for prolonged conflict. If we hadn't been ready we would have crumbled under the first wave, every planet and person lost forever.'

The man's stare darkened. 'But for all that, Robert, the Thargoids saw it as little more than a border skirmish. We don't know exactly what is happening inside their space, but we do know they are heading this way again. With the Federation fighting the Imperials over Villist and other planets, and the Alliance stabbing them both in the back, who is going to fight the Thargoids? Who?'

Robert didn't answer. He couldn't answer.

'The Federation would protect its citizens to the last soldier,' Brown said, his eyes narrowed. 'They—'

'The Federation is a bloated cesspool of corruption and bureaucracy,' interrupted the man. 'They couldn't launch a defensive fleet if the Thargoids linked in a month early to announce their arrival.'

He turned back to Robert, both arms up. He stepped forward. Robert didn't stop him. 'Robert, tell me what you would do. We tried to warn them. We left clues, messages. We tried to carefully guide governments to prevent war but all our messages were ignored. No one wants to look to the future when all they care about is the eight year presidential cycle. So I ask again, Robert, would you want to face the Thargoids with a strong unified force or separate fleets so busy squabbling with each other they can't turn and face the real enemy? What would you do?'

What would he do?

Robert opened his mouth, but no words came out. No one could unite the Empire and the Federation. Not without war.

Millions of voices, mothers, fathers, children, screaming for life, screaming for salvation, screaming for him, screaming for him to save them.

War wasn't the answer.

He shoved his gun's barrel under the man's chin. 'And that gives you the right to murder millions? Women? Children? Babies? The war you tried to start would ravage humanity, not save it.'

The man pushed forward onto the barrel, driving Robert back. His eyes were red, moist. 'Do you think I wanted to do this?' His face was carved into sharp lines and crevasses. 'Do you think I don't dream every night of the people that would die? I'm not a sociopath, Robert. Every time I look at my grandson I think of the children that will die under my orders. Every time I close my eyes I see fire. I hear screams.' The man stopped to breathe. He put his hand in his pocket, clutched something. 'I'm not a monster, Robert, I'm a man charged with responsibilities to the human race; the race, Robert, not the individual. We made an oath to protect humanity. If I could have done that without a single death, I would have.

'But the men in charge of the galaxy don't think like that. They only understand violence, they only respond to violence. To make them understand that all of them could die, I have to kill a good percentage of them.

'So I'm not the monster. I'm the one trying to make the monsters understand.'

Robert saw clear conviction in the man's eyes, but the pupils danced rapidly. The man believed everything he said. He believed it more than he believed in gravity or solar radiation. Robert stepped back, his pistol dropping to his side.

'What are you doing?' Brown asked, bringing up his own pistol. 'Shoot him or take him into custody.'

Robert shook his head. 'I can't kill this man. He is me, just a version of me that has gone way off the spectrum and around the corner. He doesn't need death. He needs pity.'

Robert stepped away, staring at the old man whose eyes were pleading. Not for his life, but his cause.

'Take him prisoner, Brown. Do what you like with him, then take your Starburst and leave us the Fates alone.'

Brown holstered his pistol, pulled a zip cord from his pocket, yanked the man's arms behind his back and tied him up. 'Let's go, Grandpa. And don't try anything on the way out.'

'I have no need. The rest of our leadership have already evacuated. Do you think the Circle can be defeated that easily?

'Yes,' said Robert. 'Without Soontill you'll be reduced to pissing into the wind, trying in vain to stop pirates. I'll take that over galaxy-wide murder any day.'

Brown pushed the man out the far doors and out of sight. The doors closed with a thump, leaving Robert alone in the massive room.

He stood a moment, absorbing the detail, the cold electronic beeps, the muted satellite feeds showing small, insignificant ships fighting above the planet surface, nameless statistics rolling down various displays.

He could almost understand how the Circle had become so callous about life, about the innocents of the galaxy.

He stepped up to the viewscreen, standing exactly where the man had been a few minutes earlier.

This place was his; his by birth, his to control. He could have been the next leader of the Circle of Independent Elite Pilots. Would he have been the same person? Would he have been at Villist? Would his father have brought him up as Scottish?

He turned from the viewport. He wouldn't have liked his Ceeper self.

He strummed around the consoles, pressing buttons, running his hands over the cool steel then found the emergency controls. There was a self-destruct option, already primed. All it required was verbal access. A message from the cloaked man, or had he meant to go down in a blaze of glory?

Robert pressed the button.

'Voice activation required,' chirped the computer. 'Oberon Ryder.'

The computer chirped again. 'Voice activation required.'

Robert frowned, tried to imagine what his voice would sound like in sixty odd years. Old, stretched, brittle. He tried again.

'Voice activation required,' chirped the computer. Robert tried again, using more chest in his voice.

'Self-destruct sequence activated. This facility will self-destruct in ten minutes.'

Robert ran for the door.

'Garry!' roared the voice, booming down the hallway. 'You killed him you bastard.' The voice reverberated off the pre-fab walls, vibrated along the floor. 'I'm coming for you pirate!'

The depth, the anger, the arrogance, all rolled up into one fingernail-on-hull shivering voice.

Criddoch.

Robert skidded to a stop. Gunn.

No.

Criddoch couldn't have beaten her. Couldn't have.

His breathing echoed in the confined passageway. Criddoch's voice sounded behind him. Robert's fingers tightened around his pistol. His chest rose and fell as his heart rate climbed an elevator to infinity.

She wasn't dead, people like her didn't get killed by people like Criddoch. She wasn't dead.

'I made her scream.'

Robert spun. Now Criddoch sounded in front of him.

'I disabled her ship, Garry. I boarded her. She screamed long and hard for her life and then I ripped her apart.'

Robert doubled over, his lungs paralysed. The air tasted thin, almost non-existent, gulping in a vacuum like he'd done too many times before.

'But I'm not going to go that easy on you, pirate.' Now Criddoch sounded to the right. 'I'm going to make you pay for what you did to him. I'm going to take you apart piece by piece. I'm going to make you beg me to kill you.'

Robert forced himself back upright, still gasping, still trying to get his lungs back in the game. Ahead was an intersection. Straight would take him to the airlock. Criddoch's voice had come from the right. He had no idea where left went.

'Warning: this facility will self-destruct in five minutes. Please evacuate.'

Robert's knuckles tensed around his pistol. He clenched his teeth so hard pain shot up his skull.

He stepped up to the intersection, stared ahead to where he imagined the airlock – and freedom – waited.

He wasn't going straight.

No chance.

He didn't leave people behind.

He was always the last one to leave. Robert turned right.

Chapter 22

Robert burst through a fire door out onto a gangway running across an open cavern. Dim light refracted through the glass dome a mile overhead, down to the terraces below, filled with greenery and fruits. The air felt moist, tasted almost salty. And it was warm, like the jungles of Vega.

Electrical conduits and flexible plumbing ran beside the gangway in big loops.

Robert stepped forward.

The far door opened. A hulking figure stepped through. Criddoch.

'Warning: this facility will self-destruct in four minutes. Please evacuate.'

He glanced backward. The fire door hung ajar; an easy escape route, a spaceship, freedom and the rest of his life.

He turned back.

No way I'm leaving.

They stood at opposite ends of the steel grating gangway. Criddoch's legs were spread, arms loose by his side. He cracked his neck. He clenched his fists, a stretched and slimy smile; a devil's smile.

Robert couldn't remember the last time he'd slept properly or consumed anything other than coffee. He'd run on empty for so long. But he couldn't feel any of that now. The fatigue, the continual adrenaline, everything faded away until there was just him and the blood surging through his body, bringing oxygen and fuel to his tired muscles.

He ran.

Legs and arms pumping, eyes narrowed. Criddoch started running. They closed in.

Robert ripped out his pistol, aimed for Criddoch's head. Fired as he ran.

The laser pulses ricocheted off Criddoch's personal shield generator. The pistol's hum died. Robert slowed, gaze drifting to his pistol, realising he'd been duped.

Criddoch's cackle echoed off the walls, an entire chorus of laughing Criddochs.

Robert dropped the pistol. He sped up. He was about to die, but he wasn't going to give Criddoch the satisfaction of an easy victory.

What were his weaknesses? Huge arms, bigger chest, an absolute wrecking ball. Quick too, or he wouldn't be a good pilot.

Not many weaknesses. Criddoch lunged at him.

Robert leapt onto the handrail, slipped, grabbed the electrical cabling and swung out over the cavern. He reached the end of his arc, swung back in, feet raised together, straight into Criddoch's chest.

Criddoch stumbled back, Robert landed, stabbed his foot out. Cartilage cracked, Criddoch dropped.

Another kick. Criddoch's hands flashed out. Fingers grabbed Robert's foot. The walls blurred past. His head hit the floor, jarring his vision. A fuzzy Criddoch loomed over him.

Legs scrambling, Robert leapt up. Criddoch's leg kicked out. Robert jumped, breathless. Feet back to the floor, turning, running, toward the far door.

A brick wall smashed into his back; the grating slammed into his face. An iron grip grabbed his chest. Walkway and walls flashed past. He was in the air, staring up at the dome, the structural reinforcements, fans spinning in the walls. He tried to wriggle free but the iron grip strengthened, pushed him higher.

Then he was free, the far wall flying toward him, the railing shooting past below him.

Robert reached out. Two fingers touched the railing, slipped.

Into a tangle of wires, they pressed into his face and his chest, pulled at his legs.

He swished around in the tangle; power, lighting, coolant. He tried to put his feet down. The wires wouldn't stay still. Criddoch's face appeared above him.

'I have my own gun, you know. I don't suppose you still have your personal shield?' He smiled as Robert's eyes widened. 'I didn't think so.'

Criddoch reached behind him.

Robert grabbed the sgian dubh from his ankle sheath.

Criddoch swung the gun in a long arc; a mean industrial lead thrower. Robert grabbed the coolant tube.

Criddoch fired.

Robert twisted aside as he sliced the tube.

Icy wetness soaked his face. Coolant burst upward. Criddoch dug at his eyes as he stumbled out of view, screaming.

Robert reached up – his stomach stretched – and pulled himself over the railing. He kicked Criddoch in the balls and grabbed his gun. Criddoch pulled backward, Robert pushed the gun up and crushed Criddoch's trigger finger down.

Explosions boomed through the cavern. Glass cracked and clinked. The gun went dry.

Criddoch dropped the gun but his other fist streaked forward. Pain smashed through Robert's cheek and he flew back. The railing slammed into his chest. Air exploded from his lungs. Robert twisted back around, gasping.

They stood there, watching each other. Criddoch squinting through red eyes, his face blistered and blotching. His mouth stretched into a grimace equally pain and anger. Coolant dripped from his saturated hair, hung from his nose and ears and chin. He clenched his arms. They doubled in size, veins visible through his pressure suit. His shoulders rose until he looked like some drowned golem from a fantasy feed. He didn't move, just breathed, chest rising and falling, rising and falling.

Robert's hand dropped to his cramping stomach. It came back red. 'Warning: this facility will self-destruct in three minutes. Please evacuate.'

There was a door behind Robert. Forty metres away, fifty tops. But he'd never make it. Criddoch was faster than him. If he took a backward step Criddoch would attack. He had to kill Criddoch. Throw or topple him over the edge, or take the gangway down, with both of them on it.

Criddoch cracked his neck. His voice dropped to a bass boom. 'Show me what you got, pirate. Show me you're a man and not some yellow-bellied girl.'

Robert rushed in. He had to stay inside those big arms to nullify their strength. He saw a blur, ducked under a swinging right, raised his own right to block Criddoch's left then jabbed at his throat, trachea denting under the blow.

Criddoch gasped. His leg flashed out. Robert reflexively jumped back, looked up.

Knuckles crunched into his nose and he flew back. Grating banged into his head. He smelt copper, tasted it.

Glass cracked above, spider webs spreading from the centre. Air hissed, escaping outside.

Robert's hands and feet grabbed at the cold grating. Pushing up, Criddoch's boot thumped into Robert's chest. He dropped, shuffled backward, got his feet underneath him.

The big boot flew forward. Robert's head snapped back and down. Criddoch filled his vision, vicious smile on his face. Thick fingers encircled Robert's neck, squeezed, lifted.

The dome clinked, exploded.

Air rushed past them, sucking, pulling, the wind roaring past their ears. 'Warning: this facility will self-destruct in two minutes. Please evacuate.'

Criddoch tightened his grip, Robert's gasps dying away. His body compressed under his pressure suit.

'We're going to die,' Robert croaked. 'We have to get out of here. If we don't run we die.'

'Then we die!' Criddoch boomed. 'You took him from me, pirate. You think just because he doesn't treat me like a child that he didn't love me? Do you think you're the only person who can have a loving father?'

Pain shot through Robert's jaw as Criddoch lifted him upward. His mouth shrunk, choking. Black tendrils enclosed his vision.

Robert tensed. With his last strength, his neck as a pivot, he kicked Criddoch in the groin. Pressure suit squished beneath his foot.

Criddoch inhaled.

Robert dropped, gasping, half blinded. Fire burned inside, the fire of survival. His hand closed around the railing, pulled himself up.

'Warning: this facility will self-destruct in one minute. Please evacuate.' Robert ran.

Nothing left to lose, weakened muscles groaning, stabbing pain in his stomach. Every nerve ending focused on the door, no more than fifty metres away.

The railing clanged behind him, louder and louder; forty metres. He felt the beast behind him.

Thirty metres.

A hand grabbed his shoulder.

Robert swung his fist as Criddoch spun him.

'Fuck you,' Robert spat, crunching Criddoch's face. He slammed his fist out and in, again and again, rage and desperation fuelling his arm. Criddoch's nose burst open, his eyes puffed up, his cheek split.

Criddoch's arm blurred forward and Robert's head slammed against the railing and down. Criddoch dragged him up, held him against the railing. The steel dug into his back.

Criddoch raised his fist; held it there, five mounds of destruction hovering half a metre from Robert's face.

Criddoch slammed his fist down.

The world turned red, spinning darkness. Ears ringing, everything numb.

'Warning: self-destruct sequence activated.'

Explosions ripped across the greenhouse. Fireballs rose from below. The walls shattered inward, dust and smoke filling the cavern. The closest door exploded, flying forward in slow motion, bouncing along the bow of a shockwave.

Criddoch seemed oblivious.

'You took him from me,' he spat.

Robert's left eye crunched closed, his right a slit of red. Nose crushed, sucking breaths through swollen mouth. Everything else felt dead, unresponsive, inoperable.

'You took him from me!' Criddoch screamed, an almost mortal wail.

Fire raged up around them, burning his back. The gangway screeched below him. It sagged. Robert stared blankly up at the broken dome.

The dome smashed apart. A black shadow raced inward. A bird of prey, long sharp beak and pointed wings.

A laser beam erupted from the shadow's nose and slammed into an overhead steel truss. The truss groaned and twisted. It pulled away from the wall, falling straight toward them.

Criddoch dived away. The truss landed across the handrails, millimetres away from Robert. The handrail sagged, crushed, and caved inward.

Steel shrieked. The gangway dropped; jarring to a halt, rocking Robert forward onto his hands and knees.

The black bird soared downward, engine wash streaming from its rear. Gunn.

But Gunn was dead, which meant Robert was dead too. Was this where the Fates had sent him for eternity?

Where was the Bruce?

Where was Dad?

The railing flattened under the truss. The gangway bent downward, pulling at its centre down into a 'U' shape.

This wasn't Damnation. He wasn't dead.

Not yet.

The Saker fired its retros, burning the rapidly escaping air. The boarding ramp lowered.

Robert slowly turned. Criddoch climbed toward him through the twisted remains of the truss. His red eyes almost glowed, an inhuman determination forcing him through when any sane person would have run the other way.

Robert wiped his face; half a good eye, half a good brain, barely enough oxygen to power them both. But Gunn edged the Saker closer, the boarding ramp less than a meter from the railing, and Robert figured it out.

The gangway groaned. The grating crushed together at the centre, pushing against itself and twisting as the gangway bent further and further down.

He felt the snap of steel through the gangway. It dropped a metre, snagging on a loop of wires. Then they tore out. The gangway dropped. The second loop took the load then snapped. The gangway lurched downwards, closer and closer to the simmering fire a mile down.

He shakily climbed the first railing, his knees against the second. The gangway dropped another half metre. He swayed forward, caught himself.

The next three loops shattered as one. He was in freefall. Robert climbed to the top railing.

Criddoch emerged from the truss. The ramp flew up at him.

He caught his balance, tensed himself, swung his arms back-

Criddoch put one foot forward. He leapt. Robert leapt too.

The gangway dropped away. He floated, Criddoch's screams fading away as he plummeted to his death.

He crashed into the ramp, the edge slicing into his ribs. He screamed, sliding backwards, fingers frantically reaching for a hold. The embossed floor was too flat, there were no other points.

He caught a hydraulic ram and jarred to a halt, one arm free, legs dangling over the edge.

The walls disappeared behind the ring of fire. The shattered remains of the dome fell past, hitting the remains of one wall then spinning down to the floor and smashing apart.

The Saker twisted around. Robert's legs twirled overhead. He flew over the ramp, into the ship and against the far wall. The ramp clamped shut.

Robert blacked out.

Chapter 23

Robert awoke. A hand stroked his face. He opened his good eye. Gunn's face was close, her eyes focused on his forehead as she wiped with a blood stained cloth. Her gaze dropped to meet his. Her mouth spread in a wide beautiful smile. Everything seemed brighter. Her lips parted.

'Hi,' she said.

'Hi.' His guts clenched and pain shot through his stomach. She stepped back and he doubled up for a moment before laying back again. He lay in an acceleration couch on the bridge of an Explorer.

Gunn leant back in and stroked his hair.

'He told me you were dead,' he whispered, 'he told me he'd killed you.'

'Almost,' she said, still stroking his hair, pushing it back off his face. Her fingers were soft and warm. She could have kept doing that forever. 'Ambushed me in the fog, I detonated a mine a little too close then went silent. Lost a wing but it convinced him.'

'I wanted to kill him. And he didn't have anything worth stealing.' She smiled, megawatts of radiance, stroked him again.

'I know.'

They looked into each other's eyes, Gunn's green and wide, her pupils dancing back and forth as she scanned his one open one. Then he coughed and doubled over again. She gave him room. He put a hand to his stomach. It throbbed like heck but it wasn't bleeding. He glanced up at her. 'Your work?'

She shook her head and nodded to the right. Robert turned, his gaze tracking over a cracked viewscreen, dangling and blackened consoles, and to Malin. She leant against the pilot's couch, arms crossed and her upper lip curled in mock disgust, but her eyes had a mischievous twinkle. 'Hello stranger.'

'Hi. You put me back together?'

'Don't I always?'

He smiled. 'You two make a good rescue team.'

The two women glanced at each other. Their eyes narrowed slightly but then Malin laughed. 'She's okay, for a Viper.'

Robert coughed a laugh then stood. He staggered forward to the viewport, each swing of a leg like dragging a bulk freighter.

Soontill filled the bottom half of the view, split in two by the crack in the viewscreen, black and white space above, uniform brown mud below. Ships fluttered down and back up. Cobras, Eagles, Adders, Kraits, and that bloody Constrictor.

'We won?' he asked. 'We won.' Malin said.

Robert shook his head. 'No. We haven't won. Not yet.' He gave them both a solid stare. 'This planet has to be destroyed.'

Gunn snorted. 'With what?' 'The Starburst.'

Silence filed the bridge. 'Will that work?' Malin asked finally.

'It has to. This planet can't be controlled by anyone. It has to be removed. Regardless of whatever Thargoid threats are happening out there, humanity will handle them. Or it won't. But today, tomorrow, next week, next year, there won't be any more innocent deaths, not because of this planet. We have to destroy it.'

The women looked at each other then back to Robert. Gunn nodded first, Malin a second later. 'Okay hun.'

Robert limped to Malin's chair and activated the link. He cleared his throat. 'This is Robert Garry. Thank you everyone for your efforts. Thank you for staying around to help us win the war. For your losses, I am so very sorry. I will spend the rest of my life mourning them. But we have made a difference today. Be proud. Stand tall. And fill your cargo holds with whatever you can find. But be off the planet in two hours' time because we are going to supernova it.' He shut the link before anyone could reply, but Brown's voice pushed through the inter-Explorer link. 'What is your plan, citizen?'

'I saw the damage the Starburst did in the airlock down there. It burrowed right down through the soil, must have gone for kilometres. Gunn's buddies said the planet was seismically active. I say we hit a fault line and let Soontill do the rest for us.'

Gunn found Robert a coffee pouch. He could feel it spread through his numb body. He closed his eyes as Malin and Gunn talked battle, showing manoeuvres with their hands.

'It's time,' said Gunn. Robert opened his eyes. She was in the sensor station couch, Malin in the pilot's seat.

'This time you're following me,' Malin said across the link to Brown.

'My pleasure.'

They tightened into Starburst formation, a single coupling connecting the ships. He counted the pirate ships as they flew up, one a time. He ignored their continual queries. They wouldn't understand.

'Okay,' Robert said, 'let's do this.'

Malin dropped them to a few kilometres above the surface. She fired the Starburst. Soil exploded into geysers as she arced the beam across the planet. The Thargoid hulk disappeared under the beam. What looked like mines disintegrated in clouds of dirt. The dead Thargoid hive or whatever it was shattered into dust. The remains of the Circle base crumbled under the attack. She destroyed everything artificial.

'We're getting close,' Gunn said. She pressed a button and a targeting box appeared on the viewscreen.' Malin adjusted the Explorer's vector. She spun them around until they hovered nose down above the coordinates.

'Ready?' she asked everyone.

Robert looked down at the planet. He'd spent his entire life hearing about the place. His father's final words instructed him to find it, his birth planet, the place where his ancestors had lived and breathed and died; a tool too powerful for any person to handle.

He nodded. 'Do it.'

Malin fired, Brown in sync. The double beam shot down, enveloping the target box. Malin kept the trigger down. The ground shook, slowly at first, then more and more violently until a fissure ripped across the landscape, stretching to the horizon. Lava spewed out across the brown soil. The planet shook like a resonance bomb.

'Climb, climb,' Robert urged and Malin fired the retros. They pulled back to orbit and watched as the planet ripped itself apart.

The shaking settled down. The planet was still in one piece but a roiling sea of lava covered the surface. Hopefully any remaining Thargoid tech was destroyed or hidden forever.

'Is that enough?' Malin asked.

'It'll have to be,' came Brown's voice from behind them. Robert turned. Brown held a pistol at a casual hip height, but the sharp end was pointing in Robert's general direction.

'Again?' Robert asked. 'Can't people just stop pointing guns at me? Just for one minute?' He collapsed back into his couch facing away from Brown.

Magnetic boots clicked on the steel floor. Brown came into view and holstered his gun. 'I need to take this ship home with me.'

Robert nodded. 'We had a deal.'

'And I held up my end.'

'As will I.' He surveyed the damaged bridge then nodded to Gunn and Malin. 'Better organise some transport off this wreck.'

'I have the Saker,' Gunn said, stepping toward him. 'It has two seats.'

'Are you going to take me into custody?'

'No, stupid,' she rushed. She glanced at the floor, kicked an invisible dust mite then looked back up, but her eyes only got as far as his shoulders. 'I'm just, I'm saying I'd like to fly with you again.'

Robert reached out to her chin and pulled it up so he could look into her eyes. When those eyes weren't bent on his destruction they were the most amazing sight in the universe. 'I'm still a pirate, Gunn.'

She shook his finger away, anger flashing across her face, darkening her nose freckles. 'No you're not. Haven't you listened to yourself lately? Nothing you've done here today has been about piracy. You're not a pirate, Robert. Stop hiding and stop pretending.'

'She's right you know,' Malin said. 'You're a lousy pirate. You don't kill half enough people and you barely make enough profit to stay afloat.'

Robert ignored Malin. He grabbed Gunn's shoulders. They were firm, strong, but tender. It would have been nice to hold those shoulders more, every day, maybe. He wondered what kind of life that would be.

But it would never happen. What would they do? They had different lives, they wanted different things. She was a weapon of justice, he didn't know what he was, and he'd never be quite sure if one day she'd put a knife in his back. *Maintain secrecy.*

'I can't go with you Gunn.' Her gaze snapped back to his. Her eyes quivered, tears beading at their corners. 'Maybe one d-' he started.

She whipped out of his arms, cutting him off and she ran for the far door. It slid open. She stopped, turned. She pulled herself to full height. 'I'll see you out there, Robert.' Then she slipped through, boots sucking to the floor. The door closed again and she was gone. Out of sight and out of his life.

Maybe forever.

His shoulders sagged. '… day.'

Malin slapped him around the back of the head. 'You're an idiot. I guess that means you're coming with me.'

'I'm a pirate,' he insisted. 'I steal stuff and kill anyone that gets in my way, I just steal enough to pay for my boys and I try not to kill people who aren't in my way. What's wrong with that?'

Brown pulled him around and walked him away from Malin, toward the viewscreen. He pointed out at the stars. 'Blond was a heck of a man. You two didn't see eye to eye and, well, let's just say he had an issue with his vocabulary, but he was driven and tough. If something stood in his way he trampled over it and kept going. Focused; One heck of a man, one heck of a partner.'

He stopped and turned to face Robert. 'I need a new partner. I've seen how you operate. You're a citizen, you've got the credentials. Some training will be required but we could have you back out in space with me in four months. Six tops.'

Robert turned. Brown stepped back into view. 'We save innocents every day, citizen. Sometimes things go wrong, but our overriding goal is to protect Federation civilians and citizens.'

'And what about the rest of the galaxy's civilians?'

'We do the best we can with what we got. The Federation provides the resources and we use them to protect the Federation. If we can help others like we did today, then so much the better.'

Robert nodded. 'I'll think about it.' And he was surprised to realise he meant it. Saving lives, being the hero, without anyone knowing what he did sounded pretty damn good. 'But I have a lot of friends to take home and a lot of friends not coming home that I need to say goodbye to.'

Brown shook his hand. 'Thank you.'

'For not killing you the first time we met?'

Brown smiled. 'And the rest, I won't forget. I'll be keeping an eye on you. If you make a decision, make it obvious and I'll know.'

'Will do.' He followed Malin out while Brown slave-linked the Explorers together.

* * *

Robert settled into an acceleration couch on Malin's Lion transport. The fleet broke up; The Alliance hypered out but Gunn's Saker headed out system, taking the long way home perhaps. That Saker had been his home for a few weeks of his life. It and Gunn felt like a part of him, a part slowly flying out of reach. His heart panged.

A hyperspace vector coalesced ahead of the two Explorers and they winked out of existence, leaving nothing but a shattered planet and a shattered past. There was nothing left out there but cold emptiness and memories.

Robert turned away from the viewport, away from his past and toward his future; a future of moving forward and not looking back.

A future.

About The Author:

John Harper's writing career began in his first year of school when he stood before the school assembly and read out his 'novelisation' of the movie Short Circuit.

Fast forward a few years and John is now a science fiction writer living in Wellington, New Zealand. He likes spending time with his wife and two children, and he follows the cricket and V8 Supercars religiously. John is a passionate writer at night and occupies his days working as a chartered mechanical engineer.

Facebook:
www.facebook.com/john.harper.9843499

Twitter:
@AndHereTheWheel

Join the Clan:
More about the Garry Pirate Clan: http://andherethewheel.co.nz

Other books available in the Elite: Dangerous series:

Elite: Mostly Harmless by Kate Russell
Elite: Reclamation by Drew Wagar
Elite: Tales From The Frontier by 15 authors from around the world

All the above published by Fantastic Books Publishing

* * *

Elite: Wanted by Gavin Deas
Elite: Nemorensis by Simon Spurrier
Elite: Docking is Difficult by Gideon Defoe

Published by Gollancz

* * *

Out of the Darkness by T.James

Lightning Source UK Ltd.
Milton Keynes UK
UKOW05f1832040517

300527UK00006B/317/P